JUPITER:
THE 27TH CENTURY

He was born Hope Hubris,
son of a peasant family enslaved
by the wealthy scions of Callisto.
To defend his sister's honor, he
committed an act of violence which
forced his family to flee into
high space . . . and Hope lost everything
but his courage and his will to triumph.
Now serving in the Navy of Jupiter,
he has launched the destiny that will
strike fear into his enemies . . . and
inspire the undying loyalty of those
who serve him.

BIO OF A SPACE TYRANT
VOLUME 2: MERCENARY

PIERS ANTHONY

AVON
PUBLISHERS OF BARD, CAMELOT, DISCUS AND FLARE BOOKS

BIO OF A SPACE TYRANT VOLUME 2: MERCENARY is
an original publication of Avon Books. This work has never before appeared in book form. This work is a novel. Any similar-
ity to actual persons or events is purely coincidental.

AVON BOOKS
A division of
The Hearst Corporation
1790 Broadway
New York, New York 10019

Copyright © 1984 by Piers Anthony Jacob
Published by arrangement with the author
Library of Congress Catalog Card Number: 84-90895
ISBN: 0-380-87221-8

First Avon Printing, June, 1984

AVON TRADEMARK REG. U. S. PAT. OFF. AND IN
OTHER COUNTRIES, MARCA REGISTRADA, HECHO EN
U. S. A.

Printed in the U. S. A.

WFH 10 9 8

The author wishes to thank Jim Parker for valuable advice on certain military aspects of this novel, notably the nature and use of the pugil sticks and the organization of a unit; and Zane Stein and Jacob Schwarts for assistance concerning the planetoid Chiron.

Contents

Editorial Preface

Hope Hubris, as the prior manuscript *Refugee* showed, was not originally aware of his destiny to become the all-powerful Tyrant of Jupiter. At first he was a desperate Hispanic refugee, fleeing his home-moon of Callisto when wrongfully charged with a crime. He saw his group brutalized and his parents murdered by pirates and the indifference of the established powers. He lost the first great romantic love of his life, the refugee girl Helse, to the savagery of the marauders of the Jupiter Ecliptic. He was lucky to survive at all, and lucky to be admitted at last as an immigrant to the peripheral off-Jupiter society. Certainly he was unprepossessing as a person in those early days, despite his education and intelligence.

However, his special talent with people found ready application as he entered the Jupiter Navy, and in due course he became the redoubtable military figure the texts describe today. That reputation was, of course, the springboard for his subsequent civilian success in the political arena. But the conventional descriptions omit certain vital insights, such as the influence of the sinister QYV, his relations with certain migrant laborers and pirates, and the frank use of social and sexual inducements to put together one of the strangest, yet most brilliant, staffs of Naval history.

The adult Hubris was always a man for the ladies, but rumors of his infidelities turn out to be largely apocryphal. He indulged in sex freely but fairly, and not a single woman who knew him well ever spoke evil of him, not even the fiery pirate wench he raped. Neither did the males of his association; he commanded an almost fanatical respect within his unit.

Hubris, despite his superficial indifference in appearance and manner, was a truly potent motivator of people.

Yet little of this shows in this private narrative. Perhaps it pleased him to portray himself as the somewhat naïve observer, as if others made most of his decisions for him; or perhaps he was genuinely innocent in his private reflections. But he was expert at delegating authority, and very little slipped by him. Many opponents misjudged him, until it was too late, because he understood them far more precisely than they understood him. His special genius did not show up in the standardized tests upon which most personnel judgments were made. Those tests never properly defined him. That, oddly, was one of his greatest assets.

This narrative, translated from the original Spanish, should be perused with that in mind: There was more to Hope Hubris than shows in the official records, and more than he himself chose to present. His highly unorthodox procedures were often the mark not of insanity but of genius. It was not, after all, mere chance that brought him eventually to the Tyrancy.

But some few did appreciate Hope Hubris's potential early, as we shall see, and there was one who perhaps contributed more to his success than Hope himself did, yet who received virtually no recognition for it.

No dates are listed in this manuscript, but external evidence suggests that it commences on or about June 1, 2615, perhaps a month after the termination of *Refugee*.

Chapter 1

WORRIED MAN BLUES

I never saw it coming. I thought the man was just shoving past me from behind, for the concourse was not wide, and then there was a hard blow to the side of my head. I saw a flash of pain, lost my balance, fell against the wall, and slid to the floor. The man shoved me about; I thought he was helping me to get up, but then he was gone and I just sagged there, dazed.

I don't know how many people passed me by; I was aware of them only peripherally, as moving shapes. I put my hand to my hurting head and found moisture. I looked at my fingers and saw the stain of red on them: blood. I thought about that awhile, not moving, while the foreign shapes continued to pass.

Then a shape stopped. "Kid, I think you been mugged," he said in English.

I looked up at him. He was a poorly shaven man with short, curly light hair and blue eyes: a fair Caucasian, rather than the dusky Latin of my own type. More succinctly: He was Saxon; I, Hispanic. He wore faded, worn coveralls and a sweat-stained shirt and cheap old composition shoes: a laboring man. But he represented help, and he looked great to me, a Good Samaritan. "I think so," I agreed.

"Check for your money," he advised, helping me to my feet with strong hands.

I checked. My new wallet was gone, and with it my money—and my identification. I groaned. I hadn't meant to make that sound; it just came out.

"They need more patrolmen in these public places," the man said. "Someone gets mugged just about every day. Where you going, kid? I'll help you there."

Confused, I pondered. "Looking for work," I said. "I—just checked the Navy office, but . . ." I was having trouble organizing my memory.

"Too young?" he asked sympathetically.

"Yes. He asked my age, and I said fifteen, and he said to come back in two years. Then—"

"Then you got mugged on your way to the employment office," he finished. "It happens. Here, let's introduce ourselves. I'm Joe Hill, migrant laborer, en route to a new hitch as a picker."

"Hope Hubris," I said, grateful for his easy manner. Other people were shoving by us, paying no attention. "From Callisto, refugee. I've just been granted status as a resident alien."

Joe smiled. "I'd guessed as much. You're from that batch they just processed at the immigration center, right? This your first day out on Leda?"

"First hour," I agreed, nodding. That made my head hurt again, and I touched the bad spot.

Joe brought out a large old handkerchief. "Let me mop that. It's not as bad as it feels. It's mostly a bruise with a little cut skin, and the blood's matting the hair a little. You'll get off with a headache." He patted the spot, and his reassurance made me feel better. "Look, Hope—I don't like to make you feel worse, but the fact is, this whole system isn't much better than the mugging you just got. At your age you just can't find decent work. All the employment offices will tell you the same. You've got to get a ticket to the Jupiter atmosphere—"

"They're not admitting aliens now," I said. "I have to find work out here in the Ecliptic until I qualify for citizenship." The Jupiter Ecliptic is the plane of the orbits of the satellites of Jupiter; actually, the outer moons do not match the plane of the inner ones, but it's all called the Jupiter Ecliptic anyway, or Juclip for short.

"Then you're screwed," he said, employing Saxon vernacular that was new to me. "Your age and nationality box you in. And now that you've lost your cash stake and your ID—"

"I must get them to issue me a new card," I said.

"Which will take weeks or months. I know this bureaucracy, Hope. What are you going to eat while you're waiting?"

I spread my hands, baffled. I hadn't counted on getting mugged.

"Come on," he said. "I'm running short on time, but I can get you to the alien office to put in for your card. Then—"

"Then?" I repeated, sounding stupid even to myself. I remained disorganized, and my head was hurting.

He sighed. "Then I guess I'd better take you with me on the picking gig. It's no life for the likes of you, but I can't see you stranded here. You'd wind up having to mug for a living."

"Oh, I would never—" I protested, shocked at the notion.

"Kid, when you're hungry and broke, and there's no work, and you know if you complain they'll deport you to your moon of origin, what do you do?"

I was silent. The realities of my situation were making themselves felt. Without my card I couldn't get a good job, and without the hundred-dollar tide-over stake they had issued me, I couldn't eat. They would indeed deport me on the slightest pretext. My kind was tolerated, not welcomed, here. They had made that clear enough at the outset. Mighty Jupiter, home of the free, had little use for dusky-skinned foreigners who couldn't manage their money and didn't work productively. Mighty Jupiter was not interested in listening to excuses, such as being mugged or being underage for employment. It was indeed a rigged system, but I was bound by its laws.

"Yes, I thought you were honest," Joe said. "I got a feel for people. That's why I stopped to help you." He paused. "No, that's not entirely so. I would've stopped, anyway. I can't pass up a working man in distress."

"No, you can't," I agreed.

His lips quirked. "You can tell?"

"Yes. It's my talent, too. Understanding people. I will go with you."

He laughed. " 'Sokay, Hope! But remember I warned

you: Picking's tough work. This is just to tide you through till your card comes and you can go for a decent job."

"Yes, thanks."

We checked in at the alien registration office where the bored clerk made a note. I would have to check in at weekly intervals, no oftener, until my replacement card was issued. Meanwhile I was on my own.

We walked the concourse again. I call it walking, though actually it was more like floating. Leda is the smallest outer moon of Jupiter, only about five kilometers in diameter, so it's strictly trace-gravity on the surface. Leda is really no larger than a major city-bubble, but of course it's solid instead of hollow, so must have a hundred times the mass. It serves mainly as an anchor for a series of rotating domes, each dome generating Earth-normal gravity by its spin, at the edge. Traveling between domes tends to be stomach-wrenching until you get used to it. Maybe that was part of my problem. Certainly I did not feel well, and so I suffered myself to be moved along by this well-meaning stranger.

This was, I think, the true beginning of my military career, which is why I commence my narrative at this point. But the progression was not clear at the time. That often seems to be the way with fate: We perceive its devious channels only in retrospect.

At any rate, Joe brought me to the bus. This was an old space shuttle with its guts gutted. It had been fitted with tiered bunks in the center of its cylindrical shell. Thus a ship designed for perhaps thirty passengers could house a hundred and twenty. There were a number of men hunched about the bunks, and one somewhat more solid, self-assured man near the entrance.

"This is Gallows," Joe told me, bringing me to the solid man. "He's hard but he's fair." He turned to the man. "This is Hope. He's not a regular picker; he got rolled, so he needs some time."

"How's he going to pay his fare?" Gallows asked.

"I'll cover it," Joe said. "I've got a little to spare."

"It costs money?" I asked, startled. "I don't have—I can't—"

"There ain't no free lunch, kid," Gallows pronounced.

"I said I'd cover," Joe said, producing some bills.

Gallows accepted them. "Better teach him the ropes, too, Joe, if you don't want to be stuck." He checked his list. "Bunk forty-nine."

"I'll repay—" I said, embarrassed. "I didn't realize—"

"Here's the bunk," Joe said, indicating the one marked 49. "We'll have to split-shift it. You sleep four hours, I'll sleep four. I couldn't afford two bunks. It'll work out."

"Yes, certainly," I agreed. "I'm sorry you had to pay anything for me. I'll try to make it good as soon as—"

"I know you will, Hope," he said easily. "I told you, I have a feel for people. I know what it's like to be in trouble."

"Trouble!" a man exclaimed a few bunks down the line. "Kid, if you like trouble, Joe's your man!"

"That's Old Man Rivers," Joe said. "Him and me, we see eye to eye on—"

"Nothing!" Rivers agreed jovially. "Kid, you better know right now you hooked up with the biggest rabble-rouser in the Juclip! Watch he doesn't incite a riot with your head in the middle!"

"You two are friends?" I asked, perplexed, for I perceived that there was an edge to this banter. I also had a moment's hesitation about the word Juclip; I have defined it here, but this was my introduction to it.

Joe laughed. "Friends? Never! But what Rivers says is true. I'm a union organizer. That's why they gave me my song."

"Your song?" Was this more slang?

"You asked for it." Joe sat on the bunk, hooking his heels under it so as not to drift away in the trace gravity, and sang. His voice was decent but hardly trained:

I dreamed I saw Joe Hill last night, alive as you and I.
"But Joe," says I, "You're ten years dead!" Says Joe, "I didn't die!"

And now the others in the ship joined in: "Says Joe, 'I didn't die!' "

It was a rousing song with a catchy tune, and the men sang it with gusto. But I didn't understand it. "A dead union organizer?" I asked.

"Several centuries ago," Joe said. "But it's a good name."

"Do the others have songs, too?" This was another aspect of the culture I had not known about. I had always been one of the most fluent students in my English class, and I could speak the language almost faultlessly; now I realized that there is a great deal more to understanding than fluency.

"All of them. That's what safeguards a man's place. His song."

"He just chooses any song he likes?"

Joe laughed again. He was really at ease here. "Never! It has to be given to him by the group. Since this is your first trip, Hope, we'll figure out yours on the way."

"But I hardly know any English songs!"

"You'll learn this one. We'll work it out, never fear."

"But suppose I don't like it?"

"Tough stuff," he said with a smile. "Your song is you." There was a murmur of assent by the others.

I shrugged. It wasn't a vital matter. My head hurt, and I just wanted to rest. I lay on the bunk, secured by its restraining strap, as the ship gradually filled up. Most of the workers seemed to know each other at least casually; they had been out on similar jobs before. The atmosphere was one of familiarity rather than festivity.

"Hey, I hain't seen you before!" a man said to me.

"I'm new," I admitted.

"Then you have to be initiated!" he exclaimed, grinning in a not entirely friendly manner. "You know what we do to—"

I saw his gaze go to Joe Hill, who had come up beside me. Joe had drawn a monstrous dagger and was using it to carve his dirty fingernails back.

"He's with you?" the man asked Joe.

"Uh-huh. He got mugged and needed help, so I thought we'd help him. It's the neighborly thing."

The man's eyes flicked to the dagger, and away. "Uh, yeah, sure. We'll help him. But he's got to—"

"Have his song," Joe finished, making a small, significant gesture with the blade.

"Just what I was going to say!" the man agreed. "We've got to tag him with a song."

"Once we get moving," Joe said, putting away his knife.

"Right." And the man moved on to his assigned bunk.

I realized that Joe was an excellent friend to have while I was among strangers. He might have a soft heart for a person in trouble, but that was only one facet of his character. He had not been fooling with that dagger! I owed him another favor.

I must have slept, because suddenly the ship was moving, accelerating from its dock. My head still hurt; the vertigo of initial motion didn't help. I lay on my back and listened.

They sang songs. Each man really did have his song, and he sang it with assurance, though few people had good voices. That didn't seem to matter; enthusiasm was what counted, and the assertion of possession. No one interrupted when a man started his song; then, after a few bars, they joined in, following his lead. The songs were unfamiliar to me, but I knew I would pick them up readily enough. I was, perforce, now a member of this culture; I would adapt.

Then, abruptly, it was my turn. "This is Hope's maiden voyage," Joe said. "We must select his song." He turned to me. "First we have to know about you. How did you come to leave Callisto?"

"That's a long story," I said. "You probably wouldn't be interested in—"

"We love long stories," Joe said. "They fill our tired evenings when the songs give out. But right now we're only doing your song, not your story. Can you summarize your life in one hundred words?"

"I can try," I said, realizing that this was not a joke. Now that I was active, my headache was fading. "My family had trouble with a scion, and we had to flee the planet in a bootleg bubble powered mostly by a gravity shield. Pirates came and—" Suddenly the horrible memories overwhelmed me, I choked up and could not continue. Only four months ago my family had been united and reasonably happy. Now . . .

"I think I understand," Joe said. "They killed your family?"

I nodded.

"And you alone survive?"

"My—my sisters—" I said.

"Survive? Raped and taken as concubines for private ships?"

"One. The other, younger, she's called Spirit, and she's twelve. Got a . . . a position on a ship, concealed as a boy—"

"And you don't know where she is now," Joe finished. He looked around at the bunks. "I think we have enough of the picture. You Hispanic refugees come through a hardball game."

There was a general murmur of agreement. "A kid sister hiding among pirates," Rivers said. "He's got reason to worry."

"But his name is Hope," Gallows said. He was the foreman, but he was evidently also part of this group.

"Hope is a worried man," Rivers said, looking around.

Slowly the others nodded.

I looked up, perplexed. "What?"

"Oh, that's right," Joe said, as if surprised. "You don't know our songs. We'll have to teach you. Anybody want to do this one?"

"I'll do it," Rivers said. He turned to me. "With your permission, Hope, I will sing your song."

"Sure," I said doubtfully.

"This time only, I lead Hope's song," Rivers said formally. "The *Worried Man Blues.*" And then he sang, in his fine deep voice:

> It takes a worried man to sing a worried song
> It takes a worried man to sing a worried song
> It takes a worried man to sing a worried song
> I'm worried now, but I won't be worried long.

I had to smile. The words did speak to my mood and my situation, and it was a pretty melody. Because the lines repeated, it was easy to remember.

"Now you try it," Rivers said.

Singing was not my forte, but I knew my voice was as good as those of a number of the other folk I had heard here, and I realized this performance was necessary if I was to be accepted into this group. I took a breath and sang, somewhat tremulously. "It takes a worried man to sing a worried song—"

At the second line, the others joined in, and it became much easier. They were careful not to drown me out; it was necessary that I be heard, that I set the cadence. By the time we got to the fourth line, it was rousing, and I felt it uplifting me. I really did feel better, physically and emotionally. I was part of the group, participating in a performing art. Surely this rendition would never be recorded as great music, but it was great, nevertheless.

Then Rivers sang the second verse—or maybe it was the first, for what we had sung before turned out to be the refrain, repeated after every regular verse.

I went across the river and I lay down to sleep. . . .
When I awoke, there were shackles on my feet.

I had gone across the Jupiter Ecliptic—and lost my joy of life along with most of my family and freedom. I was shackled, yes.

Twenty-nine links of chain around my leg . . .
On every link, an initial of my name.

Twenty-nine initials. I pondered that and realized that my name was legion. My initials were H. H., but there were many others like me, and their initials were on the chain, too. I liked the symbolism, painful as it was. Perhaps my father's initials were there, M. H., and my mother's, C. H., and my two sisters, F. H. and S. H., and my lost love, H. H., Helse Hubris, for I had married her, almost. I liked that idea.

I asked the judge what might be my fine. . . .
Twenty-one years on the migrant-labor line!

That was, I learned later, adapted to the present situation; historically, back on Planet Earth, where all these songs had originated, it had been the Rocky Mountain Line. That was a mountain range in Earth's North America, said to be fairly formidable; presumably the line—which would then have been a locomotive or railroad line in which cumbersome steam-driven vehicles were propelled along metal rails laid on the ground—required hand labor for its initial establishment. I daresay it would have required a great deal of work to lay those rails properly in a mountain district, as the locomotives needed to operate on fairly level terrain. The technology of ancient times has always intrigued me. So the migrant laborers must have had back-straining work—as I would surely find out.

Anyway, I now had my song and my culture-nickname; I would have to answer to either Hope or Worry. They were much the same, really; opposite faces of the coin, depending on whether anticipation was positive or negative. I did like the song, and especially I liked the belongingness it made me experience. Singing together—there is something special about it. I believe every experience in life, of any nature, has some value to a person; this one had a great deal of value to me. Deprived of my family and my culture, I desperately needed new ones, and now it seemed I had them. Not as good as the old ones, but much, much better than drifting alone.

The songs continued as each man had his turn presenting his own, staking out his position in the group. But I was tired and hurting, as the exhilaration of my own song faded, and I lay on the bunk and listened and then slept. I suspected I was taking Joe's turn on the bunk, but he didn't say anything.

I woke with a start as the gravity abruptly cut off; acceleration was over. But Joe's hand was on me, holding me to the bunk, so I didn't float away. I had forgotten to strap myself down this time, since the acceleration had provided weight. Now he was putting the strap across. "Finish your nap," he advised me.

"But it's your bunk, too," I protested groggily.

"Not to worry, Worry," he said with a smile. "I can sleep floating while we're coasting."

"But when deceleration starts—"

"Kid, it's a fifteen-hour trip. I won't sleep that long. You're the one with the hurting head; relax."

I followed his advice. I had been in free-fall before and could handle it. In fact, I think the free-fall helped, for it relieved my body of the ordinary strain of gravity, allowing it to concentrate on healing. Free-fall does not help all people, but it helped me. When I woke again, several hours later, my head was virtually clear.

Joe was sleeping in air, one hand gripping a bunk rail. He looked perfectly comfortable.

Now the waking workers were swapping yarns and playing poker for pennies. I was satisfied just to listen, familiarizing myself with their qualities. These were generally uneducated folk, illiterate or partially literate, but canny enough in their limited fashion. Literacy does not equate to intelligence or humanity, after all. I was not familiar with their game of poker, but figured I could learn it in due course.

Meanwhile, as a mental exercise, I calculated, in the unfamiliar Jupiter units of miles, the location of the agricultural bubble we were traveling to. I had been raised on the superior metric system, but I knew I would have to become conversant with the system of the Colossus if I wanted to convert my alien residency to proper citizenship. Also, my lost love Helse had used the Jupiter system of measurements, so I felt closer to her with them, foolish as this may seem.

Acceleration measured in this fashion came to 32 feet per second squared, for one gee. 3,600 seconds in an hour meant—this was pretty good mental exercise, because of the irregular intervals between units—about 115,000 feet per second in an hour of gee, which seemed to be what we

had experienced. There were—I strained to remember
—5,280 feet in a mile. That meant we were traveling about
22 miles per second now, or close to 80,000 miles per hour.
Fifteen hours at that velocity would be about 1,200,000
miles. But we would not be traveling straight in toward
Jupiter; we would angle back to intercept the bubble as it
overhauled Leda in its smaller, faster orbit. The bubble
was probably about ten million kilometers out from Jupiter, compared to Leda's eleven million—oops, I had slipped
back into the metric system!

At any rate, I was satisfied that the bubble was about 90
percent of Leda's distance out, in this miniature Solar System that was the Juclip, and that we would not be carried
far from Leda in the ten days Joe said we would be picking.
That reassured me; I didn't want to get lost and not be on
hand to recover my identification.

We did indeed arrive on schedule, decelerating at gee for
an hour and docking on the bubble. Our ship simply
hooked onto a rack awaiting it and hung nose-out, suddenly upside down as the gee resumed. The bunks were
made to take it; they could be used from either side. The
bubble was rotating one complete turn every minute and a
half, so that centrifugal force brought our weight at its surface to almost gee, Earth-normal gravity.

We climbed the ladder-tube up into the bubble. Inside,
we stepped out of the lock onto the great, curving inner
surface. I stood, dazzled by it.

The bubble was a virtually hollow sphere about a thousand feet in diameter. From a mirror in its center shone
the sun; or rather, the twenty-sevenfold magnified image
of the sun, projecting the hellish intensity of Earth-normal
solar radiation to the broad, curved expanse of green
plants. I knew I would not be able to tolerate that very
long; the radiation would soon blister my skin.

The bubble was, of course, oriented so that its pole
pointed to the sun. Otherwise the light would have been
flashing on and off in sub-two-minute cycles, not good for
the plants. This way, the bubble's rotation was irrelevant;
the mirror moved independently, beaming the light to
cover one-third of the inner surface, rotating in the course

of twenty-four hours to complete the circuit. Earth plants preferred the Earth cycle, and produced most abundantly with it, and so they got it. That, in addition to the absence of all Earth diseases and predators and inconstancies of nature, meant that these plants were many times as productive as they could have been on Earth itself.

"Get over to the harvest station," Gallows told us. That turned out to be a pavilion a short distance away, on a terrace up the slope. Gee was only full and vertical at the bubble's equator, of course; the terraces became increasingly steep as the poles were approached. Otherwise, the plants and soil would simply have tumbled in a jumble to the equator. We hastened to comply, scrambling up the path.

Organization did not take long. We were issued broad-brimmed hats, gloves, and heavy shirts to protect us from the concentrated sunlight, and each of us was given a large plastic bucket on a belt. This was a pepper dome; we were to fill our buckets with the red peppers. About one hundred peppers filled a bucket. When we brought a filled bucket to the foreman, he would issue a ticket worth a dime. The more buckets we filled, the more dimes we earned. It was a remarkably simple system.

Theoretically the average worker would fill one bucket in five minutes, twelve per hour, and squeeze it up to about a hundred buckets in the full eight-hour working day. The overall mathematics of it generated a schedule for our thirty-man crew to complete the full harvest of three million peppers in ten days. That seemed simple enough.

But the polite math did not take much account of the human element. I discovered that harvesting is indeed not light work. I was assigned a terraced segment of the acreage to harvest that seemed huge but was probably small. The entire acreage of the bubble might have been seventy-two, though the terracing and loss of usable area toward the poles may have caused me to misjudge it. Only a third of it was lighted, and we were working on only part of that this day. In fact, I now realize that the average man had to harvest less than a quarter acre per day—but that was ten thousand peppers, and it was an enormous task.

The plants were spaced in wide rows, so there was plenty

of room to walk between them without brushing, and that was important, because I saw that these were long-term producers. We had to pick only the ripe peppers, not damaging the greater number of developing ones; other crews would harvest those in other months.

I went to work on my segment, and Joe Hill had one adjacent. I watched him picking, to get a clear notion of how it was done, then proceeded. Each plant had one ripe pepper, readily distinguishable by its bright red color; I took hold of it and broke it free of its stem with a quick twist and set it in the pail. That was important, too, we had been cautioned; we were not to bruise the peppers by tossing them in. There were farmhands patrolling the rows, watching to see that no plants or fruits were abused. They did no harvesting, they just watched.

I thought I was making good time, but I was last to bring my first bucket in to Gallows for my ticket. I resolved to do better, and I hurried back to my section. I did speed up, but now I was getting hot in the heavy shirt, and the clothing was chafing. It was necessary to hunch over to reach the plants, and my back began to feel it. I sweated profusely and had to take gulps of water from the fountain every time I delivered a bucket, to alleviate dehydration. Within an hour the work became unpleasant; in two hours it was torture. But I had to keep picking, for everyone else was, and I was falling behind.

There was no break for lunch; we had to keep picking feverishly to make the quota. I hardly felt hunger, anyway; the fatigue of my limbs and discomfort of my body drowned it out. The curving landscape blurred; only the nearest bushes remained in focus. I was no longer concerned about future days, or even future hours; my life was measured only by the bucketful. My two hands moved of their own volition, grasping, twisting, carrying, depositing. Now each pepper was a challenge!

"This is no life for you, Hope," a voice said.

Dazedly, I looked up. A young woman stood before me, brown-haired and pretty. Her eyes were immeasurably sad.

I blinked the blur away and recognized her. "Helse!" I

cried, and lurched forward to embrace her. Helse, my love, my bride—

But she faded into nothingness, and I fell face-first to the ground. Now I remembered what I had never forgotten: Helse was dead and butchered for the key she carried. The key of QYV. "Kife, I'll kill you!" I cried in blind, hopeless rage.

"Worry! Come out of it!"

It was Joe, heaving me off the ground. I shook my head, realizing that I had suffered some sort of seizure.

Joe made me stop picking for the day, though I had filled only forty-five buckets. That put me further in trouble, for the morning and evening meals cost two dollars each, and the bunk two dollars per night. Most workers also bought a jug of rotgut for a dollar, and some paid another two dollars for fifteen minutes in a shed with the bubble prostitute. One more dollar was withheld each day for the return bus fare, until that five-dollar charge was met. The foreman didn't want any worker stranded without busfare back to Leda! As they put it, Gallows didn't want anyone hanging. It was said, not quite jokingly, that a fellow could have "A loaf of bread, a jug of wine, and thou" each day and come out even. Many of the men did exactly that.

Joe carried me. He was able to pick more than the minimum, and he gave me enough chits so I could eat and sleep. I was embarrassed to accept his further largesse, but I had no choice. Next day I was more careful and did not faint, but only picked sixty-five buckets. So it went, day by day; I was literally in debt to Joe, and could never quite catch up to it.

At night, in the ship, it was better. I rested and recovered, and gave Joe his turn on the bunk while I worked on my song and learned to play poker. I refused to play for money, since I was already in debt, and this dampened things somewhat, but I did learn the game, and my special perception of people enabled me to grasp their bluffs. Soon I was playing well enough so that they were glad it wasn't for money.

There was a good deal of time when everyone was awake in the ship, as we were not permitted to wander the bubble freely when off-duty. Naturally enough we were crowded and bored, which was why a game like poker was important. Trouble was easy to come by. I was, to my shame, responsible for some of it.

I was telling my story in nightly installments, for next to singing and poker that was the prime entertainment. Most of the others knew each other's histories, but I was new and unfamiliar, so was the present object of attention. It was like having a new holo-show for them to watch, instead of an old, familiar one. I told how my family had to depart our city of Maraud at night and catch a bootleg bubble to Jupiter—and the betrayal and tragedy that ensued. On the first night only half a dozen people paid much attention, but my audience grew on succeeding nights, and when I got to sixteen-year-old Helse, all thirty of them, including the foreman, were listening raptly. I did not spare myself, for I wanted to forget none of it: my gallant family, my first experiences with sex, the rigors of the hell-moon Io, and Helse's horrible death.

"Say," Rivers said. "For a tale like that, Trixie'd give you tail for free!" Trixie was the generic name for prostitutes.

I was silent. The thought of sex with any other woman appalled me. *Helse, Helse!* I was not even conscious of the tears streaming down my cheeks.

Joe Hill launched himself at Rivers. His fist scored on the man's gut. Rivers buckled, gasping for breath. "You had no call to say that!" Joe cried, standing over the fallen man.

I jumped up, frightened at what I had unwittingly instigated. "He meant no harm!"

Rivers caught his breath. He was a larger man than Joe, and more powerfully constructed, and it was already evident that the two were not friends. But this time he backed off. "I had no call," he agreed. "I wasn't thinking."

Joe turned away, satisfied. I was to learn by experience that fights were often this way, inchoate, terminated as quickly as they began; an unwritten code among the pickers militated against extremes of violence. But at this time I wasn't aware of that; I feared there could be a continuation. I went to Rivers. "There's no offense! I didn't mean for this to happen!"

"Joe's wrong about most things," Rivers said gruffly. "This one time he's right. I owe you one, Worry." And he, too, turned away.

Why had he backed off? It had been a fairly innocent remark, and he surely felt no personal awe of Joe Hill. Rivers had accepted a spot humiliation, a certain loss of status, and that bothered me because I didn't understand his motive. Mysteries of motive are always important to me, because I encounter so few of them.

Gallows began his song, effectively changing the subject:

> Hangman, hangman, slack your rope
> Slack it for a while
> I think I see my father coming
> Riding many a mile.

After the first refrain, the others joined in, and the song session was on.

> Papa, did you bring me silver?
> Papa, did you bring me gold?
> Or did you come to see me hanging
> By the gallows pole?

According to the song, Papa had no money to free the victim, and neither did the mother; but the sweetheart did, and so the victim was saved. I appreciated the aptness of the song, for Gallows was the one who counted out the money for the hapless workers. Without that money they would perish.

We went on to other songs, mine included, and I felt more strongly than ever the camaraderie of this group. I knew this collection of people was essentially random, just those who had been looking for work when this job was available, but the grueling day labor and the songs by night unified it rapidly. And, of course, the subculture of the pickers spread its broader unity over all such groups.

There is no need to dwell unduly on this aspect of my life. We completed our ten-day stint, and my work improved, but I remained in debt to Joe. So when we returned to Leda on the space-bus, I told him I would take another tour with him, to repay that debt. But that was only part of the reason. The rest of it was this: I had been cast adrift by circumstance, and migrant labor gave me a home and a livelihood and companions. It wasn't much, but it was what I needed.

But I knew that eventually I would have to heed Helse's warning in the vision. There was no real future for me in this life. As a child grows out of the comfort and security of his family, I would have to grow out of this.

I took the next tour, to a bubble growing potatoes, and this was grueling work. Some of the crew overlapped that of the pepper bubble, and some were new, but the songs continued. Rivers was there, and he and Joe had another altercation, for Joe openly condemned the low wages and hard work, while Rivers said that if a man didn't like it, he was a fool not to go elsewhere.

I caught up on my debt to Joe, but I wasn't ready to leave. My replacement ID card had not yet arrived, and this was the only type of work I could obtain without it. Anyway, I still needed that migrant culture.

So it continued for months, and the people changed while the nature of the employment did not. The bad blood between Joe Hill and Old Man Rivers intensified as pickers got sick with degenerative, malnutritive, and stress-syndrome diseases and lost ability to work. The bubble-farm guards were not always aloof; sometimes they beat the pickers. Sometimes the bubble-farmers cheated the work crews, and there was very little to be done about it. Joe's talk of forming an effective migrant labor union became more strident, and Rivers's opposition more implacable, and the two fought and fought again. Somehow they always shared a job, though; they never split to separate ones. That, too, I wondered about.

Gradually the union sentiment spread, for Joe's analysis was compelling: Only unified force could bring the tyrannical bubble-farmers into line and make them improve conditions and pay for the laborers. "A strike!" Joe urged. "If all the workers refused to pick and the crops started rotting in the fields—that would bring them into line soon enough! All we want is a living wage, a bit more of the fruits of our labors!"

"All you want is to take over the power for yourself!" Rivers objected. "A corrupt union boss is the worst thing there is!" But the tide was turning against him as the unfairness of the system became more apparent to the body of the laboring force.

Joe led them in a new (though old) song:

Men of the soil! We have labored unending.
We have fed the planet on the grain that we have grown.
. . . Man ne'er shall eat again, bread gained through blood of men!
Who is there denies our right to reap where we have sown?

Of course, it wasn't exact, though updated for space. We were in fact reapers, not sowers. But the essence was there: that the laborer should share the fruits of his labors. I felt it, as the power of the song took me. In unity there was strength, and in strength there could be justice! We had to unify and act!

"You're crazy!" Rivers warned. "Do you have any idea what would happen if you pulled a strike? They'd bring in the goon squads and beat your heads in!" Rivers was no advocate of the present exploitation; he merely believed that what Joe was doing would make things worse, not better, for the pickers.

"Not if we outnumbered the goons—and stood together," Joe retorted.

There was no decision yet, for though the union sentiment was gaining, it was far from unanimous. Slowly the pressure increased while the work continued. Each shift of jobs brought contact with new faces, and these people were increasingly interested.

One memorable, if not critical, episode occurred after

about six months. I was in a potato-bubble, part of a large crew with a number of unfamiliar faces and several new songs. I had been sleeping early, for grubbing potatoes is a dirty, wearing business. I woke early when I heard someone singing *Worried Man Blues*. Electrified, I bounced off my bunk and charged into the group. "That's my song!" I cried indignantly. The theft of a song was a serious business, sure provocation for a fight. I had to defend my song, or I would be in poor repute.

The man stopped. He was old and grizzled, with deep lines around and through his face. "It's *my* song," he said mildly. "Had it for thirty years."

I backed off, embarrassed. Of course, songs could duplicate; I had seen it happen to others. There were hundreds of songs, and thousands of workers. It just hadn't occurred to me that *mine* could have another owner. I now look back at this adolescent naïveté with a certain wonder; but the loss of innocence does seem to be a lifelong chore.

The man smiled. "It's good to meet a brother," he said, and extended his lined hand. "Haven't run into one in three years."

I took his hand, grateful for his attitude. "Mine's only six months."

"It's still authentic. Who named you, Worry?"

"Well, really, it was Joe Hill and Old Man Rivers. They're on another shift right now."

"Them brothers!" he exclaimed. "If them two agreed on anything, it must be right!"

Brothers? Not in the sense of matching songs. Song-brothers were those who shared a song, and they did not.

"Well, come on, Worry," he said. "It don't matter how long anyone's had it, it's ours. We'll sing it together."

And sing it we did. His voice wasn't any better than mine, but we complemented each other and made a richer song than either could have alone—and perhaps that is a suitable analogy for any type of cooperation in life. His version differed slightly from mine, but that only added to the appeal.

After that we talked, exchanging information and attitudes. We really were not much alike, but the rules of this society bound us together, and this man was rather like an uncle to me, and I like a nephew to him. He had been a migrant laborer all his life and knew nothing else. He was largely illiterate, so could find no other work. Much of the time, he confessed, he was on the bottle; it eased his mind, but his liver was starting to go, and that worried him—of course!—but what else was there?

And I learned that there was a duty as well as a friendship that went with the sharing of a song. If one of us died, and the other heard about it, he was supposed to come and investigate and set things to right if they needed it. Usually a few questions sufficed, and sometimes personal effects had to be taken to a blood relative, but once in a while there was foul play, and vengeance had to be sought. "But don't worry, Worry, 'about that,'" he reassured me. "My liver'll take me out within five years if not sooner, and I don't have no living relatives and nothing worth saving. I'll never be a caution to you. See that you ain't to me."

I promised not to be a caution to him, and that was it. We parted ways on the next tour, and I never saw him again. But the experience buoyed me. There was someone who would look out for me, not from proximity or friendship, but because the migrant society required it. It was the code of the song. That gave me an odd, deep comfort.

It was almost a year after my entry into the migrant labor circuit when things got ugly. My replacement identification had never come through; all I had was a temporary card that listed only my name and planet of origin: Callisto. The bureaucracy ground exceeding slow! The bubble-farmers and labor foremen didn't care, but this prevented me from seeking better employment elsewhere. So I was locked in, but as long as I was with Joe Hill, I didn't really mind.

The people changed, but Rivers was always with us. Fascinated for more than incidental reason now, I studied the relations between Joe and Rivers. Though their politics were opposite, and the two often came to blows, I noticed that the quarrels were never serious. Neither man ever drew his knife or tried for a mutilating blow. Other men in other controversies sometimes went the whole route, and once I saw one killed. The migrant code was strong, but not absolute; passions of the moment could erupt disastrously. No one seemed overly concerned about the dead man. The bubble-guards picked up the one who did it and turned him over to the police, and he did not return; maybe he was brought to trial, maybe just bounced to another orbit. It was the nuisance of violence the police objected to, not the loss of a worker or two. But Joe and Rivers never went that far. Could they, in fact, be brothers, bound by a more subtle tie than they advertised? I concluded that they did hold each other in a certain veiled respect.

Rivers was well named. He sang his song, and it was him:

> . . . Tired of livin', and feared of dyin'!
> But Old Man River, he just keeps rollin' along.

There was something about the way he sounded the word "dyin' " that sent a shiver through me. It signaled an enormous and terrible comprehension of the concept. I had seen my father treacherously and brutally slain; I had seen my fiancée's body cut open, her guts drawn out. I knew what death was!

But Rivers was no death-dealer, but the apostle of peaceful change. He argued that the condition of the pickers, which he deplored as much as Joe Hill did, would not change until underlying economics and social factors changed. Until the climate was right, he said, overt action could only be counterproductive. Joe, by inciting open resistance to oppression, was more apt to bring the storm down upon his own head, and increase the suffering of the rest of us.

I sided with Joe, of course, though in retrospect I feel I was mistaken. As the Jupiter-System economy wallowed in the ebb tide of an economic recession, and things tightened up all over the Juclip, and the slop the bubble-farmers fed us got worse, and the work harder for no increase in pay, my anger boiled up along with that of the others. Now Joe's reception was serious, not polite; the pickers were at last ready to organize, and the ones with this militant attitude were becoming a clear majority. The union songs became more strident, and the first open signs of rebellion manifested.

Then Joe got sick. His harvesting suffered, and he missed his quota. Now I carried him, paying for his meals and bunk. I was glad to expiate my social debt this way, owed for the manner in which he had rescued me from the concourse at Leda and given me support and a kind of family. I was a good picker now, well able to stay ahead, and on good terms with most of the other workers. I was, for one thing, thoroughly literate; when others had paperwork to decipher, I helped, sometimes saving them grief. Had either Joe or I asked for help, it would have been provided, but I preferred to help him myself.

I brought Joe his supper, which the foreman had served out especially for him, a generous portion. But he consumed only a mouthful and relapsed into his lethargy. There was no doctor; I could only sit by him and hope he got better.

I waited, finishing some of his meal for him, rather than let it go to waste. But my own appetite was gone, and so most of the stew was lost, anyway.

Others came by to express concern, but no one knew what to do. There were no contagious diseases in the Juclip; the bad days of personal contamination had been eliminated when man went out into the Solar System, with its natural quarantine. Only on septic Earth itself did the ancient maladies still flourish, and in occasional pockets in the major System cities. But there were degenerative maladies, such as the other Worry's declining liver. This one of Joe's was not familiar to any of us. We carried him back to his bunk in the ship where he lay unconscious.

In the night I got sick myself, vomiting out the stew I had taken. I felt awful, hurting and weak all over. I told myself it was nerves, or a sympathetic reaction, and forced myself to relax, and I got through the night, improving.

But I dreamed. I dreamed of a faceless man whom I realized was QYV, my private nemesis. He held out to me a goblet, urging me to drink, but I didn't want to because I knew he only wanted me dead. I spilled the goblet, and from it stew heaved out like my own vomit.

Stew?

I wrenched myself awake. "Poison!" I screamed.

Rivers appeared beside my bunk. "What?"

"Poisoned stew!" I said. "I ate some of Joe's stew, and it made me sick. It was served special for him—"

"For several days," Rivers said grimly. "Damn! I warned him not to stir up the animals!" He put his hand to Joe's forehead and froze.

"Is he better?" I asked.

"He's dead," Rivers said.

Numbly, I put my hand on Joe's face. It was cold. In a moment I was sure. He really was dead.

The other workers gathered around, their faces blank with uncertainty and horror. Joe Hill had been their tacit leader, and now, just like that, he was gone. My face was as blank as theirs, anesthetized by the first stun of grief. In the past year I had grown unaccustomed to death; now I had lost my friend and could not quite encompass the horrendous significance.

"Poison," Rivers repeated. "I thought he was wrong, but I guess he wasn't. Not if they had to take him out like this."

"But who—?" I asked, my lips fumbling numbly over the words, my tongue feeling thick, my face a chilled mask.

"The farmers," he said, "who must've paid off the foreman. They murdered my brother." He was silent a moment, staring at the dead man. There was no tear in Rivers's eye, no tremor to his chin; he simply stared. *Feared of dyin'. . .*

Then he reached down and took Joe's long knife. He held the wicked blade before him like a holy relic, and he sang:

I dreamed I saw Joe Hill last night
Alive as you and I . . .

The rest of us joined in, singing Joe's song, mourning him.

Rivers held the knife before him, pointing up, and

marched to the ladder-tube. He climbed, one-handed. We followed.

> Says Joe, "What they forgot to kill
> Went on to organize . . ."

As I climbed, my lethargy of horror converted to cold rage. I knew there was going to be mayhem. Vengeance . . .

The bubble-guards were stirring themselves, hearing our song. They were armed with billy clubs, and evidently supposed a gesture of force would cow us. We tore into them, crazed, knocking them out. Then we wrecked the tally pavilion. We set fire to the dry potato plants, and smoke smudged through the bubble.

The plantation owner's mansion was on the equator, between fields. We marched on it, singing. We outnumbered the defensive farm-guards five to one. In a moment the house was ablaze.

The police arrived. They must have accelerated at ten gees to reach the bubble so soon—or they had been warned ahead. They burst upon the scene with gas bombs, and in moments it was over. I inhaled and fell on the ground, unconscious.

There followed an interminable sequence of confinement in prison cells interspersed with official hearings. They kept me drugged most of the time, so I have no clear memory for detail. But I do remember being brought before a magistrate. The essence of what he said was this: There was no proof that I had either instigated the riot or done any of the damage, but I had certainly been involved. I was henceforth barred from the privilege of performing migrant labor.

Privilege? "But my ID replacement never came through!" I protested. "I can't get other work!"

"We are aware of that. Therefore, your options are limited. You are a resident alien of uncertain status. You must choose between deportation to your planet of origin or induction into the Jupiter Navy as a recruit."

"But I'm underage," I said, though I wanted no part of

deportation to Callisto, where at best I would face indefinite prison. If the Halfcal bureaucracy was as inefficient as that of Jupiter, they probably would not be able to identify me, and that could save my life; but still there was no future for me there. Yet I had tried to join the Navy before and learned that seventeen was their minimum enlistment age. I lacked six months.

"We have two affidavits attesting to your age as seventeen," he said tiredly, as if accustomed to the prevarications of migrant scum. "You are eligible for induction."

"Two?" I was amazed by this detail. "Who?"

He checked the papers on his desk impatiently. "Rivers, half-brother of the deceased, who testifies that the deceased informed him you were of age, and that the deceased was in a position to know."

Rivers! Now I remembered that he had said he owed me one. It seemed this was his way of paying. Joe might have told him I had tried to enlist in the Navy; Joe would not have lied about my age. All the migrants knew I faced trouble on Callisto, for I had told my story in full detail several times.

"He also testified that you had no part in the incitement to riot, though the deceased was a friend of yours. That you had been ill. A blood test confirmed mild contamination in your system, evidently from defective food. Rivers will be put on trial for riot, but we seem to have no reason to doubt his statements concerning you." He leafed through more pages. "The other statement is by your uncle Worry, confirming your age."

Worry! So he had been true to the brotherhood of the song!

"Nothing I can say would convince you that I am underage for induction?" I asked.

"We have the affidavits," he repeated firmly.

I sighed. *Please don't throw me in that briar patch!* I had tried to tell the truth, and they wouldn't listen. "Then you had better draft me."

And that was the manner of my enlistment as a common soldier in the Jupiter Navy, at age sixteen and a half. My career as an alien mercenary had begun.

Chapter 2
BASIC TRAINING

It would be tedious to describe in detail the whole of basic training, surely already familiar to the twenty-seventh-century citizen. The initial stage was a jumble of hurry-up-and-waits, of stripping and being reclothed completely, of taking batteries of tests for intelligence and aptitudes and skills, after a night with four hours sleep in a recalcitrant hammock. Hammocks are handy in space, because they adapt automatically to changes of thrust, but sleeping in them is an art that is not mastered instantly. I managed to make up the loss by sleeping through parts of several tests, by punching computer terminal buttons randomly in rapid order so as to finish early. I was a survivor.

I was assigned to a barracks ship similar in certain respects to the migrant-labor ships I had been in before. That housing made it easy to ferry our company to any part of the base or nearby space for the various training exercises; in fact, sometimes we were moved while we slept. We never knew what new hazard we would emerge to, and perhaps that was best.

I was part of the 666th Training Battalion, nicknamed "Hell's Rejects," for reasons relating to occidental mythology or numerology and the supposed savagery of the exercises. It had three companies, A, B, and C—I was in A for Awful—each of which had three platoons, each of which had three sections. The Jupiter Navy was trilaterally organized. One platoon in Awful was female. There were thirty trainees and five supervisory personnel in each platoonship, and additional cadre in each company, so Awful had a total manpower of one hundred fifty. But I was in regular contact only with the people of my own platoon; the other two platoons were of largely peripheral awareness, and the other companies might as well not have existed. My whole attention, like that of my fellow recruits, was occupied just getting through training.

We marched, we did grueling calisthenics, we attended dull lectures, we ate, we slept, we polished boots and brass. And of course we did KP—Kitchen Police, a euphemism for scrubbing floors and pots in the mess hall, sometimes with the same brushes. Theoretically the past five or six centuries were enough time for the military machines of our species to find ways to automate the kitchen facilities, but it had never happened. Similarly, permashine leather and brass were on the civilian market but were not available to us. We theorized that these were simply ways to keep us busy and miserable—and in subsequent years I have never found a better explanation. Likewise, inspections, a colossal expenditure of nervous energy without reward, and the necessity of maintaining entire display units of equipment that were used only *for* inspections. Some feculent personality once knotted my display towel over my hammock-cord while I slept, in the signal for early waking for special duty; not only was it not my turn for duty, it ruined my display. Some joke! I would have put his head out into the vacuum of space, had I known who it was.

We got haircuts every week, or else. For the first occasion, my full platoon was marched in step to the barbershop to be shorn, like it or not. We had been issued partial pay toward our first month's pay of eighty-six dollars—twenty per week—so we had the necessary cash. The Navy always made sure we had the cash for its requirements, and woe betide the recruit who spent it otherwise. Two dollars for a scalping; no hair on my head was left longer than half an inch. Later we would be allowed to grow some hair back; here in Basic the bald look was in.

The Navy was equally efficient about sex. Prescribed normal heterosexual relations were mandatory, and the Navy was the agency that defined "normal." There was, it was aptly said, the right way, the wrong way, and the Navy way. "You *will* indulge once a week," the platoon sergeant brayed, only he happened to employ a more explicit Saxon vernacular term in lieu of "indulge." Whereupon, for the first occasion, we were marched to the brothel ship for the maiden performance. The sanitary facilities were termed the Head; this department was, of course, the Tail. Each of us had to pay the two-dollar fee at the entrance, just as we had for the haircuts. Or, as the sergeant put it, else.

Talking was not permitted in the ranks, but I heard muttered exclamations of amazement, delight, and shock. Awful Company was largely Hispanic, made up of refugees like myself, ranging up to twenty-five years of age; many did not yet speak English, so had not comprehended the nature of this assignment until they saw the red Tail light by the door. I do not think Hispanics are any more sensitive about sex than are those of other origins, but we were ill prepared for the suddenness and dispatch of this particular requirement. We should have known; the haircutting had been as forceful and insensitive, and the physical examinations had nearly provoked riot when the medics started checking prostates. I do not know how the average recruit of Saxon stock feels about this, but to us the prostate check seemed very much like buggery. We also had suffered painful inoculations against obscure diseases to which we never expected to be exposed. Why hadn't they used the painless mists instead of the huge blunt needles? To humiliate and cow us, of course; that was common knowledge. So we should have been prepared for something akin to rape as the Navy introduction to sex; the Navy prided itself on making any natural occupation a horror. Yet, in our naïveté, we were dismayed.

One man broke ranks and fled. The Saxon sergeant turned and aimed his stunner almost casually, but caught the man in the back, a perfect shot, and the fugitive fell facedown to the floor. No one went to pick him up; he was left there unconscious as an object lesson for us all. We knew he wasn't seriously hurt—the stunner only stuns—but still, this had a sobering effect. No one else broke ranks. Numbly we waited as the lines moved forward.

In one sense it was an eternity before my turn came; in another it was an instant. The act of sex was not foreign to my experience, but I had no interest in this manner of indulging it. A uniformed matron, a female sergeant, met me just inside the door and guided me to Room Number Eighteen. Eighteen—my older sister, Faith, had been eighteen when she was brutally raped. "You have fifteen minutes, soldier," she said, and more or less shoved me through the entrance. Fifteen—my age when I watched my sister raped. I heard the door click behind me, and knew I was locked in. Both physically and symbolically.

A young woman in a pink negligee sat on a bunk. She was attractive enough in face and form for a Saxon, but her bored expression and my knowledge of her profession put me further off. I really had no sexual desire for her. Some people assume that any young man will eagerly indulge in any sex that offers; this is fantasy. For most of us, there has to be some emotional commitment, some indication that the woman is not merely willing but interested, that some sort of continuing relationship is possible. Our drives are strong but with many counterindications, so that the net effect is often doubt rather than passion.

"Well, get your clothes off, soldier," she snapped. The way she pronounced "soldier" reminded me that a soldier was the lowest form of life in the Jupiter Navy, and a recruit somewhat beneath that.

"I—do not feel inclined," I said, aware that I was blushing about as well as my swarthy skin permitted.

"Would you like me to undress you?" she inquired, as if this too were dull routine. Surely it was, for her.

"Uh—please, no, thank you. I—"

"Listen, kid, you only have fifteen minutes, and it takes five to undress and redress. I've got a schedule to keep. If you don't strip, I'll do it for you. I don't indulge with clothed men." Again, the term used was not "indulge."

"It—I think that would do no good," I said. "I—"

"You asked for it," she said impatiently. She bounced off the bed and strode to me. Without formality she unbuttoned my fatigue shirt and tugged it free of one arm and then the other. Then she went for the trousers.

I am, as it is put in English, ornery in some ways. I did not resist her; I let her undress me completely, moving when and in the manner she directed me, to complete the operation. In moments I stood naked before her, unaroused. This is, if you choose to call it that, another kind of talent I possess.

She looked at me and made a wry face. Then she shrugged out of her negligee and stood as naked as I was. She bounced a little on her feet so that her breasts lifted and fell impressively. She had the requisite physical attributes. But to me this was like a laboratory exhibit, and I did not react.

"May I touch you?" she asked. In the Navy no person is permitted to touch another without that person's permission; it is supposedly a safeguard against abuse. An inspecting sergeant asks the recruit's permission before he takes hold of the belt buckle to see whether the back side of it has been properly shined. Of course the sensible recruit does not refuse such permission, ever—but the forms are scrupulously honored, and I believe it is right that they are. Only an ignorant person would believe that the military service is a profession of physical violence; it is, in fact, a profession of social violence, at least in the training stage. The recruit's soul, not his body, is abused, generally. So this woman requested my permission before she touched me, but I was not wearing a belt or buckle for inspection at the moment.

"Yes," I said somewhat harshly, for my throat was tight.

She knelt before me and took hold of my member. She kneaded it delicately. She knew what she was doing; obviously she had had much experience. But there was no response, for my mental control, buttressed by my genuine aversion to the proceedings, remained in effect. I was impotent—and therein lay my true potency.

She got up, her lip curling with disgust. "Okay, soldier, I give up," she said. She walked to the wall and touched a button. "I'm buzzing the supe; she knows how to handle your kind."

"My kind?" I asked.

"The slobs who can't get it up."

This creature was not becoming more endearing with familiarity. "As I explained, I am not inclined at the moment."

She stared at my member. "Exactly."

The door opened behind me. I half-turned, abruptly embarrassed about my nakedness, but there was no refuge.

The one who entered was a woman in her twenties, garbed in a kind of off-the-shoulder, half-off-the-breast robe. She was beautiful, with flowing orange hair and a voluptuous body. She took in the situation in an instant. "Leave him to me, June. Take five."

"Yes, sir," the girl said, and quickly donned her negligee and departed.

Sir? This was an officer! That dismayed me further.

The woman sat on the bed. "Sit beside me, Private," she said, patting the bed. "Do not be alarmed."

I sat beside her, still conscious of my nakedness. Somehow it was worse to be naked before an officer than before an enlisted girl.

"You are young, I see," she said. "Probably admitted underage on a waiver, or by error. Fifteen?"

"Sixteen, sir," I said. Growth rates vary, and I am not a large person; still, this too was embarrassing. "They wouldn't—"

"It is all right; I inquired merely as a point of information, not as criticism. I presume you do not want to be discharged on that ground?"

"No, sir!" I said quickly. "I want to be in the Navy."

"Excellent," she murmured, and I saw how skillfully she was managing me. She had gotten me to agree with her on a matter of substance, and she had couched what could have been a threat in a positive manner. I had good reason to cooperate now. She understood motivation. "Have you copulated before?"

She had a higher-class vocabulary than did the girl, June! "Yes, sir." I said.

"With a woman?"

I felt the flush starting again. "Yes, sir."

"You object to doing it with a stranger?"

"I—not exactly, sir. I realize the Navy has its requirements. But—"

"Please speak freely, Private. I'm here to help you."

"Sir, it is better if there is love, or at least respect."

She smiled, and she was very likeable when she did that. She was the sort of poised woman who could make a man feel at ease, even in a situation like this. "Of course. But that will come in its proper time. For recruits there is only sex."

"I would prefer to wait for the proper time, sir."

"You are not homosexual?"

"No, sir!"

"Or routinely impotent?"

"No, sir."

"You are, then, normally disposed? It is merely the crudity of this introduction that has put you off?"

"Yes, pretty much, sir." I was beginning to feel guilty for my obstructionism.

"Do you understand why we do it this way?"

"No, not really, sir. It seems to me that—"

"Several excellent reasons, private. Jupiter does not permit homosexuals of either sex to serve in the armed forces, for historical and practical reasons that I personally may question but must honor. Other cultures have shown that homosexuals can make fine officers and personnel, if things are done openly so that blackmailing is impossible. But I do not make policy, any more than you do. We are all to that extent victims of the system, and must do what is required of us. This introduction to the services of the Tail represents a specific test for homosexuality; a man who is truly impotent with women cannot pass this point without discovery. The certainty is less with a woman, but whatever her underlying preference, she *will* function heterosexually, so the Navy is satisfied.

"It is also the opinion of the Jupiter Navy that the best soldier is a satisfied one. We do not care to have stifled sexual urges generating mischief in the ranks, so we see that sex is not stifled. Sexual expression is normal and healthy, and the Navy wants normal and healthy personnel. But this cannot be verified by a computerized test, and psychiatric charting is cumbersome and, in my opinion, unreliable; a person like yourself could readily distort the results. It is necessary to see sexual expression in practice.

"It is also true that some recruits are young, shy, inexperienced, or have some foolish notion of saving it for marriage or for a loved one. In reality, it is better to bring experience and competence to love or marriage, so that the relationship can be most positive where it counts most, without fumbling or accident or misunderstanding. So it is necessary to take care of this training at the outset. You are not in civilian life now, soldier; you are in the Navy, and your body is ours. Once you perform by the book in this house, you will comprehend the power the Navy has over you. Your sexual expression is no more private than your haircut or your pay. You will conform—or be compelled."

"Compelled?" I asked, alarmed at the increasingly firm tone.

She smiled again, putting her hand on mine, softening the impact. "Was I lecturing? I apologize. Don't be concerned, Private. It is true that we have drugs that will convert a mild-mannered man into a rutting billy goat, but that is pointless. It is the normal sexual bias and application we desire, not a drug-sponsored orgy. The Navy frowns on drug abuse. You will merely be prevented from undergoing further training until you meet our sexual requirement. You will remain on this ship until we are satisfied and issue you a certificate of completion. Most men meet it in a few days and have no further difficulty; some women take longer."

"Women really do have to—?"

"Indeed they do, soldier! The Jupiter Navy is an Equal Opportunity Employer; no discrimination is tolerated. Males and females have identical requirements, allowing for anatomical distinctions. Obviously a woman cannot be overtly impotent, but she can be frigid, and rape is not the Navy way, either, despite scuttlebutt to the contrary. The woman must understand and acquiesce, voluntarily, and show some reasonable response. She must, in other words, be normal, and demonstrate that normalcy exactly as the men do. We believe this is fair; don't you agree?"

"Yes, sir," I agreed, bemused.

"Now, you said you believe there should be love or respect. Love is not permitted recruits, but respect is encouraged. I gather you had a relationship with a woman you loved?"

"Yes, sir."

"And you lost her when you enlisted?"

"No, sir. She's dead."

"I understand. You feel you would sully her memory."

"Yes, sir." She had scored directly, surprising me.

"I *do* understand, Private. But what you wish is not an authorized luxury. Your heart may be your own, but as we say in the service, your ass is ours. You may feel what you feel for your loved one, but you must perform for the Navy. I believe your loved one would understand."

"Yes, sir, she would." That was a gross understatement. Helse would have urged me to go along. She had understood sex as well as any woman living.

"Are you ready to perform now, Private?"

"Not with you, sir!"

She laughed. "Of course not, though it is permissible in this special instance. Sometimes recruit girls feel easier about being initiated by male officers rather than enlisted men; it is a matter of breeding—no pun!—and perception. But for you, I mean, with June, whose office this is. You understand, she is required to make out a report; they all are. Attitude, technique, ejaculation—"

A report! Was nothing sacred? That turned me off again. "I—" I hesitated. "She remains a—"

"A prostitute?"

"Yes, sir. She cares nothing for me. She just wants to get it over with, like an item on an assembly line. There is neither love nor respect in that. That is not the type of woman I—"

"I understand, and I respect you for that attitude, Private. I really do! The Jupiter Navy does not require that you degrade yourself with a woman who is socially beneath you."

"Oh, I didn't mean that, sir! I—" But as I spoke, I realized I did mean it, at least in part. I had no status in the Jupiter society, but June was little more than a mannequin.

"You are intelligent and well educated," she said. "I'm

sure your tests show high facility in more than one language, broad information, extraordinary social perception, and an intelligence quotient in the upper percentiles. You are elite."

"No, I'm not, sir! I'm just a refugee."

"Well, refugee, we intend to do right by you, for you have a future in the Jupiter Navy. Would it help you to know that not all our women are sexually professional? Many are recruits, like yourself, who are assigned to this duty by roster."

"But if it's not voluntary—"

"That depends on how you interpret it, private. They do volunteer for the roster and are excused from KP or guard duty."

"Oh," I said. "Sir." I saw how it was. I knew that many of the male recruits I knew would be glad to exchange their places on the KP roster for one like this. Evidently it was true for some women, too. But that sort of woman did not excite me, either.

"I can see you are sincere, and I do want to help you," she said earnestly. I found I believed her. "I can offer you one other option, though a more difficult one."

"Sir?"

"As I mentioned, more female recruits have initial problems than do the males. They have been raised more restrictively, especially in your culture, and never expected to become refugees or to be obliged to join the Navy. Many understand intellectually but are unable to accept it emotionally. We have the drugs and experienced male operators, but—" She shrugged.

I caught on. "Me—and one of those?"

She looked me in my eye. Her iris was purple, and I realized she wore tinted contact lenses. "Hope, she is intelligent and bilingual, like you, no woman of the streets. You would be doing her a favor, believe me."

Her use of my name startled me; I had not realized that she knew it. But, of course, she had done her homework before coming here, at least to that extent. She was a competent officer.

"Uh—" I began doubtfully.

"A refugee does not really have the option of dismissal from the service, as you know. I hesitate to conjecture what would become of her, if . . ."

How well I understood! Perhaps some women considered sex to be a fate worse than death, but most refugees who returned to their home planets would find literal death, and the females would find sex, too, in the form of rape. They *had* to make good in the Navy. This officer had really maneuvered me; I could not refuse what she asked, as well she knew.

"I'll try, sir," I said.

She smiled warmly. "You will have an hour. I regret that we cannot grant you more time, but our facilities are already overworked. You will be under observation, you understand; we must be assured of performance. But that will not be intrusive. We do have some slight discretion. Here, I will convey you to Juana's chamber." She rose gracefully.

"Uh, sir, my clothes—"

"Yes, take them with you, by all means."

She waited a moment, gracious even in this detail, while I gathered up fatigues and boots in an armful that I carried as low as possible before me. Then I followed her out the door and down the hall. We passed into another section of the ship and entered a new chamber.

"Good luck," the officer said, and closed the door behind me as she left.

I stood there, my bundle of clothes held protectively before me. There on the bunk was a naked girl. She was hunched over, her black hair covering her face and part of her bosom. At least they didn't shave the women's heads; that would have been a horror! As the officer had said, certain allowances were made.

"Juana?" I asked. I could see she was Hispanic; it was not just her skin, as dark as mine, but the shape of her head and the way she held herself, even in this cruel situation.

She did not answer. I did not know her personally, but I knew her culture and her horror. I also knew that she knew what had to be. To her, it was much the same as rape.

And I was to be the rapist.

I turned to go, unable to continue with this. At least the regular prostitutes could not be hurt.

But then I remembered the alternative—for both of us— and turned again. I set down my clothing and sat beside her on the bed.

I saw her stiffen and hunch away from me, but she did not actually move on the bed. I began to use my power, to fathom her individual nature. I can judge a person quickly and accurately when I try. I would not call my talent telepathy—I have very little belief in the supernatural— but rather a semiconscious perception of human reaction, of body language, of tension in the voice; I suppose I am a living lie detector, though it is more than that. I relate to people more perceptively than others do. Now I related to Juana. She was frightened but not completely; it was not the blind terror of the unknown but rather an unwillingness to yield gracefully to degradation, and a horror of the inevitable. It is said that the familiar loses its horror; that is not necessarily the case.

"My name is Hope," I said. "Hope Hubris, from Awful. This is my first time here. I—I was impotent, so they put me with you."

She lifted her head, losing her horror of me. She brushed back her hair. Her face was pretty—or would have been, had she not been crying, making her eyes puffy and her chin mushy. Her irises were dark brown and glazed with moisture. "You're not—one of them?"

"Not a prostitute, or gigolo, or whatever it is called," I said. "I—sex with a stranger, just like that, like polishing boots or brass—I can't do that. So they put the difficult cases together, figuring maybe we'll understand each other and work it out."

"I'm sixteen," she said.

Helse had been sixteen! It struck me suddenly unexpectedly. I forgot where I was and what I was supposed to be doing. Helse, sixteen, and I, fifteen. She had shown me sex and love, in that order, and changed my life, and I never wanted any woman but her, ever, and she was dead. Because of me.

"What's the matter with you?" Juana asked.

I wiped my face, suddenly wet with tears. "I'm sorry," I said. "I can't do this."

"You know you have to," she said.

"Maybe with a—"

"All I said was that I was sixteen. I didn't mean it was statutory rape! I just meant I'm young, and it's hard for me. So you would understand."

"I'm sixteen, too," I said in Spanish, under my breath.

Juana's eyes widened. "You lied to get in?" she asked in the same language.

"No. I don't believe in lying. But someone did—and the magistrate didn't believe me. But that's not why . . . why what you said bothered me. *She* was sixteen."

"You have loved?"

"Forever."

"But she is gone?"

"Dead. And I want no other, ever."

"You made the trip to Jupiter?"

"Yes."

"Me, too." She was more comfortable in Spanish, speaking with greater confidence.

"Your folks?" I asked.

She nodded heavily. "Yours?"

"Yes. All dead, except my sisters."

"Raped?"

"Yes. One."

"Me, too."

"The Navy—doesn't understand about rape," I said.

"They practice it!" she said savagely. Then she smiled, and her beauty began to manifest. "Figuratively."

"True."

"I'm glad it's you, Hope. I'm Juana Moreno, from the Second Platoon. We had better get it over with."

"But if you were raped—"

"I think it will not hurt so much, with you."

I realized that she had accepted it, but I had not. "It should not hurt at all! And I—Helse—"

"Helse? That is not a Hispanic name."

"Neither is mine. But she was Hispanic, like me. Like you. But more experienced. She showed me—"

"Show me how she showed you. For it not to hurt."

"No. That memory is sacred."

"Look, Hope. I was raped by Saxon pirates. I'm afraid. I know it will hurt terribly, and I'll scream, but if I can't make it in the Navy, I have no life left. So I'll bite my tongue. You understand. I want it to be you."

I sighed. She was correct—for both of us. We had to do it, and I could be potent with her. "She . . . I was afraid. I had seen my sister raped—I didn't move. Helse did it all, the first time."

Juana shook her head. "I couldn't do that. You must do it."

"I don't want to hurt anybody that way!"

"It will hurt less with you. And it's so important. They are watching, and time is passing."

"They are watching," I agreed.

"Yes."

I glanced down. "You can see I'm not ready."

"Yes. You really don't want to. That makes it easier for me."

I shrugged. "I'll try." I raised my right hand. "May I touch you?"

She shrank back. "No!"

Then she laughed falteringly. "Sorry, Hope. Ask me again."

I got up and paced the floor, no longer bothered by my nakedness. "This—like a surgical operation—I can't do it."

"Yes."

My eye caught something on the wall. "A light switch!" I exclaimed.

Juana looked up, smiling with gratification.

I touched the switch, and there was blessed darkness. First, the language gave us some illusion of privacy of speech, and now the cessation of light gave us privacy of appearance. I felt much better, and knew that Juana did, too.

I returned carefully to the bed, finding it with my foot, and sat down. I heard her breathing beside me.

"Juana, take my hand," I said.

There was a brushing of arms, and then her hand found mine and squeezed it nervously. She was shivering and not with cold. It was warm here, and she was well fleshed. I knew she would cooperate, but would not initiate anything; it wasn't her way, and she had not been jesting about being afraid.

"May I kiss you?" I asked.

"Yes," she whispered, almost imperceptibly faint.

I drew her in toward me by the hand and quested for her face with my own. I found it and met her lips, and kissed her briefly.

Then she tore her hand away from mine but not to retreat. It was not passion, either, but the desperate need for comfort. She flung her arms about my shoulders and pulled me in close, so that we both almost fell over. "Hold me! Hold me!"

I held her. She was excruciatingly female against me, and now I reacted. Her hair caressed my shoulder, and her body was warm though her hands were cold. I felt guilty on two counts: for having to take advantage of a frightened woman; and for being aroused by someone other than Helse.

"May I pretend you are someone else?" I asked.

"No!"

Surprised, I chuckled ruefully. "That was unkind of me. I did not mean to insult you."

"You did not insult me, Hope. I know you loved her. But I wish you would try to love me, just for this hour. I have no one, and I need someone."

Helse was dead I reminded myself yet again. I was not really being unfaithful to her. She would have urged me to do this. She would never have permitted the dead to hurt the living. "I'll try."

We lay on the bed and kissed again. I was on my right side, she on her left, and it was somewhat awkward. I proceeded very slowly and paused when she stiffened, trying not to hurt her, but somehow it had to be forced. In retrospect I realize that the position was wrong, but then I thought it was my inadequacy.

"It does hurt," she whispered. "But I don't mind. You are a nice man, Hope."

"You're a nice woman, Juana." And when I said that, she sighed and relaxed a little, and it was easier.

"I think we're going to make it," she whispered.

We were already making it. "I think so," I agreed.

"I could love you, Hope."

"It's not authorized."

She laughed, then caught her breath, for that had hurt. But it helped me complete the position. We finished it, not with any sharp climax, and separated with a certain relief. There had been some discomfort for me, too, physical and emotional, for she had not been ready, and perhaps would never be ready. Sex is not always wildly exhilarating, contrary to myth, for either man or woman. Sometimes, with the best intentions, it is a chore. But we had accomplished it, and that pleased us both. Had it not been for the fertility suppressant in the base water supply that halted the female cycle, she could have become pregnant. It could have been much worse.

"Can we be friends?" she asked wistfully.

"Yes." My limited passion had abated, but my emotion was stronger than ever.

"Would you kiss me again?"

I rolled over and kissed her. This time, free of the onus for performance, it was a deep and wonderful experience. We held it for some time, not wanting to let it go. The sexual act had been a somewhat artificial thing, done by Navy command, but this was genuine.

Then I had an idea. "Juana, you know we have to come here to the Tail once a week, and it will be with different partners each time. We have no choice; we're recruits."

"Yes. But I think I can tolerate it now. I will pretend it's you."

I smiled in the dark. "And I will pretend it's you. But after Basic, when we're E2's, a person doesn't have to come here, if he has a hetero-roommate."

"I know."

"When that time comes, if we're still here in this company or this base, will you be my roommate?"

She made a little shudder of gladness. "Yes, Hope."

We lay there in the darkness, holding hands, and there was a certain affinity to love. We had worked it out.

Training continued unabated. I learned to fire a laser rifle with accuracy and to do hand-to-hand combat and to make a "jump" in a space suit, with a miniature rocket jet to propel me. And I marched. The Navy in its infinite wisdom believed that marching with full gear built good soldiers. There was an all-purpose dome with a sand path around it, and we traversed that path interminably, until I thought I had memorized every obnoxious grain of sand.

But it wasn't all bad. The Navy also believed in culture, in the form of art, music, and dance. The art was in the form of repainting the buildings. They didn't need it, in this controlled climate; that was not the point. *We* needed the experience. The music was in the form of a marching band. Those of us who could play musical instruments of the brass or percussion variety played them while we marched to the booming beat of the big drum. It was, I admit, fun to march to the drum; the beat made our feet respond, and the pace was always slow. The dance was in the form of trick marching: intricate maneuvers in unison. These were exacting but all right. Anything was better than the dreary marching in sand with gear.

We did get fleeting moments of free time. The Navy encouraged us to use it in constructive entertainments. Our ship had an excellent day room, complete with pool table, table tennis, decks of cards, chess, checkers, backgammon (Acey-Deucy), dice, dominoes, and marbles. Naturally the troops generally ignored these and concentrated on the unauthorized entertainment: the feelies.

The feelies were special programs played through headsets. Electrical currents were fed through the head in the form of trace magnetic fluxes, stimulating programmed visions. Some were benign, such as a tour of an Earthly zoo or a swim through ice water in a fissure on Europa. Most were sexual, ranging from normal Tail-type through sadomasochistic, which last extreme the Navy frowned on. This sort of thing did not appeal to me, either, but I was surprised by how many others professed to enjoy it. There were several brands that circulated, and it seemed some were better than others. Periodically there were crackdowns on the feelie-chips, but there were always more of them, and it was evident that the Navy did not take the matter seriously.

"Hey, Hope, you should try this one!" a platoon-mate called to me. "It's got your name on it!"

"Hubris?" I asked, suspecting this was a joke.

"No, Hope," he said. "Here, try it! You'll see!"

Still wary, I borrowed his headset and set it over my own head. The front of it came down to cover my eyes, and the sides covered my ears. Sight and sound came, three-dimensional and binaural, seeming to put me in a different world. The touch and smell sensations took longer to manifest, as the currents did not immediately align with those of the brain; the participant had to cooperate, to get himself into the mood, and I was not doing so. I was just looking.

I seemed to stand on the hull of a bubble in space, with the pale illumination of the sun highlighting the curve of it. Before me was a bag or package. From it poked a human arm, and the hand reached toward me. "Here is what you need," a voice said in my ears. But the hand was empty.

Then my vision panned around, and I saw the name printed on the surface of the bubble: HOPE.

I removed the helmet, controlling my reaction. "So it is," I said as I returned the headset to the other recruit. "What's it all about?"

"You okay?" he asked. "I thought you were going to fall over for a moment there!"

"I thought you were joking," I said quickly. "It was a shock to see my name on that spacecraft."

"I guess it was. I'm only a little way into this one. It's a reverse-role experience—pretty hot stuff, I'd say."

"Reverse-role?" I asked blankly. "You mean where the man's passive and the woman dominant?"

He laughed. "Naw, that's tame! Hell, you can get that in

the Tail, if you ask for it. This is where it's keyed to a man, but he's in a girl's body. I played through one the other day. It's really something, getting felt up when you're a girl. Feeling things happen to anatomy a man doesn't even have. Drove me crazy, till I caught on. Penetration—" He shook his head and rolled his eyes. "Some freaks really go for this stuff, though." He set the helmet firmly on his head and settled back in the chair.

A man's awareness in a woman's body. While that woman underwent the experience of sexual stimulation and culmination. That was surely not on the authorized list!

I read the label on the chip container projecting from the top of the helmet. Each chip was protectively encased, but the cases plugged into the helmet socket. It was easy to use. This one said EMPTY HAND—HOPE.

I went to my hammock and closed my eyes, feigning sleep. We had already passed morning inspection, and it was a weekend, so my gear no longer needed to be reserved for display and could be used for its theoretical purposes. I wanted a chance to think without being disturbed.

When my family had fled Callisto and traveled toward Jupiter in a bootleg bubble, using gravity shields somewhat the way the ancients had used sails on ships of the seas, our toilet tanks had filled up and had had to be evacuated. My fiancée, Helse, and my sister, Spirit, had gone out with me onto the hull without the benefit of magnetic boots—bubble equipment had been minimal—and guyed ourselves with ropes and done the job. But I had passed close to one of the bodies frozen and bagged and tied to the hull—the bodies of our menfolk, slain by the pirates—and suffered a vision of a dialogue with my father, Major Hubris, who had told me there was food and shown me his empty hand. That vision had horrified me, but the revelation had been valid, and we had found food.

All the people of the bubble had known of my vision, but all were dead now. All except me—and my little sister, Spirit. She alone knew the significance of the empty hand. This particular thing I had not spoken of when I told my tale to the migrant crew; it was a very private matter.

The feelie-chip was labeled EMPTY HAND, and the particular show was titled HOPE. Could that be coincidence? Perhaps, but the view it presented of the bubble hull and the packaged corpse could not. No one could have guessed about that, and I had told no one. Well, I had written it in my biography of my experience as a refugee, but that was safely out of the way; I knew no one here had seen it.

And the reverse-role theme—that also related. Spirit and I had escaped the pirates by masquerading as the opposite sex. She had become a little boy, and I a teenaged girl. We had learned that device from Helse, who had protected herself from molestation by passing as a boy. That strategy was not effective in all cases, of course, but it had worked for her. I had left Spirit on a pirate ship, in a compromise with necessity, to be the cabin boy for a reverse-role captain named Brinker.

No, this was no coincidence! That pirate ship must now be involved in the illicit distribution of this line of feelies, and Spirit, who would now be about fourteen, had sent me a message only I could comprehend.

My spirited little sister survived, and was reaching out with considerable ingenuity to find me! I had hardly dared think of her in the interim, fearing confirmation of her demise; now a portal in my heart flung open.

Until this time my life had been somewhat desultory. I had spent a year in the dead-end occupation of migrant labor and gotten into the Navy more or less coincidentally. I had lived from day to day and hour to hour. Now my life assumed meaning, for I had a mission: to rescue my sister, Spirit.

For Spirit was my life. She alone, of all people living, had shared my ordeal of refuge and survived. She alone truly understood me. She was my kin. I had loved Helse as a woman, but I loved Spirit as family and friend. Helse was dead, and I mourned her forever; Spirit lived, and I needed her.

From that moment, I had purpose. The knowledge of Spirit guided me like the light of a distant beacon. Two-thirds of the emptiness of my situation could be filled by the restoration of my sister.

I checked the other feelie-chips. They were scattered about the post, traded from unit to unit, and, of course, there was no computer-library index to them. The Navy might tolerate illicit chips, but the Navy did not encourage them or admit their existence. Everyone knew of them, but no one spoke openly of them, apart from such in-barracks exchanges as had introduced me to the first. It was an unwritten code: Do not rock the boat.

I became a collector of experience, viewing every EMPTY HAND chip I could borrow. The shows were not important to me; I familiarized myself with them only to be able to discuss them intimately with others, justifying my interest in more of the same. It was better to be judged a reverse-role freak than to have my real purpose known. In this manner I became acquainted with the programs FAITH, CHARITY, MAJOR, HELSE, and, of course, HOPE. The names of my older sister, mother, father, fiancée, and myself. But there was none for my younger sister, Spirit. And that made sense, for her own name would be suspect among the pirates. Her absence amounted to confirmation: Spirit was reaching for me and now had touched me.

But where was she? She was aboard the pirate ship, but that could be anywhere in the Jupiter Ecliptic. The pirates would not identify themselves to the Jupiter Navy!

But they did do business with the Navy, however covertly. The EMPTY HAND chips had to get from ship to base. What was their route? It should be possible to trace it backward. There should be pickup points, distribution centers, authorized agents to accept payments—that sort of thing. The chips might be illegitimate, but there had to be a framework. Pirates did not distribute chips free; they were in it for the money. The chips were free to enlisted personnel, common property; that meant that the Navy was in fact paying for them, and what the Navy paid for, it had on record, somewhere, somehow.

Part of my training was in computer research. That is, learning to use the Base Computer to ascertain such things as how many pairs of combat boots were available in storage, for each size of foot. It was not that I had an aptitude for data retrieval; I did, but they didn't know it, because I had literally slept through that segment of my placement testing program. In fact, I wondered how I had scored so well overall, considering that, but the Navy seemed to have more use for supply clerks than for combat specialists. The training computers were centuries out of date, contributing to what I now perceived as the monumental inefficiency of the Jupiter Military System. But I realized that I might be able to use them to gain the information I needed. If the monthly purchases and disbursements of boots were listed, the feelie-chips had to be entered somehow, probably under an alias. I had to look. So I picked the lock during off-hours and sneaked into the terminal room.

Alas, I did not yet know quite enough about even those primitive machines. They were keyed for trainee exercises; when I punched the coding for an unauthorized listing, an alarm was sounded in the Military Police Station. Suddenly I found myself under arrest. To add to my ignominy, I learned that the Base Computer System had no information of the acquisition or disbursal of entertainment chips. The records for gray market purchases were kept separately, by hand, so as to keep the official record clean. I had blundered badly.

My unit was notified, and my platoon sergeant came to fetch me. I knew I was in for the Navy version of hell.

Sergeant Smith was an E5, the lowest level of sergeant, though, of course, that was far beyond my E1 recruit status. He was no young soldier; he seemed to be in his forties, and the seven longevity slashes on his left sleeve showed he had twenty-one years' service. He had four slanted slashes on the right sleeve, too, indicating two years of combat duty. He should have had a higher rank by this time. He was a rough-tough soldier and a harsh barracks master; he breathed fire when we fouled up, which was often, since we were normal recruits. He was Saxon and did not speak Spanish, and there was a general suspicion that he did not like Hispanics. I had felt the heat of his wrath before, and I was afraid of him.

But Smith surprised me. He brought me to his barracks room, which was in strict military order, its hammock folded away and its furnishings sparse. There were two chairs and a table, and he bade me sit down. "Hubris, I've been watching you," he said. "You're inexperienced but hardened to work, and you're three times as smart as your tests show. Why'n hell'd you pull a stunt like this?"

"I can't tell you, Sergeant," I said, hating this.

"You broke 'n entered, and that's a black mark on your platoon and on me," he said. "It's my business to see that this sort of thing doesn't happen. You aren't a criminal-type, Hubris. You had to have reason. You were after something, and I mean to know what it was."

I sat silent. I couldn't tell him about my quest for Spirit; this was not a thing the Navy would understand. It would be better to take my punishment straight. I deserved it for my foolishness.

"Tell me why, and give me your word there will be no repetition, and I will give you minimum standard punishment," he said.

I shook my head no, fearing what was coming.

He said no more on that subject. "The barracks needs cleaning," he said. "You will scrub it down, beginning at floor level, during your free time, commencing today. Here is your scrub brush." He handed me an archaic tooth-brush.

That afternoon, and the afternoon following, I labored to clean the immense inner hull with that tiny brush. My platoon-mates saw me but did not comment; it was forbidden to talk with a person undergoing punishment. The labor was mind-deadening, but I had spent a year on the migrant circuit, so I was toughened to this sort of thing. I simply tuned my mind to other things, freeing it from the mundane blank, and proceeded, as it were, on automatic.

On the third day Sergeant Smith approached while I worked. "This isn't necessary, Hubris," he said. "You have completed minimum punishment and have served as an example. What have you to say?"

"This is supposed to be a training battalion," I said gruffly. "I did wrong and I am being punished; that's fair. But you are making me do something useless when you should be making me do something that forwards my competence as a Jupiter fighting man, even though I'm really a mercenary."

"Just what are you trying to say, Hubris? You may speak freely." That meant I would not suffer additional punishment for anything I might utter; this code, too, is honored. I could call him a fecal-consuming pederast whose hash marks were forged, and get away with it.

I elected for a less personal critique. "This is chicken shit," I said, using the age-sanctified vernacular for pointless harassment.

"You want a rationale to justify it?" he asked disdainfully.

He had the temerity to argue the case. "Yes, if I have to indulge in it." I should have known better than to challenge a military professional. The officer at the Tail had tackled my doubt head-on, and so did Sergeant Smith.

"The foundation of the military service, *any* military service," he said carefully, "is discipline. Men and women must be trained to do exactly what is required of them, in precisely the way required, and at the moment it is required. The military organization is ideally a finely crafted machine, and the individual parts of that machine can not be permitted free will, or the machine will malfunction. We want the soldiers of the Navy to be able to fight; but first they must obey, lest we become no more than a random horde of scrappers. Civilians come to the service with a number of ungainly and counterproductive attitudes; we must cure them of these, just as we must build up their bodies and their skills. Naturally, civilians resist these changes, just as they resist the first haircut and the first session in the Tail. They have other ideas —and because we must rid them of these ideas, we put them through a program some call chicken shit. It may be unpleasant, but it is necessary if they are ever to become true military personnel, able to function selflessly as part of an effective fighting force. It is, ultimately, not hardware or firepower or numbers that determines the true mettle of any military organization; it is discipline. What you are undergoing now is not useful work by your definition; it is the essence of discipline."

I paused in my scrubbing, impressed. Sergeant Smith had given me a genuine answer, instead of the bawling out I had expected. I realized that I had not properly appreciated the qualities of the man—and that was embarrassing, because I, of all people, had no excuse for such misjudgment. I had turned off my mind too soon!

Yet I resisted the logic. "In what way does scrubbing a clean hull with a toothbrush contribute to discipline that rigorous useful training would not?"

"Rigorous training is proud work," he said. "You have too much pride, Hubris. Your very name smacks of it; I daresay it runs in your family. In civilian life it can be an honorable quality, but here it amounts to arrogance. You assume that your personal standards are superior, even when you are in plain violation of reasonable regulations. We must expunge that arrogance, or you will never be a true soldier. And that would be unfortunate, because you have the makings of a fine one. So I have given you a task that deprives you of pride, because it has no meaning. Chicken shit is very good for abolishing hubris, the arrogance of pride."

He was making some sense. I realized, now that I understood him better, that I could trust Sergeant Smith. He was not the blind disciplinarian I had taken him for. He was a sighted disciplinarian. It was a significant distinction.

"Will you keep a secret?" I asked.

"No. I serve the Jupiter Navy, nothing else."

Did my quest for Spirit really have to be secret? It seemed to me now that Smith would understand, and perhaps it was best that I tell him. I could have told him before, and spared myself all this, had it not been for that very hubris he charged me with. Surely my surname was no coincidence; some distant ancestor had been so proud of his arrogance he had adopted its name for his own. This was, it seemed, a lesson I had needed. "Will you give me a fair hearing, even if it takes some time?"

"Yes." No fudging here.

"Then I will tell you what you want to know, and I will promise not to break any more military regulations."

"Come with me." He turned and walked away.

I set down my toothbrush and followed him to his room. There I told him about the manner I had separated from my sister, Spirit, and how I had received news of her survival.

"Then it was not pride so much, but need," Sergeant Smith said. "You have to try to save your sister from the pirates."

"Yes."

"You should have gone through channels. The Navy is not indifferent to the welfare of the families of soldiers. You should have come to me at the outset."

"I guess I should have. I didn't realize—"

"Lot you have to learn about the Navy, Hubris. That's why you're a recruit. It's my job to teach you, but you have to give me half a chance."

He was right. "I'm sorry," I said. "I—"

"Apology accepted." He looked at his watch. "Chow time." He touched his intercom. "Corporal, bring me dinner for two from the mess."

"Check, Sergeant," the intercom replied.

Startled, I looked at him, the question in my face.

"I have obtained some of your private history, Hubris," he said. "Now I'll give you some of mine. We'll eat here; what we have to discuss is nobody's business but ours."

I nodded, still uncertain what he had in mind.

And while we ate, Sergeant Smith told me his military background. It was amazing. He had been a master sergeant in a regiment, in charge of the specialized training the troops needed for a hazardous mission. The plan had been to make a covert raid to a planetoid in the Asteroid Belt where certain Jupiter officials were being held hostage. Smith had urged against the attempt, believing that the risk of precipitating the murder of the hostages was too great. He believed that negotiation was called for. The captain in charge had overruled him unceremoniously and ordered the preparations to be made. Smith had then gotten the job of training the men in the necessary maneuvers. He had tackled it honestly but pointed out that he needed at least two months to get the men in proper shape so that there would be no foul-ups. The captain, eager to get the job done, cut the time to one month. Again Smith warned against using this inadequately prepared force; again he was overruled.

The mission was launched—and it failed. The hostages were killed, a number of the raiding personnel were lost, and Jupiter's interplanetary relations suffered, exactly as Smith had warned.

There was an investigation. Smith was found guilty of gross negligence, reduced four grades in rank, from master sergeant E7 to private first class E3, and reassigned to the lowest form of supervisory labor: the training of recruits. That had been four years ago; he now had won back two of his lost stripes and might eventually recover the rest if he kept his nose clean.

"But it was the captain who should have paid!" I exclaimed.

"Officers don't pay," Smith said. "Appearances must be preserved. They needed a scapegoat, and I was the one."

"But you were right and he was wrong!"

"Right way, wrong way, Navy way," he reminded me.

I shook my head, confused. "You accepted wrongful punishment to support the military way?"

"You accepted it to protect your sister."

"Yes, I suppose. But—"

"When you are ready to do the same for the Jupiter Navy, you will be a true military man."

"I'll never be that sort of man!" I declared.

He smiled, somewhat grimly. "Hubris, when you finish Basic, I want you to put in for retesting, and then for Officer's Training School. I believe you would make a better officer than the captain I served."

"You are going to all this trouble, just to get me to try to be an officer?" I asked incredulously. *"Why?"*

"I owe it to the Navy to do my job the best way I know how and to produce the best fighting men I can. You have real potential. I want to straighten you out and set you on the right course. Hubris, you have a real future in the Navy—once you make up your mind to pursue it."

"A future in the Navy? I'm a mercenary, and I'm not even of age!"

"I know that. But irregularities in the induction are excused if the rest is in order. As a resident alien you are eligible for any position in the Navy, which is more than can be said for your civilian opportunities. You have a clean record, Hubris; keep it that way."

"A clean record? But I—"

"There was no court-martial. You accepted unit punishment. No officer was involved. It is off the record. Remember that: In the Navy, souls can be bought and sold for a clean record."

Probably true. "You expect me to be the sort of careerist you are? A scapegoat?"

"I think you can do better, Hubris. Get your house in order, become an officer, and I will be proud to call you 'sir.'"

"I can't do it," I protested. "My first priority is to rescue my sister."

"I will help you do that."

Again I was amazed. "How? You can't break the regulations either."

"I don't have to break regs. I just have to enforce them."

I raised an eyebrow.

"The transsex feelies are unauthorized," he explained. "It is Navy policy to tolerate them as long as they don't cause mischief. It is the prerogative of the Platoon or Company Commander to determine what constitutes mischief; in practice it's left to the noncoms. If I raise an objection, I'll get to the source quickly enough. They'll figure I'm bucking for a bribe; they'll be glad to settle for information."

I smiled. "Sergeant, if you do that for me, I'll be the best soldier I can be. And the day I get my sister back, I'll put in for Officer's School."

"Deal," he said. "But it'll take awhile to trace the supply route, because these people are cagey, understandably. They've been stepped on before. And I don't dare check with the officer who pays for the chips out of general funds; he's twice as cagey as the pirates are."

"I understand." We shook hands, and that was that. It was a great relief to me, in several senses.

Nothing more was said in the following days. But the next week, when the assignments for trainee squad leaders were posted, I was the one for my squad. I had no real authority; all it meant was that I got an armband, marched at the head of my column of ten men, and had to relay minor directives and items of information. I also had to select the men for police call (routine cleanup of refuse) and such other stray chores as were assigned. But it was my first taste of leadership in the Navy, and a signal that I was expected to set an example of good soldiering. I intended to do so.

A few days later, Sergeant Smith called me in for a squad leader conference, told me one of my men had reported for sick call twice when due for special duty formation, and to get him in line pronto. Then: "EMPTY HAND chips are distributed by the pirate fence, Chip Off the Old Block, who handles the more extreme entertainments. They're into drugs, too, and they've got a security system the Navy can hardly match. That's a dead end; we'd have to shut them down before they'd talk, and by the time that scene was done, they'd have destroyed all their records and skipped the base. Only if they get into murder, or if they seduce a general's daughter, will the Navy move firmly against them."

"All I want is information," I said.

"I know. That's why I call this a dead end. We've got to go another route, and it will take time. You don't want the pirates to get any whiff of what you're really after; your sis would pay the penalty. The Navy runs surveillance on the pirate ships in the Juclip; I'm sure there's a record of every one that connects to the Old Block fence. But no enlisted man has access to that list. You need an officer. The right officer."

"What officer?"

"Hubris, I can't tell you. I know him, but I can't violate his trust. I'll have to ask him to contact you. If he refuses—"

"I understand," I said. "You can't tell an officer what to do."

"This one's special. Give it a couple of weeks; I think he'll agree. When you meet him, you'll understand."

"Thanks, Sergeant," I said sincerely.

"Just you be a credit to my platoon."

My squad was already doing well; in due course it would be recognized as the sharpest in the company.

As it happened, the officer did not contact me during Basic Training, but Smith assured me that the man intended to when he deemed the moment propitious, and I believed him. I had to wait, but I knew this was my best chance, and meanwhile there was plenty to keep me occupied. I was discovering that despite the hard work and dehumanization of training, I liked the military life. It was another kind of family, and once its ways were understood, it was a good family. The decent food and thorough exercise filled me out physically, so that I became an unimpressive but extremely fit individual, fast and strong and confident. I was, indeed, becoming a good soldier, and I was learning a lot.

The weeks passed, and the months. The concluding exercise of Basic came in our tenth week. This was the Challenge Course. If we were true soldiers, we would make it successfully through; if not, we would be recycled for further training.

There were other inducements. Our full cycle—the entire training battalion, three hundred recruits—would run the course together. There were many more people in the battalion, of course, but the rest were cadre, training personnel, officers, and staff. The recruits were the ones that counted. The nine platoons of the three companies would vie with each other for points, and the leading platoon would be granted an immediate three-day pass. That meant free time, and free time was the Navy's most precious commodity. The leading individuals would be granted a jump promotion from E1 to E3, for performance in the Challenge Course was considered to be the measure of competence and potential. There would be nine such promotions—theoretically, one per platoon, but if all the top scorers were in one platoon, they'd get it. Sergeant Smith wanted our platoon to get the victory, for it would mean a commendation for him and facilitate his own promotion. Promotion was another great Navy lure.

The course was through the special Challenge Dome, which was made up like an Earth wilderness. There was supposed to be jungle, desert, mountains, lakes, and snow. Also wild creatures of a number of types, ranging from gnats to crocodiles. And a tribe of headhunters, who would be out to get us. They wouldn't really take our heads, of course, but anyone captured and ritually decapitated— stripes of red paint would serve to show the cuts—would be considered dead and out of the challenge. The headhunters, too, had passes and promotions to earn, so they would be alert, but they had to follow the rules and could not capture any recruit unless he made some sort of error. There would be about a hundred referees in there, personnel in distinctive black garb, who would mark individual injuries and deaths along the way and feed the information into the Casualty Computer. They would neither help nor hinder us; they merely observed, until the occasion came to mark the dead and pull them from the course. We were supposed to ignore them; to ask one for help or information was to forfeit the course immediately.

Supplies would be issued when we entered the Challenge Dome: bug repellent, croc repellent, machetes, maps, and so on. The wild animals were real, but we were not supposed to hurt them; avoidance was the key. "Getting chomped by a croc is line-of-duty-no," Sergeant Smith explained with a smile. Line-of-duty-yes was okay; sometimes legitimate accidents occurred, for which a recruit was not penalized. Line-of-duty-no mishaps were subject to reprimand. The course was supposed to take about three hours, but anyone who got through "alive" within six hours passed. Those who made it in two-and-a-half hours got a higher rating, and chances were that anyone who made it in under two hours would be among the winners of promotions. Last cycle's winner had done it in one hour and fifty minutes, with his buddy right behind.

For we were to use the "buddy" system. We would travel

in pairs, with each one looking out for the other. Loss of partner was line-of-duty-no unless there was good reason, such as the death of the buddy under honorable conditions. If two people lost their buddies, they were supposed to buddy up with each other.

I intended to score well in the challenge, for three reasons. First, I was really getting into the training and wanted to prove myself in the field. Second, I wanted to help Sergeant Smith's platoon make the best showing. And third, I had discovered that though E2's were not marched in formation to the Tail, they weren't permitted heterosexual roommates; that was a privilege reserved for E3 and up. E2's could use the Tail, or make private liaisons and clear them with their units. It was catch as catch can, not an ideal situation; most of them wound up at the Tail, anyway. I had had enough of that; I wanted to room with Juana. I was not emotionally involved with her in the sense of being in love, but I did like her, and the rooming arrangement would be more comfortable for both of us for any number of reasons. So I wanted us both to make E3 so we could do it.

I knew that it was important, in any competitive situation, to plan ahead. So I researched the Challenge Dome, learning what prior layouts had been. It changed each time, but there was a certain broad pattern, since lakes and mountains weren't easy to move. What they tended to do was use different segments of the dome, so as to include patterns with minimal effort. I found out what the pattern of patterns was, and so had a pretty good notion what to anticipate for ours.

I consulted with Juana. We had not met in the Tail again, for the Navy policy was to change combinations each time, to prevent exactly such emotional attachments as we were forming, but we met in our free time. After the first month we were permitted to wear civvies during off time, so I saw Juana in a dress and a feminine hairdo. She was lovely! She, like I, had filled out in a beneficial manner, and she had been well endowed to begin with. No one could ever match my lost fiancée, Helse, in my heart, but I realized that as a sexual partner of convenience, Juana was all that I could ask. She could easily have paired with another man, but she had fixed on me because of the difficult contact we had shared that first time. We understood each other in a special way.

She was smart, too. She had had a good education, as I had; her family had been reasonably well-to-do. That was one reason she had had such a problem in the Tail; she had expected to be a virgin at her marriage. The brutality of her rape and loss of her family had shocked her fundamentally but had not made it easier for her to indulge in casual sex; the opposite was the case. I understood this all too well, so in this sense I was right for her. I was almost sorry I could not love her, for she was worthy of love, but neither Navy policy nor my private emotional makeup permitted that. From the outset we had our understanding: we would be friends and sexual partners, but not lovers. That may seem like a strange distinction, but it was valid. Sex can be separated from love, and love from friendship, and only by recognizing this separation could I believe I was not being false to Helse.

Juana shared my eagerness to score well in the Challenge. We agreed to be buddies there, trading off our assigned partners so we could be together. That way we would succeed or fail together, and that was as it should be. Buddies were to be chosen ahead of time, since the Navy knew that strangers did not make the best buddies, but for convenience they had to be in-platoon at the start. So I paired with a handsome Saxon youth, and Juana took a voluptuous Saxon girl; then we introduced them to each other and asked if they would like to make the exchange in the Challenge. They were more than happy to oblige; they had not thought of this particular device.

Then we got down to serious planning. I showed Juana the maps of prior layouts, and she made suggestions on how to proceed. She came up with one notion that appalled me, but she showed me her research and finally convinced me she was correct. The more I considered her proposal, the more I liked it. It was risky; we could be genuinely hurt if we miscalculated. But it offered a chance to complete the probable course in well under two hours—perhaps even record time. As far as we could tell, no one else had ever tried this ploy, and it required courage for us to decide on it. But we did; it was basically double or nothing.

It took some preparation. We were allowed to bring no props to the Challenge Dome, but we could develop whatever skills we wished and had time for. So we researched and found out how to make a paddleboard from natural materials. We went swimming at one of the Base pools—Juana looked great in a suit!—where paddleboards were allowed, and learned how to use them. It took some effort, and we weren't expert, but we could make do. We also practiced our straight swimming, especially the breast-stroke–frog-kick combination.

All too soon, the day came. We were marched into the Challenge Dome. We stripped and stepped naked into the supply section. We had to choose our equipment from what was available and use it to run the course. Anyone who chose foolishly would pay the consequences soon enough. The Dome personnel quickly provided what was ordered but made no suggestions or remarks. Some trainees evidently hadn't thought about it ahead and wasted precious time making up their minds. I had memorized my list and was one of the first on my way.

I wore standard combat boots, jungle fatigues, heavy gloves, and a cap with mosquito netting that tied around my neck, so that no part of me was open to the bugs. Other men simply used insect repellent and traveled lighter and cooler, but I had my reasons to do it my way. I took a standard machete and a small hunting knife and a quadruple ration of reptile repellent. "Going swimming?" the clerk inquired wryly, in violation of the no-comment regulation, but I didn't answer. He thought I was a fool, since land was faster than water for footsoldiers. And, of course, I took one of their little maps.

I smiled as I viewed it. They had set the course just about where I had anticipated. I knew this layout in more detail than the map showed, for it was supposed to be only a general guideline, with a few minor errors to simulate real-life conditions. This was verisimilitude; maps could be out of date or simply wrong, so part of the challenge was to make do despite errors of information.

I focused on a particular area. Sure enough: There was a mismarked quicksand bog. Anyone who trusted this map and tried to swim in clear water could blunder into quicksand instead. Since clear water was infested with crocodiles, few were likely to try, however. Mainly, they would lose time, having to skirt an unexpected bog. Never trust a map too far!

I proceeded to the rendezvous point with my buddy. There were the two girls, as agreed. Juana was shapeless in fatigues and netting, as I was, but her friend was in a fake wool sweater and skirt and looked stunning. The other couple evidently planned to hike through the mountain region where the air was cool, even snowy, so they were warmly dressed. They wore spiked boots and carried coils of fine rope, so they could navigate the high pass. I had studied that route; it was a slow but sure one. They would finish in the middle of the pack—perhaps a little behind, if they dallied during a rest stop for a little romance. It wasn't that either was starved for sex; that was impossible in the Navy! It was that the Challenge Dome was a very special place and this was a special occasion; they were all worked up for it, and love in the wilderness had unique spice.

Now Juana and I were together, and we had no present interest in sex. We forged directly for the quicksand, moving swiftly over the firm ground, then carefully through thickening jungle lowlands. The headhunters were here; we saw one of their snares. But we passed through their territory unmolested, because of our silence and the fact that we wore no strong-smelling bug repellent. Juana had figured that out: The headhunters sniffed the odors and zeroed in on them for the kill.

We came to the edge of the open water by the map, and now the error of the map was plain, for this was perhaps six inches of water topping a quicksand bog. There was no question about the quicksand, because a float carried a sign: QUICKSAND. A real wilderness wouldn't have such a marker, but this was a mock wilderness and the quicksand was simulated; we had to accept it by definition. A Dome observer sat in a shallow-draft boat, ready to pull out any fools who stumbled into it and to ferry them to the morgue.

There was a stand of papyruslike reeds at the edge, as I had known there would be. I began cutting these down with my machete as Juana scouted for suitable vines. Soon we were fashioning two paddleboards: flat bundles of the buoyant reeds. When they were ready, I faced the observer and made my statement: "Quicksand is more dense than water. A person can float in it if he doesn't panic, especially if he is buoyed. There will be no need to consider us mired; we know what we're doing."

There was no response from the observer. But when we stripped, bundling our fatigues into our boots and hooking the boots to our bodies by their linked laces, and smearing croc repellent over our naked bodies, and flopping on our boards in the water, the observer made no protest. In fact, his rapt attention was on Juana's splendid body; observers seldom got the chance to observe this sort of thing in the Dome! We had a viable program.

We paddled carefully across the quicksand, keeping our arm and leg strokes shallow. This was the second reason we used no bug repellent; it was water soluble and would have been lost here. The reptile repellent was more durable in water, and we had plenty. Even so, I felt a thrill of nervousness, not so much for the actual dangers as for the possible reaction of the observer. The crocs were fangless, but if they came too close, we would be disqualified; our repellent had better work!

We swam slowly across. No crocs came. We climbed out on the far bank and shook ourselves off and got dressed again before the bugs could cluster. Then, with a cheery wave to the observer, we resumed our trek. I had not thought of Juana's body as an asset, but surely if the observer had been in doubt about whether to call a fault, this had helped keep him positive.

We had, by use of this shortcut, reduced our travel distance by almost fifty percent. It had taken time to prepare the paddleboards, but we were still a good half hour ahead of any ordinary schedule, and not as tired as we would have been had we spent that time plodding on foot.

We had to cut through a section of palmetto, and at one point heard a rattle; whether it was a real rattlesnake or a planted sound we could not know, but we gave it a wide berth and renewed our dosage of reptile repellent. The headhunters could smell this, too, but according to the map there were none of them in this region, and this coincided with my judgment.

Then we came to higher ground, and moved faster. But it was hot in our netting, and Juana was tiring; it is a fact that the type of flesh that makes a woman a delight to view is not as useful as plain muscle, in such a trek. We had to slow. I carried all our extra equipment, her pack and mine, but still we lost time. Yet she had done very well so far, and was striving hard now; I would not have traded her for a man.

Breathless, we hastened to the finish zone. We were numbers five and six, and Juana was the first woman here. So she would have qualified for the bonus even if she hadn't made the first nine. We had made it!

One day later, when the official tabulations were posted, Sergeant Smith's well-prepared platoon was shown as the leader. A cheer went up, and the troops bustled out on their three-day pass. Juana and I sewed on the single stripes of Privates First Class and moved into a room together, with the blessing of the Navy. Never again would we have to endure the rigors of the Tail.

We received a note from one Commander Dunsted, whose name neither of us recognized. It said, "Congratulations." When I checked the Base listing of officers, I discovered that this was the gracious woman who had put us together in the Tail.

Chapter 3

FIVE STEEL BALLS

My life as a PFC in the Jupiter Navy was full, but again it would be tedious to detail it. I continued my training, for though I now had some slight rank, about six months before I would ordinarily have had it, I still had much to learn. I was studying how to raid a ship; that is, how to perform as a member of a specialized crew who would board and take over an enemy spaceship. This was considered to be one of the most dangerous and challenging specialties, with a brief life expectancy. Few soldiers either wanted it or could keep its pace; therefore, promotions within it were prompt. I had jumped to E3 while most of my cycle-mates remained E1; after completing four months of training as a raider with top scores, I made E4, corporal.

Juana, not being driven as I was, pursued a more normal course and trained as a computer clerk and secretary. This was a good, secure specialty, but beneath her potential. It became apparent that she and I were not at all similar in personality, but we related well as roommates. Maybe opposites do attract. She was not keen on sex, and my preoccupation was elsewhere, but we performed our weekly stint because the Navy expected it of us, and it was said the Navy had ways of knowing.

Having said that, I must also say it was not an onerous duty, and as I came to understand Juana's nature better, I believe she came to appreciate it as I did. Indeed, though we both agreed that love was no part of this relationship, there were times when a third party might have thought otherwise. Our sex was always gentle and often fulfilling, as Helse had taught me, and I'm sure Juana gradually lost her fear of it. She did not have any strong drive to participate, but she liked to please me, and sometimes we even exceeded the minimum frequency quota. Certainly she valued the closeness of it, if not the mechanics.

In due course I was contacted by the anonymous officer Sergeant Smith had promised: the one who had the list of pirate ships doing business with Chip Off the Old Block. He was Lieutenant Repro, a psychologist attached to the Public Relations staff of the training battalion, and he was a drug addict. I quickly realized that while Sergeant Smith had been relegated to the lowly training unit as an extension of his scapegoat punishment, Lieutenant Repro had been relegated here as an act of mercy. A training battalion had little need of publicity; it did not deal very much with the outside world. Especially not when most of the soldiers were refugee orphans. So this was a sinecure, where Lieutenant Repro could drift out his enlistment in obscurity without doing much harm. No wonder he had not been eager to reveal himself; his shame was best kept private. No wonder, too, that he kept track of pirate vessels: They supplied the drug he had to have.

Why, then, had he agreed to contact me? I realized that he could not have much interest in my need to locate my sister. There had to be something in it for him. I needed to ascertain what this was, to be sure I could trust him.

Repro was a friend of Sergeant Smith's, and I learned later that Smith had pointed out that I might be a suitable pawn in a kind of game they were playing. It was a game that was to have amazing impact on my life, and this contact was perhaps the major break of my military career. But, of course, I did not know this then. Let me render this more directly.

I met Lieutenant Repro in his office in the S-5 section. I should clarify that a battalion has five special sections, each headed by an officer and designated S-1 through S-5. They are, respectively, Adjutant, Intelligence, Operations, Logistics, and Public Relations, otherwise known as Propaganda. As an enlisted man, I was hardly aware these existed; later in my career, that was to change.

Lieutenant Repro was a tall, thin, unhealthy-looking man in his late thirties or early forties—perhaps he looked

older than he was because of the ravages of his addiction—
with thinning brown hair and deepening lines on his face.
He was at the moment in command of his faculties, but I
could see he wasn't enjoying it. He must have straightened
out temporarily, for this occasion. His Class A uniform was
slightly rumpled, and his brass slightly tarnished. He was
about as unimpressive an officer as I had seen.

On his desk was a little stand, from which five steel balls
were suspended by angled threads, barely touching each
other. He showed me how it operated. "For every action
there is an equal and opposite reaction," he said, lifting an
end-ball to the side and letting it go. It swung in its arc
down to strike the stationary four, and the ball on the far
side swung out, leaving the other four unmoved. The force
of the first had been neatly transferred to the last, without
moving the intervening masses. Then the end-ball swung
back, and the first one rebounded. The principle was simple enough, but I was fascinated to see it in action.

Repro stilled the motion by touching the center balls
with his hand. Then he lifted two balls from the end. "If I
drop this pair, what will happen?" he asked.

I started to answer, then hesitated, realizing that I
wasn't sure. Would two balls beget two balls—or one ball
with twice the force?

He let go, and two balls reacted. I had my answer; a ball
for a ball, two for two.

Then he lifted three. "Now?"

Three balls. That suggested three to react, but only two
remained. What would happen?

He let the three go, and three balls rebounded. Rather,
two did, and the third carried through without pause. Fascinating!

"Action-reaction," Lieutenant Repro said. "Inevitable."

I wondered what the point was but remained too intrigued by the balls to inquire. Such a simple yet effective
way to demonstrate a principle of physics. "May I try it,
sir?"

He nodded acquiescence. I lifted one ball, let it go, and
watched the far one fling out with similar force. I let the
progression continue, noting that the size of the swinging

arcs gradually diminished, and that the row of steel balls began to get moving, until finally all five were gently swinging in unison. Friction, I realized. No process was perfect in atmosphere. In a vacuum it would work better, though there would still be some power siphoned away by the inefficiency of the supporting strings.

I tried two balls, then three, then four, then five—and smiled, for, of course, the five merely swung without collisions. Then I started a ball on each side, watching them rebound outward simultaneously. Then I started two balls on one side and one on the other, and saw the reaction proceed without hitch. The two proceeded back on the one side, the one on the other. This device could handle opposite impulses without confusing them.

Then I swung a single ball down with a double force. The opposite ball flung out with similar force.

I looked up. "How does it know the difference between two balls with normal force, and one with double force?"

"It knows," Repro said gravely.

I played with it some more. "The double-force ball is traveling faster," I decided. "That speed is transmitted."

Then I tried two balls at normal force, and then three. Two, then three rebounded. "The velocity is constant," I said, bemused. "But somehow it knows how many there are."

"It knows," he agreed again. "Action and reaction are constant, anywhere in the universe, and in any form in the universe. One has but to read the forces correctly."

"Even in human events?" I asked, beginning to catch on.

"If we read correctly."

"Then psychology reduces to elementary physics?"

"If."

I nodded. "It must be so."

He looked at me, his wasted body strangely animated. "Show me your power," he said, using a Navy idiom.

"Yes, sir." I took a breath, studying him with more than my eyes and ears. "You are intelligent—about one point three on the human scale—and have a civilian university education. You are honest but lack physical courage, so you become compromised. You see reality too clearly, but it is painful, so you dull your sensitivity with a drug—and have done so increasingly for the past decade. You had and lost a woman; that contributed. When your Navy enlistment expires, and they deny you reenlistment, you will retire without protest, step off into space, float free toward the sun, and open your suit."

He was unimpressed. "You could have gotten most of that from Personnel records."

"Had I known your identity, sir," I agreed.

He nodded, acknowledging my point. I had been summoned suddenly to an office; I could not have known. "And why did Sergeant Scapegoat connect us?"

"I have a private mission. You—" I concentrated, seeking to fathom this specific aspect of his nature. My talent is normally a general thing, a perception of fundamental biases, rather than a detailed itemization of traits. It did take time for me to understand a person properly, and this was sudden. Mostly, in the Navy, I had not bothered to use my talent on the soldiers around me; it really wasn't worth it. I had used it on Juana, and on Sergeant Smith, once he caught my attention, but there was no more point in using it on everyone than in studying the complete Personnel files on everyone. It requires an effort to form an informed opinion, and the Navy does not leave a trainee much surplus energy. For routine life and work, it is often best simply to accept people at face value—particularly in a regimented system where deviance from the norm is not encouraged. "You need contact with someone who can apply instinctively the principles you have studied professionally. Such a contact would—would provide some meaning for your life, and you value meaning more than life."

"Purpose," he said. "Purpose more than meaning, though the two may overlap."

"Purpose, sir," I agreed.

"I have measured out my life in chicken shit."

"Yes, sir!"

"Shall we deal?"

"Help me recover my sister, sir, and I'll do anything you want, within reason and legality."

"What I want is reasonable and legal but too complex for you to fathom at the moment."

I concentrated on him again. There is nothing supernatural about my talent; I merely read people quite well. I can, to a large extent, discover their moods and natures from peripheral signals, but I cannot read minds. Intelligent interpretation, not telepathy, is my secret. Now I saw in this man the signals of an enormous ambition but not one to be expressed in simple things such as promotion or riches or romance. He craved power but not any ordinary or competitive type. Rather it was a kind of vindication he sought—vindication in his own eyes, by his own complex code. He sought, perhaps, to change the course of Man, in a devious fashion that only he himself could properly understand. This was a fascinating man! "Yes, sir," I agreed. "But I will cooperate to the extent feasible."

"Your destiny may change," he warned me.

I was aware that he believed he was understating the case. I began to believe it myself. "I have not determined my destiny," I said. "I only want to recover my sister. Then I must become an officer, to fulfill my commitment to Sergeant Smith, so I suppose that means a career in the Navy. I'm satisfied with that."

He lifted a ball. "Perhaps you are now," he said. "This is me." He indicated the ball he held. "This is you." He indicated the far ball.

"Yes, sir," I said noncommittally.

He released his ball. It swung down and struck the group, and my ball rebounded. The implication was clear enough. He intended to apply force to move me, according to his complex will, and I would have to react predictably. He was a strange yet well-meaning man, and his effort would have power, but as I watched the return swing of my ball and the thrust it imparted back to his ball, I knew that once he started me going, he would be subject to my force as much as I was now subject to his.

"Yes, sir," I repeated.

The balls swung back and forth, acting and reacting and

re-reacting and slowly declining, until at last the entire group was gently swinging. "And there is the Navy," Lieutenant Repro said.

What we did would have a subtle but definite effect on the entire system. That was a grandiose ambition of his, yet it seemed a credible one.

"I think of these balls as a physical representation of honor," he said.

"Honor, sir?" I asked, surprised.

"Do you know what honor is, Hubris?"

"Integrity," I said.

He smiled. "I will educate you about honor. It is not integrity or truth. It is larger, a less straightforward concept. Honor has aspects of personel esteem, respect, dignity, and reputation, but it is more than these. Honor is an intangible concept, based more on appearance than reality, but its fundament is based on reality, and to a considerable extent it fashions its own reality. Civilization is a function of the honor of the human species. You must master the nuances of honor, to know personally what input will bring about what output." He started the balls rebounding in a complex clicking pattern by releasing them sequentially.

"What do I have to do with honor?" I asked. "It's hard enough just getting through training."

He shook his head ruefully. "I can see my work is cut out for me." But he was not upset by the challenge. "How can I help you recover your sister?"

I explained about the need to check the list of pirate ships doing business with Chip Off the Old Block, especially the one that handled EMPTY HAND chips.

"Yes, I have access to that list," he agreed. "It is considered part of Publicity, because no other department wants to touch the touchy matter of Navy trade with pirate vessels. We do keep track, but we don't advertise it, because then the question might arise why we don't stamp out that trade."

"Why don't we?" I asked.

"That is an excellent question, to which I can proffer no adequate answer. Do you wish to stamp out piracy?"

"Yes!" I said fervently.

Abruptly he stood up, and I saw just how tall he was. "Private First Class Hubris, I have a temporary detail for you. Come with me." This interview occurred before I was promoted to corporal; it is difficult to maintain a perfectly chronological narration when separate threads come together.

I realized that he did not feel free to talk frankly with me here in the office. "Yes, sir."

We walked out into the hall system that linked the various offices, and on to the officers' recreation section. "Do you play pool?" Lieutenant Repro asked.

"Yes, sir. Not well." I had learned all the available games; it was necessary for proper integration into the system.

"I will show you how to play well."

"Yes, sir. Am I permitted to play in the officer's room?"

"You are if I say so." He brought me to a pool table, and we took cues. "The monitors are unable to pick up sounds well in this vicinity," he murmured as he racked the balls. "Just keep your voice low and don't gesture expressively or react overtly."

"Yes, sir." I wasn't certain whether he was paranoid about being spied on, or whether there was justice to it. I can read much of a person's nature, but human nature is largely subjective. Probably there was both paranoia and justice.

"You hate all pirates because of what some did to your family?" he asked, not looking at me as he made his shot.

"Yes. I swore an oath to extirpate piracy from the system."

"But first you must recover your sister from the pirates."

"Yes."

"Suppose you discover that certain powers in the Jupiter hierarchy don't want the pirates extirpated?"

"I will find a way." I realized that he did have some notion why the Navy traded with pirates.

"First you must place yourself in a position to take direct action against the pirates. Then you must have an organization that is capable of doing the job."

"I will find a way, sir."

"I have amused myself by formulating in my mind the elements and personnel of a unit that would be capable of doing any job required of it, despite the opposition of the hierarchy. This unit could be turned to the extirpation of pirates."

"An imaginary unit, sir?"

"Part of my ambition is to make this unit become real."

"But the Navy would not let you assume such a command, sir," I said, perhaps undiplomatically.

"True. I can not assemble it myself. But an officer with the right credentials could."

"Who is that, sir?"

"That officer does not exist at present. I confess this is a weakness in my scheme."

"Then how—?"

"It will be necessary to bring him into existence."

I was silent, not following his logic.

"But first things first," he said abruptly. "The pirate trade with military bases is tolerated because there is graft. Therefore, any direct action against the pirates must be organized in secret. Once we locate the ship on which your sister is hostage, it will be necessary to provoke a conflict with that ship, so that it may be captured without affront to the powers that do not wish to disturb pirate ships."

"You can plan such a mission, sir?" This was obviously the right man to talk to!

"I? No. For that we require a good S-2 officer, for the necessary intelligence, and a strategist for the actual mission."

"Just to capture one ship, sir?"

"To capture it without the loss of your sister's life, and without disturbing the Naval status quo. Both are vital."

"I see, sir." This was becoming more complex than I had thought, but of course I hadn't thought it through. Sixteen is not the most thoughtful age.

"I will get on it, Hubris. You continue your training. Chance may put you in the position you need to accomplish your mission."

"Chance, sir?"

"We'll call it that." He smiled. "Patience, Hubris. A program of significance may be inaugurating here."

"Yes, sir." I did not quite realize or believe it then, but he had spoken absolute truth.

Lieutenant Repro was as good as his word. He was an addict, but he was competent. It is an error to suppose an addict is necessarily an inferior person. This one was a driven person.

In two weeks I had the name and location of the ship that handled EMPTY HAND: the *Hidden Flower,* now drifting in the inner Juclip. It was one of the more disciplined pirate vessels, having originally fled one of the Uranus navies and retaining a fair percentage of military personnel.

That was definitely the ship I had left Spirit on! My premonition of eventual victory grew.

When I completed my raider training and made E4, early in the next year when I was just seventeen, I went on for further training in related areas: infiltration, use of nonstandard weapons, disguises, small-ship piloting, practical emergency medicine, and similar. I was in continuous training, and I liked it. I wanted to be skilled at everything I might possibly need. The continuing availability of EMPTY HAND chips assured me that my sister remained functional.

I made E5, sergeant, at age nineteen, and was put in charge of my own highly trained raider squad. I was ready for action, but there was no action to be had because the pirates were behaving themselves reasonably well in local space, molesting only refugees and incidental stragglers, and it was Naval policy (facilitated by graft) not to make waves. I was helpless.

Then I received a cryptic message. It was a spacegram from Jupiter: Do you have it? It was signed "Q," with no return address or other identification.

I pondered that. Why should an obscure nineteen-year-old sergeant in the Jupiter Navy receive a message from Jupiter? As far as I knew, no one on the Colossus planet knew me. Of course, my enlistment record would be available there, but it was undistinguished. I had spent virtually all my time training for a mission that might never be scheduled. Could the spacegram be an error? That hardly seemed likely; it would have required specific information to locate my name and assignment. I was not a name to be read by mistake in an address directory.

What of that signature? Why was it merely an initial? This anonymity prevented me from responding, even to ask for clarification. Did the sender assume I would recognize him from that single mysterious initial? Why?

I pondered, and suddenly it came to me. I did know of someone whose name started with a Q, and I did have something that person wanted. The name was QYV, pronounced Kife, and the thing was the key that my fiancée Helse had carried. I now wore it on the chain with my dog tags, bound lengthwise so that it wasn't obvious. It was always with me: my sole physical memento of my lost love.

This had to be QYV, who had finally tracked down his lost key to me. That could not have been any easy job, for most of the people his courier Helse had encountered were dead. Certainly the pirates who had been responsible for her demise were dead; I had seen to that. Technically *I* had killed her—but only technically. She had died in our defensive action against attacking pirates. The memory still hurt; it would always hurt. But four years is a long time to a teenage youth, and I was now able to face the truth without more than an internal flinch.

I had no knowledge what lock that key might fit; I valued it solely because it had been Helse's. I was not about to give it up. If QYV wanted it, he would have to come and get it.

My feelings about QYV were balanced. I was sure he was a pirate, an illegal operator, probably a smuggler. I knew that his name was respected and feared throughout the pirate realm; no one dared cross QYV. I had sworn to extirpate all piracy, but I wasn't sure that oath included QYV because QYV had made it possible for Helse to travel to Jupiter as his courier for the key. That key had enabled me to meet and love her. It was true that I had also lost her, but QYV had not been responsible for that, and certainly had not approved it. QYV protected his couriers. He might be a criminal, but he had done no direct harm to me.

Now he was searching for his lost key and probably also for revenge against those who had balked his courier. I had the key, but I also craved revenge. To that extent, our purposes aligned. However, I knew the enemy of my enemy was not necessarily my friend, and I wanted no contact with QYV. Certainly I would not give up the key.

So my answer to this cryptic message was no problem: I ignored it. But I knew that it had to be merely a preliminary signal; I would be hearing more from QYV.

I did. I received an anonymous vid-call. The screen showed only the letter Q. "Do you?" a nondescript voice asked.

"Show me your power," I replied, and hung up.

A week later new orders came through for me. I was to report for space duty to the destroyer *Hammerhead*. Its mission was to capture an errant pirate ship, and it turned out that the ship was the *Hidden Flower*. The very ship I wanted.

In my mail, the last one before I transferred to the ship, I received a sealed note. Inside was a square of paper bearing the single letter Q.

QYV had shown me his power, indeed! How had he known of the thing I most wanted: the chance to rescue my sister Spirit? But still there was no deal, no demand for the key. This was only a demonstration, not the negotiation. But it was doubly impressive, for it also showed the potency of QYV's graft. I no longer considered Lieutenant Repro to be paranoid about pirate influence in the Navy; that influence was real.

I bid farewell to Juana; our two-year tenure as roommates was over. "There is another sergeant I can room with," she said bravely through her tears, so I wouldn't worry.

"Make him happy, Juana," I said. "We shall meet again."

"Yes, we shall," she agreed determinedly. There was theoretically no love between us, but I was aware that she had not entirely kept faith, and I myself was moved more than casually by the sudden separation. Juana was a good woman, and her supportive presence had done much to alleviate my own heartbreak over Helse. We had always known separation would come; enlisted personnel could not marry. Well, they could come close; E4's could be reassigned as units, and E5's could even have a child, using a counteragent to block the universal contraceptive. But that child would be a ward of the Navy and could be taken away at the convenience of the Navy. True marriage and family status, Navy-style, was reserved for officers. Juana could not join me on this hazardous mission, nor would I have wanted her to. Her skills were wrong, and so was her temperament; she was no adventurer. So it was circumstance rather than desire or regulations that separated us. Perhaps this was just as well; it would have been too easy to stay with her for life. Certainly she could attract another roommate; she could attract a hundred! She had been beautiful at age sixteen; at nineteen she was ravishing.

"And if you want to, when you use the ship's Tail," she murmured, "you may pretend it's me." Then she kissed me one final time, and I realized it was no joke. It would be uncomfortable sex on the ship after two years of Juana. Not because she was anything really special in this particular way, but because I did indeed care for her.

This mission had been arranged by QYV, I knew. But there had to be an official pretext. There had been several deaths from contaminated drugs, and the *Hidden Flower* had been implicated. It was probably a put-up job, but pirate ships had little recourse to legalities. It was to be a surgical strike, without fanfare; we were to capture this vessel undamaged and turn its personnel over to the proper Navy authorities. Except for one civilian hostage aboard it . . .

I met the captain of the *Hammerhead* and his crew; they would pilot my crew to the rendezvous with the target vessel. I do not name these people here because they are peripheral to my narration.

We boarded and accelerated toward the *Hidden Flower.*

Of course, this was not a straight line; there are few straight lines when traveling in space, contrary to popular illusion. It was a closing spiral as we moved from our position in the skew-ecliptic of the outer moons of Jupiter to the true ecliptic of the inner moons. Acceleration provided our pseudogravity, and it was not confined to single gee. We moved rapidly in toward the colossus planet, though, of course, we would never arrive there. As we neared the detection range of our prey, we set our snare.

It would of course have been virtually impossible to close on the pirate ship unobserved. All pirates were alert for Navy vessels and quickly took evasive action. We had more drive power and could have run the *Hidden Flower* down and holed her with a single shot, but destruction was not our purpose. We also could have haled her and demanded surrender, but she would have fled or fought or destroyed all her records and contraband before yielding to us. Those records were vital, theoretically. So we used a subterfuge.

We became a virtual derelict. We turned off our drive and drifted in orbit in the approximate path of the pirate. The *Hidden Flower*, like most pirates, was a scavenger; she took anything she could use from any ship she could disable. The EMPTY HAND trade was only part of her activity, not enough by itself to sustain her. She would not pass up a choice morsel like this.

We were a very special derelict. We had a double hull. The outer one was of the standard thickness and strength; the inner one was much stronger and was largely self-sealing.

We drifted for several days, Earth time. Little of significance has occurred on Earth in five centuries, but its time retains its hold on us, as do its several languages and cultures. Man never truly left Earth; he merely expanded Earth into the Solar System. At any rate, this delay was necessary to abate any suspicion on the part of the target ship.

In that time, we occupied ourselves in whatever manner we selected. Some played dominoes, either the spot-matching type or the physical collapsing-structures type.

Some took on the lone girl representing the EM Tail in shifts, trying vainly to wear her out; she must have been nympho. Some viewed feelies. There was, ironically, one chip of the EMPTY HAND brand, the best of the lot; one of my men mentioned his regret at having to take out this particular ship. Some practiced their various combat proficiencies: barehand, sword, club, garrote, and so on. We were all proficient in several martial arts, but true expertise took many years to develop, so competitive practice was always welcome. Because of my talent and intensive training, I was one of the better practitioners, but my ability suffered when matched against the proficiency of strangers whose natures I did not yet know. So mostly I rested and exercised and reviewed raiding strategy in my mind. And got to know my men.

We knew the layout of the *Hidden Flower;* it was on record, and we had studied it to the point of memorization. We could now move competently within it blindfolded. Indeed, we would do something very like that, for all power in the ship would be stifled. This was necessary to incapacitate the self-destruct system. The pirates thought they were safe from boarding, because of that system, but our technology was ahead of theirs. So it meant a hand-to-hand struggle. We could not use a pacifier for the same reason they would not be able to blow up their own ship: All electric or electronic equipment would become inoperative while the suppressor field was in place.

"Alert," the captain murmured on the intercom. "Prepare for mission."

It was time. The *Hidden Flower* had sighted us and was closing. I got into my space suit and rendezvoused with my squad. Ten good men, all suited and ready. We did not use names on this mission; I was One, my corporal was Two, and the rest were Three through Eleven. "Remember," I said unnecessarily. "We want them alive—and you alive, too." We knew how to knock out a man bare-handed but also knew that some of those pirates had had similar training, and they would be desperate. So it was no sure thing.

The *Hammerhead*'s crew were also suited. They were Navy men, somewhat disdainful of the soldiers of the enlisted ranks, but they knew what this mission entailed. If this mission malfunctioned, and the pirate ship self-destructed, the Navy personnel would be lost, too. They were dependent on our raider squad to do the job properly. They would have to sit and wait, for this part of it.

"Stand by for holing," the captain's voice came. We had the double hull, but still it was not comfortable waiting to be fired on and holed. If the pirates had a lucky shot, that penetrated the inner hull, too, we would have a rougher time of it than we liked. That was why everyone aboard the *Hammerhead* was now suited.

The missile came. The ship rocked as a shell detonated against the hull and rocked again as another struck. The third one holed it, and the air blew out; then the bombardment ceased. This was the manner of operation of this pirate: Hole the ship to make quite sure it was dead, then board and clean it out. It was an efficient operation, virtually risk-free, but it forfeited the normal pirate delights of rape, slave-taking, and bloody hand slaughter. Most pirates seemed to crave literal blood, using swords to hack at helpless victims. How well I remembered seeing my father die that way!

I controlled my black rage. These pirates were just as murderous, and I had no sympathy for them, but my mission was to recover my sister alive, and I needed to be coldly objective, to be sure that nothing went wrong. Navy justice would take care of the others.

Now there was silence among us, for we were theoretically dead. The inner hull remained tight, but I led my squad quietly out the lock and to the outer hull. In the darkness we could not see the hole but did not need to; we waited by the main airlock. It was now useless as a pressure lock, but the pirate ship would use it for attachment, to keep the ships conveniently together for the plundering. Once they used the lock, we would strike.

I heard the clang of contact and felt the shudder of the ship. We were in vacuum, but sound is transmitted through substance, so as long as we remained in contact with the hull, our ears could guide us. They guided the Navy captain, too; when that airlock opened, he would turn on the suppressor. Then it would be up to us. We estimated that there were about thirty pirates aboard the *Hidden Flower,* three times the number of our raiders, but we would have the advantage of surprise and planning.

The lock opened. And the gentle vibration of the pirate ship's operating systems ceased. Our suppressor had blanked out both ships, freezing them electronically. This included the life-support systems; the air would soon be going stale. The mechanical systems of the suits were unaffected.

Now was our time. The first party through the lock, in suits, didn't know what had happened. We closed on the three of them in the dark and took them physically prisoner, three to one. We simply disarmed them and carried them to our inner airlock and put them in, after making sure they had no knives or other purely physical weapons tucked out of sight. The Navy personnel would know what to do with them. The pirates could not communicate with their ship, since their suit radios were now nonfunctional. Not that their fellows would have paid much attention; they had problems of their own, now.

But I knew that Captain Brinker, of the *Hidden Flower,* was not stupid. Brinker was a woman masquerading as a man, and she kept her secret and her position by ruthless cunning. She would know the moment the power failed that the *Hidden Flower* was under siege, and she would react immediately. My hope was that she would not know by whom she was being attacked, so would not use Spirit as a hostage. I intended to give her no leisure to think of this; speed was essential.

We operated the airlock—all airlocks had manual controls, since emergency use could occur when power was off—and sent in a party of three. These were our scouts, specially versed in stealth; they would tap a signal if all was well, and another if there was trouble, and we would be guided accordingly.

The all-clear signal came, and three more of us went through. The corporal had been in the first party; I was in the second. I operated the lock controls in the darkness without hesitation; I had practiced carefully for this.

Number Two, the corporal, gripped my arm. I touched my helmet to his. "Three more here," he said. "Unconscious."

"Take them out," I said, "I'll secure the center passage."

He loaded the bodies into the lock, having no difficulty because this was the weightless region, then accompanied them back through. That made six pirates out of the way; perhaps twenty-four to go. The more of them we could take out piecemeal, the better off we would be. At this point they could still overwhelm us, if they made a concerted effort.

I moved toward the center of the ship with four men, leaving one to guard the lock. Why weren't there more pirates here? They had been set up to plunder a dead ship; they should have had a dozen on duty, not six.

Answer: The captain had caught on when the power failed and had immediately reassigned all but three already outside and the three waiting to follow. But where had they been reassigned? This could be trouble.

It was. This ship was too quiet. There was none of the noise of confusion there should have been. Captain Brinker had probably set a trap, an ambush, and now was waiting for us to blunder into it.

I thought of the five swinging steel balls on Lieutenant Repro's desk. For every action, an equal and opposite reaction. Force translated exactly. We were now in the role of swinging balls. The *Hidden Flower* had bombarded and boarded us; we had reacted by neutralizing her electronics, capturing her boarders, and boarding her back; and she reacted by laying an internal ambush for us. The speed of the pirates' reaction bothered me. It was almost as if Captain Brinker had anticipated this raid.

Anticipated it? How could she have, unless someone had tipped her off?

Kife! I muttered subvocally. QYV had set up this mission; he could also have set up a countermission. What did I know about him? Only that he operated ruthlessly, and that he wanted my key. Why not lure me to the pirate ship, my sister as the bait, then capture me and the key and the Navy ship, too? It would be written off as a mission that failed; the Navy would cover up its embarrassment in the usual fashion, and I would disappear.

Very well: Accept the notion of a pirate countertrap. How could the pirates hope to deal with the *Hammerhead* when the suppressor controlled both ships? It would not be enough to kill or capture me and my squad; the Navy ship would remain supreme. There was no way the *Hidden Flower* could prevail as long as the suppressor operated.

In my mind, one steel ball swung into another, and a new one rebounded. Now I understood!

I touched the man next to me. Our helmets met. "Back," I said. "Evacuate. Fast. Spread the word."

He was a trained man. He did not question the order. He acted like a cog in a fine machine. He touched the man behind.

In moments we were hastily retreating. We met the corporal with the other arriving men. "Out. Quickly," I said to his helmet. "To the inner hull."

We crowded out through the lock, and on to the inner hull, after tapping out the recognition signal. No one balked or hesitated. How glad I was for the type of discipline Sergeant Smith had instilled in his recruits! Now our lives depended on it.

When we were back in the inner hull, in air, I lifted my helmet so I could communicate more freely. "I must talk to the captain immediately."

He came to me in the dark. "You aborted the mission, soldier?" he inquired with a hint of contempt.

"We have been betrayed," I said. "The pirates knew we were coming. They have set a countertrap. We have to nullify it or we're in trouble."

"What trap, soldier?" he asked skeptically.

"I believe there is a traitor among your personnel," I said. "He is going to turn off the suppressor so the pirates can use power weapons to overwhelm the raiding crew. They are hiding now, waiting for that."

"Among my men?" he demanded, outraged. "Among yours, perhaps, if any traitor exists. Not mine!"

"Sir, the ship is yours, but the mission is mine," I reminded him. "I must act to accomplish the mission and to save your ship and the lives of my men. You must facilitate this."

"Sergeant, facilitation of the mission is one thing; an accusation of treason against my crew is another."

"Yes, sir. We must hurry. I must interview each of your crew members in the next few minutes."

"You have some nerve! This is highly irregular."

"It is necessary to the mission, sir."

"That statement gives you authority of a sort," the captain conceded grudgingly. Anger fairly radiated from him. "I shall cooperate. But there will be an investigation of this matter when we return." That was definitely a threat.

"Yes, sir. Please move it along."

Someone had lighted a candle; now we could see. The captain's aristocratic lips quirked. "Start with me, Sergeant."

"You're clean, sir."

"Just like that, you can judge me?"

"Yes, sir. For this purpose. Please expedite this; we don't know how long the pirates will hold off."

"Your arrogance is phenomenal!" But he gave the order, and one by one his officers came to be interviewed by the sergeant.

Because speed was essential, I had to proceed bluntly. My talent served in this instance as a lie detector. Of each I demanded, "Are you a loyal member of this mission?" Each, of course, asserted that he was. Most considered the question an indignity and would have refused to respond had not Navy discipline required it.

When I came to the ensign in charge of special equipment, I got a false reading. He was lying about his loyalty.

"Place this man under arrest, Captain," I said. "He is our traitor."

The captain was too outraged for a moment to speak. I filled in the gap by addressing the ensign. "I know it is you, sir. You have a choice: Tough it out and take your chances with the court-martial when we return to base, or turn state's evidence and help us now. I am the one pressing the charge; I will give you opportunity to resign without being charged if you cooperate."

"Preposterous!" the captain huffed.

"It is your choice, Ensign," I said evenly. "You have thirty seconds. I will be generous, if."

The ensign looked at me, then at the captain. The ensign was an officer, while I was an enlisted man, but it was evident that I was sure of my ground. His gaze dropped. "I'll cooperate," he said.

The captain's mouth dropped open.

"What is the pirate trap?" I asked.

"I was to turn off the suppressor when all of your squad was inside the pirate ship," he said. "Then I would pie the electronic fire-control system. The pirates would have their destruct system reactivated, putting this ship in check, and we would be unable to retaliate in kind. Then their raiding party would board us—"

"Thank you," I said. I turned to the captain. "Sir, I suggest you confine this man to quarters for the duration of this mission. No charge will be filed against him, and there will be no note in his record."

"The man has committed treason!" the captain exclaimed.

"No, sir. He has informed us in timely fashion of a plot against this mission. He never acted; he merely kept silent until the moment was propitious."

"But his intent—"

"Who can speak for intent? It is the action that counts. I gave him my word, sir. He is to be allowed to resign for personal reasons without dishonor." Sergeant Smith had told me in Basic that souls could be bought and sold for a clean record; I had learned the lesson well.

"Sergeant, you can't presume to tell me—"

"For the good of the mission, sir, I must insist."

The captain clenched his fist. Then he backed down as I had known he would. He realized that I had already saved his ship and probably his life, not to mention his reputation, by the deal I had made. "*He* shall not be charged," he agreed. "But you and I will settle in due course, Sergeant."

The ensign was conducted away. He shot back one glance of gratitude to me. He had gambled on me and won.

"Now, sir, we must regroup to complete our mission. Have one of your men turn off the suppressor—"

"What?"

"Long enough to satisfy the pirates that their plan is working. They will proceed to the counterraid. Half my squad will be inside the *Hidden Flower,* ready to take their ship; the other half will deal with the pirate raid."

"Half your squad—five men—can handle the whole pirate ship?" he demanded.

"Yes, sir, in this circumstance. The pirates will radio you to demand your surrender; you must avoid committing yourself. They will then issue an ultimatum: If any of your men resist their raiders, they will blow up both ships. You must accuse them of bluffing, but you must sound uncertain."

"I comprehend the ploy. Any other orders, Sergeant?" he inquired ironically.

"Just keep alert, sir. This is no sure thing, because those pirates are primed for action. Turn the suppressor on again when my corporal tells you to. Mistiming could be fatal, for they will surely use their destruct system when they realize they are being outmaneuvered." I turned to my second-in-command, who had been waiting silently behind me. "When you observe their raiding party clear their ship, take them down without warning, with your stunner beams. Then turn on the suppressor—before they can activate their destruct system—and come in after me, in the *Hidden Flower.* Fast. The rest as before."

My corporal nodded. He knew what to do and how to do it. I had confidence in him, and now he had confidence in me.

I took five men and returned to the lock. It was chancy doing this, for the pirates might wonder why we were going back and forth. But they were waiting for the suppressor to stop, so probably thought we were just ferrying our captives out. They had sacrificed six men to lull us; the rest would wait for us to bumble inefficiently into their trap.

We entered, then crowded into equipment-storage alcoves and waited. After a minute, the suppressor went off; the captain was following orders.

Almost immediately there was activity in the pirate ship. The lights did not come on; they were too canny for that. But we heard the faint noises of the supplementary airlock being used; their raiding party was sneaking out, and their communications officer was surely getting in touch with ours to deliver the ultimatum. Other men were coming toward us, armed with power weapons that we supposedly believed were inoperative. A man using a knife against a laser pistol would live or die according to the state of that pistol! But we were similarly armed and warned, and they did not know this. This was our counter-countertrap.

I heard a man come into the access passage, followed by others. They did not speak, but I knew they were perplexed. Where were we? We waited, unmoving.

When discovery was incipient, I fired my stunner at the nearest. He went limp without a sound, for I had taken him in the throat. We had to keep them silent, to avoid giving alarm before my corporal's party took out the external raiders. My men followed suit. In a moment we had stunned five pirates.

That took care of eleven, here. I judged that a dozen more would be out with the raiding party. That should leave only about seven in the ship, one of which was Spirit. The odds were now just about even.

We waited, and the suppressor came back on. The corporal had scored! We put away our inoperative power weapons and moved on toward the pirate control room. The remaining pirates should be disorganized now, caught by the restoration of the suppressor; we could put them away relatively efficiently.

It wasn't quite that simple. The pirates, aware that something was wrong, were now playing the same game we were. My men spread out, delving like deadly snakes for their hiding prey. I dropped silently down the center tunnel to the control area. The ships were spinning end-over-end, Navy-fashion, so the centrifugal gee was greatest at the extremes. I touched the ladder lightly with alternate hands, controlling my fall and pushing myself away from the wall, since such a fall seems curved. I reached the floor and paused, listening.

There was someone near. My suit was designed for completely silent life support; his was not; therefore, it was not one of my men. I pictured him in my mind, getting his position clear; then I moved in and ran my metal needle into his main oxygen tube.

Now he was in trouble, for I had holed his tube between the tank and the regulatory valve. Oxygen hissed into his suit under unrestrained pressure, bypassing the valve. The outer puncture sealed itself, but not the tube; he was inflating uncomfortably. He had no recourse but to remove his helmet to relieve that pressure, and then I caught his head and jammed my armored finger at a buried nerve complex under the ear, and he was unconscious. I left him on the floor and moved on.

I entered the control room. It was empty. Since the suppressor made all the electrical controls inoperative, including the self-destruct system, it was pointless for them to man it. I moved on to the captain's office and paused again. There was only one entrance to the office, and it would be dangerous to use that.

Again the image of a steel ball striking another came to my mind: Open that door and trigger a devastating reaction. Captain Brinker was no shrinking violet, though she was the true hidden flower. I needed another way.

Quickly I removed my suit. There was air here; the suits were in case the ship got holed, or its stalled life-support system was insufficient. There was air at the moment, and I would use it.

I set up the empty suit before the office door. Then I stood to the side and extended a hand to draw the entry panel aside.

Something thunked into the suit. It fell over. I waited. I knew Captain Brinker could not afford to leave the suit there long; it would serve as a signal of her presence.

I heard her come out. She wore no suit, either, knowing it interfered with nocturnal combat.

I could have knifed her, but I wanted her alive. I went after her bare-handed, launching myself in a tackle.

She heard me and moved. I sideswiped her, managing to catch hold of one bare arm. I yanked on it, getting her off-balance, and swept at her ankles with my foot, using a judo takedown. I had not seen her body in the blackness, but my glancing touch had provided me with a suggestion of amazing femininity.

She jumped and swung at me with her free hand. By the way she moved, I knew there was a knife in it.

I caught that hand, clasping it with my fingers, squeezing it, seeking leverage on the knife. We fell together to the floor, torso to torso, and I confirmed that she was not only naked but voluptuous. How had she concealed her sex so effectively?

Then I felt the fingers of her hand and realized that her little finger was missing. "Spirit!" I whispered.

She froze. "Hope," she responded after a moment.

"I got your message. EMPTY HAND. Where's Brinker?"

The cold metal of the blade of a knife touched my neck. Suddenly I knew where Captain Brinker was.

I was trained in combat, but so was Brinker. She had reflexes no other person could match, and iron nerve. She had the drop on me with the knife; I knew I could not escape it. I had her ship by this time, but she had me. She had sprung yet another trap, using my sister to put me off-guard. What a callous ploy that was: Spirit, believing I was a pirate raider from a rival ship, could have killed me, or I her. Captain Brinker, the bloodless female pirate, didn't care; either way, she had her chance.

I held Spirit, savoring her presence after four years, though I had not rescued her yet. "What is your offer, Captain?"

"Life for life," she said. "Yours for mine."

"Agreed." And the knife withdrew. I kissed Spirit, then disengaged and got to my feet. "You can take your lifeboat out, as I did before."

"Yes. I know you are a man of honor, Hubris."

Honor. Lieutenant Repro had lectured me on it, and increasingly I accepted his definition. Truth can be a liar, when incomplete; honor is more than integrity. Honor obliged me to follow through on the spirit of the agreement as well as the letter. There would be no treachery, no loophole.

"Spirit," I said. "Go get dressed, then stay clear while we deal."

Spirit moved away in the dark, and Captain Brinker did not protest. Brinker knew that Spirit had been forfeited as a hostage the moment she was used to decoy me.

"What other deal?" Brinker asked.

"A secret for a secret. Yours for Kife's."

"Agreed." She paused momentarily, knowing that I protected the secret of her sex by not even naming it. "Kife offered a Naval vessel for a key you wear. He set up the trap; I was to deliver the key. I do not know what the key is for."

"He honored his bargain with you," I said. "He betrayed me, but I caught on. How can I reach him?"

"Communications were anonymous. I was to mail the key to Box Q, New Wash, USJ, 20013."

"Company," Spirit murmured, returning.

"We're done here," I said. I raised my voice. "Navy in charge here. Is the ship secure?"

"Secure, Sergeant," one of my men agreed from the control room. He was the one Spirit had heard.

"Losses?"

"One, inside. No report from outside."

"Go check. Tell the captain I am releasing the pirate lifeboat; let it go without molestation. Turn off the suppressor when satisfied that all is secure."

"Right." He moved off.

"I'll lead; you follow, Spirit," I said. I set out for the *Hidden Flower*'s lifeboat, Captain Brinker behind me, Spirit following her.

One of my men guarded the lifeboat access. "Hubris here," I told him in the dark. "I have made a deal. I am releasing this pirate to the lifeboat."

My man moved aside, not questioning this. Captain Brinker entered the lifeboat. "Perhaps we shall deal again, Hubris," she said.

"Perhaps," I agreed noncommittally.

She closed the hatch. She would not be able to take off until the suppressor field stopped, but she was aware of that. The key element of our deal was that the lifeboat would not be fired on as it departed.

Then I found Spirit's hand in the dark and drew her in to me. We embraced and kissed again like long-lost lovers. She was my closest kin and best friend; now my life had shape.

As I held her, noting her newly strange adult body so like that of my older sister, Faith, and yet reminiscent of the twelve-year-old child I had left, I knew there would be complications to negotiate. I would have to persuade the Navy captain to make no protest over my handling of either the traitor or the pirate captain. But a successful mission would make his record, too, look better. He could spare himself embarrassment by going along, and I rather thought he would. Spirit was a more complicated problem. I wanted her with me, now and always, but she was a civilian.

A civilian? She had had four years experience aboard a pirate ship! She surely knew more about handling a spacecraft than any ordinary person did.

"You are going to join the Navy," I informed her.

"Of course," she agreed, as if there had never been any question. Perhaps this was true; she had always had a clear notion where she was going, though she generally had not shared her insights with others.

Then the power returned. The lights came on, and we had to separate slightly. The lifeboat took off. Things were busy after that.

Chapter 4
CHIRON

True to my deal with Sergeant Smith, who was now back up to E6, I put in for Officer's Training School and was accepted. I had thought Basic Training was bad; this was worse. But I struggled through for several months while my sister Spirit breezed through Basic. I emerged an ensign, O1, the lowest form of officer, and she became a private. I continued my training, and so did she, and when I was twenty and she seventeen, she, too, went in for officer's training. In due course I was a lieutenant j.g., O2, and she was an ensign. One tends to think of the distaff as weaker, or at least gentler, but Spirit seemed to get through the rigors of training and qualifications, Tail and all, with less difficulty than I had.

Now Lieutenant Repro presented me with the next stage of his ambition. "You must achieve your own command," he told me. "You must gather within it the most capable officers available, so as to make it the best unit in the Navy. But you must not let the upper echelons realize how good it is, or they will destroy it."

I smiled. "I'm only a junior-grade lieutenant," I reminded him. "It will be decades, if ever, before I command anything—and at such time as I do, I'll be more interested in wiping out pirates than in forming the perfect concealed showcase unit."

"Not so, Hubris," he said. "You are a man of destiny. Your talent is the understanding of people. You will be a leader. You will indeed go after the pirates—once you have your position."

That interested me. "I have sworn to extirpate piracy from the System," I said. "If your ambition aligns with that, I'm with you."

"To abolish the illicit drug trade, it is necessary first to abolish piracy," he said. "That is part of my ambition."

I gazed at him. He was an addict, of what particular drug I felt it was not my business to know, but it continued to devastate him. He had grown more gaunt in the past three years. I had to believe him; he wanted the drug trade stopped. But if it stopped, his own supply would be cut off. His motive remained too complex for me to fathom.

"Your first target is Lieutenant Commander Phist," he said. "Draw him into your orbit. He is the best logistics officer in the Navy."

"How can an O2 lieutenant draw in an O4 commander?"

"You won't stay O2 forever," Repro said. "But he will remain O4 forever, just as I will remain O3 forever. You must find a way to snag him before he resigns from the Navy."

I was now in charge of a maintenance platoon, doing routine inspections of Navy equipment. It was a standby operation, and I had time on my hands. I got to work researching Lieutenant Commander Phist.

Gerald Phist was thirty-five years old. He had been a rising logistics officer, highly competent, with an impressive number of citations for excellence. It had been his job to oversee the Navy's acquisition of supplies and equipment, and he had done that well.

Then he had blown the whistle on a billion-dollar cost overrun that was bilking the Navy of hard-pressed resources and reducing combat efficiency. But in so doing he had stepped on the toes of certain profiteering commercial interests. Strings had been pulled, and instead of being rewarded for service to the Navy and, indeed, to Jupiter herself, Phist had been passed over for promotion, removed from his position, and assigned to irrelevant duties. His Navy career was essentially over, because he had done his job too well. He was described as a pleasant, handsome, conscientious, and extraordinarily capable man of conservative philosophy and absolutely honest; but these qualities, it seemed, counted for nothing in this situation.

Lieutenant Repro was right. There was the smell of something rotten in the Navy, and Commander Phist was the kind of officer I wanted at my side when the going got tough. But how could I, a lowly Hispanic lieutenant, keep Phist in the Navy, let alone bring him to me? What miracle did Repro require of me?

I discussed it with Spirit. As a surviving sibling of a devastated family, she was permitted to serve in my unit; the Navy did have some slight conscience about such things. At seventeen she was a lovely young woman, with luxuriant dark hair and a classic figure. Her face was not as striking as Faith's had been, partly because of the faint scar tissue from a mishap we had had as refugees with a rocket motor, and her left little finger was a stub; but Spirit remained a woman of considerable esthetic appeal. Her mind, too, was laser swift; she was more intelligent than I, and more incisive. She also had more nerve, though it seldom showed overtly.

"I will fetch him for you," she said.

Again I looked at her. My talent has this limitation: It loses effect when my own emotions are involved. I could not read my sister. But I knew she was capable of things I would hesitate to speculate about. "How?" I asked.

She merely smiled. "Just give me a little time, Hope."

Spirit had always been able to bluff me out, the only person who could do so. She was, in a subtle sense, my strength. She would reveal her design to me in her own fashion and time. "I don't know whether there's any real meaning in Lieutenant Repro's ambition," I said. "He has worked out a slate of ideal officers as an intellectual exercise, not necessarily during his lucid periods. It may be no more than a pipe dream."

"It's a good dream," she said.

Weeks passed in the normal routine, and the dream faded into the background. In the Navy one must live with delays; they are part of the bureaucratic fabric, without which it would doubtless fall apart. Every so often I dropped in on Sergeant Smith, who was still training recruits; he always grinned as he saluted me. I represented a victory for him; he had decided I was officer material, and he had been vindicated. He was doing the same with other selected recruits, steering them right. I was gratified to have come through for him. Yet so far my life as an officer was no more progressive than it had been as an enlisted man. Military life, if the truth must be told, is not nearly as dramatic as the recruiting posters pretend. Of course, it might be different during a war.

Then I got another vid call from Q. "What price?" the blank screen asked.

"I asked you to show me your power," I said angrily. "You showed me your treachery!" I had not followed up on the Box Q lead I had from Brinker, wary of another trap; better that QYV did not know what information I had. When he was satisfied that I could not locate him, then I would follow up. I had time, and my position on QYV was no longer neutral.

"Never trust a pirate," the Q voice said. "Sell it."

"I don't do business with your ilk!"

"Do not force my hand, Hubris. There is more than you know."

"It is an empty hand!" I snapped, and disconnected.

A week later new orders came down: I was to command a platoon in a company of a battalion that had been placed on alert status. This meant space duty, possibly extended. It would separate me from Spirit.

I had little doubt that QYV had shown me his power again. I was angry, but I had no choice; I had to go where assigned.

My platoon was infantry, somewhat surly about being commanded by a Navy officer instead of an Army sergeant. It was a conflict that had smoldered for centuries, ever since the various military services of Earthly nations had merged with the exodus to space. Because ships were essential in space, the Navy dominated; the Army had been reduced to enlisted status. The several other military branches—Air Force, Marines, National Guard, and such—had simply faded out. One might have supposed that time would have eased the internecine rivalries, but that had not been the case.

This would be no pleasant tour. All three platoons were holding GI parties—that is, pointless and savage scouring of their barracks—as I arrived, preparatory for an inspection. I had never liked inspections; most of them were merely makework, unpleasant exercises that irritated the men. My assumption of command at this moment was unfortunate; my men would forever associate me with it. I had to do something in a hurry to modify that association, or turn it to my advantage.

The sergeant in charge snapped to attention as I entered the barracks area. The men did not; they were on work detail. "Sir, Sergeant Fuller reporting."

"At ease," I said. "I am Lieutenant Hubris, your new commander." I looked about, noting that a good half of the men were dusky in the Hispanic manner. Deliberately, I removed my hat and jacket and handed them to the sergeant, symbolically stripping myself of my rank. "What chicken shit is this?" I inquired loudly in Spanish.

My judgment was correct; half the laboring men paused and looked up, startled. The sergeant evidently did not speak Spanish, but he knew something was up. "You wish to talk to the men, sir?" he inquired respectfully.

"I do not see any men," I continued in Spanish. "I see a bunch of scrubwomen. Did they enlist for this?" I was rolling up my sleeves.

Baffled, the sergeant did not reply. Some of the men were stifling grins. This was a good show!

"Well, might as well do my part in this foolishness," I said. I picked up a brush, found a spot, and got down on my knees to scrub.

"Sir!" the sergeant protested.

"Hi, soldier, what's your name?" I asked the man next to me.

"Rodriguez, sir," he said, bemused.

"Hope, here. From Halfcal, the hard way. You?"

"Dominant Republic," he said, smiling. "Same planet."

"We're neighbors!" I exclaimed. "We share sunshine."

"Yes, sir. But you—an officer?"

"First refugee, then migrant, then enlisted, then officer. Each in its turn. I don't know which is worst." I looked down at my brush. "This isn't so bad. Last time I was on this detail, I used a toothbrush. The sergeant seemed to think that was more effective." There was a general chuckle; they knew about toothbrushes, and about sergeants.

"Sir," the sergeant said worriedly. "Commander Hastings—"

"Ooops! Have to put on the monkey suit," I said. "Forgive me, neighbor; it's guard-duty time." I scrambled up and dived into my jacket and hat.

"Loco!" someone muttered admiringly.

When the martinet arrived, I was pretty much in order. The sergeant looked as if he had swallowed a scrub brush, and the men were scrubbing savagely. I had soap spots on my knees.

Lieutenant Commander Hastings glanced at the scene. "You seem to have a knack for discipline, Hubris," he remarked.

"They're good men, sir," I said, straight-faced, in English.

Someone coughed.

This platoon was mine.

Next day the *Cannon Dust* weighed anchor and cast off from her mooring at the pier. Since the pier was a rotating cylinder, this sent the ship moving away from Leda at approximately thirty-two feet per second. When she had suitable separation, she oriented and cut in her main drive. Naval vessels seldom bothered with gravity shields; those were too slow.

Perhaps I should mention one technical aspect: The Navy uses the most effective mode of propulsion, which is the CT drive. CT, of course, stands for contra-terrene matter, which might be described as the mirror image of normal matter. CT atoms have negatively charged nuclei surrounded by positrons, so their charges are opposite to those of normal matter. When CT encounters normal matter, the result is total conversion to energy, the most potent explosion known. I am not a physicist so can't go into detail, but in general the drive consists of a magnetic chamber in which a rod of CT encounters a rod of normal matter, at a controlled rate, with the resulting energy directed to the rear of the ship. In short, one savagely powerful propulsive jet. The CT is fashioned in isolated space laboratories in which gravity shielding is employed to generate controlled black-hole conditions that allow manipulation of fundamental matter in a manner not possible otherwise. Blocks of CT substance are handled and stored magnetically, so that they never touch normal matter until the proper time. Only small amounts of CT fuel are kept on any given ship, to militate against unfortunate accidents, but a small amount of CT goes far. The power of the acceleration of a given ship is determined not by limitation of the fuel but by the capacity of the ship to withstand the rigors of high gee. I trust this makes this aspect clear; the average man prefers not to think too much about CT.

This was the comfortable part of the voyage. We accelerated at gee for almost a full day, to almost two million miles per hour. Of course, this was a largely misleading figure in space. What it meant was that in just under two days at this velocity we could travel one Astronomical Unit; that is, the distance from the sun to the planet Earth. Our Earthly heritage remains with us in a number of incidental and archaic ways, but actually the AU is a fairly useful measurement for Solar System distances. Jupiter is just over five AU from the sun, and Saturn nine and a half, and Uranus nineteen. That did not mean that we could travel to Saturn in nine days, assuming we wanted to; Saturn was not aligned with Jupiter at the moment, so we would have to cross a fair secant to reach it. But it provides a notion of the scale.

As it turned out, it was no planet we traveled to. When Commander Hastings briefed the officers on our mission, it turned out to be the planetoid Chiron. Chiron is a tiny body about 150 miles in diameter, orbiting elliptically between Saturn and Uranus; in due course it intersects the orbits of each. It was colonized by both major planets and has had a savage history, as the representatives of each planet tried to assume full control. Violence was flaring again, and we were going there as part of a temporary United Planets peacekeeping force. This was supposed to be a routine operation, no actual combat, but in that volatile region, we had to be prepared for anything.

We traveled for a week in free-fall before spinning the ship for the remaining part of the month. Cmdr. Hastings believed that it was good discipline to endure the rigors of null gee. Cmdr. Hastings was a polished nugget of chicken manure; all agreed on that. We had frequent free-fall drills. We were, as I put it in Spanish (never in English!), the Chicken Express. By the time we went into deceleration, my men were ready for the kill, and Commander Hastings was the leading candidate for the chicken ax. I kept them in line largely because of my talent and my Hispanic identity; I spotted the potential troublemakers early and persuaded them to keep the lid on. It was effective; I was, I discovered, an excellent leader of men. I was an officer and they were enlisted men, but we came to understand each other well enough and we had mutual respect. I made things as easy for them as I could; I could not do much, but I knew they appreciated the effort.

We also had indoctrination on our destination. It was my duty to absorb the often tedious detail of the holo tapes and digest it so that I could make it palatable, or at least intelligible to my men. Chiron was named after a famous centaur, the wisest of the herd. Indeed, the planetoid was shaped vaguely like that mythical creature, with a torso 60 miles in diameter and 140 miles long to the tip of the extended tail. This is what the "about 150-mile diameter" translated to. Its present population was about 600,000 people, four-fifths of them Uranian and one-fifth of them Saturnian. It had been under Saturnian domination for three centuries despite its Uranian majority; then when it swung close to Uranus it had been taken over by the empire of Titania, the Uranian moon, and held for another century. There had been a number of petitions for "enosis" or political amalgamation with the Uranian system. When this was denied, there were riots. Ninety-five percent of the Uranian-derived population wanted that unification with the mother planet. At last Chiron had been granted independence, but still the problems erupted, with the Saturnian minority insisting on partition, since they believed they were suffering discrimination. A terrorist campaign had started, and at one point there had almost been war between the parent cultures on Uranus and Saturn. Now the interplanetary peace force was supposed to cool things off.

I rephrased all this for my men, delivering summaries in English and Spanish. "Those people probably feel about the way we do," I concluded, "after a month in space tasting chicken. All we want to do is get back to base and unify with our regular women: enosis." That brought on an approving laugh, for the men were sick of the all-male condition of this mission, and of the long lines for the inadequate Company Tail. They knew that the officers were little better off in this respect; there was only one O-girl. She was less busy than the E-girls but also offered less variety. Things were rough all over.

The nominal entertainment facilities received heavy use, too. There were no feelies here, because Commander Chicken (surely Satan reserved a red-hot pitchfork for his posterior!) believed them to be effete, or worse: fun. But there were boxing gloves, pugil sticks, and an in-ship obstacle-course racetrack. I shed my jacket when I could and played table tennis, chess, and pool with my men. I was not expert in any of these, but I made it a point to be an excellent loser. While I played, I talked with them, getting to know them better, and I encouraged positive interaction among them. This did not mean I tolerated indiscipline; I knew better than that. When I donned my silver bars, I meant business, and this was quickly apparent. No one, I knew, respected an easy officer. I had discovered this the hard way as an enlisted man, from Sergeant Smith. Tough but fair—when it counted.

And so we arrived, ready for trouble. Chiron looked like a narrow punching bag, with its extended tail. It was a planet, for it orbited the sun, no bigger than a moonlet, as perhaps it had once been or would in future be. It was well domed, the domes spinning in the manner of Hidalgo's or Leda's, generating the necessary internal gee. This was the only way for these tiny bodies; they lacked the mass to have enough natural gravity for gravity-shielding to concentrate effectively. Actually there is nothing wrong with spin-gee, for ship or for planetoid. It's just less even.

We docked near the ships from other regions. I recognized the emblems of several Uranian nations; they must have been summoned before us, since they had a longer voyage here. At present, as I understood it, Chiron was about the same distance from Saturn and Uranus, which was one reason for the current strife; neither side had a clear legal or geographical advantage.

We did not go on peacekeeping duty immediately; first we were treated to the standard background briefing, which repeated much of what we had already learned. Greek and Turkish were the official languages here; fortunately the long involvement of Titania had made English a language most Chironiotes comprehended. We would be able to get along.

For me and most of my men, the cultures of this planetoid were equally opaque; neither was remotely Hispanic. I instructed my men to avoid trouble whenever possible and to stay away from the local women until some were inspected and cleared for free-lance Tail subcontracting. I reminded them that though venereal disease did not exist in the Jupiter region, other planets had different standards, and infection was possible. "Herpes," I said firmly, "is line-of-duty-NO."

We were assigned a segment in one of the Greek-Chironiote domes. My three sections were to take three eight-hour shifts, covering our beat around the clock. I would be keeping an eye on all three shifts, of course.

This seemed routine, but I was wary; something about it didn't feel right. For one thing, QYV had evidently pulled another string to put me into this mission, replacing the lieutenant originally supposed to go. Maybe QYV was just trying to unsettle me, but maybe he had more in mind. I had foiled him when I recovered my sister; he might scheme more carefully this time. I worried peripherally about Juana and about Spirit, though I knew they could take care of themselves. It was the key I carried that QYV was after, not any of my associates.

Our first day on duty went without trouble. The Chironiotes were tolerant of our presence, and even friendly; they knew we were here on invitation, not as invaders, and they did not seem to want further bloodshed. In fact, they offered my men little gifts, which was a problem because we were not supposed to accept gratuities, but we realized that to decline might be to give offense. We solved that by giving back little gifts of our own, so that it became an exchange. We had little packets of Spanish candy, Toron, sealed in aluminum so there could be no question of contamination, and they liked these. It was the principle that was important: We were not taking without giving, and we were not being aloof.

Trouble came so suddenly and personally that it almost caught me off guard. I was walking through a shopping district, on the way from one station to another, admiring the olives, melons, grapes, and citrus fruits the local farmdomes produced, when I turned and saw a striking woman smiling up at me. "Will you come with me, officer?" she asked in accented English, giving a little shake to her low-slung décolletage.

"Thank you, no," I said politely. "I am a member of the United Planets peace force. We are not permitted to mingle." That was, of course, a euphemism. We were encouraged to mingle socially, but not sexually, and she was evidently of the latter type. Her garb and manner were like commercial advertisements.

"But, officer, I insist," she said, taking my left arm firmly.

This was a more forward approach than I had anticipated. I pulled away from her. "I regret—no."

She leaned into me. "Note the men on either side; they are armed," she murmured. "Do not embarrass us with a scene. We only wish to talk."

I glanced to right and left. Two men boxed me in, and each turned back a lapel to reveal the glint of steel. Firearms and other powered weapons were forbidden here, because of the social unrest and vulnerability of the domes to damage, but knives existed.

I had been trained to deal with knife attacks. I was sure I could handle these two men and get away. But I paused, for I did not want to make the scene the woman urged me to avoid; it would reflect adversely on my unit. An officer brawling? Some example! Also, I was curious what they wanted; this did not seem to be ordinary mischief. So I touched my alert button, signaling my platoon sergeant.

The woman saw my motion and snatched away my communicator and dropped it to the floor and stepped on it. That would prevent my sergeant from tuning in on me. Then the armed men took my arms and hustled me into a nearby building. I did not resist.

The woman preceded me up an ancient-fashioned flight of stairs and through a solid fiber doorway. I felt the gee easing with the elevation; that's a consequence of spin-gee. The door was simulated wood; there was no genuine wood here, as Chiron was too far out from the sun to farm trees effectively, though a few eucalyptus trees were grown for symbolic purpose. But woodlike fibers were manufactured and used freely, and so this was very like a wooden room.

I stepped into it, then reached back almost casually as if about to scratch myself and caught hold of the knife the man to my right had shown me. I whirled, assuming a knife fighter's stance, facing the second man. He had had to fall back, to follow his companion through the doorway, and was at a momentary disadvantage. "Stand aside," I told him.

Foolishly, he went for his own knife. I knew better than to bluff; I slashed at his moving arm, laying it open. Then, as the blood welled out, I caught the door with one foot and slammed it in his face.

This had taken but a moment. Now I faced the disarmed man, my knife poised. "Balk, and I attack," I said. He now knew how fast and sure I was with a blade. "What did you want with me?"

"You forgot to protect your rear, officer," the woman said.

I whirled again and found myself facing a rapier. I had indeed been foolish! My knife was no match for such a weapon, if competently wielded, and I saw quickly that this one was. The woman was more than a decoy; she was the main agent of my abduction. She stood before a green divan, poised.

My back was now to the disarmed man. He took this

seeming opportunity to grab for me. That was his mistake. I had not neglected my rear a second time. I reached over my own right shoulder to catch his right lapel with my left hand, and hauled him around me in a judo wraparound throw. I never let go of the knife in my right hand. Few people untrained in martial art comprehend the devastating nature of a properly executed wraparound throw. He landed hard before me, half-stunned and under my control. Now I had a human shield. "What did you want with me?" I repeated, touching the point of my knife to his neck just behind the right ear.

"The key," the woman said, evidently not unduly alarmed by the threat to her henchman. I was using my talent now, studying her; I knew she was irritated but not afraid. I should have focused on her before; I had been careless in that respect, too. We learn the costs of our carelessness the hard way!

Suddenly it fell into place. "Kife," I said.

She nodded. "Turn over the key and go unharmed. The key is all we want."

"How do you know I have it with me?"

"Your belongings have been rayed," she said. "It is not there. It has to be on you."

I stalled. "Why do you want it?"

"It is Kife's property. Yield it and be free."

I sensed that she was bluffing, in part. I counterbluffed. "Tell me what is so important about that key, and I will spare his life." I nudged my blade against the henchman's neck so that he flinched.

"I could run you through," she said, her rapier point aiming at my face.

"Then you had better do it quickly." I dug in with the knife, drawing blood.

"Wait!" she cried.

I paused, knowing I had figured her correctly. She could kill me while I killed her henchman, but that was not an exchange she wanted to make. It was not that she cared for the henchman; she did not want to kill me.

"The key opens a particular lock," she said. "No other key fits."

She was lying. "I'll make a copy for you," I said. "The original key has a sentimental value for me." It did indeed; it was my only physical relic of the woman I had loved.

"We must have the original," she said. "It is not the physical key; that's only for appearance. There is a unique magnetic pattern that is the actual key."

Now she was telling the truth. "So it's a magnetic key," I said. "What does it unlock?"

"This is Chiron, the Key," she said. "The symbol for Chiron is a key."

"Very nice alignment," I agreed. "Kife seeks to fetch a key at the key. But you haven't answered my question."

She hesitated. "I don't have full information."

"But you have more than you have told me," I countered.

She smiled, deciding on another course. "Let the man go, and you and I will talk without weapons."

That was an improvement. I stepped back from the henchman, knowing he was no good as a hostage, anyway.

"Leave," the woman told him. The man scrambled to his feet and went out the door, closing it behind him.

The woman put her rapier on the floor and stepped away from it. I set my knife down similarly. I knew she did not intend violence. I didn't trust her; I trusted my reading of her motive.

She walked to the divan. "Sit, and we shall talk."

I had something she wanted, but she also had something I wanted. Obviously she wished to obtain the key without killing or hurting me, so that there would be no wider attention called to this matter, while I wanted to know the full nature of the key and of QYV. I was willing to play the game of seduction, to learn what she knew. Up to a point. I joined her. "What does the key unlock?" I repeated.

She adjusted her décolletage to show more cleavage. I almost smiled at so obvious a ploy. But when she leaned forward, I had to concede that she had a lot to show. "Do you understand cryptography?"

I was aware that this was relevant. I looked where I was supposed to look but did not let the view distract me in the manner intended. I always appreciate the female form, but at the moment I was far more interested in the key. "Very little."

"For centuries man has labored to develop an unbreakable code for private messages," she said. "The closest we have come is computer-assisted. The elements of the message are converted to numbers, and the numbers are scrambled according to a special pattern. We call it encryption. Only a person with that special scrambling pattern can decode the message."

It began to make sense. "And this key's magnetic pattern is the key for a particular message."

"A vitally important message," she agreed. "I don't know what that message is, but Kife must have it."

"But that message is years old now!" I protested.

"It remains vital." And I knew that she was telling the truth, as she knew it. She held out her hand. "Now the key."

"We agreed to talk, not to exchange the key," I said.

"True," she agreed. "But the key is of no use to you. Will you sell it to me?"

"What price?" I had no intention of selling it but was curious about the monetary value QYV placed on it.

She made a negligent gesture. "Money is of no account. Name a figure."

Something rang phony. Again I had a vision of a steel ball striking a line of balls with no ball rebounding. Why should money be of no account? Because they had unlimited funds, or because I would not be permitted to live to enjoy the money? As a military man I had no use for any large illicit windfall, anyway; it could only prejudice my career. "You can offer better than that."

She smiled. "You are cunning, officer. I, too, am available, if that is your desire." She touched the rounded hollow between her breasts. She had been doing her best to make it my desire, and certainly her anatomy put that of the ship's Tail to shame. QYV could afford the best in bodies.

"We do not mix with the local women," I said. "However

much we might like to. I think you have something of
greater value to me."

"Your life," she said.

"I don't think you mean to kill me. You had the chance
before, and to take the key from my body."

"It is better to bargain than to kill."

She was to one side of the truth again. "Let me conjecture: Kife is not sure the key I carry is the original. I have
had opportunity to hide the original or to give it to someone else, and I have had prior warning of Kife's methods. If
you kill me, then discover the key I carry is a duplicate,
you have lost your mission or at least walked into another
extended search for the original. That key is worth more to
you than my life or my death, and my death would bring
suspicion on you. The Jupiter Navy is implacable in the investigation of the murder of one of its officers, and Chiron
is a sensitive assignment; such an investigation would
surely expose your activity here. So you want the key—and
my silence—and my life is safe until you have verified the
key's authenticity, which is not something you can do
soon."

She smiled again, more warmly. "I grow to like you, officer. Your conjecture is correct. I must deliver the key to my
superior and wait for confirmation. If I myself were to discover the nature of its message, my life would be forfeit.
We thought to take the key from you and let you go, since
you do not know its message either. Thereafter we have no
further interest in you."

"So you never planned to kill me. In what sense, then,
are you offering me my life in exchange for the key?"

"There is danger to you not of our making. We can get
you removed from this situation before that threat materi-
alizes."

QYV had put me on this mission; he could probably take
me from it. He could move me about like a pawn on a chess-
board, but he could not conveniently get my key. I did not
like the smell of this. "No deal. I'll take my chances."

She sighed. "Then we must take the key by force."

"Then I must escape by force," I said.

"We have overpowering force available."

She was bluffing. "So do I, when my sergeant zeroes in on the region of my disappearance. Shall we set some guidelines for our encounter, so as not to generate an interplanetary incident?"

She smiled again, genuinely appreciative. "You amaze me, officer. I wish you were on my team. What do you have in mind?"

"First, no bloodshed. Bare-handed, action ceasing when opponent yields or loses consciousness, and the defeated party retires from the fray. By bare-handed I mean no power weapons, pacifiers, blades, or chemicals. Second, no telling. If you win, you will take the key and return me to my unit with no word of what really happened; if I win, I will not turn you in or make any report. This is a private contest. Third, no future action on Chiron either way; now decides the issue."

She considered. "Let me consult." She rose and went to the door. There was a murmured exchange. Then she returned and settled herself again. "It is agreed. A mock conflict. Bare-handed, bloodless, silent, and no further issue. Escape this building with the key and you are free; otherwise, it is ours. If we prevail and the key is false, you will guide us to the real one."

"Say when," I said.

She gave me a direct look. "When."

I launched myself at her from a sitting position, but she was already moving. Her legs came up to fend me off. I caught her left ankle and shoved it aside, but her right leg slid past on my other side, and suddenly she had me in a scissor hold about the waist. I had thought she would try to flee the couch, to alert her associates; instead, she was trying to pin me there, and she had strong legs. Women may be weaker than men above the waist, but not below. I had miscalculated because I could not use my talent to interpret her training; her reflexes were largely automatic, not subject to conscious planning. She had countered my motion reflexively, and so had caught me. I tried to lean forward, to get a choke hold on her, but she squeezed me tightly and held me back so I had no leverage. I grasped a handful of her upper dress, to haul her in to me, but it ripped away. No purchase there!

Well, there were other ways. I could have dumped us both on the floor, but the thud would have alerted her henchmen that the engagement was on, and they would have rushed in to overpower me while she pinned me with the scissors. Our silence was literal; she did not scream for help. I realized that she was enjoying the challenge of this combat; she was a very physical woman and wanted to do this job herself. If our struggle should lead to seduction, she would not object.

I took another handful of dress and ripped it away, exposing her low-cut halter beneath. Then I ripped that away, leaving her bare above the waist. She had reason to be proud of her body! Still, she did not scream, but continued to squeeze me unmercifully in her scissor hold. That hurt physically, despite my conditioning. I had to break her grip, and I did not want to strike her. Even in this combat I retained a certain diffidence about violence toward a beautiful woman, as perhaps she knew.

I put my hands to the nether portion of her dress and ripped that away. Soon I had her entirely naked, but still she did not relinquish her grip on my waist. I considered ramming my hand into an intimate place, but knew that would not make her let go; she was too close to victory to give in because of pain or indignity.

I reached suddenly for her face, and when she batted my arm aside with her forearm I caught that and hauled it in to me. She fought me savagely, but my strength was superior, and I got hold of her long black hair and used it to draw her head close. Now I was able to move to a so-called "naked strangle," perhaps appropriate for this occasion. One forearm was behind her, my fist anchored in her hair, my other forearm levering into the side of her neck, squeezing the buried carotid artery. This would not render her unconscious quickly, as the artery on the other side of her neck still conveyed blood to her brain, but I could make the hold extremely uncomfortable.

She relaxed her scissors grip and spun out of my strangle. But I caught her in another, this time from behind, and this one was secure, and it put pressure on both carotids. She had played into my hands.

I did not try to put her out. "You are my shield," I murmured in her ear. "We shall march outside together."

"My men will grab you, anyway," she gasped. "I'll tell them to!"

"We'll see." I marched her to the door. "Stand back!" I called. "I have your leader hostage, and she'll be the first to suffer." Then, to her: "Stop trying to pull at my arms, and open that door. We're about to test your men."

Confident that I was now playing into her hands, she did so. The door opened, and there was a henchman ready to spring.

His eyes widened as he saw the naked, buxom form of his leader. Obviously she was no common man's sexual plaything, and he had never been presented with this particular view before. He stepped back.

"You see, no bluff," I said, following him. "I have her in pain; she will not tell you to free her."

The woman tried to do just that, but now I was attuned to her physical reactions, and I tightened up my strangle into a choke just as she started to speak, so that only a gasp emerged. It must have seemed to be a sufficient confirmation of my threat, for the man retreated farther. A choke hold can be impressive; the victim's veins swell in the head, and eyes protrude, because of the blockage of flow from the jugular vein, though this is neither as painful nor as incapacitating as the less-obvious pressure on the carotids. And, of course, the victim's breath is restricted; that's no fun at all.

"Lead the way downstairs," I told him. "With your companion."

The man hesitated, and his companion did not appear. I figured the missing man was lurking in ambush, waiting for me to pass. I also figured there were only two of them; the woman had been bluffing when she mentioned "overwhelming force." Had she really had it, she would not have bargained with me; she would have used that force immediately.

"Now!" I snapped with authority, and I eased up on my

choke while kneeing the woman in the rear. She had a plush posterior; I half-regretted having to treat it this way. She made an involuntary screech, caught by surprise. That was exactly what I wanted.

The second man appeared from an alcove down the hall. "That's all of you?" I asked, making sure.

They exchanged a glance. "No," the nearer one confessed. He was lying.

I propelled the woman forward. She didn't even struggle. If there was one thing I had learned well in the course of my Basic and officer's training, it was how to apply a submission hold. I had mastered a number, ranging from finger-breakers to potentially lethal nerve grips, assuming such proficiency would be useful—an assumption now confirmed. My present neck hold was a compromise, maintaining the subject in a suitable state of consciousness without permitting her freedom of speech or resistance; I could put her out in seconds if I had to. Control is all important, not mere power. There is something very persuasive about pressure on the windpipe; the victim knows that struggle will only make it worse.

The two moved down the stairs, helpless before my certainty. Each time they paused, I nudged the woman's bare bottom with my knee, she obligingly squeaked, and the men moved with alacrity.

It was, after all, that simple. We made it down and out the door and into the crowded street. "Get back inside," I told the men, and they did.

Then I released the woman slowly, so I could tighten up if she tried to attack me, and so she could recover her wind and poise. There was a mark on her neck where my forearm had pressed so cruelly. "I believe I have won the round," I said.

She took a moment to rub her neck and get her bearings. "Conceded, officer," she agreed hoarsely. She touched her behind where I had kneed it. "I trust you enjoyed our contact."

"Indeed," I agreed. "I regret it could not have been more intimate."

"It could have been; why do you think I didn't scream?"

She leaned close and kissed me on the mouth. Then she turned and reentered the house.

There was applause from the crowd that had instantly gathered. I made a little bow, adjusted my clothing, and went on my way.

I completed my inspection of my unit, then retired to my office in the ship to ponder. I believed the agent of QYV would keep her word; I did not know her name but had gotten to know her well enough to know she was dealing honestly in her fashion. My key was safe from molestation while I remained on Chiron. But there were two other matters.

First, this showed that QYV was going to keep trying to acquire the key. I would have to take better measures to protect it—and myself. In fact, I might have to deal directly with QYV. I had his Jupiter address; perhaps it had been a mistake not to follow that up.

Second, there had been that reference to trouble on Chiron, not of QYV's making. It sounded serious. This was a place where violence could break out at any time. Something must be in the offing—something bloody. I had better do something about it.

I followed the book. I went to my supervisor, the Company Commander, Lieutenant Commander Hastings, the martinet. He was not pleased to have me intrude on his time. I wasn't sure what he did all day, as little evidence of it filtered down to the units. But he had to see me when I put in the request, by military protocol. "What is it, Hubris?" he snapped.

I was aware that, among things, he didn't like Hispanics, and therefore held me in automatic contempt. Prejudice does exist in the Jupiter Navy, as elsewhere, but I had long since learned to live with it and often to turn it to my advantage. I was much closer to the men of my platoon than I would have been if I had been Saxon. I was also helped by the fact that I had come up through the enlisted ranks. Hastings had not; he was an Academy graduate and exemplified the liabilities of that. The best and the worst were Academy, because of that lack of leavening.

"Sir, I suspect that serious trouble is brewing," I said

carefully. "Perhaps a deliberate program of mischief by terrorist revolutionaries. We should take special measures to—"

"You *suspect*, Lieutenant?" he demanded nastily. "On what evidence?"

I could not give my source; that was part of my deal with the QYV agent-woman, she of the delicious bottom. "It is just something I heard, sir. A passing reference to—"

"Are you an expert in Intelligence, Hubris?"

"No, sir. But it is wise to pay attention to—"

"It is wise to confine yourself to your area of expertise, Hubris. Perhaps you should return to scrubbing floors with the grunts."

I made one more attempt. "Sir, I feel a report should be made, and a warning issued—"

"Forget it, Hubris! Leave policy to those whose concern it is."

So much for that. I had received the anticipated response. "Yes, sir." I saluted and turned away. He didn't bother to return the salute.

I had played it by the book. There would be a recording of my suggestion, putting me on record to that extent. Now I had to put my own program into effect, for I had no intention of being a scapegoat. I also had no intention of getting myself killed, or of allowing disaster to strike my unit through any neglect of mine.

My options were limited since my superior had rejected my petition. I could not take any official action. But I did act unofficially. I informed my platoon sergeant that I had gone to Commander Hastings with my concern about a possible outbreak of violence and had been put in my place. "I do not necessarily regard this as a private matter," I concluded.

"Yes, sir," he said. I had just provided him with some hot gossip, and signaled that he could spread it freely. In fact, I had hinted that he should do so. He was one Saxon who had quickly learned how to get along with a Hispanic officer.

"Inform the men that I will be available for personal dialogue in the rec room," I said. That meant that my enlisted men could come and talk to me informally.

News travels at close to C (lightspeed) in a unit. I had hardly sat down at a table and set up the dominoes before several of my Hispanic troops appeared. "Sir," one said in Spanish. "What are you up to this time?"

"I am up to nothing," I replied innocently in the same language. "I have been instructed to leave significant matters to those equipped to comprehend them, and to concentrate on my floor-scrubbing. I would not presume to do otherwise."

They grinned knowingly. "Everyone knows how stupid Hispanics are," one said. "Scrubbing is all they understand."

"Only a very stupid man would believe that a program of riot and possibly assassination could be in the offing," I agreed. "Or that interplanetary peace-force troops and officers could be the target. Far better to scrub floors!"

The grins faded. "What do we do, sir—off the record?"

"I believe we should try to ingratiate ourselves further with the natives," I said. "To treat them well and try to get to know them as friends. Entertain their children. Study their cultures. Listen to their concerns with real interest and help to what extent we can, as fast as we can."

"But we are not supposed to get social with them!"

"No sex with their women," I said. "But other favors, other forms of social interaction are permitted. Off-duty personnel should be friendly, like brothers. We want them to like us." I paused. "And if any of them mention things in confidence, such as the secret movement of weapons, we must protect their secret. We must never betray them in any way. But *I* want to know, off the record, immediately."

Now they understood. "Spy work," one said.

"Social work," I clarified. "Commander Chicken has forbidden spy work to floor-scrubbers. But we want the local Chironiotes to be concerned if anything should threaten us."

"You really think something might, sir?"

I nodded grimly. "My evidence is thin, but I am very much afraid it might. We need to be careful."

"We shall spread the word, sir."

"I realize this is not very dramatic," I said. "But it's all I can think of. I'm not expert in intrigue. Let's hope my concern is groundless."

"Yes, sir." They departed, ready to spread the word.

Naturally, for a week thereafter, things were perfectly quiet on Chiron. But my men, showing more faith in me than I felt in myself, labored diligently to be Good Guys. They found a number of ways. They arranged little parties for the children, giving out token prizes and singing songs. They helped old ladies do their shopping. They even filled in for ill men, doing work in their off-duty hours. They chipped in to help a poor family make an overdue payment on a mortgage. They spread cheer.

News of this foolishness spread through the other units. Jokes abounded. We were the *loco* platoon. But my men merely shrugged and continued. They had never tried being Nice Guys this way before, and they found they liked it. And the natives, originally diffident or even covertly hostile, became friendly very quickly. They began inviting favored soldiers to meals and parties. All it took was our genuine effort to relate.

Ten days after my alert, one of my men brought me a slip of paper. "A little Greek boy," he said almost apologetically. "I helped him carve a sailboat. He gave me this. Sir, I don't know if it means anything—"

I unfolded the paper. One word was crudely printed on it in Spanish: *hoy.*

"Did the child speak Spanish?" I asked.

"No, sir."

The word was *today.* Innocent, by itself; it could mean anything. "We'll find out," I said. "We must continue as usual, so as not to betray our informant. But watch it, and be ready."

"Yes, sir," he said doubtfully, perhaps thinking I was being kind to take the note seriously. Perhaps I was.

We proceeded as usual, though the word spread throughout my unit and no one slept. Nothing happened.

But during the night shift, most of hell tore loose.

Firearms were forbidden in the domes because of the

danger they posed to the environment. One small hole in the seal meant a pressure leak, and a large hole could mean explosive decompression. A city of a hundred thousand people could be suffocated in seconds. But now there was the sound of guns firing.

I knew when I heard the first shot that this was serious. "Full alert, all shifts!" I barked into the unit intercom. "Double the present duty shift. The rest form a section with me—Hispanic." Because neither the Greeks nor the Turks understood Spanish well; it was a code language.

My sergeant saw to the disposition of men. I took my Hispanic squad—ten men and a corporal—directly toward the sound of shooting.

Men were in the streets, tough-looking Greeks, but they were not rioting. "Lieutenant," one called as I approached. "Do not go abroad."

"It is my duty to keep order," I said, pausing.

"There is no disturbance," he said. "See, our streets are quiet."

"Yes? But there is gunfire in the next section."

"Lieutenant, you have been good to us. We forbade the terrorists to come here. But in the other sections you are not safe."

So my policy had paid off! These were our friends. But I couldn't stand idly by while a riot or insurrection proceeded. "I have a job to do."

"Please—you do not understand. Foreign officers are being executed!"

"Then I must get there immediately!" I broke into a run, my squad double-timing behind me.

The Greeks kept pace. "Lieutenant, you force our hand! We do not wish harm to come to you!"

"I'm sorry," I said. "I am here to keep the peace. I must do it. Please return to your homes."

"No. We must come with you. There is great danger!"

I sensed the mood of these people. They knew more than they were telling, but they were uncertain. They had assumed that I would stay at my post and not interfere with what occurred elsewhere. Ordinarily, I would have. "Come if you wish, but do not interfere with my men."

We jogged to the next section. I saw I was already too late; two uniformed men lay in blood. A wild-looking Greek stood over them, waving a pistol, haranguing the crowd in Greek. Here was a terrorist leader!

"Halt!" I cried. "You are under arrest!"

The terrorist whirled, bringing his gun to bear. I carried only my billy club, and my men were no better off. We had been keeping the peace without power weapons, not even stunners. I realized that I had indeed been foolish to charge here, knowing we would face firearms. My life might well be forfeit. Yet this policy had been necessary to assure the folk of our region that we were basically men of peace.

The terrorist aimed at me. I threw myself to the side. "Take cover!" I yelled.

Then something flew through the air and struck the terrorist in the chest. He cried out and staggered and fell. The handle of a knife protruded from his body. I knew one of the Greeks from my sector had thrown it, for my men did not carry knives on duty either, here.

I reached the bodies. One was a corporal, part of the office staff of our company. He was dead; he had been shot through the head. The other was Lieutenant Commander Hastings. He was dead, too.

I faced the Greeks. "The other officers?"

"I fear all are dead," the Greek leader said. "The terrorists, the leaders—"

"Well, *I'm* not dead!" I snapped. "Until I verify who survives, I'm assuming charge of this sector. I hereby declare martial law. All citizens will confine themselves to their homes until further notice. Only international troops will remain on the streets. Any Greek found abroad fifteen minutes from now will be subject to immediate arrest."

The Greeks exchanged glances. "Yes, sir." They dispersed.

It would have been awkward if they had balked! But they trusted me, and my decisiveness. I turned to my corporal. "Take five men," I said in Spanish. "Check the whereabouts and condition of all company officers and

NCO's, and report to me at my office in the ship. Be on guard against gunfire."

"Yes, sir!" Quickly he chose five, and hurried away.

I picked up the fallen pistol, checked it, and tucked it into my belt. "Now we return to the ship," I said to the five remaining men. "Form a cordon around me; I believe I am now the prime terrorist target."

They did, and we proceeded to the ship without further event. We heard distant shots but none in this region.

At the ship I used the intercom to clarify that one officer survived: Commander Waterman. He had barricaded himself in his office instead of going out on the street. He was, in fact, a coward. He had done nothing to stop the violence.

I went to his office, and he let me in. "Commander, I believe all the other officers of the battalion have been assassinated," I said briskly. "I suggest you appoint me Battalion Executive Officer and let me carry on from there."

He stared at me, trying to fathom my motive, so I spelled it out for him. "Commander, when I was fifteen I saw my father and friends slaughtered by pirates, and my sister raped. I swore vengeance and have been taking it. I had more blood on my hands before I entered the Navy than most careerists ever see. These terrorists are in the same class as pirates. I can handle this; it's not new to me, it doesn't touch me the way it does others." Actually, I never liked killing, but I had learned to function amidst it. "But I need authority to act. I'm not trying to usurp your authority; I'm trying to salvage the situation. Support me, and I will support you."

Waterman considered. He remained severely shaken, but now he realized how his inaction would be interpreted. "Scuttlebutt has it you forced an officer to retire—when you were a sergeant."

"There was no blemish on his record, sir."

"I retire in ten months."

"Retire with honor, sir."

He nodded. We had an understanding. Even in an institution as wedded to spelled-out formality as the Jupiter Navy, much of the real business is done by unwritten understanding. He activated the intercom, and it was answered by the private filling in for a slain sergeant. "Cut the orders for Lieutenant Hubris to be Battalion Executive," he said. "Temporary field promotion to O3 and complete authority to act for me for the duration of the crisis."

"Yes, sir," the private said.

"Thank you, sir," I said, saluting.

I deputized my trusted men to fill the vacant offices, and we cleaned up the mess, extended our area of control, and got things restored to a facsimile of normal until reinforcements arrived. As it turned out, the violence had largely passed. Evidently the terrorists had intended to precipitate a riot and revolution by assassinating the officers of the peace force and haranguing the populace, but when the segment controlled by our battalion remained orderly, the effort lacked sufficient momentum to continue. I was able to track down and arrest the inciters, thanks to the cooperation of our Greek friends, and that looked very good on my record. Things settled down.

Commander Waterman was permitted to retire in due course, without prejudice, and my promotion was confirmed. I received a commendation, a ribbon, and a medal for heroism. It was more than I deserved, but I did not protest. For one thing, I had issued a number of emergency promotions, putting privates into NCO spots and granting a field promotion to an ensign to fill my own vacated position as Platoon Commander. I kept my mouth shut, sparing the Navy embarrassment, and every one of those promotions was confirmed. The Navy had tacitly paid me off.

When notice came that our battalion was relieved of peace duty, we flung a party like none the Greeks had seen before. The Greeks who had helped us were given special attention, and our stores were raided for presents for them all. This wasn't strictly Standard Operating Procedure, but no protest was heard.

Chapter 5
MIGRANT

Again, I must plead dullness as the pretext to skim over much of the ensuing eight years. Military life is not generally filled with excitement; tedium is its ordinary nature, except for fleeting periods of devastation, as happened on Chiron. I organized the company I commanded as well as I could, given the restrictions of the Book; it became a haven for ambitious Hispanics. Perhaps this amounts to segregation; well, there is more of that than the Navy admits. Other units were generally glad not to have to deal with aggressive Spanish-speaking men and officers; as long as neither they nor we protested, the Navy went along. There is a lot of live-and-let-live in the military.

My sister Spirit abruptly transferred to another base, one orbiting closer to Jupiter, and entered into a term marriage with Lieutenant Commander Phist, the whistleblower. How she managed that on either practical or social levels I hesitate to conjecture; she was always more clever than I at manipulating her circumstances. I still tended to think of her as the twelve-year-old child I had left among pirates; at eighteen she was a long way from that, but even at twelve she had been nervy and tough in a crisis, always ready and able to do what had to be done. Her restored presence was enormously gratifying to me, and her renewed absence was hard for me, though I knew she would return. She and I could never truly be separated again.

I attended their housewarming, and Commander Phist, a handsome man in his mid-thirties, informed me politely that he would be happy to oblige his wife in any legitimate way within his power.

I explained about Lieutenant Repro's model staff, and

Phist said he considered himself honored to be included in that roster. That was all; since my command did not warrant any such staff, it remained only theoretical. Spirit had delivered; the most competent logistics officer in the Navy had elected not to resign and was now in our orbit. I pondered the ethics of this, and concluded that since no deception was involved, and Commander Phist understood why Spirit had come to him and was satisfied, that was satisfactory. The truth was, Spirit had an extraordinary amount to offer any man; I was in a position to know.

Now Lieutenant Repro presented me with the next name on his list: that of the most brilliant unrecognized military strategist to be seen in this century. "The test scores are virtually unbelievable," he confided. "I thought there was a typo or computer glitch, so I double-checked it and found it was true. This person by rights should be put immediately in charge of the entire Jupiter strategic initiative. But that will never happen."

"Why not?" I inquired innocently.

"Three reasons. First, no connections. You have to come from the right family and the right political spectrum to have any reasonable prospect of achieving anything approaching policy-making status."

All too true. I, as a young Hispanic officer, understood that well. "And?"

"Second, you have to be of the proper race. This one has a visible percentage of black ancestry."

That, too, I knew. The Navy was an equal-opportunity employer, but there were few black officers and very few ranking ones. Two strikes.

"Third, you had better be male."

I was startled. "A black woman of the wrong political persuasion?" Three strikes indeed!

"Lieutenant j.g. Emerald Sheller," he concluded. "Age twenty-two. Go get her, Hubris; your sister has shown how."

"But she's young!" I protested. Young: my exact age now.

"That, too, is a liability," he agreed. "But genius knows

no age. Be warned, Hubris: She's brilliant, aggressive, and bitter. It will be a significant exercise of your talent."

"I've got to have her?" I asked dispiritedly.

"You've got to have her. One day you'll tackle the pirates on the field of battle, and you will have a reasonable chance of success if Sheller is on your team, and little chance otherwise. She's a wild one, but believe me, Emerald is a jewel."

He was serious, despite the pun, and this was his life's hobby. The ravages of his addiction were more prominent now, but I trusted his competence in this. I had to have wild Emerald Sheller. I nerved myself to get on it.

Locating her was no problem. They had her supervising the filing department of the Base Records Division. Their tests showed her to be the most promising strategic genius available, yet this was the use they put it to! She had a right to be bitter.

I sent her a message: Lt. Hope Hubris Requests Date with Lt. Emerald Sheller. That's an Approved Navy approach. She responded promptly: 1800, this date. A pun, perhaps, on the social and calendar aspects of the word, but nevertheless an acceptance.

I presented myself in my dress uniform at her residence at the appointed hour. I had thought she might dress civilian, as was customary for women in this circumstance, but she met me in her own formal uniform. She was a small, angular woman with short jet-black hair and brown skin, no beauty by the standards of her race or mine, but fit and brisk. Every inch the efficient, virtually sexless clerk. I anticipated a dull evening, but a challenging one intellectually. I was half right.

We shook hands, as it was our first meeting. "I thought we might go to a restaurant and talk," I said.

"I have made arrangements," she announced briskly.

So she had. She conducted me to one of the licensed private shops on the post where we bought two bean sandwiches in bags. Then we went to the capsule tower, which was a mild form of entertainment. Opaque small bubbles were released to be drawn in by Leda's trace gravity. The descent was not far, but the bubbles moved slowly and could take an hour to land, or longer if jostled out of the direct line of fall. They were known as love capsules, for they were commonly used for brief dates. I had never used one before, being already familiar with free-fall and preferring more comfortable settings for my romantic engagements and was surprised Emerald had chosen this. But I said nothing, letting her play it her way. I had, after all, been warned about her aggressive nature and sought no quarrel.

Thus we found ourselves floating down, isolated. We ate our sandwiches, catching stray beans out of the air. And the woman tore into me verbally as if I were a pirate.

"So the lordly Hispanic Lieutenant Senior Grade, hero of Chiron, craves some black nookie. What possessed you to seek out this particular stranger? Surely not my voluptuous ass!" She patted her petite military flank.

My talent works best when there is interaction. I can gather a sense of a person's character in minutes that others might not discover in years. But this woman was complex, and as yet I had no grasp of her. "I am informed that I need you with me," I said.

"You are *informed*, Lieutenant?" she demanded, in a parody of the martinet. "Don't you have a mind of your own?"

I smiled, refusing to be baited. "Sometimes that is in doubt. You see, I have one ambition, but other people are formulating its realization, and they know more than I do. Thus I am supposed to enlist you in my cause."

"Why do I get the feeling this is not a simple sex-liaison?" she inquired, frowning as if in doubt. She was good at her mannerisms, and I found myself liking her.

"Because it isn't," I said. "I have no particular interest in your body, no offense intended. I need your service as a strategist. You may be the best of this century."

"Let's leave it at the sex. You aren't turned on by my body?"

She remained hostile and difficult to read. There were so may complex currents in her that I still could get no firm sense of the whole. "I asked you for a date because I wanted to talk with you," I said. "It is your mind, your ability I am interested in. I prefer not to advertise my real purpose. No one need know what passes between us here."

"They'll figure sex. And that's what it's going to be."

"I need your strategic genius, not your body," I insisted doggedly. "This isn't any ploy for sex! I won't lay a hand on you. I'm simply asking you to join my mission, because it should represent an excellent challenge for you, and its success may hinge on your ability."

"Well, I still figure sex," she said. "So get your clothes off, spic."

I had not heard that term in some time. It was a hostile reference to a person of Latin descent, specifically Hispanic; its precise application and interpretation had changed in the course of centuries, but it was generally considered grounds for combat when addressed to a person of my background by a Saxon. This woman was only half Saxon but was prickly indeed! Combat was what I did not want. "I only want to talk to you," I insisted. "I have no designs upon your—"

"Yeah, sure," she said. "Get 'em off, Lieutenant Loco, or I'll take 'em off for you."

I was irritated by her perversity but was aware that this was her intent and refused to be baited into open anger. So I removed my clothing and folded and bound it carefully in the null-gee, and floated naked before her. I experienced *déjà vu,* the feeling of having been here before; it was my memory of my first encounter in the Tail. I would handle this woman as I had the Tail-girl, June, if I had to.

She looked me over. "You're in pretty good health. Well, so am I. We'll wrestle."

"I don't wish to—"

But quickly she divested herself of her own uniform and floated nude before me. It is a peculiarity of the English language that a man unclothed is naked, while a woman unclothed is nude. I have never fully understood the distinction and tend to ignore it, but in this case I appreciated it. Nakedness is embarrassing; nudity is intriguing. Emerald was slender rather than lush, but she was indeed in good health, and her form was well assembled. Sometimes clothing diminishes blemishes or malformity; in this instance it had rendered severe a form that was in fact esthetic. My lost love, Helse, had masqueraded as a boy by strapping down her breasts and wearing boy's clothing; Emerald had in effect done much the same. I had not seen a brown girl completely exposed before and was interested. Her midsection was very small, and her breasts and buttocks quite well rounded.

But I had no intention of indulging in sex with her, because that had never been my intent and because I needed to prove to her that it was her strategic ability I valued. I must confess it had become a certain challenge for me to demonstrate my lack of sexual interest in her, though her body was in no way repulsive to me. Quite the opposite; the overly soft, fleshy women of the Tail were not strongly conducive, while the taut, vibrant, artistically molded flesh of this one—

"Try for a fall," she said, taking hold of me.

A fall—in free-fall? It was impossible! I simply fended her off. But she went for a pain hold, and that sort of thing can be effective in free-fall, so I had to counter. I was stronger than she, and I had had excellent training in several species of martial arts, but most importantly I was increasingly able to fathom her physical strategies. Her mind remained largely unfathomable, but not her body. One might argue that bodily action is a product of the mind behind it, but in practice this is severely limited by the physical chemistry of that body, and its signals are much more evident. So I understood her body, using my talent, and she could not make headway against me.

"One fall for you," she said when this was apparent. "But I can make you perform sexually."

"I've been trying to tell you—"

She grasped my private anatomy and kneaded it. I was surprised, but I remembered the Tail and let her proceed without reacting. This was a considerable challenge, for she had a flair for this sort of stimulation. Then she put her face down and used her tongue in a manner that caught me quite unprepared, and caused me to react despite my intent. In moments I converted, as the saying goes, from rubber to iron. Then she grasped me about the hips and drew me in close to her as we both floated in the sphere, and spread her legs to take me in. She had a kind of internal muscular control that amazed me, and in that manner she had her will of me. I gave up the struggle and clasped her body tightly and thrust urgently within her. "One fall for you!" I gasped as I shuddered to conclusion. She acknowledged by coming further alive against me. Juana, though more luxuriantly endowed, had never reacted like this. Emerald had shown me a new level of sexual experience.

But she wasn't through with me. "You figure you're a leader," she said as she separated from me. "That business with the *Hidden Flower*—you were just lucky they blundered worse than you did. If you had planned and executed it properly, you could have saved your sister without risking your Navy ship. And the episode in Chiron—blind luck was sixty percent of that, and again your own life was on the line. Those were Pyrrhic victories; too many of them and you'll be finished."

"That's why I need you, to plan and execute my strategy," I said humbly.

She considered momentarily. "Very well, Hubris. I'll marry you."

I had not, of course, proposed marriage to her. But in the Navy, term marriages were the norm for officers, just as heterosexual rooming was for enlisted folk. Emerald Sheller had concluded that she could achieve her own ambition more readily by being with me than on her own, and marriage was the most expedient way to get her reassigned to my unit.

We signed the forms that evening, for a one-year term, renewable, and next day she was transferred to my unit. For the second time in the Service, I had a liaison with a woman in which convenience was the motivating force, rather than emotion. But Emerald took her wifely perquisites seriously, and I must confess that I liked it. She was motivated to succeed at anything she tried, and her definition of success was demanding. She saw marriage as a legitimization of both sex and common interest, and she was quite good as both sexual partner and intellectual partner.

I think I could have loved Emerald, had she wanted to be loved, and had I wanted to love. Certainly I respected her. She was indeed a kind of genius. When our year was up, we renewed without question, and again the following year. Each time I told her: "I married you for your mind, but you conquered me with your body." And each time she said: "I know it." But the word *love* remained forbidden.

Emerald assumed the management of my career, and as my success as a leader led to promotion, her career profited, too. She was doing what she lived for, strategic planning. In three years I was a lieutenant commander, O4, and she was a lieutenant, O3, and my company was achieving a reputation as a fortunate unit.

Emerald, however, did not get along perfectly with the others. She had a certain acerbic way of expressing herself that came across more in tone and look than in content, and in this way she distanced herself from male and female alike. That seemed to be the way she wanted it. My sister Spirit, when she returned to the unit, resented this especially, yet she was the first to recognize what Emerald was doing for my career and the reputation of our unit, and she was also aware that Emerald and I were using each other, quite consciously and amicably. Spirit remained my closest friend and associate; *she* was the one I loved.

I should clarify an aspect of the military system and how it related to us. Some navies were organized on strictly impersonal lines, with officers rotated every six months and enlisted personnel having absolutely no certainty of assignment. The Jupiter Navy, however, favored the so-called Regimental system popularized by the Uranian moon of Titania, in which both officers and enlisted personnel tended to remain for prolonged periods in the same units, changing assignments only if dissatisfied with present ones. Promotions were generally within the unit, so that the commander had years-long association with the unit he took over. This led to much greater esprit de corps and satisfaction. Fewer people retired early, and performance tended to be better. I endorsed this system wholeheartedly, as it enabled me to gather in those people I knew to be good, and to retain them. For example, I got my old roommate Juana to be my secretary. She was now a sergeant, E5, and I promoted her at the earliest opportunity. She was a bright woman, good at her task, but our association was more than that. She knew my ways and would never betray my interests. Emerald was not entirely pleased, knowing our prior connection, but in this case I put my foot down. I wanted a secretary I really understood and trusted. There was, of course, no further sexual contact; Juana was enlisted, and officers did not mix that way with enlisted. But Juana and I remembered our first encounter in the Tail with a certain fondness; we had been good for each other and remained so, and that was what Emerald distrusted. I could talk candidly to Juana; she would understand, and she was never abrasive. I think it is possible for a man to be closer to a woman after the flame of sexual appetite has burned out; at this time true friendship becomes feasible, and that is as rewarding in its fashion as sex.

I also gathered in a considerable number of the Hispanics I had commanded during the Chiron mission—and some of the Saxons, too. They had never forgotten how we worked together to befriend the Greeks and how many lives had been saved when the violence erupted. They also remembered how I had scrubbed the barracks floor. Some called me, privately, *el cepillo,* the brush. But only those who had been there at the time; they were a select group. And I also picked up a few Chironiotes, young folk who had emigrated and been inducted as resident aliens. They had petitioned to be assigned to my unit, and I was flattered.

Of course, I got Sergeant Smith. Mine was not a training battalion, so my company had no recruits, but we did have need of instruction and discipline, and there was a better future for Sergeant Smith with us. We were an action unit, similar to the one on the Chiron mission; we could be sent out to fight at any time. I wanted my men ready, and Sergeant Smith was the one to get them ready. When he transferred in, there was some muted protest by my regulars because he was a Saxon outsider, but I put out the word: He was also the one who had put me on the track to officer's training. Without Sergeant Smith, I would not have become an officer, and this unit would not exist. Sergeant Smith was amazed at the welcome he received then, and the cooperation he received from a class of personnel who had always given him trouble before.

But mainly I was assembling my elite administrative officer corps. As commander of a company I did not warrant a special staff, so this remained largely in the imagination of Lieutenant Repro, but we had designated the positions and placements that would occur at such time as I commanded the battalion. In that fantasy, I was the commander, and Emerald was my executive officer. She was planning my promotion and acquisition strategies, devising ploys to gain key personnel, and doing comprehensive research on battle tactics, anticipating the time when we would put them into practice against the pirates.

Spirit was to be my S-1, or adjutant, the chief administrative officer. She would be responsible for all paperwork, finance, mail, personnel records, promotions, legal problems, and my official correspondence. Juana was really her secretary as much as mine, and the two got along well together, perhaps because Juana never opposed her will to Spirit's. Spirit was, in fact, running my company now, and all others knew that when she issued a directive, I backed it even if it hadn't originated with me. Because she was also Hispanic and spoke fluent Spanish, my Hispanic enlistees accepted her on her own merits.

Gerald Phist was to be my S-4, Logistics. He was not presently connected to my unit, but thanks to Spirit he was ready to join when this became feasible. He would be responsible for keeping the unit supplied with whatever it needed to accomplish whatever mission it had: ammunition, food, fuel, repair, spaceships, and so on.

Lieutenant Repro was to be our S-5: Public Relations, or propaganda. He remained ravaged by his addiction, his Achilles' heel; we had to help him mask it, but his mind remained sharp. I was increasingly curious about the nature of the drug he took but still hesitated to inquire, knowing I could do nothing about it.

Still our roster was not complete, even theoretically. I needed more rank, and promotions did not come readily to brash Hispanics. Emerald brooded on it, seeking a suitable avenue for rapid progress, and in this we were all with her.

Things broke one morning, abruptly. Spirit came striding into my bedroom, trailed diffidently by Juana. "Rise and shine, Hope!" she cried, waving a news printout. "Our mission is on the horizon."

I blinked sleepily. It was 0500. "What?"

"Get up, brother!" she said, catching my top sheet and whipping it off the bed. I slept naked, as she knew, so this was a rather forceful inducement to wake and dress.

Of course, Emerald also slept nude, and she was not entirely pleased to be exposed before my sister and Juana, both of whom were somewhat more generously endowed than she was, physically. "Get out of here, you canine!" she snapped, sitting up.

"This concerns you, too, Exec." Spirit said, unfazed. "The news just broke—" She paused, staring at Emerald's torso. "Of course, if you're too tired after mauling my brother all night, perhaps it should wait."

Juana stood near the door, repressing half a smile. I winked at her, keeping my own mouth shut. Spirit and Emerald were the two most forceful personalities in our group, and sparks often flew when they collided.

"Speak your piece and clear out, Adjutant!" Emerald snapped. She managed to pronounce the word *speak* with a short vowel sound, hinting at that cultural slur again.

"Or if you prefer to take thirty seconds to work your black magic again, before he gets away—" Spirit continued.

Thirty seconds! Slur and counterslur! They might as well have been fighting with knives.

Lieutenant Repro arrived at that point, forestalling Emerald's response. "Got here as soon as I could—" He broke off, taking in the situation. "Just what kind of a mission *is* this?"

"You summoned him, too?" Emerald demanded of Spirit.

Commander Phist arrived. "Have I missed anything?"

Emerald, sitting on the bed, threw back her shoulders

and spread wide her legs. "You tell me, sir," she said. "See anything here your busy wife hasn't shown you recently?"

Phist actually blushed. He turned away and almost collided with Sergeant Smith, who was just arriving.

"Sit down, all," Spirit said. "I called this staff meeting because time may be of the essence. We all know our futures are tied to Hope, and he needs a promotion. I think we have a chance at that now, if we act quickly."

They sat down around the bed, except for Sergeant Smith and Juana, who felt that enlisted personnel should not presume. If Sergeant Smith was perplexed at the manner of Emerald's dress and mine, he was too diplomatic to show it.

"Well, spit it out, woman," Emerald said, realizing that Spirit had pretty much skunked her on this encounter.

"Hope, you have had experience in the agricultural sector," Spirit said to me.

"Yes," I agreed. "Eight years ago, before I joined the Navy."

"So you should have an understanding of the issues; that gives you an advantage."

Phist lifted an eyebrow. "Perhaps I am slow, Spirit. I don't perceive the relevance."

Spirit waved her newsclip. "The Aggies are rioting. The Navy has been asked to intervene."

"Let me see that!" Emerald said, snatching the newsclip. "Why didn't I know about this before? It's a golden opportunity!"

"Well, if you'd been on your job instead of—"

"Because we lack an S-2," Lieutenant Repro said quickly, though even he ran an appreciative eye over Emerald's torso. It seemed he did have other interests beside the drug and his dream. "A top Intelligence man would have alerted us to this long before the public news broke."

"And what S-2 man do you have in mind?" I inquired.

"That's awkward," Repro said. "Which is why I haven't brought this up before. Your ideal hidden S-2 is acquirable only by one means, and your sister isn't his type."

"I should hope not," Phist said. His eyes were wide open about Spirit's reason for marrying him, but he loved her.

He was thirty-nine, she twenty-one, but they made a splendid couple. "Who *is* his type?"

Repro coughed apologetically. "Emerald."

Emerald straightened again, frowning, then quickly shifted gears. "Is he young and handsome?"

"Middle-aged and sickly, like me," Repro said. "With a potbelly and severe emotional disturbance. But he's the Intelligence man we need."

"Well, we can live without him," Emerald said. "I'm not going out whoring for discredited personnel."

Phist flinched, and Spirit's eyes flashed. Emerald had scored that time!

I changed the subject. "First, there is the matter of this prospective mission. I don't want to strong-arm migrant laborers. I still identify with them."

"Precisely," Spirit said.

"Damn, we need to organize for this," Emerald said. "We need our S-3, too, Operations. I can't plan strategy without knowing what we've got and how it's organized."

"Sergeant Smith knows," Spirit said. "He can handle S-3."

"With all due respect," Lieutenant Repro said, "I believe the psychological thrust is most important here. We can certainly volunteer for the mission and get it, because no commander in his right mind wants to tangle with rioting migrants who have little to lose and are very likely to destroy vital crops and make a messy scene regardless of what the Navy does. They aren't pirates or Saturnians; they're underprivileged Jupiter nationals and resident aliens, and there's a formidable bleeding-heart contingent on Jupiter that will raise one hell of a stink if any migrants are abused."

"They *are* abused!" I said angrily. "Sometimes a riot is the only way to make their case!" I had never looked in on the migrant scene after joining the Navy, knowing my friends there were dead or imprisoned; now I felt guilt for my neglect.

The members of my staff exchanged significant glances. "Let's go for it," Emerald said. "A bloodless settlement, by a minority-culture Navy officer who knows the migrants.

Excellent press! That'll bump Hope up to O5 right there, with luck."

"My thought exactly," Spirit said. "But we do need that Intelligence officer, or we risk flubbing it."

Emerald bit her lip. "Yes, we do. I've got to target every migrant leader, his background and nature. Precise dirt. Must have that S-2."

The others slowly nodded. "But he needs a competent and understanding woman, of a certain physical type. You realize what that means," Repro said.

Emerald slammed her fist into the pillow. "Whoring for personnel. Damn it!" she swore, angry tears in her eyes. "I liked it better with a man who understood *me!* I'll get you back for this, Spirit!"

"She didn't suggest this," Repro said. *"I* did. Sometimes we just have to make sacrifices." But I knew he was being gallant; Spirit had known.

"You damned junkie!" Emerald snapped at him. "Get out of my life!"

Repro hastily exited, and the others got off the bed. Emerald turned to me. "But I'm not through with you yet, Commander. If I've got to go whoring, I'll whore for you one more time." And she took hold of me, commencing a furious act of passion even before the others were clear of the room. Even as I enjoyed the experience, as I always did with her, I wondered what kind of man could only be won by such an aggressive display. Emerald really wasn't much on understanding, but she was supremely competent. I hoped that S-2 would be worth the sacrifice that I, too, was making, in giving up this Class A sexual experience.

And so it was that my marriage to Emerald was dissolved by mutual consent before our third year together was finished, and I volunteered my company for participation in the Navy action relating to the migrant riots, and Emerald, as she insisted on putting it, went whoring for personnel. Spirit had indeed torpedoed her rival for my attention, and I had to go along with it, though I had been well satisfied with Emerald as wife. The organization of my unit, orthodox on paper, was not nearly as regular and disciplined in practice; it was a hodgepodge of luck and sex and connivance and obscure understandings, guided by the mad dream of a drug addict. But we had purpose, and an extraordinarily fine cadre—and now we would put it to the proof.

Emerald acted swiftly and decisively, as was her wont. That evening she brought Lieutenant Mondy in to see me. He was as represented: about forty-five, pudgy, balding, and with nervous mannerisms. There were bags under his eyes, suggesting he was chronically short of sleep. He was O3, and had been there for twenty years, a derelict who evidently had not resigned when passed over for promotion repeatedly because he had nowhere else to go. He certainly was not physically imposing. But I knew better than to judge him by appearance; Lieutenant Repro called him the best available, and my talent was rapidly confirming the internal complexity of this man.

Nevertheless, I tested him. "Show me your power."

"You lost your family to pirates and swore to extirpate piracy from the System," he said without hesitation. "But your resolve has been blunted by circumstance. Your sister Spirit has become the backbone of your effort to organize a truly competent and low-profile antipirate force. She hesitates at nothing to promote your interests, and that attitude has spread to your other associates, even to your wife, who is now willing to sacrifice her personal comfort on your behalf."

He was on target so far. I felt no uncertainty in him as he spoke; his nervousness stemmed from personal concerns, not professional ability. "And?"

"You wish to capitalize on the current agricultural sector disruption," he continued. "You hope to succeed so well in this inclement assignment of migrant laborer pacification that you will earn a promotion to full Commander. Unfortunately you are not a schemer, so may fail to exploit your opportunity properly."

Emerald turned her head, surprised at this. "Clarify," I said, intrigued.

"Considering the risk you are taking of being punished as a scapegoat if you fail, you should make this double or nothing. Your entire unit must be given pressing incentive to succeed. You must name a price commensurate to the challenge: a blanket promotion."

"A what?"

"One grade for every member of your command. Private to PFC. Sergeant to SFC." He glanced at Emerald. "Lieutenant s.g. to Lieutenant Commander." Emerald gave a start. None of us had thought of this!

"That can be done?" I asked.

"The Navy is prepared to pay for its most challenging and risky missions, if the price is made clear at the outset. This is not by the Book, but the Book is commonly honored more in the neglect than in the letter. Consider the challenge: About fifty farm bubbles are involved, with a thousand others watching to see the outcome, and a sizable element of the Jupiter population ready to react politically no matter which side wins. The Navy doesn't want this assignment, considering it to be a sure disaster, but cannot refuse it. The migrant workers demand better conditions, more pay per basket picked, and a recognized union to represent their interests in the future. The owners claim they can't afford more pay without raising prices to the point where consumers will balk, and they absolutely refuse to recognize any union. So the workers have gone on strike, and hunger has caused them to riot at three bubbles. They swear to die before they return to work under the old conditions, and not all of them are bluffing. The crops are spoiling. Prices have begun an anticipatory rise on Jupiter, making the political climate volatile. This will be remembered at the next general election. It has become an extremely sensitive matter. The Navy will be instructed to end the strike within seventy-two hours, and it looks as though there will have to be martial law and summary executions of resistant migrants. About a third of the workers are of Hispanic descent, and this use of force could further complicate Jupiter politics. In sum: If this job is bungled, the current government could fall." He smiled grimly. "I think a blanket promotion is not too much to ask for a quick, peaceful, amicable, and lasting settlement."

He certainly had the essentials! I had not comprehended the ramifications. "But can our unit succeed?" I asked.

"Very likely—with the proper information, strategy, incentive, and nerve. You can arrange everything except the information. I can supply that."

"Will you join us?" I asked, certain now that this was the officer we needed. A scheming genius!

"I am of course available for a price. But the ethics are uncertain."

And I saw that he was concerned with ethics. That was an excellent sign. "This morning Emerald and I were in the third year of our term marriage," I said. "We dissolved it by mutual consent so that she would be available for you. We were satisfied with each other, and faithful to each other, but we were not in love. It was a marriage of convenience. We deeply regret having to separate, but the need of the unit overrides our personal preferences, and we have done it. Promotions and the chance to establish our unit formally, with its full slate of officers, would make up for whatever private personal misgivings we have." I saw Emerald nodding. She wanted, more than anything else, to be a true military strategist, and the blanket promotion would be a giant step in that direction. "If Emerald marries you, she will be true to you for the duration of that marriage, and I will find another woman. Our unit is more important than our marriage. I trust she has already shown you what she can do for you." Again I saw her nod. Her demonstrations were impressive.

"You don't understand," Mondy said. "I am aware of the inhuman discipline you both possess, and the hard-nosed tactic by your sister who resents your sexual captivity by another woman." Emerald gave another start; evidently she had not told him of that. "You are making me an offer I am unable to decline, and I must compliment Lieutenant Repro on his Machiavellian perception in using my own system against me. But my awareness that Emerald would return instantly to you if she could, and that I can never have her love—"

"I never had her love," I said.

"Nor your secretary's," he agreed. "It becomes a matter of definition. You have more than you suppose."

He had researched all of us intimately! "It is true that Emerald has an unkind manner of phrasing it, but—"

"Whoring for personnel," he said. "And I have no pride in this respect; I will accept her on that basis. Her demonstration was persuasive in more than the physical sense. A unit with such dedication to its welfare—" He shrugged. "I would certainly like to be part of that unit. But I am not merely an unattractive man eager for young flesh. I suffer from posttraumatic syndrome. I am not easy to live with."

"I believe that should be between the two of you," I said. "If she believes she can handle it—"

"I can handle anything I have to," Emerald said, though she seemed shaken by Mondy's knowledge of the situation. How had he discovered our dialogue of the morning? Emerald had shown him her power; now he was showing us his.

"I will not bore you with my South Saturn experience," Lieutenant Mondy said. "I will just say that it continues to haunt me, after twenty years, and has ruined me as a conventional officer. I wake screaming in the night; I go on drugs sometimes by day, not from addiction but from inability to function otherwise. I am literally afraid of the dark. I am terrified of being alone, but even in company I cannot necessarily relax. I need someone to talk to, about things that are not pleasant to discuss. I need a nurse. No woman has been able to put up with me for more than a few days. I am no sweet, cuddly teddy bear; I need a woman with guts and stamina and comprehension as well as a body."

"I can handle it," Emerald repeated grimly.

"We offer you more than a woman," I said. "We offer you a family. Give us what we need, and we will give you what you need. It seems a fair exchange."

"I'll take it," he said.

And so we got our S-2 officer. I won't say Lieutenant Mondy was easy to get along with. He did, indeed, wake screaming in the night, and on occasion I had to come and help Emerald restrain him from hurting himself or her. It was not that he was vicious, but that he suffered hallucinatory episodes of horror that caused him to flail uncontrollably. It was not feasible to put him in restraints; his reaction to that could have killed him. But he did like young flesh, and it did have a pacifying effect on him, and at age twenty-four Emerald was young enough. As he came to know and trust her, this became more effective, even during his worst spells. She had to be with him constantly, at first, day and night, literally holding his hand, speaking softly to him, sometimes literally seducing him into relaxation. She was tough, and she was showing more compassion now than I had realized she possessed, but this was a strain on her; she lost weight and sleep. But gradually she got on top of it and recovered much of her former animation. "I never knew when I was well off," she muttered once to me, and I was deeply flattered. She was making a real sacrifice for the unit, and I wished there was more I could do for her, but our code forbade it now.

Mondy did produce for us, and we all came to respect his mind. He had an intimate understanding of the vulnerabilities of the military system, and he knew, often literally, where the bodies were buried. He came up with information about the migrant leaders that amazed me. We used that information to formulate a daring strategy.

We got the mission, of course; it was ours for the asking. And Lieutenant Mondy had no trouble transferring in immediately; the Navy didn't value trauma-ridden officers any more than it did ambitious Hispanics or blacks or addicts or whistle blowers. And, after a week's bureaucratic delay, we got our deadline exactly as Mondy had predicted: seventy-two hours from our scheduled arrival at the Agricultural Ring. That wasn't much time!

I briefed my company. Most of the top men had a pretty good notion already what was up, and they were for it. I stressed that we intended to get the migrants back to work without violence, and that we would do our best to relate to them, speaking in Spanish or whatever language made them most receptive. "But these are tough and desperate people," I concluded. "For two weeks they have held out against the owners and the government itself. So first we shall show them our power."

Then I turned it over to my staff for implementation. We were preparing for a battle, but not for bloodshed; we intended to convert the migrants to our side by means of a finely orchestrated campaign.

According to Lieutenant Mondy's information, rioting had gutted three bubbles, and these had already been evacuated. They were scheduled for demolition and replacement; it was easier to bring in new bubbles from Jupiter, paid for by calamity insurance, than to repair the old ones in space. We requested and received permission to use them for target practice during our mission; Mondy had known what channel to use to get immediate affirmation. But the missiles Lieutenant Commander Phist arranged for us to stock were not standard ones; they were heavy-duty planetoid busters, seldom used in the Juclip. But Emerald had specified that kind, and I concurred. We were ready to show our power.

We selected our first bubble carefully. The leader of the workers here was Hispanic and had a checkered history that we could exploit psychologically. Lieutenant Mondy had briefed me thoroughly on this; that information, plus my talent, should put the migrant in the palm of my hand. We hoped.

We closed on the bubble, landed, and hooked on well away from the migrant bus; no sense inviting early trouble. A picked squad charged in, armed with stunners and ready for action. The way was clear, and I followed with a picked squad of my own. We carried no visible arms, but my sergeant had a pacifier: an electronic device that could deprive people in the area of their free will, unless they were protected by small personal interrupters as my own troops were. I didn't want to use the pacifier, as it would not solve the long-term problem; it was merely a backup in case things went wrong.

This was a pepper bubble. The sight of its rows of green plants stirred me to nostalgia, for I had first worked as a migrant picker in a pepper bubble. This was one reason we had selected this one to start. Still, I felt the impact. Nine years—how brief it seemed, suddenly! The subjective impression sometimes bypasses objective reality.

The workers were spread out around their ship exit, looking bedraggled and hungry. This strike was hard on them, because the bubble-owner normally provided most of the food, selling it to the local foreman. Naturally the food was the first thing cut off when the workers balked. They did have some supplies of their own but not enough for comfort. They had to have been subsisting largely on peppers for several days, which was no joy. We had brought extra food, but we said nothing of this now.

"We represent the Jupiter Navy Order-Restoring Force," my sergeant announced in English as we approached. "We want to talk to your leader."

A large, swarthy man in his thirties stepped out. "I'm Joshua. I'm the foreman, and I'll speak for the workers here."

Now I spoke. "I am Lieutenant Commander Hope Hubris, in charge of this expedition. I speak for the Jupiter Navy. I have no politics; I am only here to see that you return to work before any more of the crop spoils."

"You going to arrest us all, officer? That won't pick these peppers."

"I don't want to arrest anyone. I just want to see this thing amicably settled."

"Easy enough," he said. "Just give us decent conditions and better pay and our union, and we'll be glad to work."

"I can't promise any of that, especially not the union," I said. "But I can help negotiate something, if you will return to work first."

Joshua spat on the ground and turned his back. It was his typical reaction to affront, as Mondy had informed me.

I was ready. "Don't turn your back on me, gringo!" I snapped in Spanish.

The man whirled, his face abruptly charged with fury, a knife appearing in his hand. But I was already moving, and a knife was in my hand, too.

He paused, surprise tempering his anger. "You're bluffing, Navy man. You don't know how to use that thing."

"Take my word, picker: I know how."

"Watch it, Josh," one of the migrants said. "Either way, you're dead. They've got power weapons."

"There is another way," I said. "Sergeant."

The sergeant stepped forward smartly. "Sir."

"The rubber knives."

"Yes, sir." He lifted a case and opened it. Inside were two handsome knives. He removed first one and then the other, flexing them to show their nature clearly. They looked real, but they were toys.

Joshua stared. "A joke?"

I smiled. "You have doubted me twice," I said in Spanish. "I don't want to stop your doubt by killing you. Try it with these, and doubt no more."

He shook his head. "What the hell." He put away his real knife and took one of the rubber ones. I did the same.

He came at me suddenly, but I was already moving aside. Few amateurs can match the proficiency of one who has trained seriously with such weapons. In a moment I had his knife arm in a standing armlock, and my own knife poised at his throat. I had him.

Joshua froze, then relaxed, as Lieutenant Mondy had predicted he would. He was a man of bluff and give, as my own talent had confirmed, seldom pursuing an unprofitable course too far. He laughed, converting his defeat to a joke. "Okay, Navy man; you can use a rubber knife. You say you can negotiate a better deal for us?"

I let him go, and we returned the rubber knives to the case, and the sergeant put the case away exactly as if a genuine duel had been fought. "I can negotiate—if I have your help. Not for the union; the farmers will blow up their own bubbles before they give on that. But the rest, yes. I need to get the top leaders of the striking migrants together with the most intransigent farmers' representatives and have them bargain together in good faith. The only way I can get them together is if one of their own endorses my effort. The farmers say they'll meet if I can get the migrant leaders to come. So I am asking you to come with me and help persuade the other leaders to board my ship. I promise to treat them with respect and return them all safely to their locations, regardless how the negotiation works out."

He squinted at me. "Do I doubt you a third time?" He

gestured with his hands. "I guess I've got to believe you. You could have mowed us all down with lasers instead of talking. You could have taken me on with a real knife and killed me if you'd wanted to. In fact, you could have killed me with the fake knife! Sure, I'll do it. What I want is a fair settlement, not a lot of fighting." He glanced at his workers. "But maybe—"

"To show my good faith to your people while you are gone, I will leave some of my personnel with you, unarmed." I turned to the sergeant. "Send out Corporal Allen with some food."

"Food?" one of the migrants asked involuntarily. Yes, they were hungry!

The sergeant spoke into his mike. In a few minutes Corporal Allen arrived with three privates, hauling a chest on wheels. "Corporal Allen reporting as directed, sir," she said, saluting smartly. She spoke in Spanish.

The migrant workers stared. Corporal Allen was not only of mixed Hispanic descent, she was stunningly pretty—and so were the three female soldiers with her. Their uniforms had been tailored to enhance rather than diminish their qualities.

"Remain here and serve these good men a good meal," I told her. "We'll pick you up when we return with Don Joshua." At that, Joshua gave a start; I had referred to him with respect, Spanish-style. Such little signals can carry powerful freighting.

As we departed with Joshua, the girls were opening up the chest to reveal a relatively sumptuous array of hot meats and vegetables and cold fruits and wine, with spices on the side. They smiled winningly at the hungry workers, who were covertly wiping the dirt off their faces and combing their hair. There would be no quarreling with the Navy in this dome!

Joshua paused to look back, half-longingly. "By the time I get back, my men'll vote to take anything you offer," he muttered.

"That's better than bloodshed, isn't it?" I inquired innocently.

Food and attention were awaiting Joshua on the ship.

He was treated with deference by our personnel, as if he were an honored dignitary. He well understood the psychological ploy, but he enjoyed it. The fact that we were making the effort was as impressive as the effort itself. The bubble-farmers had spurned him and his cause; we were doing him the signal honor of taking him seriously. Dignity and respect—these can be magic.

We detached and jetted to the next bubble on our list, as carefully targeted as the first had been. Lieutenant Mondy and Lieutenant Sheller had choreographed this precisely; I was merely the officer implementing their strategy.

The second leader was a straight Saxon original-stock illiterate leader type, stupid but strong. He was not about to fight the Navy but also not about to be moved. His name was Laredo, and I remembered the song that was from. I left Joshua Jericho in Juana's care, feasting on Spanish-style food, and took my squad out into the bubble. The preliminaries were similar to those of the prior session, but this time I spoke no Spanish and made no challenge with the knife. Instead I glanced at the acreage filled with tomato plants. "That certainly doesn't look like such hard work to me," I remarked.

Now Laredo was an excellent tomato picker. He didn't know that I had developed a good technique myself, in my year as a picker. I could move tomatoes about as fast as anyone, without bruising them. He assumed I had always been a Navy officer.

"Shipman, you couldn't do no work like this," he asserted. "It takes speed, stamina, and a sure touch. This ain't soldiering; this is real work."

I shook my head, disbelieving him. "It seems to me anybody could do this sort of work."

"Oh, yeah? Well, soldier boy, why don't you just try it yourself? Then maybe you'll see what we're striking about."

I pondered. "I'll tell you what. If I show you I can pick as well as you can, will you come on my ship and negotiate with the farmers to end the strike?"

He laughed, and so did the other workers, who well knew the pitfalls of the simple-seeming job of tomato picking. Too fast or hard, and they bruised and were rejected. There were many migrants who couldn't pick tomatoes, because their touch was too heavy. This was a chance to put a snobbish Navy officer in his place without getting into further trouble! "You're on, mister!"

We set it up. The deal was to pick ten buckets of tomatoes and deliver them to two migrant inspectors for checking. The winner would be the one who completed the job first with fewer than ten tomatoes rejected for bruising. Each of us had a row. My men became my cheering section, while the migrants favored Laredo. We took our buckets, and started picking at the "go" signal.

It had been eight years since I had picked, but a skill once mastered is never forgotten, and I had had considerable training in the interim. I had muscle and stamina, and I could handle explosives rapidly without a slip. Also, I had rehearsed during the trip to the Agricultural Ring, with tomatoes on the ship, recalling and sharpening my technique. I was ready for this.

Laredo, on the other hand, was a foreman. He had not actually done much picking in the past two years, so was rusty.

My hands moved rapidly, plucking the fruits, twisting them expertly from their attachments without damaging the plants, and setting them gently in the bucket. The migrants gaped, then frowned, realizing that they had been suckered. I delivered the first bucket before Laredo did, and started on the second.

Laredo now realized that he was in a serious contest. He *was* a good picker. He buckled down with increasing speed and skill, getting back into the familiar routine. I had a slight lead but could not improve on it. No doubt he thought I would fade, but I was too fit for that; I continued without slacking. He began sweating, for he was heavyset; his eyes flicked often to my bucket.

I brought in my tenth just ahead of his. My troops cheered.

But there was a hitch. "Too many rejects," the man who checked my total announced. Sure enough, there were a number of badly bruised fruits.

I knew I had not bruised them. The migrant checker had done it himself, to disqualify me. That was one thing we hadn't counted on: cheating.

Laredo went over to inspect my tomatoes, frowning. "Them's all recent bruises," he said. This was the premium variety, very delicate, that discolored almost immediately.

I shrugged, knowing complaint would only seem like an excuse. "I guess I wasn't as good as I thought I was."

"Man, I saw you setting 'em in! You never—" Then he paused. He was an honest man, but he didn't want to accuse his own worker of cheating. "It don't matter. You proved you could pick. I'll go on your ship."

So I had won what counted. We brought out the food, as before, this time served by petite Saxon privates, and Laredo boarded the ship. "You was a picker," he said to me challengingly. "You never learned to pick like that in the Navy!"

"Before I joined the Navy," I admitted. "We rioted, too." Then I proffered my hand, and he took it. I had another man with me in more than body, which was the point of the exercise.

The third bubble was the toughest. The strike leader was an old-timer, as tough as they came, named John Henry. Neither physical force nor picking expertise would move him, we knew; he would settle for nothing less than victory. His workers were expecting us, too; they had a barricade set up, and they were armed with knives and clubs. Any attempt to roust them out would result in bloodshed, and that could set off the remaining crews. The migrants had set up their own minor radio network, so they were current on our activities.

This was an apple bubble. Small apple trees covered its inner surface, hardly more than bushes, loaded with ripe fruit. I saw that dry brush had been piled in one section, glistening with oil; the flick of a lighter would set it blazing, and the fire would be hard to stop because the brush extended to the trees; flame-dousing chemicals would damage the trees.

But if I could get John Henry to negotiate, I could get the rest. This was a crucial encounter.

This time I brought Joshua and Laredo with me. Both of them stood before the barricade and pleaded my case: I was Hispanic, I had been a picker, and I just wanted to help them get a fair settlement without violence.

"Yeah?" John Henry demanded. "We heard how those Navy dolls've been turning your heads, but I'm too old for that. If he was a picker, where's his song? You schnooks ever think of that?"

Joshua and Laredo fell back, dismayed. Of course, a Navy man could arrange to fight or pick; that didn't make him one of them. Had they been taken in?

Now I stepped out alone. I took off my hat and jacket and rolled back my sleeves as if preparing for a heroic effort. Then I sang:

It takes a worried man to sing a worried song . . .

"God Amighty!" someone cried. "Wasn't you with Joe Hill?"

That was the single break I needed. This was a large group with many old-timers, but Mondy had not been able to ascertain whether any had shared crews with me. The odds had been about two to one in my favor, but it had remained a gamble. It seemed one had been there—or at least had known of me.

"Yeah, I was with him," I agreed aggressively. "You got anything to say against Joe Hill?"

"He's dead!"

"Joe Hill never died!"

The man stared at me a moment, then nodded somberly. He knew what I meant. The spirit of Joe Hill lived in the striking laborers, as it had for centuries.

I finished my song, and some of them joined in. Then I started Joe Hill's song, and soon they were all singing. And John Henry was mine; of course, he had known of Joe Hill and what he stood for. I had shared Joe's life; I had rioted at his death. No better credits existed.

It was downhill after that. We picked up several more

leaders without difficulty; the radio network was helping us now. It was the long shadow of Joe Hill that did it. I was still in his debt.

But I had to explain that the farmers remembered Joe, too, and that they still feared him; no way would they let a union get started. Not this year or next. That was their real balking point. The migrants could go for the Galaxy in other matters, if they yielded on this one.

The leaders greeted this with stony silence, as had the owners when I had mentioned how generous it would seem if they were to upgrade the working conditions in the domes. We had two unfortunately intractable sides here.

We rendezvoused with the yacht carrying the lawyers who represented the farmers. We were ready for our negotiation session.

"But first, if you don't mind, there is a little errand I have to do," I said. "Bear with me, please; it won't take long."

The migrant leaders and the farmer's lawyers were sullen; they were not at ease with each other. They had come to the meeting, but it was obvious that neither side cared to compromise. I had made an impression on the migrants, but that was personal; it would not persuade them to desert their fundamental interests. Good food and pretty girls can only accomplish so much. That was why we had scheduled this "errand."

We accelerated to one of the derelict bubbles. I did not explain what the errand was, and our guests did not inquire.

Our ship oriented on the bubble. "Has there been any change?" I inquired of my Exec gravely, in the presence of my guests, as the viewscreens were activated to show the bubble.

"None, sir," Emerald replied as gravely. She was in full uniform, very severe.

"No response to our final communication?"

"No, sir." She looked grim indeed.

I frowned. "Unfortunate." I made a small sigh of resignation. "Well, it has to be done. Proceed with the alternative measure."

The image of the bubble magnified on the screen, becoming quite clear to our guests. They watched. They had nothing else to do at the moment. They did not know this was a derelict.

"Fire one missile," Emerald said clearly into her mike.

Our ship rocked as the missile was launched.

A lawyer looked about, startled. "Missile?"

"Do not be concerned," I reassured him. "This is an incidental action."

The planet buster struck the bubble. It detonated. There was a brilliant flash, prevented from being blinding only by the automatic dampers on the viewscreen. From the flash emerged a cloud of debris, fragments flying outward in an expanding kaleidoscopic pattern. It was one devastatingly beautiful explosion.

"The—you—" the lawyer exclaimed, for once failing in eloquence.

"Let's hope such discipline does not again become necessary," I said somberly. "I dislike certain measures, but I learned long ago not to indulge in half-measures." I turned to our guests. "My apologies for this delay. Now let's get on with the negotiations. I'm sure something can be worked out."

"But that bubble!" Joshua exclaimed. "You blew it apart!"

I shrugged. "Sometimes my hand is forced." Then I paused, as if realizing something. "This is not one of your bubbles, of course. You are cooperating. We were not able to obtain representation from either side from this one. Naturally I would not discipline a bubble involved in honest negotiation."

The migrants looked at each other, then at the lawyers. The two parties seemed to draw closer together. "In your resumé," a lawyer said cautiously to me, "there is a reference to the slaying of a number of pirates, when you were a refugee—"

"They were criminals. That's ancient history."

"You ain't changed much," Laredo muttered.

The lawyer glanced again at the dissipating cloud, unwilling to accept the implication, but shaken. He licked his lips nervously. "Perhaps we should get on with it."

"By all means," I agreed heartily. "Now let me summarize the points at issue. As I understand it there are three. Working conditions—"

"Can be upgraded," a lawyer said quickly, glancing at the others for confirmation. "The farmers are not unmindful of the practical comforts of the workers. They are willing to provide better food, and to space the working hours for greater worker convenience. Internal discipline can be ameliorated or placed directly in the hands of the migrant foremen. There really is no problem there, so long as the work is properly done."

"Excellent," I said. "I was sure your employers were reasonable men. Now the workers say they want a union—"

"Uh, if we get what else we want, maybe the union can wait," John Henry said, his eyes also on the dissipating cloud, and the others nodded agreement. "One thing at a time, I always say." It was amazing how readily peripheral elements could be dispensed with when the hint of violent destruction was made. Civilians were not inured to such measures. I had obliquely shown them my power.

"Excellent," I repeated. "It is generous of you to postpone such a heartfelt issue. We all remember Joe Hill." I took a measured breath. "Now the central issue: the rate of pay for work performed. Now this does appear low compared to the prevailing Jupiter scales—"

"This is not Jupiter," a lawyer said. "Minimum-wage scale does not apply—"

"Yet," John Henry said meaningfully.

"Our clients have formidable problems of supply and transportation that make the standard scales inapplicable."

"Yeah, they prefer slave labor," Laredo said.

"The migrants work voluntarily!" the lawyer snapped.

"We ain't working *now*," John Henry said.

"We volunteer to work instead of starve," Joshua said. "That is not much choice, my friend."

"Pardon me for interrupting," I said. "But would it be fair to say that the migrants would be satisfied with a higher rate of pay per bucket, nothing else? No unemployment insurance, medical coverage, retirement benefits—"

"Retirement benefits!" the lawyer exclaimed, appalled, while the eyes of the migrant leaders widened with appreciation. They had not thought to try for anything like this!

"I understand your problems of supply and shipment," I said to the lawyers. "We have them in the Navy, too. Let's concentrate on the central thing: the pay per bucket picked. If you pay the workers more, you will have to raise your prices in Jupiter, putting you at a competitive disadvantage."

"Exactly! We compete with pseudo-produce, and there are cut-rate imports from Uranus and Saturn—"

"But you see, the workers' rate has not changed in years, while the cost of living has," I pointed out. "The workers are being severely squeezed. That is why they are restive. If you gave them more to work for, you could save some of the cost by reducing your supervisory personnel, that we all know are really guards. Satisfied workers reduce your overhead."

"Well, if we could afford—"

"Suppose you key the workers' pay to the retail price of the produce?" I suggested. "That would alleviate the criticism some make that the farmers ignore the increasing cost of living of the workers while increasing their prices."

The farmers, and therefore their lawyers, were quite sensitive to such criticism. "Well, we have no objection in principle—"

"Perhaps five percent," I said.

"Five percent!" a lawyer exclaimed indignantly. "Preposterous!"

"Normally, as I understand it," I said, "the fee for a significant service rendered, one necessary to business, is ten percent or more. Five percent seems modest enough, considering the importance of the service."

"But it has never been done before!"

"We are all progressive people, willing to try new things when the old ones prove inadequate," I said blithely. "This is, after all, the twenty-seventh century. Suppose the arrangement is publicly posted: Of each dollar retail price, five cents is allocated for the picker.''

"But the men will not work, if it is not tied to the bucket!"

"Tie it to the bucket, then. If a bucket contains one hundred peppers whose retail value is five cents per pepper, or five dollars to the bucket, the picker gets twenty-five cents."

"Twenty-five cents!" the lawyer cried as if in pain. "That's two and a half times the present rate!"

I shrugged. "I suppose we could publicize the fact that the farmers are unwilling to allocate more than two percent for harvesting, while paying more than that to keep discipline among the distressed workers, and see how the Jupiter public reacts. Perhaps the public will agree this is fair."

The lawyers blanched, knowing the outrage such statistics would incite on civilized Jupiter. "Perhaps three percent, which would represent a fifty percent improvement in—" one began.

I glanced at him. "What is the basis for your own fee for services rendered?"

The man backed off hastily. "Perhaps if the percentage was publicly posted, so the consumer would know the reason for the increase in price—"

"I think it might appear unpatriotic for the buying public to refuse to pay a few extra cents to allow the pickers a living wage," I said. "I doubt you would lose much in sales—if that were the extent of the increase."

The lawyers pondered. They knew the farmers would not object to a settlement that successfully passed along the added cost to the public. But I suspected that when the time came to publicize the prices, the public would demand that the five percent be taken out of the original price, and the farmers would discover that they could, after all, afford it. Regardless, the principle of a fixed percentage for the pickers was the key to a long-term settlement. My staff had hashed this out beforehand and rehearsed me on it; I was not nearly as quick or informed as I appeared. That was the beauty of a good staff; it made the commander look good, when it was important that he do so.

That, essentially, was it. We made a temporary agreement, and the foremen promised to put their workers back in the fields, and the lawyers promised to allocate five percent. If the remaining migrants or the farmers did not ratify the agreement, the five percent would still hold for the work done during the temporary period. After that, the strike would resume. But we all knew it wouldn't come to that. We had worked it out.

We returned the migrant leaders to their bubbles, and picked up our girls. Joshua was right: The migrants were ready to sell what remained of their souls, after enjoying the hospitality of our lovely personnel. They would ratify.

Before we parted, Joshua spoke to me privately. "That bubble you blasted—rubber knives?"

"You're smarter than you look," I said.

"Thought so. You're not really a killer."

"Not of migrants," I agreed.

The agreement stood. There was no further violence. We got our blanket promotion: I advanced to full Commander, O5: Repro, Spirit, Emerald, and Mondy to Lieutenant Commanders, O4; and right on down to our lowest E2's becoming PFC's. We had gambled big, and won. And my name flashed across the Jupiter news of the day. Commander Hubris was momentarily famous.

And perhaps I had repaid Joe Hill for his kindness.

Chapter 6

PUGIL

There are set routines for promotion and assumption of commands, but Lieutenant Commander Mondy knew how to circumvent them. Our next step was perhaps unique for the time: my company expanded into a battalion; my three platoons became companies; and my squads grew into platoons. New personnel came into this framework mostly from below. We simply fissioned away from our former battalion and became our own.

Now my battalion staff became official. Lieutenant Commander Phist transferred in to be my S-4 Logistics officer; he had not been part of our unit before, so had not shared in the blanket promotion. I now ranked him and could include him in my command.

Now our training commenced in earnest. Some of it made little sense to the troops, but they worked at it, anyway, because the penalty for unsupport was to be transferred out again. You see, it wasn't just physical training, it was social.

I required each man to learn a song, and that he always be ready to sing it in public. I had been reminded of the power of song by my experience with the migrants. The migrant laborers had a special kind of camaraderie, and I wanted it for my battalion. This was my first major step. The men grumbled, but they picked out their songs in the migrant manner and rehearsed them. We had regular singing sessions where enthusiasm counted more than skill. There were a good many duplications of songs, and those who shared songs were supposed to look out for each other's interests, even if they had no other bond.

I had Sergeant Smith, now E7, instruct a program of special training in judo, fencing, and pugil sticks. Why? Be-

cause I wanted my men to be expert in hull-fighting. You
see, there are several ways to take out an enemy ship in
space. You can blast it to pieces, which I deem to be wasteful; or you can disable it and force surrender, which is
risky when dealing with dishonorable folk such as pirates;
or you can board it and take it over from inside by using a
pacifier or gas grenade. To board it you have to land suited
men on the hull, who then operate the airlocks and get inside to do their work. A stun-bomb flung through as the inner lock opens is very effective. But a smart ship's captain
will post guards on his hull to prevent exactly such intru-
sion, and those guards have to be dealt with quickly and silently.

Picture the problem: There you are, just arrived on the
hull, your magnetic boots clinging to the metal surface,
the centrifugal force of the ship's rotation pulling you outward. (Technically, there is no such force, but it is more
convenient to deal with that imagined force than with the
more complex input of the vectors of deviation from rest.)
You are, in essence, hanging upside down, with little leeway for error; the moment your feet lose contact with the
hull, you fall out into space. The boot magnetism is not
great, because you need to be able to move individual feet
readily; falling is all too easy. And here is this enemy soldier coming at you—

Perhaps the best way to illustrate this is to describe an
episode of the training in which I was personally involved.
We did not have many discipline problems, because of the
spirit of unity we cultivated, but any organization has
some. This one involved Corporal Heller, a huge, tough,
canny brute of a Saxon who went in for all the violent activities. He wasn't popular, because he had a sarcastic
mouth and was apt to hurt people by too-vigorous physical
competition, and he had a bad attitude. But he insisted on
remaining in our unit, and he was competent and worked
hard, so we tolerated him.

When an opening came for a squad leader, there were
two prime candidates: Corporal Heller and Corporal Valencia, a qualified Hispanic. I interviewed both men, for
even small decisions of personnel were important to me

and the lower officers had not wanted to touch this particular case. I made my decision in favor of Valencia. He was designated squad leader and was promoted to sergeant.

Heller was furious. He claimed I had discriminated against him as a Saxon. Actually, I had seen that however well qualified Heller was otherwise, he was unsuitable as a leader of men, because he had little sensitivity to the needs of others. This was a largely Hispanic squad that would be more responsive to one of its own, and Valencia spoke Spanish. He could not compete with Heller physically, but leadership is more than physical. He would do a better job, and his squad would have higher morale and fewer gripes and superior performance.

However, a sizable segment of my unit did not see it that way, including many Hispanics. Sergeant Smith explained it to me succinctly: "We're training to go out and fight pirates, right, sir? Pirates are tough, so we need tough leaders to match them, not just good organizers or nice guys. Heller is tough."

"Would you have given him the job?"

Smith laughed. "No way, sir! You can't train men by breaking heads! But that's the way some of the men see it. There'll be discord, sir."

I called in Lieutenant Commander Repro. He had a spaced-out attitude, but he was functional. That addiction bothered me increasingly, and I knew I could not forever postpone taking action. "Are you familiar with the Heller/Valencia case?"

"Certainly, sir." Personalities were in his bailiwick.

"What's your advice?"

"You'll never satisfy Heller without giving him promotion and responsibility, and he's not fit for it. You need to find a slot for him that has rank and responsibility without direct command of men. Is there such a spot?"

I looked at Sergeant Smith. "Is there?"

"Yes, sir."

"But you must also satisfy his pride," Repro continued. "He's so angry, and so are a number of others in the unit. They think you have been unfair, and they're taking flak from their peers in other units about reverse discrimination. You've got to give them some satisfaction."

Leadership has its limitations. "How?"

"A challenge match, sir." Repro's brow furrowed. "Odd, though, that Heller even made an issue, when he could simply have transferred out. Something's not rebounding."

A steel ball not favoring the pattern; I knew what he meant. But his advice seemed good. That was why I arranged a challenge match with Corporal Heller.

We took off our marks of rank and set it up as a public training exercise, with the rest of the unit watching. We started at the center of the ship, back to back in the fashion of a duel. We each carried a foil, a pugil stick, and a bomb in addition to our standard gear, attached by snap-free fasteners. They looked clumsy but added only about fifteen pounds to the thirty-five-pound suit assemblies. We could handle the weight, especially in free-fall and with suit-jets to propel us.

This match was well refereed; just about every enlisted man wanted to see the old man defend his turf, so to speak. (Age has nothing to do with the designation; it is the slang for any unit commander.) It was not necessary for me to win to retain their respect; it was necessary for me to show the same qualities I required of them: skill, courage, stamina, and fighting spirit. But if I lost, I would have to appoint Heller squad leader, and that would be a minor disaster. There was also the matter of pride.

Sergeant Smith gave the command: "Move out!"

We bounced away from each other and floated toward opposite airlocks. I was the Raider, and Heller was the Defender; these roles had been chosen by lot. It was my job to disable the enemy ship, and his to protect it.

I spun the wheels and worked the handles of the inner panel of the lock. Everything was manual, of course; airlocks are too important to trust to powered machines. There was an art to navigating an airlock swiftly, and it was important now; the first man out had a definite advantage.

The portal opened; I jumped down in, for there was gee

here at the rim of the ship. Gee, of course, is more than an abbreviation for gravity; it means weight in space, in whatever manner it occurs. I closed and secured the inner panel, then struck the pressure-release valve. The air of the lock bled out rapidly into space. This might be considered wasteful, but it was fast, and a powered air pump would be suspect during battle conditions, as well as slower. What use to save a little air and lose a ship? Simplicity and speed were of the essence.

My suit became rigid as the pressure dropped, but the hinges in the limbs kept it flexible where it needed to be. Civilian suits are flexible all over, and the really good ones fit like a second skin; in fact, a healthy young woman can be spectacular in space, the more so because she's untouchable. But the military suits were old-fashioned, bulbous-limbed, and heavy and rigid between the hinges. But they were cheap and reliable, and they provided a convenient cushion of air around the body that enabled a person to remain in space as long as his oxygen held out, and sometimes that was critically important.

I dropped out as the outer panel opened, caught one of the external handholds, and flipped over to plant my magnetic boots against the hull. These boots certainly would have been useful when I was working on the hull of the refugee bubble, so long ago! Then I had had to depend on a tether to keep me from drifting free in space, and it had been nervous business.

The panel slid back into place automatically, spring-loaded. I stepped on the fiber panel, where the force of magnetism was muted, and squatted. I waited for the buoy to come into sight; the spin of the ship brought me around to it in a few seconds. Then I leaped as hard as I could toward that buoy. I seemed to depart the ship at an angle, but this was mostly illusion, because the ship was spinning under me. *Over* me; I was falling away from it. I had compensated for the tangent of my centrifugal departure when I jumped; I was right on course for the buoy, which was two miles away. I was traveling at close to forty miles an hour, so would reach it in about three minutes. The buoy represented the halfway point in the course; in an actual mission I would make a jump correction here and home in on the enemy ship. This time it was trickier; I had to loop around the buoy and return to the *Copperhead*, now redesignated as the Enemy Craft. That meant using my suit-jets to kill my inertia and get me moving back. That could be awkward, but my officer training had prepared me well for this. I could make the loop with fuel to spare.

Now I spotted Heller. He was way behind me and proceeding slowly, no more than twenty-five miles per hour. Good enough.

I approached the buoy, oriented, and used my jet to decelerate. I may have mentioned that technically there is no such thing as deceleration, only acceleration, but the old concepts remain useful even when erroneous. Why say negative acceleration when deceleration makes it so much clearer? At any rate, I was braking, reducing my velocity relative to the buoy.

I came to a "halt" in space just beyond the buoy where three enlisted men, referees, perched in their suits. They saluted cheerfully, and I returned it, though no salutes were required in this circumstance. I nudged to the side, then accelerated again, having looped it. The enlistees waved. Heller was only now coming close.

Then I remembered: He was the Defender. He didn't have to loop the buoy; he just had to defend the ship he started from. He had come out slowly not to race me but to stop me, and he had saved all his fuel. Now he was meeting me, and my challenge had just begun. All he had to do was grab me and haul me out to space; if I used my jet to oppose his, my fuel would run out before his, and I would not be able to reach the target craft.

My best bet was to outmaneuver him: to get past and accelerate so that he could not catch up. But now he used his jet, angling to intercept me. I could not stay on a straight-line course.

I tilted my body and jetted to the side. Heller tilted and jetted, again on an interception course. Maneuvering in space in a suit takes skill; I had it, but so did he. In fact, he was better at it than most enlisted men were; he must have had more aptitude for this than our supervisory personnel had judged. Why hadn't he transferred to a unit specializing in this sort of thing? Inexorably he closed on me.

He had equivalent skill and more fuel remaining than I did; I could not avoid him. I would have to fight.

I reached over my shoulder and drew my foil. This was a long, thin, round-bladed sword with a button on the end. On a real mission a rapier would be used, the sharp point being used to puncture the enemy's suit. This was the manner that swords came to space, anachronistic as it might seem: There was hardly a more efficient method to dispatch a person in space than simply poking a hole in his suit. Small hand-lasers could be devastating on bare flesh, but the material of military space suits resisted this, spreading the heat rapidly and dissipating it harmlessly. A ship-mounted laser could readily take out a suited man, of course, but a hand-laser was a mere toy in comparison. It was not true that a mirrored surface could stop a laser, as many folk believed; the ray ignored the polish and melted the backing, as it was not strictly a visual phenomenon. A mirror might help deflect a glancing shot, and some suits were polished with this in mind. But only hand-lasers made glancing shots; a ship-laser could send a beam several feet in diameter, bathing the whole suit, and there was no defense. The heat had nowhere to dissipate to. Of course, it was uneconomic to take out a single man with a ship-laser; such power is by no means cheap. So the net effect was to eliminate lasers from this action. Small projectile weapons were notoriously unreliable in a vacuum, even those supposedly designed for it. They tended to misfire or explode in the hand, and the recoil could set a man spinning wildly. Thrown knives or bombs depended on the accuracy of the throwers and could be dodged if any distance was involved. So it came down to the recoverable sword point, which had no permanent recoil and could be used as often as needed. Not the slashing type of sword; that was too easy to parry or blunt, and was too unbalancing to swing unless the user had good anchorage. But the direct thrust of a rapier was difficult to avoid or counter.

So we did indeed have old-fashioned swordplay in modern space, and swordsmanship was a viable Navy skill.

The foil, of course, had a blunted point. The button of the tip would, when depressed with sufficient force, complete an electrical circuit that registered as a score. A score anywhere on a space suit suggested a puncture, and that, in a real combat situation with sharp points, would be lethal. It did not have to be a vital area of the body, and no blood had to flow; a sleeve puncture was just about as fatal as a heart puncture. A pinhole leak could be patched before significant deflation occurred, but a sword puncture would blow out the suit too rapidly for remedy, and if it didn't, surely the victim would be too busy trying to stop the leak to continue the fight and would be easy prey for the next strike.

But this discussion becomes tedious. Heller had his sword out. He wasted no time; he jetted right at me, the sword point leading. I reacted automatically, countering his thrust and using the contact as leverage to move myself out of the way. I could have struck forward at his torso, but that would only have resulted in mutual scoring. Who won if both died? The suicide ploy was only for those who were dying, anyway. He shot past me harmlessly.

Harmlessly? I realized that I had seen something alarming. Probably a misperception, but I wanted to be sure.

He spun in space, using the catlike gyration needed to reorient when there was nothing to push against. It is an acquired skill, but military men are so often exposed to free-fall that most pick it up readily. The body had to be oriented so that the fixed suit-jet would aim in the desired direction; orientation plus thrust equaled motion.

This time I jetted toward him, my point extended. The niceties of fencing don't work well in free-fall, because the body is not braced. Heller did not seek to parry me; he extended his own weapon. We were ready to suffer mutual "death."

This time I saw the point, uncapped. He had a rapier, not a foil!

This man was out to kill me, literally.

Abruptly I parried, shoving him out of the way. I spun in place and jetted at him again immediately. The ship was now directly behind me, and my fuel was low; this was the last such maneuver I could make. I would lose this aspect of the match if I got stranded in space, but that was not my present concern. I had my life to protect!

Heller spun to meet me, his sword coming at me. I parried it again—and grabbed it with my other hand. I let go my own weapon, putting both hands on his rapier, wrenching it from his grasp. He hadn't expected this! I put my two boots up against his chest and shoved him violently away from me. He spun out toward the buoy, and the recoil sent me spinning toward the ship as I had planned.

I reoriented and used the last of my fuel to accelerate toward the ship. I now had a head start, but Heller had plenty of fuel. Would he come after me without his rapier?

He did. He gained on me and would have intercepted me before I reached the ship, but now I had his rapier, and I menaced him with it, keeping him at bay. Rather than risk my thrust, he avoided me and preceded me to the ship. I could not prevent that; he would have the advantage of being set on the hull as I arrived. I had no choice except to continue my course; I was out of fuel. If I missed the ship, I would be helpless.

But I had faced death before and had seen my family and friends die. I had no liking for violent death, but this immediate threat only galvanized me to better performance.

As I moved toward the ship, I pondered. Why was Heller trying to kill me? He had a grudge, true; but he could settle that by defeating me in this match and getting his promotion. He was throwing that away, for he had to know he faced court-martial and summary execution the moment he tried seriously to kill his commander. His life was on the line now, and he hadn't had to put it there. There was a missing element.

There were more witnesses floating beside the ship. I could signal them at any time, but they did not know how this contest had changed and might only get hurt themselves, so I let them be. This was my own fight!

Someone must have put Heller up to this. His insistence on staying with my unit, and trying for a position for which he was unsuited, now fell into place as part of a more insidious plot. But who or what could have caused him to go to the extreme? Well, if there were some understanding within the Navy, so that he would face a lenient court, and if he claimed he hadn't known his weapon was pointed—an error by Supply—and I were not alive to refute him, he just might get off with a nominal punishment. A year in detention, reduction in grade, a general discharge from the service. Then he could collect his private reward: perhaps enough money to make the risk worthwhile.

Heller was surely a tool. Who was behind this? Who had sufficient money and influence to arrange this—the murder and the nominal punishment? Who had motive to eliminate me?

There was an answer: QYV.

QYV had left me alone for years, ever since Chiron. It seemed his activity had resumed. He still wanted that key and knew I would not yield it while I lived. So he was trying to kill me and somehow recover the key from my body, gambling that it was the original. It made a certain sense.

I experienced two reactions, of roughly equal and opposite nature. The first was curiosity. Who was QYV, and how did he wield so much power? What secret did the magnetic coding of the key unlock, that was at once so quiescent as to be able to wait for years for recovery, yet so important that people could be killed for it?

My other reaction was anger. Twice QYV had set traps for me, and twice I had survived them. Now he was doing it a third time. I fancy myself an intelligent rather than a vindictive man, but there are limits. It was time to deal with QYV.

These thoughts took only a moment. Now I was sailing in toward the ship, and Heller, the agent of this annoyance, was waiting for me with his pugil stick.

The pugil stick is a training device dating back six or seven centuries. Surely the name derives from the English word *pugilism*, itself derived from the Latin *pugil*, a boxer. In other words, it was a boxing stick. It was originally designed to resemble, in mass and length, the primitive projectile weapon of historical Earth called the rifle. You see, the liability of all projectile weapons is that they constantly require new projectiles, the old ones being lost by use. When the ammunition is exhausted—as might happen when a unit is surrounded or has its supplies interrupted, or when the press of battle prevents timely reloading—the empty rifles, laser pistols, blasters, or whatever become clubs or swords. A knife could be affixed to the end of the ancient rifle, so it came to resemble a crude spear, and in that condition was called a bayonet. Unfortunately bayonets were not ideal for training, being too clumsy and deadly. So the pugil stick became a mock-up of the bayonet, padded and rounded so that it was difficult to actually harm an opponent. The center was narrow, for a handy grip, while the ends were cylindrical masses; the whole vaguely resembled an ancient barbell. Protective helmets were worn for such practice, and heavy gloves, and crotch armor. Still, it was possible to inflict quite savage punishment with such a device; a blow solid enough to knock down an opponent was not lightly dismissed. On occasion, in the early days, men were beaten to death with the pugil sticks, and on occasion, such pugilism had been banned. But I had instructed Sergeant Smith to train my men with it, and the present case was an example why.

In the Jupiter Navy we used the sticks in new ways. They were, of course, useful for inculcating an aggressive attitude in trainees; it might fairly be said that there are no pacifists with pugil sticks. The man who hesitates to strike is doomed to *be* struck; he soon learns to fight back. The exercises are competitive with squad, platoon, and company champions. I had become a platoon champion in my day, using my talent to comprehend the nature of an opponent. All this had been standard in military training since the pugil stick was developed, but in space and/or free-fall, there is a new dimension, literally. The stick is no longer a substitute for a more effective weapon; it is a weapon itself.

I could tell by the way Heller held his stick, and by his stance on the hull, that he was expert in this form of combat. He was large and strong; there he had a natural advantage over me, for I am of average dimension. But already I was coming to grasp his nature—as I should have done before this match ever started!—and this would enable me to compensate. There is more to pugilism than mass and strength. This would be a fairer match than he supposed.

Several more referees were on the hull. They watched without interfering. As yet, none of the observers realized the actual nature of this encounter.

It was Heller's evident intent to bash me as I landed. If he could knock me loose from the hull before my magnetic boots found firm attachment, I would drift helplessly through space, my mission incomplete, and the victory in the match would be his. On the other hand, if I could land and knock him loose, I would then have the advantage: He did have fuel remaining, so he could return; but I could intercept him as he did so.

I rotated so that I came at him boots first. Then I hurled the rapier at him. He had to dodge aside lest his suit be punctured. The throw also provided me some braking action, slowing my approach. As he dodged, the weapon smashed into the hull and rebounded back into space, and I landed safely before he could attack.

Heller strode into me, thrusting at my head with one of the padded ends, but I was ready. I blocked his pugil stick and quickly countered with a butt stroke to his groin. A point is scored when a contestant lands a solid blow to a vulnerable region: the head, throat, chest, stomach, or groin. Of course, our suits protected all these regions of the body, but the referees would tally the score for any such blows made. In addition, there was the knockoff strategy: to knock the opponent loose from the hull and into space. This would be the object on an enemy hull: literally, to hurl the defenders away.

Heller readily blocked my stroke, and struck swiftly at my shoulder. I ducked and dodged aside, letting the padded end graze my shoulder while I countered to his briefly vulnerable midsection. I scored on his stomach solidly enough to rock him back, and I knew the referees were making notes.

But something was wrong, and in a moment I realized what it was. There was a scratch on my shoulder where his strike had scraped across it.

Scratch? From the soft, padded end of the pugil stick?

I fenced with him, watching his stick. The ship was spinning, so that we were in effect hanging by our shoes with light and darkness alternating frequently; as we swung back into "day," I saw the bumps in his stick. Originally the pugil sticks were wooden rods wrapped in polyfoam, enclosed by canvas bags at each end; today they were wholly synthetic but similarly padded and enclosed, and the materials were still called "foam" and "canvas" and "wood" though they were not. There should have been no bumps in the canvas. Heller's stick had to be spiked with hard or sharp objects fixed between foam and canvas. They showed only slightly, but any solid blow would bring their sharp surfaces into direct contact with the opposing surface: my suit.

I slashed viciously at his head, forcing him to counter. Thus his canvas struck mine—and mine tore. Now I had confirmation. His supposedly harmless pugil stick had been rendered into a deadly weapon, here in space. He was still out to kill me, and the referees still didn't know it.

I could retreat, grab a referee, and have Heller arrested. But wise as that course might be in the practical sense, it would not be good in the social sense. No officer should flee an enlisted man in a situation like this, or pull rank to get out of a difficult situation. I would be entirely within my rights in this instance, but I could suffer a critical loss of respect in my unit. I needed that respect, not for personal pleasure but to enable me to forge an absolutely dedicated corps. I wanted troops who put the welfare of the unit ahead of their own, and I had to set the example. This remained *my* fight, win or lose, regardless of the handicap. After all, in real battle situations the unexpected had to be dealt with, too.

I continued to analyze Heller's style. He was strong and skilled, but I was flexible; already I grasped his patterns. This was my talent, and it was of inestimable value to me in a crisis. It was as if he were calling his shots in advance, while mine were surprises. Now that I knew his weapon, I guarded against it. The tide of battle was turning in my favor.

Heller became aware of this. He strove desperately to take me out, smashing brutally at my body with alternate ends of his stick, but no shot touched my suit. My own pugil stick was in shreds, however. When his intemperate effort put him out of position, I countered devastatingly; I chopped at his feet, sweeping both his boots free of the hull. He fell away from the ship, and in the moment he did so, I lofted him on his way with a stick-end uppercut that caught in his padded crotch and shoved him out. He was on his way!

Of course, he used his jet to brake and return, but that took precious seconds, and in that time I charged the airlock he was supposed to be defending and spun the exterior wheel. Heller returned before I got the lock open, but I was mindful of his progress and paused to bash him back into space. On his next return he was more careful, landing at a small distance so he could anchor his boots before encountering me, but by that time I was inside the lock.

He jammed his pugil stick into the closing aperture, preventing me from shutting him out. I grabbed the stick, opened the panel, and hurled the stick away into space; but that gave Heller time to scramble into the lock with me.

Now it was the third phase of the contest: hand-to-hand. This was where the judo came in. Judo is one of the old Earth martial arts, and though in its full scope it includes all of the blows and holds known by man, its essence is the technique of throwing. On Earth this meant throwing the opponent to the ground on his back hard enough to knock the fight from him, and perhaps holding him down; the idea was to overcome him without having to hurt him. The term *judo* meant, in the original Japanese, "gentle way," in contrast to the necessary violence of striking with fist or foot. In that respect judo was superior to most other martial arts; it provided an avenue of limited or measured force, regardless of the effort of the opponent. Such an avenue was invaluable when it was necessary to subdue an intoxicated friend, or an enemy one preferred to reason with.

Here on the hull of a spaceship, the thrust of the judo throw was reversed. Now it meant breaking the opponent's magnetic contact and hurling him into the void. The seemingly opposite techniques were not too different in practice; the presence or absence of gee made all the difference. But in the close confines of an airlock, it was another matter.

Strength counts for a lot in hand-to-hand combat, but skill counts for more. Here I had the advantage; I had spent more time in a space suit, and had faced worse hazards than had Heller. I maneuvered him into an armlock that was just as effective in suits as it was naked; he could not move without dislocating his elbow. I maintained the hold with one arm and my body and feet, pinning him to the wall by using the leverage in my magnetic boots as well as bracing against the opposite wall. With my free hand I sealed the lock, pressured it, and set off my bomb.

When the inner panel opened, my "nerve gas" spread rapidly into the ship. It was actually colored, perfumed vapor, harmless, but it made the point: I had taken the ship and won the match.

Now I signaled Sergeant Smith. "Arrest this man," I said as my helmet came off. Respect was no longer an issue.

The referees recovered the rapier and doctored pugil stick; there was no question what Corporal Heller had tried to do. But before taking any further action, I interviewed him in my office.

"Corporal," I said briskly, "you have your choice of summary unit discipline or a formal court-martial. I recommend the former."

"Sir?" he asked, perplexed.

"I am prepared to deal," I said.

He understood. "Unit discipline," he said immediately.

"You may have information I want. Provide it freely, and I will assign nominal punishment." I remembered how Sergeant Smith had said this to me, years ago; I had learned from him.

"Sir, you know I tried to kill you," he protested.

"You are not the first," I said dryly. "I know you are only a tool. I want the mind."

"Sir, my life—"

"Is forfeit to the Navy. I will protect you."

He yielded, knowing the nature of my commitment. "I will tell you anything I know."

"Who hired you to kill me?"

"Kife," he said, his mouth seeming to be reluctant to form the syllable.

That surprised me. Not the answer; I already knew that. But the fact that he answered without evasion. Few who betrayed QYV, I was sure, survived long. In fact, he could have been hired indirectly, not knowing his true employer. QYV was being less devious here than I had expected.

I got the story from him: Heller's family was poor, with no real prospect for improvement. He had been sending most of his service pay back home; the normal Navy allotments for dependent parents were not sufficient in this case for the medication required. QYV had offered instant, anonymous settlement of the family debts, and a handsome reward upon discharge from the Service, so that the family would be secure and Heller himself would have much-improved future prospects. Heller trusted QYV because QYV always kept his word; in any event, the debt settlement had been arranged before Heller made the attempt on my life. If he died in the attempt, or was executed, his family remained better off. "It was the best I could do for them," he concluded.

"Now that you have failed—"

He smiled grimly. "No bonus. I'm on my own."

"If you had succeeded—"

"I was to fetch a little key from your body and fling it into space."

I was surprised again. "You had no delivery route?"

"No, sir. Just to fling it away. After that, Kife would send a lawyer to plead my case in court-martial and get my sentence reduced."

With such a lawyer, and the strings QYV could pull, I knew Heller would have done all right. But he had failed, was now a liability to QYV, and so had accepted my terms instead.

That was the extent of his pertinent information. I knew he was telling the truth, because of my talent.

"You have no personal animosity toward me?"

"No, sir. I respect you. It was a put-up job; I'm no good for command, just for fighting. We knew you'd have to turn me down, giving me cause for challenge. You're not bad at combat yourself, sir."

I pondered. "I can't give you riches, but I can give you life and a clean record." I had not forgotten the potency of that offer, either. I knew he would respond; when he made a commitment, he honored it all the way. "Will you serve me loyally henceforth, if I give you the chance?"

He spread his hands. "You beat me fair, sir. You've got me, if you want me. *I* wouldn't want me."

"Then you are hereby assigned to my personal staff. Your record will not be affected, and your family will not know."

He was amazed. "What about the punishment, sir?"

"You will be my bodyguard. If I am to be killed, you will intercept the attempt to the best of your ability. If you die or are wounded, that is your punishment. You tried to take my life; until you save it, you have not paid."

"Yes, sir!" he agreed.

Another person could not have afforded the risk, but my talent made it feasible for me. Heller would be the best bodyguard I could obtain. He owed me life and knew it.

"Uh, sir—"

"Yes, Corporal?"

"Something I heard, can't be sure it's true—"

"Yes?"

"There's another attempt on you slated. Some other way to get the key from you. But I don't know how. Just that there's someone or something on the ship. Indirect, maybe."

"Thank you, Heller." I wasn't surprised. QYV had tried three times; why not four?

I had survived the encounter with no more than some

chafes about my body, owing to the unexpectedly strenuous nature of it. I didn't bother with sick bay, preferring to assume the pose of indestructibility. I rubbed some salve on the sore spots, had a light meal, and settled down in my hammock for a nap, alone. When I had been married, I had rated a bed; I missed it, but single enlistees or officers had hammocks, and I was no exception.

Several hours later I awoke, feeling odd. The room was dimly illuminated, the way I preferred it for sleep; there was sufficient light for vision. I looked at the ceiling, for I had caught a flicker of something there, something in a dark color, oblique to my vision. I could not quite focus on it, seeing it mostly peripherally as it flowed gently by. I was not alarmed; the sight was pleasant. It occurred to me I was dreaming, for there was no holo-projector here, yet I knew I was awake.

Now the image changed, becoming brighter, more defined, undulating iridescently, as though an ocean of rainbows were heaving by. Bands of color separated from the mass, forming into arcs, semicircles, spirals, and loops. Other bands realigned, forming patterns of lines that somehow passed through the individual curves without interference. Perhaps it was like the petals of flowers floating on a heaving sea, the waves distinct from the objects yet interacting in a curious, intangible fashion.

I closed my eyes, and the sight changed but did not disappear. Rather, it became muted, an underlying grid of color, as if this were the fundamental form that filtered through my eyelids. I opened my eyes again, and the grid was clothed with new ornaments, symmetrical motifs, that slowly turned in space three-dimensionally, like galaxies or rare ancient urns, each more lovely and significant than the others, each a vessel of sheerest wonder. Faster they turned, like spinning planets, spraying out colors like gravity waves, more and more rapidly until their outlines blurred, and even then they were impossibly beautiful.

Abruptly, all was gone. I saw only my room, stark and bare. There are no loose items in a Navy ship, for they could become missiles during accelerative action. No pictures or paperweights. All is secured and little is esthetic. I lay still, hoping for a return of the pretty visions, but they were gone. I felt a loss so great it brought tears to my eyes and a burden to my chest. Paradise lost!

I stirred, sitting up, causing my hammock to swing slightly—and suddenly there was sound. Fragments of marvelous music flitted about me, as if some profound orchestra were tuning up. The room seemed to tilt as I moved, throwing me off-balance; everything was askew. I steadied myself, but though my body was still, it also seemed to be turning; the room was turning, too, in the opposite way, and my legs were rotating in diverse directions; yet somehow all was organized so that I neither twisted apart nor lost my position in the room. The sound clarified, and I heard a distant, lovely, vaguely familiar melody, one I longed to appreciate more closely but could not approach.

But I tried. I got to my feet and found I was not dizzy despite the motions of the universe and my body. Beautiful bass notes sounded as my feet struck the floor. I walked melodiously to the door in pursuit of the distant theme, passing through the complex tapestry of colors that reformed, without disturbing it. Geometric patterns played across the door, and the latch-release panel was somewhat like a painted goblin's head, but I touched it and the panel slid open.

Beyond was flickering fire. Intense orange flames leaped up and came through to touch me, but they had no heat; I was invulnerable to this sort of illusion. I stepped into the inferno, following the melodic theme.

The flames remained, reminding me somewhat of the savage surface of Io, but once I was fairly in them I discovered new aspects. They had discrete shapes of their own, and these were animate, almost alive. There were flame-flowers blooming from their twining flame-vines, more beautiful than any I had ever seen. The smells of them came to me now, the essences of perfect nature, compatible with the music that enfolded them. The geometric shapes flitted in from the other chamber, becoming angular and sine-wave bees and butterflies and hummingbirds without sacrificing their mathematical identities, and carried

sparkling pollen from flower to flower, mating them.
There were small, satisfied flashes of light as the sex or-
gans that were the flowers received their gratifications,
their completions. Then the flowers faded, for nature has
little use for anything whose function is past, and were replaced by fruits on the vines, becoming full and juicy and
delicious.

As I gazed at those fruits and understood the symbolism
of their generation, I felt the stirring in my own loin, the
need to merge my own pollen with the ovules of the female,
to generate my own fruit and the seeds of my own type of
life. The flames became half-naked young females of human persuasion wearing skirts without panties, shawls
without halters, dancing, twisting, shaking, writhing,
their breasts bouncing and quivering with the fullness of
their motions, their legs lifting, spreading, closing beck-
oningly. The nymphs twined like serpents inside their
decorative ornaments, impossibly alluring. Now I saw
flame-men, too, with fire phalluses that jetted sparks into
the crevices of the female flames. I longed to jet my sparks
also, but the flame-girls were intangible to my flesh. I
needed my own kind.

I resolved to search for a human woman of suitable configuration and youth. I strode forward, and suddenly my
environment shifted again. Horror fell on me like nocturnal rain, soaking me through the flesh to the bone, and
through the bone to the marrow. I shivered, terrified of
everything. Things came at me, threatening; I was aware
of teeth, claws, eyes, and thin sucking-type proboscises. I
fled their chill menaces, but there was nowhere to flee; the
very shadows reached their barbed extremities toward me.

I spun to the side, and the scene obligingly shifted, sliding past me laterally, vibrating; when I stopped, it continued more rapidly, carrying the monsters along. But this
was dizzying. I clapped my eyelids down; the clang as they
slammed closed echoed loudly across my skull and set the
jelly of my brain to vibrating. That was worse than the
monsters, so I reopened my eyes, cautiously so the orbs
would not burst loose from their sockets in the vacuum,
but it was all right; they were contained. Now I saw my

hand before my face, outlined in double contours without and within, so that it was at once skeletal and ballooningly fat. The contours tripled, quadrupled, quintupled, sextupled, until I blinked, reminded of something by that last description; I had been in quest for a woman. Then the multiple lines vanished, replaced by solid colors, red contrasting sharply with green, blue with orange, yellow with brown. But underneath remained the hand, the empty hand, proffering what was more horrible than anything it could have held. I wrenched away again, trying to scream, trying to blot it out.

And a man loomed before me, but the sounds he uttered were unintelligible, a meaningless roar. I peered into his face, but it was blank, devoid of soul. As I looked, I saw a progression of features on him: human, ape, feline, reptilian, with staring eyes. I realized he was but a shell, an incubus, a golem of no account. I shoved him aside, and he moved with strange lightness, as if he were canvas filled with foam, and I went on to the next, and he, too, was nothing. I continued past a crowd of them, until I came to the master-entity, a monster in vague man-shape, foul smelling. I saw it take hold of a man and crush him in a bear hug so hard that flesh pulped under the skin, so that he was rendered into a shapeless mass. Then the monster sank a hollow fang into the top of the victim's head and sucked out the multicolored juice, and the skin-sac shriveled as the substance was depleted. When the bag was empty except for the rattling bones, the monster blew foul air through its tooth, inflating the sac until it was as turgid as a space suit in a vacuum. The man was restored as a soul-empty shape, a balloon, a doppelgänger who moved about among the others who did not notice the change. Who accepted it as an ordinary person.

Now the monster came for me, for I still had juice in me, and I could not flee him. There was blood all around me, pooling on the floor, spattered on the walls. Evidently some had leaked from the victims of the monster while they were being squeezed. I didn't want to step in it, knowing it would somehow destroy me, but the monster was reaching for me. I was too frightened to think straight or even fight, knowing I was doomed.

Words came through from the confusion of notes and blood. "Hope . . . Hope . . . Hope . . . Hope . . ."

I paused, seeking the source. "Who calls me?"

"Repro. Repro. Hope, you have been drugged. Drugged! Do you understand?"

"Drugged," I repeated. It did seem to make sense.

"Hallucinogenic, evidently. Are you in a vision?"

"Vision," I agreed. I was not surprised that I could talk to him. At the moment, nothing surprised me.

"We don't yet know what drug it is, so can't neutralize it. But I can help guide you through the vision till it passes. I have had experience with hallucinogens. Just listen to me, and all will be well. Do you understand?"

"Understand." Then I essayed a more relevant thought, as my mind was quite clear, regardless what my senses were doing. "There's a monster here, about to squeeze me to a pulpy mass, suck me dry, and blow me up again as a doppelgänger. I can't flee it; there's blood spattered all around."

"That sounds like the *boraro*," he said after a pause for thought. "An ancient spirit of South America associated with the jungle and with visions. I have encountered him in the past. He carries a quartz crystal to make him fierce. Do you see that?"

I peered at the monster. Sure enough, now I saw the bright crystal held by one paw. "I see it."

"If you can take it away from him, he will not attack you."

"Take it away from him!" I exclaimed. "I don't dare get close to him!"

"Then give him milk and honey; that will pacify him, and you can escape while he's eating. Both milk and honey have a seminal character, so are potent in magic. The *boraro* loves potency. He is a manifestation of a person's repressed instincts, so—"

"I have no milk and honey!" I cried as the monster took another step toward me, bear arms extended, sucking-tooth ready. He seemed larger and fiercer than ever.

"Then you must find him."

"I *can't—*"

"Now listen to me, Hope," he said. "This is your vision, and you have the power. You merely need to know how to use it. You are in your vulnerable human form now; you can change it to something the *boraro* can't hurt. In South America, the jaguar was very strong. Change to a jaguar."

"A jaguar? A feline animal? I can't—"

"Yes you can. I know how these things work. I have been there before you. Just—change. You can do it if you try."

The *boraro* took another step toward me, his pulp-squeezing arms almost enclosing me, and suddenly I was a jaguar. I was on four lithe feet, and my limbs were finely muscled, my torso lean, my senses keen. I felt exhilaration and strength.

"But beware," Repro's voice came. "The jaguar embodies death—"

I ignored him. I leaped at the *boraro,* and he fell down, terrified, no further threat to me. I charged on through the jungle, exhilarated. This was my alter ego, my true self; now I could act out my deepest desires with impunity.

I sniffed, winding female. Ah, yes, I could not touch the flame-forms, but there were others. I followed the currents of the breeze, zeroing in on the scent I wanted. I found a hill and entered a tunnel in it, going down into the subterranean world where the females were lurking, hiding. I burst into a great nether ballroom where women were dancing. I took hold of the nearest and spun her about, and she was made of flesh and her eyes were alive, but she screamed with terror.

I realized what was wrong. "I have not come to consume you," I told her. "See, I am really a man!" And I resumed human form, confining as it was, giving up the jaguar alternate.

But still she flinched away. "I am not really a woman," she told me. "I am a deer in human form."

I stared at her and realized it was true. There was a doe-eyed, furry quality about her. She had fled the hunters and concealed herself in this manner. All the dancing women were animals. Still, she was female, and flesh, and that was what counted. I drew her into me hungrily. She tried to resist, but her efforts were ineffective, for she was not a fighting creature. This was, as Repro had pointed out, my vision, and I had power.

"I will do it," another female said, interceding. I looked at her, and she was full and beautiful. She had taken the form of Juana. I let the deer-woman go and turned to her. I had always liked that particular form.

"This way, jaguar," she said, and led me to a separate chamber within the mountain, where there was a bed. I wondered what kind of animal she was in reality but did not ask, lest her present attractive form be lost. Perhaps she was a female jaguar.

Then all was immersed in the colors, sounds, odors, and touchings of hallucination, and I lost myself in the raptures of pollenization and closeness and warmth, and finally slept.

When I woke I was in my own room, and Commander Repro was sitting by my hammock. I was back in the mundane world. I felt tired but not ill. Had it been a dream, rather than a vision?

Repro saw me stir. "Over, sir?" he inquired.

I nodded. "What happened?"

"You were dosed with a potent hallucinogen," he said. "It sent you on a several-hour trip. I don't know when it began, but it was well advanced when I was summoned. I tried to talk you through it, for that often helps, but lost you—"

"I remember," I said. "I changed into a jaguar and went rutting after—" I paused. "Maybe you had better tell me just what happened next."

"You charged into the enlisted women's barracks—"

"Oh, no! I thought it was a subterranean cavern filled with, er, animals."

He smiled. "In human form. I have been there, too. Fear not. Juana was there, and she took you in hand."

"Some hand! I—"

"I explained about the drug," he said. "The girls understand. They are amused. And Juana—was glad to do it. Your secret will not escape this ship."

Probably true. My personnel were loyal to me and to the unit. "I should apologize to—"

"No need. They rather enjoyed the episode, once they realized what the problem was. Your new bodyguard, Heller, was alarmed, however; every time he approached you, you yelled about the monster. He figured you hadn't forgiven him for past offenses."

"I didn't recognize him," I said.

"What we must do now is discover what the drug was, and when and how you were dosed. I think we know who is behind it."

"Kife," I agreed. "Heller warned me that something was in the offing. But how could dosing me with a hallucinogenic drug—?" I had had to explain about the key to my staff, so they could be alert for QYV.

"Some of these drugs are addictive," he reminded me. "Generally, the more potent the effect, the greater the addictive potential. Some are primarily physiological, some psychological, but once you're hooked, you're hooked. I happen to know."

An understatement! Suddenly I understood. "If I were to become addicted to a rare drug, and Kife was the only source—"

"You would do almost anything to assure your supply. The key would be only the beginning. You would become the creature of the supplier. There are nameless drugs today that put to shame anything known historically. Believe me, you do not want to go my route. That is why it is essential that we run this down immediately. We must eliminate the guilty party. A single dose should not habituate you, but a very few repetitions could. This appears to be the most potent hallucinogen I've seen, considering that it leaves no measurable residue in the body. You can bet that Kife uses only the best."

I saw his point. He was the expert here, and now I was selfishly glad he was an addict. His guidance had indeed helped me get through the vision. "This wouldn't by any chance be similar to what you—?"

"No. Mine is not hallucinogenic. It merely enables me to function. I am on it now."

Just so. I had never inquired into his addiction, because if I ever officially learned of it, I would be required to discipline him—a pointless exercise. I knew he would die if deprived of his drug. Only in this privacy could the subject be mentioned at all, and only now was he trusting me with this confirmation. My staff had given him the song "Beautiful Dreamer," but there was nothing beautiful about it. Commander Repro was on a spiral sliding slowly to Hell, and the best I could do for him was to try to implement his dream of the perfect unit—and use it to extirpate both piracy and the drug trade from the face of the Solar System. Certainly I did not wish to join him on that spiral!

We reviewed my activities immediately prior to the episode in detail, and concluded that the drug must have been slipped into my food. These chemicals could be tasteless and colorless, so potent that a few milligrams did the job. Therefore we launched a rapid private investigation into both the food supplies and personnel associated. With excellent computerized records and Commander Mondy's insights, we were able to accomplish in hours what once would have required weeks.

Food and personnel were clean. We had to assume this had been a one-shot deal, leaving no trace. It was frustrating, but we were stuck. QYV was indeed a slick operator. But I felt no compulsion to take more of whatever drug it was.

Then I had another vision. This time the geometric and color patterns were fleeting, and I proceeded directly to the action. I became the jaguar, hunting prey. The colors about me formed a rainbow, and that converted to a huge python, and that became a bolt of lightning that returned to thunder and rain. The rain fell so heavily that it formed a huge, branching river, and I saw that rivers, like snakes, were both male and female. The mouth of the river was its female orifice, and to ascend by that mouth was to indulge in symbolic copulation. I did this and saw the water nymphs swimming; I resolved to catch one for my own, but she eluded me, being more versatile than I in this medium, and so the jaguar had no woman.

Repro was there again when I came out of it. "Must have been a smaller dose this time," he said. "That's fortunate; your intoxication was not as intense."

I agreed, relieved. Not only had the duration been less, so had the intensity of the experience. I had enjoyed it but felt no strong compulsion to return to it. I remained unaddicted; but where had the drug come from?

My food had been monitored this time, just to be sure; there had been no drug in it. We searched everything, and tested the water I had last drunk: nothing. We had the air ducting gone over and the rest of the life-support apparatus. Nothing.

"Maybe it was only a flashback," Repro said doubtfully. "That does happen. Many of the visual effects are the result of phosphenes, subjective images that originate within the optic system itself. It's a common phenomenon, and phosphenic patterns appear in many art forms. Drugs stimulate them, but they can occur spontaneously. Many hallucinogenic drugs produce phosphenes of geometric motifs; these are not true visions, but an intermediate form."

"Maybe," I agreed uncertainly. I was deeply disturbed by this demonstrated ability of QYV to penetrate our defense.

Next day I had another vision. This time I entered a quiet jungle glade where natives were playing flutes formed from bones and the shells of snails. This was a haunted spot, dangerous to visit, because spirits of slain animals were present. When I intruded, the spirits of those animals turned on me and riddled me with tiny arrows: their vengeance for being hunted. "But I'm not a hunter!" I protested. "I'm a refugee!" Then they faded away; I knew that none of this was real, and I snapped out of it.

When I told Repro, he was perplexed. "That was a vision, not a phosphene," he said. "Yet very mild, almost a daydream. You must have been dosed—"

I shrugged, and touched one of my healing scrapes, which were not after all the wounds from tiny psychic arrows. The medicinal salve had really helped.

Salve? I had used it three times. . . .

"Test this salve!" I exclaimed.

That was the answer. The salve had been heavily laced with an extremely rare, potent, highly addictive hallucinogenic drug whose chemical description was meaningless to me but caused Repro to whistle, shaken, as he reviewed the lab results. "You have had three doses; you should be addicted now. This stuff is like a shot from a laser cannon!"

"I'm not addicted," I protested. "I have no craving for it."

Indeed I was not. There are ways to test for drug susceptibility, and Repro knew them, and we used them. I was now immune to this particular drug. My system was developing antibodies against it, protecting me.

"I never heard of that before," Repro said. "Apparently you cannot be habituated; your body treats addictive drugs like disease and fights them with increasing effectiveness on repeated exposure."

Just as my mind was able to tune in to the natures of other people, rapidly enabling me to protect myself against them. And my emotion had developed a block against the shock of threats against my life, so that the horror of death had not caused me to suffer from post-traumatic stress in the manner of Mondy. I had not before realized that there was a physiological component of my talent, but it made sense. I was blessed with an unusual, subtle, but quite useful system.

It developed that I remained vulnerable to other types of drugs. My immunity was only to this specific one, and to a lesser extent to closely related drugs, and it did take time to develop. We found that I had used the salve before, but only irregularly and in very small amounts, so that the full effect had not been triggered and I had suffered no visions. But my body had gotten a head start on defending against it. Otherwise, my second and third major episodes could have been far more intense than they were, though I still could not have become addicted.

Repro shook his head. "I wish I had your immune system."

"I wish I could share it with you." But, of course, I could not.

We agreed to keep this matter private. We couldn't even discover who had doused the salve; it had been part of my private supply for several months. Evidently QYV had set this up as a sleeper, knowing that sooner or later I would use it. That had been correct, and only my unusual body chemistry had prevented this insidious ploy from being effective.

But QYV might now suppose that I was addicted. Quite possibly I could turn that supposition to my advantage when the right time came. Mondy was the one who perceived how: "Have Commander Phist put in a requisition for some of the components of that drug," he suggested. "We cannot duplicate it precisely, but this will suggest we are trying to. Kife will get the message and may come forward with an offer."

I smiled like a jaguar. "You are an evil genius!"

Mondy nodded, pleased. He was doing very well in our unit.

One other matter I should mention here. We were adding considerable personnel during this expansion phase, and I left most of the details to my Adjutant, as is normal. But officers and key enlisted personnel I interviewed myself, to be quite sure they were what we wanted. In the Navy a commander's powers of choice are limited; some higher and somewhat erratic power directs the movements of personnel. That was one reason we had to use marriage to fetch our most vital members; it bypassed the red tape without betraying the nature of the larger plan. But the commander can do quite a bit to encourage particular people to remain or to move on, and this I did, whichever way was called for. Most were all right, for they knew of me and my unit and wanted to join; many were Hispanic, but others were ambitious Saxons or minority factions, highly motivated. We promised fair treatment and no-fault advancement for those with merit and loyalty, regardless of background, and it seemed this was unusual in the contemporary Jupiter Navy. So now we were getting skilled personnel without going after them, apart from the marriage acquisitions.

Spirit surprised me one day by bringing in a civilian clerk. The Navy did employ a number of civilians, because they were cheaper for mundane purposes such as kitchen police and janitor service and clerking, and often better suited for these jobs. It made little sense for the Navy to draft qualified personnel, run them through expensive training and conditioning, grant them generous medical and retirement benefits, then put them to work scraping dirty pots. Also, the job requirements for specialized noncombat positions are beyond what is normally available in the military system, especially when sophisticated computerized equipment is involved. For these positions civilian specialists must be hired, theoretically temporary until qualified Navy personnel are assigned; actually, they tend to be more permanent than most Navy assignments, since they are not subject to whimsical rotation. The local commander can hire and fire directly, without significant interference from above. Thus he has greater control, and often the truly key personnel in a unit are almost invisible civilians, known in the trade as technical mercenaries, hired out by civilian companies. This process was so advanced at this time that unit commanders sometimes vied competitively for desirable civilians. The rates of pay were fixed by Navy regulations, but there were off-the-record inducements. Some civilian employees lived quite royally, with government meals and the pick of enlisted (and sometimes commissioned) roommates of the opposite sex. For centuries it had been said that a master sergeant had things as good as anyone in the Service; today it was the choice civilian mercenary. As a military mercenary myself, I was quick to appreciate the situation. But in fairness I must also say that most civilian employees were simply that: hirelings with no job security and not a great deal of respect.

This one was a woman in her forties, slender and serious. "Isobel is a resident alien," Spirit said. "She migrated from Titania as a child and lost her papers."

"I know how that is," I said. "It took over a year for my

lost papers to be replaced, and then only because I joined the Navy—and even then my age slipped by them."

"She's a skilled military-computer operator, and conversant with navigation in space. But she does not want any security clearance."

I looked more carefully at the applicant. She had shoulder-length brown-red hair and color-matched painted fingernails. Her eyes were deep gray. Her face was poker, giving nothing away, and she had no body mannerisms to signal her thoughts. I could not read her, yet she was oddly familiar. "We can use her qualifications," I said, "but the position we need her for requires a clearance or personal assurance by the commander. Does she have good references?"

"No," Spirit said.

I glanced at her, annoyed. And paused, for Spirit was virtually quivering with excitement. Something was afoot.

I looked again at Isobel. "Speak to me," I said.

"As you wish, sir," Isobel said.

Then it struck me. "Captain Brinker of the *Hidden Flower*—in drag!"

She grimaced. "It is the only way to conceal my identity. A necessary evil." She glanced with distaste at her nails.

I had made a deal with Brinker, sparing her life in exchange for mine, and preserving the secret of her sex in exchange for information about QYV. The deal had been honored by both parties. She had spent her adult life as a male; how ironic that she now had to hide by reverting to her true nature.

But hiring her in my unit?—I really did not want any further association with this pirate. Yet my sister had brought her.

I returned to Spirit. "You know this woman a good deal better than I do. Do you speak for her?"

"I don't like her," Spirit said. "But she treated me fairly and kept my secret, and she is the most competent fighting woman I know. If she will serve you, you can't afford to turn her down. I gave her my word not to betray her to the authorities."

"That word shall be honored, of course," I agreed. "But she is a pirate!"

"Was," Spirit said. I saw that despite her personal distance from Brinker, she did want the woman to be hired.

I turned to Brinker. "My friends died because of you."

"I lost my ship because of you," she said evenly. "It happens, in war."

So she viewed piracy as a state of war. Well, perhaps it was. It was true that I had done her about as much damage as she had me; several of her officers had been executed. It was also true that I had recovered my sister, who probably would not have survived on another pirate's ship.

"With your qualifications," I said, "you can hire out elsewhere. Why come to me, the one who knows your secret?"

"I can't return to space without protection. I am confined to low-grade clerical tasks and subject to the whims of men."

The whims of men. Yes, women had little sexual privacy in the Navy, and civilian employees could have difficulty retaining their positions if they differed too obviously from Naval norms. If she wanted to be inconspicuous, she had to go along. "Are you homosexual?" I asked. Even today, some people distinguish between homosexuality and lesbianism, but they are the same: sexual preference for one's own sex.

"No. I don't like sex at all."

I glanced again at Spirit, who nodded. In this manner I had the answer to a question I had not been able to ask before: whether Spirit had been subjected to same-sex sex. I knew Spirit could handle anything she had to, but the information gratified me. I had feared what I might have left her to, among pirates.

But now this woman wanted not only employment, but also protection: from the attentions of men, and from revelation of her history. And she wanted to get out of the clerking trade. She wanted a lot, and I could not see my way clear to giving this pirate any of it. I would much prefer to put her on trial for her past.

But Spirit spoke for her. I had to hedge.

"Bring Repro," I said to my sister.

Spirit made a military turn and departed, leaving me alone with Isobel Brinker. "The things you want can be arranged, if I choose," I said carefully. "You could be assigned a male roommate whose sexual interest matches yours. You can be assigned compatible work. Your past can be private, with certain exceptions. Lieutenant Commander Repro is our unit psychologist and our S-5. He and my other key officers would have to know."

"Your word governs them?"

"Yes."

"Then do as you will."

"You know I have sworn to extirpate piracy from the face of the system."

"I have no loyalty to piracy. It was a necessary expedient."

"You would serve in this cause?"

"Yes."

Spirit returned with Repro; he must have been close at hand. I outlined the situation briefly to him. "What is your advice?"

He considered. "She was not on my list, because I did not know of her. She belongs on it. Hire her."

"But she is a pirate!" I protested again, dismayed by his ready acceptance.

"Sir, you swore to eliminate piracy. You can do that by conversion as readily as killing. You must be ready to accept those who genuinely reform, otherwise you are no better than Mondy was."

"Mondy?"

"He has killed as many as you have, in much the same manner, and now cannot escape his conscience."

Conversion—it did make sense. Why had I never been able to see it before? Because I was overly obsessed with vengeance. I did not need to consult with my other officers; I knew they would agree with Repro. Captain Brinker, former pirate, was not really the issue; my attitude was.

"It seems I have been overruled by my staff," I said. I turned to Spirit. "Hire her."

Brinker and I both knew the commitments implied.

Brinker would not attempt to kill or harm me and would serve in whatever capacity assigned with complete loyalty and effectiveness. I would protect her from certain types of exposure. Objectively I knew it was a good deal for both of us; she could return to space action in no other way, and she could do our unit a lot of good, for she was highly competent. Still, there was a bad taste.

Repro was right; it did work out. Brinker served me better than I could have anticipated. My unit even gave her a song: "Who's Going to Shoe Your Pretty Little Foot?," which concludes, "I don't need no man." Brinker sang it with a certain pride.

Chapter 7

QYV

Time passed. In due course we sought and got another inclement assignment: the elimination of the pirates of the Juclip. My sister Spirit, my S-1 Adjutant, had been keeping her eye out for this opportunity, and Mondy had advised her when it was coming; when it arrived, we pounced.

The pirates had been getting bolder. It seemed the flow of illicit refugees from the Hispanic planet-moons had ebbed, and the ships that normally preyed on them had had to turn to other areas in order to sustain themselves. I state this dispassionately, but, of course, that is illusion; Hispanic refugees are very much my people. But I had been powerless, hitherto, to strike back at the pirates; I had to remain in military channels or lose my position. Now, however, the pirates had taken to raiding pleasure craft, including some wealthy yachts; a prominent debutante had been kidnapped, raped, and ransomed. That finally got the attention of the Jupiter governments. The authorities had chosen to ignore the increasing raids on agricultural bubbles, and, of course, refused to acknowledge the brutal decimation of refugees. "Hell, they're doing us a favor!" one high government official was reported to have remarked about that aspect of pirate activity. I smoldered; there were bigots in high places, and I hated them in much the way I hated the pirates, for they were almost equally responsible for the murder of refugees such as my father. But the rich girl had been beautiful and purest Saxon and well connected, her family vested with enormous wealth; she made excellent news copy, and her family was a major contributor to the party in power in North Jupiter. So the word went out: *Do* something about the local pirates. Teach them a lesson. And we were ready. We had spent three years preparing our battalion.

I had four hundred Hispanics in my unit. When I announced our intentions to go out after the pirates, they raised a cheer that shook the ship. Most of them had had at least peripheral experience with the pirates; many of them had scores to settle as savage as mine. It was for this I had forged my fighting force, and for this these Hispanics had flocked to my banner. But the non-Hispanics were, for different reasons, as eager for action. They wanted the glory and promotion attendant on success, and many of them sincerely believed that piracy was evil.

Lieutenant Commander Phist, our S-4 Logistics officer, now had the authority to requisition the best equipment, thanks to this pressing mission, and he knew exactly what that was. Logistics can be the lifeblood of a mission, and now it showed.

As a commander I was entitled to a cruiser, but there was considerable leeway in the definition of that designation. The *Copperhead* was a reconditioned ship, originally commissioned in the year 2600—by a nice coincidence, the year I was born—and renovated in 2625. There was a general prejudice against reconditioned ships, as though they were damaged goods, but that was foolish. The fact was that an old ship was a proven ship, and renovation in no way damaged its reliability or performance. Phist assured me of this, and I soon saw that he was speaking from extremely solid information. The *Copperhead* had been assigned to me, a Hispanic officer, because as an old ship she was considered to be inferior, but she was in fact an excellent fighting vessel. We had then had to go through the inconvenience of the renovation, which had forced our unit to occupy other ships on a temporary basis, no fun; that was part of the covert harassment the Navy dealt to our ilk.

Under Phist's supervision, she became a better ship. She was rated at 3.2 gee acceleration for twenty-four hours, which was plenty of power for a ship of her class, but Phist requisitioned seemingly minor modifications that increased her actual performance to 3.7 gee. That's more significant than it might seem; it meant she could outrun most other cruisers, and in a battle situation that was important. She mounted nine eight-inch guns and twelve five-inch laser cannon, as was standard, but it turned out there was a difference in guns, too. Phist got them replaced by more accurate, higher-muzzle-velocity guns; these required better-trained crews, but we were quite ready to provide them. Now we could outshoot most cruisers, too. I was quick enough to appreciate the advantage; I had not before realized that it was possible to change the specs on things like acceleration and big guns. I was learning. Phist might well have saved the ship and all our lives from some future destruction, and he had done it through only quiet paperwork.

We also acquired three escort ships, each only half our length and one-sixth our mass of 17,000 tons, and two destroyers, smaller yet but faster. Spirit finagled that, finding authorization in an obscure naval directive about battle theaters. We were going out to do battle with pirates, and the Juclip was our theater, so we qualified. Phist made certain they were good vessels—he knew more about military specifications than I had dreamed there was to be known—and he conspired with Emerald to get sophisticated torpedoes for the destroyers. Mondy's information was that most of the pirates had devices to foil the guidance systems of standard Navy torpedoes; these were proof against that. And, of course, we had half a dozen tugs.

I should mention the song the group gave Lieutenant Commander Phist, as it certainly fitted him: "Old King Cole." In the song, King Cole calls for all manner of personnel, who have all manner of equipment, but generally settle for beer. It was funny, but "King Cole" Phist was also able to requisition the finest quality beer for the "fighting infantry."

As fleets went, what we had was minor, but it was enough to do the job. If I failed, I would be through, perhaps dead, for those pirates were no gentle creatures. But if I succeeded, I would rate another promotion—and I needed that, for this time it would be to Captain, O6, and mean command of a larger force, with attendant upgrading of many of my personnel. I wanted that power to pursue my personal mission properly: extirpation of *all* piracy in the Solar System.

We moved out. We had been drilling for this for some time, with our pugil stick and space-raider training; we were ready. We knew there was danger and that there would be bloodshed; this would be our blooding as a true fighting unit.

Mondy had done his homework, cooperating with Repro; he had the current information on the location of every private vessel known to the Jupiter Navy. That was only a fraction of the total, of course, but a large fraction. Many of the others would be part-time pirates, or pirates of opportunity: legitimate vessels preying on what they could get away with, whatever happened to be in their paths. My older sister Faith had been taken by such a ship, a merchanter whose men were simply on the prowl for sex. Merchant ships don't handle sex the way the Navy does, forthrightly, and so they have problems with it. The refugee-bubbles were considered fair game for sex by any males in the vicinity.

Faith—I had not thought about her much. Spirit was really my closest sibling, the one I cared about. Faith, my senior by three years, had always been somewhat aloof, too mature and too pretty, and her humiliation too savage. It was as if she had died, in my mind; psychologically I could no more bring her back than I could my parents. I believed she was alive but did not act on it. I can't justify this attitude, for surely I loved my big sister; I merely say that is the way it was. I hoped she was well, somewhere out of space; perhaps she had managed to marry a merchant captain and settle on Jupiter before her beauty faded.

Our strategy was simple: We plotted a route to intercept the nearest pirate vessel on our chart, and proceeded at gee. We could accelerate at more than triple that, of course, but sustained multiple-gee is uncomfortable and wasteful of CT fuel; we saved that for direct pursuit when the time came.

Perhaps I should qualify that. Theoretically it is just as

efficient to reach a given velocity at two-gee acceleration as at one gee, if the drive is geared for it. There is, after all, no significant friction in space. At the velocities normally used for travel between moons or planets, loss of efficiency owing to relativistic factors is too small to be noted. So we could accelerate for half a day at two gee, instead of for one day at one gee, and use the same fuel. But what would be the point? We would not arrive soon enough to justify the awful burden of sustained double weight, since acceleration is only part of the trip, with inertial drifting being the major part. Only if it was urgent to travel faster would we use more than one gee. If we sustained high-gee to cut our total travel time, that would use more fuel, which we might need later.

Actually, distances within the Juclip are such that a few hours of gee suffice for any travel needed, and our plotted route to the nearest pirate ships cut that down in some cases to mere minutes. We had no problem there. Accordingly I am skipping most reference to periods of acceleration and free-fall. We spun ship while coasting, so we had gee at hull diameter most of the time, keeping our men in shape. We also continued exercises and drills; it was our intent to capture ships whenever feasible, not depending on the pirates' choice of surrender or flight. We did not want to depend on the pirates for anything.

We also worked hard to enhance the spirit of unity. Every day, sometimes every shift, we sang our songs, and when we were singing there were no ranks, either enlisted or officer; we were all worthwhile people in our own rights. Elsewhere in the Navy this singing was ridiculed, but now there were more petitions to transfer in than we could accommodate, and very few transferred out. I can't say the songs were responsible, but I am sure they helped. We had the feeling of togetherness, of family.

It had taken some time for the group to complete the selection of songs, but in most cases they were apt, and a person could indeed be judged by his song. Emerald, the strategist, had "The Rising of the Moon," a ballad of organization and battle; Mondy, locked in his prison of the soul, had "Peat Bog Soldiers," deriving from inmates of a concentration camp in an ancient war; Sergeant Smith had "Stout Hearted Men," since he was deeply involved in the often-difficult training exercises. My secretary, Sergeant Moreno, whom I always think of as Juana, had "Early One Morning," a song of a maiden mourning the lover who has deserted her; I have never been quite certain I comprehend the relevance. Perhaps I simply do not wish to. And my sister Spirit—hers was "I Know Where I'm Going," whose key line seems to be "I know who I love, but the dear knows who I'll marry." That implies that she did not marry the one she would have liked to, but I know that she never had an interest in any man other than Commander Phist, her husband. Yet the group agreed that this song fitted her, and she agreed. It continues to perplex me.

We zeroed in on our first target: the *Caprine Isle*. The pirate ships generally retained their prepirate designations, since theoretically they were law-abiding traders; this led to anomalous nomenclature. This one was notorious for gunrunning to guerrilla groups on the Hispanic moons. The pirates had no special sympathy for revolution; they merely went for money, and it seemed weapons brought excellent money. *Caprine Isle* was also a prime suspect in the abduction case that had triggered this mission. We expected her to be tough, to try to fight or flee, and we expected to make an example of her. In fact, we were primed for it; I intended to give the destruct order personally. Many people are naturally squeamish about killing, and that is a thing I understand and respect, but when it came to pirates I was ready to do it. The image of my father, cut down treacherously by a pirate sword, was before me; the red of his brutally spilled blood threatened to blot out all else, as I viewed the pirate vessel on the screen. Vengeance was to be mine, and I reveled in it.

We matched velocities and course with the *Caprine Isle*, and set our destroyers before and after her, torpedoes ready. She could not escape; in fact, she made no attempt to flee. Perhaps she assumed this was a routine challenge, a harmless posturing to demonstrate that the Jupiter Navy still controlled this place of space. We would quickly disabuse her of that!

We radioed her, and I sent a beam to HQ at Leda, putting the complete proceedings on irretrievable record. The Navy wanted to show that it was taking firm action; I would oblige. Repro, as Public Relations officer, had suggested this aspect. Mondy endorsed it for a different reason: He wanted there to be no possible recrimination against us when we did what we expected to do, should public reaction be adverse. We were not playing with rubber knives this time.

Our operator made contact with hers, establishing the identities of both ships. Then I spoke directly to the *Caprine*'s captain, who was indeed a goatlike man, bearded and shaggy, named Billy. Billy the Kid. Pirates tended to use professional pseudonyms, for obvious reason, and seemed to prefer the names of animals. There was a certain crude art to this, showing some humor, but probably the roots were deeper. Migrant laborers had identifying songs; probably the pirates needed similar marks of distinction in an undistinguished profession.

"Billy, we are cleaning up the Juclip," I announced. "You have one hour to consult your crew and surrender your ship and personnel to us for impoundment and trial according to Jupiter law."

"Yeah, spic?" he demanded in the screen. "What if I don't?"

"Then we shall give you final warning and blast you out of space." I hit the sound broadcast cutoff so that the cheer that rose from my eavesdropping men was not transmitted. They got an almost sexual thrill from speaking this way directly to a real, live pirate. It was the feel of vengeance. We *wanted* to blast that ship! But we didn't want to appear bloodthirsty.

Billy considered. He knew we had the firepower to do it. No doubt he now regretted addressing me by epithet. "What if I do?"

"My men will board you, disarm the ship, confine your personnel, and pilot the *Caprine Isle* to the Navy base at Leda where you will be interned and put on trial for piracy."

"But that's death!"

"For those found guilty in court," I agreed. "You will, of course, be adequately represented by counsel. For those who demonstrate extenuating circumstance there will be variable terms at hard labor."

He laughed. "You're crazy, spic! You ain't taking us in!"

I believe I speak dispassionately: He had sealed his fate with those words. It is not that I am intolerant of the colloquialisms; Emerald and I had in the time of our marriage exchanged words like spic and nig as ironic endearments. It was that this pirate evinced open contempt for us and had announced his intention not to cooperate with the law. Now the status of the Jupiter Navy was in question. Discrimination might be covertly tolerated in the Service; no non-Saxon ever made admiral. But this was public insult to a ranking Naval officer, and defiance of a legitimate Naval thrust. Jupiter was watching, literally, via my rebroadcast. Billy had talked himself and his ship into deep trouble.

"I am obliged to advise you," I said formally, "that if you have not professed surrender under the terms defined, by the expiration of this hour's grace period, and do not do so upon my re-challenge, I shall order my torpedoes launched. I strongly recommend that you reconsider. Surrender, and you will be treated fairly, now and at your trial."

"Stuff it up your drive-jet, immigrant!" he snapped. He went on to describe my supposed racial and cultural status in unkind detail, concluding with some rather imaginative sexual preferences involving mutilated animals. I listened impassively, and we rebroadcast it all. At last he shut off transmission, and we relaxed. His foul mouth had damned him in Jupiter's eyes. Even the Bleeding Heart faction would not rise to this one's defense.

Emerald glanced up at me from her seat before her own vision screen. Her eyes virtually glowed with the joy of battle. "I think we have our example, sir." She had planned for this: to make a public example of the first pirate, so that the remaining pirates would heed. She was probably correct; it was a language pirates should understand. But it was more than that. For her it was the beginning of her vindication as a strategist. She had the training, aptitude, and motivation to be the best, and now she was at last implementing her ambition. For me it was the beginning of the execution of a vow. For others—

We waited out the hour, pacing the pirate, the two destroyers keeping the *Caprine Isle* targeted. We were in no danger; Mondy had researched the armament of all the local pirate ships and assured us they had no cannon capable of penetrating our guard. We were a military vessel; they were civilian. This is somewhat like the distinction between a fourteen-year-old girl and a hardened gladiator in full battle dress. Only through avoidance or trickery could she hope to prevail, and it was an anemic hope. In a David and Goliath situation; the smart money is generally on Goliath.

Of course it would be trickery. Mondy had even advised me what type it would be. Emerald had planned our strategy accordingly.

We heard singing elsewhere in the ship. This was theoretically bad form in a battle alert, but song was part of us.

The hour expired. I signaled the *Caprine Isle* again, on the common channel, and resumed our live broadcast to Leda. "The moment of decision is at hand," I said, enunciating clearly. "We shall have your surrender within one minute, or we shall launch our torpedoes."

Billy came on. He looked nervous. "We surrender," he said. "Hold your fire!"

I glanced at Mondy, then at Emerald. Both nodded, concurring with my own diagnosis. The pirate was lying.

"Very well," I said. "We are sending a tug to pick up your officers. When they are in custody, we shall provide replacement officers to guide your ship to our base. Instruct your crew accordingly, and be ready to board the tug in five minutes."

"Yeah, sure," Billy said ungraciously.

The tug accelerated toward the *Caprine Isle*. Tugs were small, squat ships with enormous propulsion, capable of moving far larger vessels. They were useful for minor chores like this. This particular tug was special, however; it went unmanned, controlled by a pilot aboard the *Copper-*

head. It also contained some rather special equipment. My staff had planned for this moment carefully.

The tug docked at the *Caprine Isle.* I gave them five minutes, then spoke again on the radio. "Have your officers boarded?" I inquired.

A pirate technician answered. "Yes, sir. They're all there, and the tug's sealed. You can call it in."

"I must advise you of one other thing," I said. "Aboard that tug is a general-purpose detonator. Its range is limited to the interior of the tug, but it is controlled from this ship. The detonator field is harmless to living personnel, but it will set off any explosive aboard. Have you loaded any explosives aboard the tug?"

"No, sir, of course not," the technician said. "Just our officers."

"Then you will not object if we activate the detonator."

The technician swallowed but tried to bluff through. "It's okay, sir."

"You are sure?"

"Yes, sir."

I turned to our remote-control technician. "Detonate."

He touched the button.

The pirate ship exploded. It flew apart, its air puffing out through the suddenly gaping hole in its side. Pieces of it radiated out into space to disappear in the distance. Some passed close to the *Copperhead* shrapnel, but our magnetic shield deflected them.

We all watched silently. Mondy had predicted they would plant a powerful bomb on the tug, in an attempt to get it adjacent to our crusier and blow a hole in our hull. He even knew what type of bomb. We had been ready, and had turned the pirates' treachery against them. We had dealt honestly with them, and had even advised them of the detonator; had they honored their agreement to surrender, they would not have been hurt. It was all on holotape, transmitted live to Leda for all to see. I was sure the major news programs of Jupiter would carry suitable excerpts. We had made our demonstration.

But even so, my mouth tasted of something like ashes. There had been, according to our information, seventy-two people aboard that ship. Now all of them were dead. The responsibility was mine.

"Captain off the bridge." I heard the announcement and realized that I had indeed left the bridge. I did not feel well, but it was not a malaise of the body. I retreated to my cabin and fell into my hammock and closed my eyes, but the bursting ship remained in my mind's eye. Seventy-two living people—and I had killed them. I had thought I was prepared for this, but the reality showed me that I had deceived myself. What I had done as a refugee I had done in desperation and paid a hideous price; this time I had done it deliberately, with no threat to myself. Now I was truly a mass murderer!

I became aware of a presence. A hand was on my shoulder. I knew immediately the touch of my sister Spirit. I reached up and caught her four-fingered hand in mine, finding special solace in it. I brought it to my face and kissed it and found it wet—wet from my tears.

She came down to the hammock and embraced me, hugging my head to her bosom in the manner of a mother, and I cried into her comfort. I had not realized how vulnerable I was, or how strong she was, or how much I needed her, until this moment. She understood what I felt, for she shared my heredity, my culture, and my experience. She, too, had seen our parents die; she, too, had lost our friends to pirates. She had lost her little finger to a pirate and taken her vengeance. Spirit was my true strength; without her I had been adrift, and only the promise of her return had motivated me, and only her presence at my side truly sustained me. I loved her as no brother ever loved a sister, and she loved me. That was the love I had to have. To me, women were merely women, some more important than others; I could take them or leave them, as I had done with Juana and with Emerald. To Spirit, men were merely men, and she did with them what she found necessary. Love was not truly a part of that. Our truest love was for each other.

After a time we talked, the words sparse, the meaning deep. "I never killed before like that," I said.

"It was their bomb, their deceit," she pointed out.

"But I *knew* of it!"

"You *suspected*. And you warned them."

True. Now the justification of my act became more convincing. The pirates had set up their own demise. Like a person who strikes at another and scores on himself instead. I had known—or suspected—but I had honored the rules of the situation. I had given fair warning.

"They intended that bomb for us," she said.

They had indeed! Had we not anticipated their treachery, it would have been our blood sprayed into space.

I still felt the blood on my hands. But now I could handle it.

"Are you better now?" Spirit asked gently.

"Vital signs stable," I agreed.

"Now you hold me."

It was indeed my turn. I sat up straight and held her head to my chest and enclosed her in my arms while she cried. She felt the same pain I did. But she was stronger than I. She always had been, even as a child of twelve.

In due course we went to see the other officers of the staff, for the shock had hit all of us. It is no gentle thing, to be blooded, even though the signs may be subtle. We did not see Mondy and Emerald for two days.

We left one of our escort ships to conduct salvage operations from the largest fragment and proceeded to our next rendezvous. We had a job to do, and it had only begun.

The second pirate ship bolted the moment we hailed her. We fired one torpedo and rendered her into another derelict. Again we suffered reaction, for again we had killed, and this time we had done it directly. But our pain was not as bad as before; already we were getting hardened. So were our crews; they had played no direct part in the destruction, but they supported it, and they felt its impact. Lieutenant Commander Repro, as Morale Officer—some of us wore more than one hat, as is standard practice in the Navy—had his hands full. Oddly, his addiction seemed to fade in this period; he was better able to handle this reality than were the rest of us.

I don't want to make our following campaign seem less than it was, but repetition fatigues me, and most of it is in the official record, anyway. We were in space on the Juclip cleanup mission for almost a year, for though at first the ships were easy to catch, the pirates soon learned to take evasive measures long before we came near, and it took time to run them down. Some vacated the Juclip entirely. I will proceed to the high points.

The third ship we hailed surrendered honestly. We took her over and sent her to Leda in good order, and the event made the news; there was no question about fair treatment being rendered. Of course, the pirate officers were executed after being convicted. The fourth yielded similarly. The fifth tried to bolt; we disabled her with a suppressor torpedo and boarded her with our pugil team and took her over but did not advertise how we had done it, lest others take warning. In this manner we eliminated forty-seven pirate ships, and it was becoming so routine it was almost dull.

No pirate had a chance against us; we could blast any of them out of space, from well beyond their return-fire range. In space, of course, a missile could proceed indefinitely until captured by some planetary body, so there was technically no such thing as a limited range, but accuracy was certainly limited, and beyond certain parameters, any missile could be balked or avoided. A laser cannon generally could not penetrate the hull of a spaceship, but it could heat and detonate an explosive missile if the range was great enough to provide time to track it with precision and lock on. Our lasers were far more potent and accurate than those of any converted civilian ship, for our power source and computer specialization was greater. Our eight-inch shells were fired at twice the velocity a pirate could muster. Our big shells were also far more heavily armored than theirs, so they were in effect largely invulnerable to premature laser detonation. Our torpedoes were slower but also more massive and better armored, and they were fired from much closer in, so the effect was similar. A pirate could fire at one of our destroyers, of course, but the fact was, a single destroyer was more than a match for the average pirate vessel. Virtually laserproof and swift enough to dodge any shell large enough to damage it, a destroyer was—a thing that destroyed.

We were, as the ancient saying went, shooting fish in a barrel. Phist had seen to that, by providing us with the best equipment the Navy had to offer. With that hardware, we were supreme. I blessed the day my sister had gone out to bring him in, for I also liked the man personally. Phist was, as I mentioned before, conservative, honest, and competent; the very model of a modern Naval officer, who should have been an admiral by now if only the Navy had valued his sterling qualities.

The news of our campaign was now making the headlines of the Jupiter news services. The civilians, secure in their great atmospheric city-bubbles, loved the vicarious adventure of cops and robbers, and kept running score of our "kills" as if this were one big game. I became the hero of the hour: the token Hispanic officer making good in the free society of Jupiter. Little note was taken of the fact that I had never been granted Jupiter citizenship, so remained a Callisto national-in-exile, a mercenary fighter. In the Navy this made no difference, but the moment I left the Navy I would revert to resident alien status. I *had* to make good in the Navy, and so did most of my Hispanic troops; we had nowhere else to go.

So it went, as I said, for forty-seven ships; but the forty-eighth was special. It was the *Purple Mountain,* taken over by mutiny fifteen years back, preying on refugee-bubbles and unwary pleasure craft in the normal manner. She had no armament to speak of, and it was surprising that she had survived this long without being taken over by another pirate. "There's something odd about this one," Mondy muttered. "We'd better take it intact—and carefully."

No problem about taking it; the *Purple Mountain* surrendered instantly when challenged. There were no tricks or booby traps; the news had long since spread that we were alert to such things, and this tended to discourage them—as we had intended. The complication came in this case when we processed the crew. They were the usual motley bunch of cutthroats, the scum of space—except for one, the cabin boy.

He had the mark of QYV on him. He was a courier. That,

of course, was why he had been spared; no pirate dared interfere with a QYV courier. It seemed this ship had sacked a refugee-bubble, discovered this lad, and undertaken to deliver him to his destination, but he had not known where to go. So they had held him, pending communication with QYV, and in the interim no other pirate had bothered this ship. QYV's protection had thus been extended to the *Purple Mountain*.

I interviewed the lad in a private cell with only my bodyguard Heller present. I started carefully, getting the feel of his nature. "What is your name?"

"Donald Beams, sir. Are you going to shoot me?"

He was trying to be facetious but was uncertain. He was about fifteen years old, which had been my age when I was a refugee. Now it seemed so young! "Have you murdered anyone?"

"No, sir!"

"Then you will not be shot. What does the term *Kife* mean to you?"

"That I can't be touched, sir."

"You are no longer among pirates. This is the Jupiter Navy. We can touch you."

"Yes, sir," he said, unconvinced that his charm of immunity should thus be voided.

"Let me explain something to you," I said. "When I was your age, I loved a girl. She was a courier, like you. I killed her and took her item."

"Sir!" It was not the boy, but Sergeant Heller.

I glanced at him inquiringly.

"Sorry, sir," he said, embarrassed. "I didn't know."

"If you loved her—" the boy said, perplexed.

"Why did I kill her?" I finished his question. "It was not because she wasn't true to me; we were getting married. It was because pirates were raiding, and I had to kill everyone in the bubble to get them before they got us. She was in the bubble. Then I took the item because it was all of her I could keep. That was thirteen years ago, and I still have it."

"But Kife—"

"Tried to take it back from me three or four times," I said. "He failed."

"I don't believe it!"

I nodded at Heller, giving the cue to speak.

Heller shook his head. "Believe it, kid. This guy ain't afraid of Kife. I was one of the three or four, and now I serve Commander Hubris."

"You got the mark of Kife on you?"

Heller shook his head. "No. I wasn't a courier, I was a killer."

Now the boy's certainty was shaken. "Whatcha going to do with me?"

"I am going to use you as a hostage against Kife. If he wants you, he will have to meet my terms."

"But Kife don't deal with nobody on nobody else's terms!"

"If he refuses, I will take your item and add it to the one I have. I think Kife will prefer to deal."

"Yes, sir." Now Donald was distinctly uneasy.

"Tell me how you were supposed to make contact with Kife."

He didn't know, but with careful questioning I learned that he did have an address in a dome on Europa to which he was not supposed to go. I smiled.

We rejoined my staff. "Treat Donald as a hostage," I told Spirit. She took charge of him, knowing I had made progress.

"Ready an escort ship," I told Sergeant Smith. "Program it for Europa."

"Sir," Heller protested. "You can't go there! It's obviously a trap!"

"What other person should I subject to such a risk?"

He gulped. "Me, sir."

"You suppose you aren't marked for death by Kife now?"

He was scared and showed it, but he stood his ground. "If I am, then at least I have saved your life, sir, and repaid my debt. You've given me three good years. If you die, I'm washed up, anyway. And so is the battalion."

Mondy arrived. "He's right, Commander. We can learn

a lot, if we play this correctly. This may even be a setup: Kife's way of contacting you. Send the sergeant, with news of your hostage—and an empty jar of salve."

"Salve!" I exclaimed, seeing it. "He will think I'm—!"

"Precisely, sir. Kife wants *you* to contact *him* this time. He believes you are ready to deal. He won't harm the envoy."

QYV thought he had me in his power now—and just might find the tables turned. Mondy's sinister intellect had come through again.

Sergeant Heller went, nervous but proud. The ploy worked. Heller brought back QYV's envoy: a woman of about fifty with the aspect of a clerk. She requested a private interview.

We ran her through decontamination, nominally because we wanted no planetary diseases introduced to our fleet, but actually to assure ourselves she carried no weapons. She was clean, carrying only a purse with harmless routine items. "Unless she's better at hand-to-hand combat than she looks," Mondy said, "she poses no physical threat to you."

"Just make sure she never gets close to our hostage," I said. "That's the pretext for this meeting, and we both need that pretext."

I met with the woman in a private chamber. She was neatly dressed, heavyset, with fashionable iron-gray hair and trifocal contact lenses that gave her eyes preternatural brightness. Her name was Reba Ward, and she was nominally a Jupiter government research assistant for a minor USJ congressional committee.

I wasted no time with introductions or explanations; she knew, or thought she knew, what we were here for. "You are empowered to deal?"

"I am."

"I want information. You want your courier. We'll trade."

She smiled, as I had expected. "Try another exchange."

Uh-huh. "Be more specific."

"I will trade a product for an item."

"Try another exchange."

She squinted at me, not understanding this balk. She thought I was desperate for the drug. "We can provide an unlimited quantity—"

"Of information?"

She shrugged. "Very well. First we shall discuss courier versus information. Then we shall discuss a second trade."

I shrugged, too. "You can meet my price on the courier, at least."

Now she was really perplexed. "What information do you seek?"

"The nature of Kife."

"Seek other information."

That was really sensitive information! Of course, I had known that if Mondy couldn't run it down, it had to be exceptionally closely guarded. But it was against my nature to leave any potential threat uncomprehended, and QYV had made four savage attempts to take my key. Once I knew the nature of this enemy, I could consider how to nullify it. "That is the only information for which I will deal."

"Then ask for something tangible instead."

So I made an impossible demand, rhetorically. "Promotion to Captain, and a fleet to go after the nest of pirates in the Belt." That was the so-called Asteroid Belt, where the most flagrant piracy in the System flourished. This Juclip mission had been only a warm-up, and it was almost done.

"Done."

I was startled. "You can authorize that?"

"My employer can. Will you deliver the courier to me now, or do you prefer to wait for confirmation of your promotion and assignment? It will take two weeks to flow through channels."

I had dealt with QYV before. He had honored his prior bargain on Chiron. It had been years before he tried again for the key, and I considered that sufficient. I did not appreciate his subsequent moves against me, but there had been no actual breach of faith, so it remained possible to deal. "You may take the courier with you." Reba Ward was hard to read, but I was making progress and realized now that the courier was not important and probably carried no item. This had been merely a device to enable me to contact QYV. Reba had called my bluff on the promotion, and now I had at least to discuss the other matter. In this sense I had been outplayed.

"You know what we want," she said. "We have what you want. I presume that the matter of the courier can be publicized among your officers while the other is completely private."

It was time to end this. "The courier carries nothing, and I am not addicted. I will deal only for information, and the key will not leave my possession."

She took stock, realizing that I could not be bluffing about the drug. She had been lured here for nothing. "Then I shall provide the information."

Just like that! "You are ready to promote an addict to O6 before answering a question about Kife, and now you give the information, anyway?"

"The promotion may be considered amends for past indiscretions. The key you have is more valuable than our secrecy. The information is the price of last resort."

"That key was transported by the woman I loved," I said. "I killed forty-five pirates and twenty-two children along with my fiancée, and the key is all I have left to show for it? How can you hope to return any part of my loss to me?"

"We did not properly understand the nature of your attachment before," Reba said. "Once we did, we altered our approach."

"By trying to kill or addict me?" I asked tersely.

"I can explain that—if we are engaged in negotiation for the possession of the key."

"We are not." Yet she had excited my curiosity considerably, and I was mindful of her remark about the promotion being an apology for those thrusts of the past. I really did want to know about QYV, for QYV had really been the source of my acquaintance with Helse, my love. If QYV was now ready to deal positively rather than negatively— well, I would see.

"I am assuming that we are. I must clarify that Kife is not a person; it is an organization. Individual technicians are assigned to cases as circumstances warrant. We are chronically overextended, so some accounts lapse until it is convenient or necessary to expedite them."

An organization! That explained a lot! "You are saying that one person elects to negotiate for a lost key and another will try more violent persuasion?"

"Exactly. Your own account has been outstanding for thirteen years and has had several technicians. I assumed the account after the last effort malfunctioned."

"After they canned the fool who botched my murder?"

She smiled briefly. "Just so. And when it seemed that the addiction ploy had failed or been countered. Later it seemed that it had succeeded, but it was too late for that particular technician. I was prepared to follow up, but now it appears that the original judgment of failure was justified."

"So you, personally, had no hand in that?"

She nodded agreement, and I could tell it was true. I had already had my vengeance on the one who caused me mischief. "It will benefit me to succeed where others have failed. I believe in positive measures and fair exchanges. I am pleased to have been able to bring you to dialogue. I believe we can deal."

This woman continued to surprise me. "You are merely a technician—a low-ranking officer—taking over an old and difficult case, and you have the power to dictate my rank and assignment merely as a way to get my attention?"

"True. I believe you have noted our power before."

"I had. But I thought you had reasonable limits."

"We don't."

"Then why don't you simply cut orders for me to be court-martialed on a trumped-up charge, condemned without appeal, executed, and the key stripped from my body?"

"We could do this," she confessed. "But negative approaches have been counterproductive in your case in the past; you have been far more savvy in your defense than anticipated. We also dislike being obvious. We prefer to work with the current. That way, failure carries less consequence."

"And if you fail now, some other technician will take your place—with some other approach?"

"I will not fail."

And she believed that. I now appreciated this woman's motive for success. I knew QYV played hard ball; any organization that kept ruthless pirates in check had to be tougher than they were. She might have great power, but her own position was on the line. Success—or extinction.

"Kife is not, then, a pirate outfit," I said.

"It is an agency of Jupiter," she said. "Bear in mind that this is privileged information."

"Agreed. But my staff must be advised. My officers know more than I do, and I depend on their expertise."

"Your sister," she said. "Commanders Mondy, Repro, Phist, and Sheller."

She had done her homework! "And Sergeant Smith, who is filling in for Operations. And Juana."

"Your de facto S-3 and your confidential secretary," she added reluctantly. "I suppose if you cannot trust your former supervisors and mistresses, you have little certainty in life."

"We checked you for physical armament. We should have checked for mental," I remarked.

"Success is facilitated by information, as it seems you are aware. I don't suppose you care to advise me how you avoided addiction after using the hallucinogen?"

"Ask some other question."

She sighed. "Very well. You may brief these personnel with appropriate cautions. But further information is yours alone."

"Spirit."

She sighed again. "We gave you back your sister. I am not certain that was not an error."

"You used her as a lure to trap me. I *took* her back."

"And the pirate we bribed. That was typical of our misjudgment of you. Very well; her, too, for this. No others."

"No others," I agreed. "You are very trusting of my word."

"It is possible I know you better than anyone other than your sister does."

"Oh? Show me your power."

"In a moment. Will you deal on the key?"

She had me halfway hooked. She was a dowdy, middle-aged female, but she was a gladiator. I knew now I had to play her very carefully, or I would find myself committed for more than I intended. "I will consider it. I make no other commitment."

"Here is part of my power: the empty hand is that of your father, whom you consumed."

She had scored. Of all people living, only Spirit and I knew of our necessary cannibalism for survival. Except—

"You have seen the manuscript!"

She nodded. "I have it hostage, Hubris. Will you deal?"

"How could you even know of it, let alone acquire it?"

"Commander, I have traced all your contacts. The scientist to whom you sent it is dead. His family is not aware of its significance."

The scientist on the terrible hellface of Io: Mason, the one who had befriended Helse and me! The news of his demise struck me like a blow of a pugil stick. "He—how—?"

"Natural causes," she reassured me. "He was old, and time has passed since you knew him. He treasured your manuscript and kept all your secrets till the end of his life. I assure you the material is safe with us."

"As safe as your key is with me," I said. I remained shaken; I knew people did die of natural causes, but I felt this loss with a special poignancy. Mason had known Helse and me together; now another intangible link to her had been broken. This agent of QYV had touched me with her masked finger of steel.

"Precisely," she said. "Do you care to exchange?"

"No. If you went to that much trouble to fetch the manuscript, it should remain with you. It has served its purpose." For in truth I valued my single tangible token of Helse more than my own narration of my experience as a refugee, and I would not allow this cynical organization to use my own words, literally, to deprive me of that token.

"Suppose we arrange for it to be delivered to your family, after your own demise?"

Hard ball indeed! What would relatives of mine think of

that history? But only my sisters survived with me, and they already understood the realities of refugee existence. QYV had no leverage there. "Good enough. I will make a similar allocation of the key."

Reba shot me a glance of wry appreciation, as if I had made a telling shot. "We need the key now."

"It has waited thirteen years. It can wait another."

"Not readily. We must recover it as soon as possible."

It seemed QYV wanted the key more than I wanted anything from QYV. "I fail to see the urgency."

"Our hireling at Chiron informed you of the manner in which we use an unbreakable code to convey private messages."

"She did. The key I possess has a magnetic pattern containing the key to an important message. But what message could be so important, after so long a delay?"

"The problem with the closed encryption technique is that the decoding pattern must be physically transmitted to the recipient before the message can be read."

"Yes. So you need my key. But—"

"That problem would be solved if a public encryption key could be used. Then no one could intercept the decryption key, in the manner you have done, and the transmission of secret material would be enormously facilitated. We have been able to function hitherto by courier; now we must reduce our dependency on that system."

"I can see why," I agreed. "You must lose a lot of messages among the pirates." And, of course, I was now cleaning out the pirates—and intercepting couriers.

"Yes. They cannot decrypt the messages, but they can deny them to us. We take stern action when we discover the culprits, but a better system is needed."

Stern action—an understatement! "But with a public encryption key, anyone could read your messages."

"No. Anyone could *encrypt* messages to us; only we could decrypt them."

"I don't understand how that would work."

"You don't need to. All you need to know is that over the centuries, no system of public keys has survived; all have been broken and become useless. But at last one isolated genius has developed the truly unbreakable public key. And the secret of that key—"

"Is contained in the key I carry!" I exclaimed. "This *is* precious! But you could go back to your genius for another copy."

"No. He spent fifteen years developing it, encrypted it, started it on its way to us—and died. He left no comprehensible notes. For the past decade our experts have labored to duplicate his feat, without success. It is truly unbreakable. Your key is it—the secret of the century."

"An unbreakable open code," I repeated. "With that, this problem would never have happened."

"Exactly. We have suffered too much already and exhausted our other avenues. We must have that code. The health of Jupiter requires it."

I shrugged. "Maybe so. But I have no abiding passion for the Colossus. I am a mercenary, denied citizenship. Jupiter turned my bubble away, costing the lives of my mother and companions—and my fiancée, who carried your key. There is an irony! I owe Jupiter my service but not my devotion. The key is mine."

"We offer citizenship," she said quickly.

"Too late. I no longer need it. When my family and I passed inside the orbit of Amalthea and met a Navy ship and our refugee-bubble was towed back out to space—that was when we needed acceptance. You cannot restore what indifferent Jupiter took from me."

"We can perhaps restore part of it," Reba said.

"Some way you have gone about it! Trying to kill me and throw the key out into space—"

"Where our instruments would have intercepted it promptly. But that was the action of my predecessor. If you will only allow me to offer you—"

"Bring me back my love, and the key is yours," I said bitterly. *Oh, Helse! Oh, my love!*

"We can provide you another woman you could love."

"I doubt it," I said. "I have had access to some good ones but have not loved them."

"I am aware of that. Nevertheless, I will show you

another part of my power." She opened her purse and brought out a single picture and held it up to me.

I froze. "Helse!"

"Megan."

I remembered. "The girl who so resembled Helse! Mason's niece!"

"Megan resembles Helse in few respects," she said. "At a young age, she looked very similar to the way Helse did when you knew her. But Megan is older, and Saxon, and her intellect dwarfs Helse's."

I felt pain in my hand and discovered that my fist was clenched so tight that my fingers were being crushed. The person who spoke ill of Helse—!

I forced myself to relax, so as not to be prey to this tough woman. "Helse was—nice."

"Certainly she was. She was a lovely girl, despite her background. It in no way diminishes her to say that Megan is a more lovely woman than Helse ever could have been. Your love for Helse was a product of your situation. Even while it existed, you loved your sister Spirit more. You would love Megan more."

She was persuasive, not so much by her words as by her attitude. Reba Ward was totally convinced. She had researched me in depth and knew my nature, and evidently she knew this woman Megan's nature, too. And—I had been attracted to Megan, when I was with Helse, seeing her picture in the dome on savage Io. A single glimpse of heaven, there on the hell-planet! It was more than coincidence of appearance; it was that a good man had helped us both in our time of dire need, and helped our refugee-bubble, and I bore him a phenomenal debt of gratitude that his death prevented me from repaying, and Megan was of his blood, his niece. If I could love any woman other than Helse, it would be Megan, though I knew next to nothing about her.

"We can give you Megan," Reba said.

For a moment temptation almost overwhelmed me. Love—restored! It might be possible! But then I knew that this was not the way I could accept it. Not as the cynical handout of a ruthless secret organization. How would they give me this woman? By blackmailing her with some closetal skeleton in her family? I would not take her that way!

Reba saw my temptation and my rejection. "That offer remains open," she said. "Be assured that no dishonor can stain this woman; she cannot be forced. What we offer you is, in fact, the means to win her honorably." She brought out a piece of paper. "Contact me at this designation, Europa, when you change your mind."

Numbly, I took the paper. I was not at all sure I would not change my mind.

We released the courier boy to Reba Ward and transported them back to Europa. Then we chased down two more private vessels, bringing our total to fifty. Then my new orders came: promotion to Captain and command of the Task Force destined to eradicate piracy from the Belt.

The publicity suggested this was a merit assignment, because of my superlative record in the Juclip mission, but I knew it was the action of Reba. Once again, QYV had shown me its power.

But I still possessed the key.

Chapter 8
FIRST BLOOD

The pretext was dramatic: Trouble had erupted in the Belt, that zone of planetoids that existed between the orbits of Jupiter and Mars. Theoretically the Belt was an independent, disorganized conglomeration of settlements, analogous to the widely scattered islands of Earth's giant Pacific Ocean; actually they were the meddling ground for the interests of Jupiter, Saturn, Uranus, and scattered lesser powers. A good deal of interplanetary spying went on there, and several major battles of the Second System War had occurred there. These days the planetary spheres of influence overlapped in the Belt with uneasy tolerance.

The greatest officially unrecognized complication in the Belt was the rampant piracy there. The pirates owed no allegiance to any planet but seemed to have obscure but potent ties to several planets. Perhaps bribery was involved; such information is difficult to come by, for an obvious reason. At any rate, the pirates were a force to be reckoned with in that region of space, and they, too, were tacitly tolerated.

But now the pirates had overstepped their bounds, as they had in the Juclip. They had moved in force on the Marianas, a protectorate of Jupiter, taking over a whole cluster of bubbles and planetoids. The settlers there spoke English, and many of them possessed Jupiter citizenship. Angry protests followed, but the pirates claimed the territory was historically theirs. Centuries ago it had indeed been overrun by pirates; they had preyed on passing Jupiter ships, so in due course Jupiter had sent down a warship, rousted them out, and settled the section itself. It really wasn't so much; today it was mostly agricultural, taking advantage of the more intense sunlight of the inner system, so that smaller focusing lenses were more necessary there than at Jupiter. Probably it cost Jupiter more to maintain the colony than the colony returned in benefits, but once Jupiter had Made an Issue, it had to maintain a presence there. This was the way of planetary powers.

Incursions had occurred before, of greater or lesser severity. Saturn's moon, Titan, embarking on a program of expansion that included several other moons and a segment of Saturn itself, had precipitated Jupiter's entry into the Second System War by sending a carrier fleet to bomb Hidalgo; the drones had devastated Jupiter's Belt-based fleet. When that war ended, Jupiter had defeated and occupied Titan, and the two were now firm allies. But this was only one historic example of the effect episodes in the Belt (Hidalgo, as a planetoid, was considered part of the Belt, though it ranged widely) had on System politics, and helped explain why Jupiter was especially sensitive to incursions against its Belt properties.

It was our public assignment to rid the Jupiter-aligned territory in the Belt of pirates. Privately, I was advised in no uncertain terms that Jupiter wanted to make an example of these criminals, so that no similar episode would occur in the foreseeable future. First the Juclip abduction, now this; the Colossus was annoyed. This was supposed to seem like a routine cleanup mission, nothing special, which was one reason they were assigning a captain instead of an admiral. But in actuality it was a demonstration of imperial will and power, which was why they were providing me with a full fleet.

I would have been more impressed with the rationale had it not been for two things: First, I knew this had been arranged by QYV; second, no self-respecting admiral would embark on a mission against mere pirates. This was work suitable for the riffraff of officers and units. In short, me and my unit. If I got myself killed and my fleet humiliated, they would have a suitable pretext to send an admiral of proper Saxon stock, with an overwhelming fleet.

That was all right. I had wanted this mission, and I would accomplish it. My objection to pirates was not a matter of appearance or politics; I owed the institution of piracy for the destruction of my family and fiancée, and now was my chance.

So we were supposed to punish the pirates as well as clean them out of Jupiter territory. This I intended to do. Unfortunately, the pirates were ready for us. Somehow they had known that Jupiter would make only a token effort, initially, and they were set to turn it into another splendid embarrassment to the Colossus of the System. What they planned to do when Jupiter's anger intensified was unclear; presumably then they would decamp, leaving Jupiter with nothing to step on. That would add insult to injury. Oh, the flies enjoyed plaguing the tiger!

At the moment the pirates were massing most of their available hardware at the Marianas base, which was more than I had in my fleet. Thus they had a triple advantage: superiority of force, the convenience of short supply lines, and the fact that somehow we had to drive them off without hurting the Jupiter settlers they held hostage. No wonder this was no task for an admiral!

I discussed it with my staff. Our decision was simple: We would surprise the pirates by attacking at their weakest point, well around the Belt. Once we had established a solid base in the Belt—a so-called beachhead—we could move on the Marianas pirates at our convenience. If they remained concentrated at the Jupiter base, we would continue to attack elsewhere, expanding our territory. Since I intended to eliminate all pirates, not just some of them, this was a feasible strategy for me. By the time the original-target pirates were brought to bay, they might be at a disadvantage. In fact, with proper deployment, we might compel them to desert the Jupiter base, so we would not have to risk damaging it. In any event, the pirates would not return to their old ways after we departed the Belt, for there would be none left. In this sense my strategy was like that of the Mongols of Earth's medieval period, who simply exterminated all potential troublemakers. That system had worked very well; there had been little internal dissent in the territories of their conquests. Not that I endorse bloodshed as the solution to political problems; this is just an analogy.

My task force was impressive: one battleship, one carrier, two cruisers, six destroyers, fifteen escort ships, and a number of service boats and patrol craft. True, the *Sawfish* was neither the largest nor the most modern of battleships; she was hardly larger than a modern cruiser, massing 40,000 tons and being 650 feet long and 100 in the beam. She could make 2.8 gee, and carried nine sixteen-inch guns and a commensurate number of laser cannon. Her crew was two thousand. In her day she had been considered a member of the finest class of battleship in the system, but that had been twenty-five years ago, and modern capital ships dwarfed her in mass, firepower, and acceleration. But Commander Phist assured me that she was a good vessel, soundly constructed, maneuverable, and versatile. "There were no lemons in this class," he said. "By the time we get her revamped, she'll be fit for service."

Having seen what he could do in this line, I was reassured. The fact was, a battleship was normally commanded by a rear admiral, and a task force by a vice admiral; my present rank of captain barely qualified me to command this expedition. QYV must have pulled very hard on the string to install me here. But if I succeeded in my mission, I would soon become the first Hispanic admiral in the Jupiter Navy. So I could not complain if my battleship was small and old, and my cruisers minimal; it was the best I could expect.

The carrier, the *Hempstone Crater,* was, of course, no giant of her type. Carriers, in the ancient days of Earth ocean ships, tended to be named after islands and bays—at least they were in the particular navy from which the Jupiter Navy claimed theoretical descent—so Jupiter's carriers followed in such suit as they were able. The *Hempstone Crater,* I think, is on Charon, Pluto's moon, about as distant and inhospitable a body as exists in the Solar System; there may be a scientific study mission there but not much else on any regular basis. *HC,* as we called her, was an escort carrier, much smaller than the contemporary ones. This, more than anything else, is useful to place our mission in perspective: a modern carrier is about 1,000 feet long, displacing some 80,000 tons (that is, if one were to set it into an ocean on Planet Earth, it would squeeze aside that weight in water; actually the calculations are now based on more refined data, but the archaic terminology remains), accelerating at 3.5 gee, carrying 100 drones, and with a crew of 5,000. The *HC,* in contrast, was 500 feet long, displaced 10,000 tons, accelerated at 1.9 gee, carried 28 drones, and had a crew of 800; that is, an eighth the mass and a quarter the payload and half the gees of the modern one. That was how serious the Navy was about cleaning out the pirates of the Belt. QYV had fetched me a minimal mission.

"We know what they're doing," Repro said heartily. "They're sending the troublesome riffraff off on an impossible mission. They believe we will never return."

"Of course," Phist agreed. "We were supposed to flub the prior Juclip mission; instead, we became heroes. They think we were lucky, but now they have upped the ante."

"They?" Spirit asked.

"The powers-that-be of the Jupiter Navy," Phist clarified. "The ones who are uncomfortable with ripples in the grand old order. It embarrasses them to have a ragtag outfit officered by a scapegoat, a delayed-stress-syndrome derelict, an addict, a whistle blower, a black female file clerk, and a couple of Hispanic refugees, to have such a collection make good. It is not the Navy Way."

"They just can't believe there is any real competence in our unit," Repro agreed, looking more satisfied than ever before, for his dream unit was coming true. "That is the beauty of it. If they suspected our potential, they would instantly yank the rug out."

"That they would," Phist agreed somberly.

"Nevertheless," Emerald put in, "we're going to have to scramble on this one. We aren't facing inferior forces this time. No one has been able to make a permanent dent in the piracy of the Belt before."

"No one's really tried," Mondy said. "The pirates are into a number of endeavors that cause politicians to hesitate."

I shrugged. I had this mission and a fine unit; I was not going to hesitate. My whole prior career had been in preparation for this. Already I had arranged to promote Phist, the longest in grade, to full commander, O5, and would see to the others as feasible. We would succeed.

Phist did his usual with the equipment specs, upgrading the battleship to 3.2 gee and the lesser ships to more. He saw to special weapons. It was amazing that the powers-that-be in the Navy did not realize the transformation that was occurring in our combat capacity; apparently, the bureaucracy chose not to comprehend the kind of logistics competence Phist possessed.

Task forces are not formed and launched on a dime, however. It was eight months before we set off for the Belt, and that in itself was a miracle of logistical organization. Work was still being done as we launched, but we were glad to be on our way at last.

I have said I can match every body in the Solar System to the continents and islands of prediaspora Earth. The notable exception is the Belt. The so-called asteroids (they really are not small stars, they are fragments of planetary matter) can be matched with the old Pacific islands, and the planetoid Hidalgo aligns nicely with Hawaii, as does Chiron with Cyprus. But I don't believe the old Earth islands ever had as savage a concatenation of evils and corruption as did the Belt. There were countless pirate vessels, roughly organized into several major bands—the Bands of the Belt. Each band had a specialty of crime and a territory, generally, though not perfectly, honored by the others. The most powerful bands were like six nations. I knew that the pirates of the Juclip were only limping rabble compared to those of the Belt. Criminals who lacked the strength or courage to go for the big time skulked around the various planets, preying on helpless craft such as the refugee-bubbles; those with real ambition went to the Belt. Such was the power of the Belt pirates that most legitimate planetary trading fleets paid toll to guarantee safe passage. It was cheaper than going to war. So the pirate kingdoms flourished, and in their lee, the rabble-pirates of the other regions survived. I had always known that taking out the Juclip pirates was only tokenism; they would regenerate the moment the Navy mission ended, unless the real pirate bastion in the Belt was eliminated too.

We took our time traveling, picking our spot. We could have reached the nearest section of the Belt in two weeks, but instead we elected to go a quarter of the way around to intersect it at the zone of the Carolines.

The Carolines were the least of the major pirate bands. Their biggest ship was an ancient cruiser, and that had been refitted as a printing shop and warehouse. The Carolines were specialists in pornography and illicit publication, and they handled the best. I had seen some of it as an enlisted man, and it was eye-popping; Juana had required me to burn it, because she said it degraded women. Perhaps she was correct, but I was male enough to enjoy it no matter whom it degraded. The illicit sexual feelies were also wholesaled by the Carolines; the *Hidden Flower* had merely retailed the transsex line of those, putting her own brand name on them. That was how Spirit had reached me with the EMPTY HAND message.

I did not have a consuming passion against the Carolines; in fact, I felt that pornography was relatively harmless as a vice, and that its suppression was a manifestation of the abridgment of free expression. But pirates were pirates, and Mondy had pinpointed this band as the weakest militarily, and Emerald had decided to start with it so as to test our mettle in true combat without undue risk. I concurred. I was not expert in either Intelligence or Strategy, which was why I had followed Repro's script to acquire personnel who were. A commander is only as good as his staff and his men, and he has to honor his staff's informed judgments. A good commander is to some extent a figurehead, a focal point for the expertise of his unit. So I set out to destroy the power of the Carolines (by that I mean the pirates thereof), a decision viewed with a certain regret on my part, and a certain righteous glee on my secretary's part.

Emerald was neutral about the social implication; she didn't care about pornography one way or the other. She viewed this purely as a strategic and tactical exercise, and it was her intent to give us the cleanest possible victory with minimum loss. She explained the essence to us with pride, for this was her moment.

"The operative concept is Kadesh," she said. "This was one of the earliest Earthly battles of which we have record. The Egyptians met and defeated the Hittites in the vicinity of the town of Kadesh in 1299 B.C."

"Now wait, Rising Moon!" Commander Phist protested, using her song-nickname. "Those were marching land armies; this is space! There's hardly a parallel!"

"You worried about your hardware, King Cole?" she inquired with a glance at his trousers. "I'm trying to protect it for you." She went on to describe the broad outline of her strategy. "Of course, the tactics are critical," she concluded.

"Tactics?" I asked. "I thought you just described them."

"I described strategy," she said. "That's our effort to bring our forces into play advantageously. Strategy occurs before the combatants meet. Tactics are what happens once the battle begins. A winning strategy can be ruined by losing tactics."

"Oh, you mean like setting your opponent up for a knockout punch and then missing the punch," I said.

"Close enough, Worry," she agreed wryly.

It turned out that the Carolines, having noted our coming, had gathered reinforcements. They still had no capital ships, but they had borrowed another cruiser, and this was a good one, a match for one of ours. They also picked up several more destroyers; as a result, they now had six, matching ours.

Emerald bit her lip. "I hadn't counted on this," she said. "We don't want to commit the *Sawfish,* and without it, the sides are too close to even."

"Why not use the *Sawfish?*" I asked innocently. "She could gun down the enemy ships before they could get within their torpedo range."

"Same reason you don't use your queen to mop up pawns in a chess game," she said. "In close quarters a battleship has less advantage and becomes vulnerable. We'll hold the *Sawfish* out until we have access to another battleship, or at least a cruiser. We'd be fools to risk her in a destroyer battle."

Emerald wanted to be able to direct the battle personally, which meant she couldn't remain aboard the *Sawfish*. I designated the destroyer *Discovered Check* to be her command ship and went along myself. I wanted personal involvement, too.

"I don't like this, Hope," Spirit said darkly. "That little ship is a lot more vulnerable than the *Sawfish.*"

"Also a lot less obvious," I pointed out. "We'll be observing, not fighting. The enemy will never suspect."

"If the battle comes near you, I'll bring the *Sawfish* in to fetch you out," she warned.

"And take your bodyguard along, sir," Sergeant Smith said. "Here, I'll assign another dozen men—"

"I don't need any dozen men!" I protested.

"Take them, Captain," Mondy said. He was pale and drawn; he had no love for battle. But he was not nonfunctional; now that the challenge was on him, he was holding steady. Emerald had been good for him these past few years. "In fact, I would like to accompany you myself."

"This may be closer to the action than you like," I warned him. "There is no need for you to expose yourself to this."

"Yes there is, sir. My wife will be exposed."

His wife, my former wife. I knew what a woman Emerald was. I was proof from love, but evidently it was a different case with Mondy. He did not want to live if Emerald didn't. She had married him because our unit needed him, and he had proved his value to us many times. But he had needs of his own. Our unit was bound together in special ways. "Come along, Peat Bog, " I said. His song-nickname, no affront.

"And stay out of mischief!" Spirit called as we entered the linked airlocks, transferring to the *Discovered Check*.

"We know where we're going," Emerald called back, paraphrasing Spirit's song. Songs became more important as tension mounted.

The destroyer was a nice ship. Commander Phist had requisitioned some very special equipment for her, which was one reason we were using the *Discovered Check*. She was the fastest of our ships, capable of an astonishing 4.5-gee acceleration in her upgraded condition, which meant she could probably outrun any ship in the Belt. Her torpedoes were of the most modern type, fifty percent faster than standard, with magnetic repulsion fields that made physical interception of them in flight almost impossible. When they homed in on their target, the magnetism was programmed to reverse. Her hull was plated with laser-resistant alloy, and her own laser cannon was oriented by computer to destroy any oncoming missile. She was also armed with "depth" bombs—that were hurled by catapult slowly through space, but so powerful that they could disable a small ship by a proximity explosion. This was, in short, one potent ship, and about as safe as a destroyer could be. Commander Phist had taken a great deal of pride in it, justifiably. He had not been able to upgrade the other destroyers similarly; most were not designed for such changes, and as a unit we had already pushed our luck about as far as we could. Had the officers in charge of these matters possessed Phist's insight into performance, quality, and costs, they would never have let us get away with many of our requisitions. But these officers, like much of the Jupiter Navy, were essentially asleep at the helm.

The problem with the Asteroid Belt is that it obscures things. Much of it is sparse, and, of course, the orbiting rocks are readily avoided by ships that travel outside the Solar Ecliptic, the plane in which most of the planets revolve. But there are more small chunks than large ones, and there is considerable sand. In some regions there are whole clouds of dust. This interferes with radar and makes it easy for ships to hide; the radar can't readily distinguish between rocks and ships. It was in this manner that we sailed into the pirate ambush.

We were advancing toward the main Caroline base on a half-mile-diameter planetoid. Because of the debris in the area, we were strung out along a natural channel that the pirates normally used. There really wasn't any other way; the Belt was constantly changing its configuration as planetoids ellipsed in and out, stirring up sand and throwing dust about in their wakes. Maps had to be constantly updated, and, of course, we lacked the latest. Only the pirates themselves knew the latest details, and they weren't giving out that information to the Navy. So we used the main channel, watching for pirate ships, but we had underestimated the care with which their ambush had been laid. Or so the pirates believed.

All six of their destroyers materialized from the debris, bare light-seconds from the center of our fleet. In that region we had only two destroyers, a frigate, two sloops, and half a dozen gunboats. Our fleet had started in compact order but had become dispersed because of the differing accelerations of the various types of ships. Our battleship was at the head with two destroyers and several escorts, while our carrier was far to the rear, with two more destroyers and a cruiser. The center was by far the weakest region, lacking either the firepower of the *Sawfish* or the drones of the *Hempstone Crater*, without even a cruiser to bolster its striking force. The pirate fleet of six destroyers was much more than a match for our widely spaced eight ships, and, of course, the second pirate cruiser, the battlefit one, was waiting in their rear. They could cut our column in two, and then concentrate their remaining ships, which were surely deploying invisibly in the debris of the Belt. When our carrier arrived, they could mass against it. We could lose half our force before we got properly organized. Then they would retreat, escaping retaliation, awaiting a new opportunity to strike.

Emerald showed her teeth in no friendly smile. What I have described is the way it was supposed to seem to the pirates—and now they had taken the bait. Kadesh, when the Hittites had pounced on the Egyptians' weak center as the Egyptian forces marched in columns. Perhaps the Egyptians had not planned it that way, but we had. Our vulnerability was a good deal more apparent than actual.

Our light cruiser, the *Inverness,* thirteen thousand tons, had already rotated in space and commenced acceleration back toward our center as the enemy destroyers made their move. Our radar wasn't good in this region, but we had known what to expect, so had been able to track their ships approximately. The *Inverness* was armed with a dozen six-inch guns and another dozen five-inch lasers, compared to the four five-inch guns of each enemy destroyer, and her acceleration of 3.5 gee matched theirs. Of course, she was really decelerating, reducing her inertial velocity, but in the situation that was a quibble. When everything is moving at a given velocity, that becomes your basis for orientation in space, and it is convenient to treat your formation as if it is at rest. The enemy craft were matching our velocity, and the *Inverness* was rapidly closing the distance, and she was a considerably more potent fighting piece than they. Her six-inchers had greater muzzle velocity and accuracy, which translated into greater effective range.

One of our two destroyers in the region was the *Discovered Check*. She was not here to fight, of course; she was the temporary command ship. If things got difficult, she could outrun any of the enemy destroyers, but it wouldn't come to that. And our frigate was another upgraded ship, as were two of our corvettes. In fact, our supposedly weak center was a good deal stronger than it appeared.

"Corvettes, evasive maneuvers," Emerald was saying into her scrambled radio connection. "Frigate, fire on your nearest." She glanced up at me, the light and delight of battle in her eyes. "It's only a pair of three-inchers she can orient without changing course, but they may not know that." The problem, of course, was that small ships could not fire effectively sidewise; their heavy guns were oriented forward, since their spin made side-oriented guns highly inaccurate. The larger ships had special independent artillery belts, which did not spin with the rest of the ship; that was another reason our battleship was like a chess queen, while the destroyers were like deadly pawns. Versatility in firepower was critical in battle!

Of course, normally attacking ships simply matched velocities, then rotated to point at their targets; destroyers were highly maneuverable this way. But it did take a few minutes, and they were vulnerable while correcting their attitude, as it was called. The enemy destroyers were closing on our ships at an angle so they could fire forward at us, but that meant they presented a larger and steadier target for return fire by any ships in our column that could fire sidewise. That was why the frigate's effort should be slightly unnerving to them, until they discovered that only two three-inch guns were involved. Theoretically one three-incher was enough to score, but it was unlikely at this range.

The Caroline destroyers were coming within effective range of their five-inchers. Our corvettes, not daring to drift in space while changing their attitudes, were maneuvering by irregular acceleration. When a shell approaches at an angle to the target ship, the rate of the target's acceleration has to be taken into consideration. If the target accelerates faster than allowed for, the shell will miss to the rear; if it accelerates slower, the shot will miss to the front. So the attacker has to get close enough to increase its accuracy and to read the acceleration of the target correctly. Even so, the chances of any one shell scoring, even when correctly aimed and timed, are only about one in four at close range, and close range is dangerous when a number of ships are involved.

You may be wondering why ships don't simply loop about, the way ancient Earth vehicles did. Certainly I wondered, at first. The answer is that they can't. Not when they are spinning for internal gee and external stability. They can change course a little, but any sharp turn at speed would encounter precessional resistance that would tear the ship apart before the maneuver could be completed. Those old stories of spaceships making neat loops in space to engage their opponents, on a scale of seconds, are fantasy; any loop they might reasonably make, unless they are almost stationary in space, would be so big as to be useless in a close encounter. Here in the confined channel of the Belt, the attempt would be disastrous. So maneuvers of this sort are sharply limited, and the keys become proximity and rate of acceleration.

Now the *Inverness* came in range. Immediately her six-inchers opened up, and the Caroline destroyers were in trouble. They had to refocus on the cruiser, because otherwise she would concentrate her firepower and pick them off one by one. The chances of a single shot scoring, in ideal conditions, may be one in four, but our destroyer would fire hundreds of shells. That shifted the odds.

Actually, six destroyers could normally take on a single cruiser. The cruiser would probably knock out a couple, but then the rest would be within their effective range and would be able to fire so many shells that the cruiser's lasers would not be able to handle them all. Saturation shelling was an excellent tactic. So they ignored our lesser ships and oriented carefully on the *Inverness*.

Meanwhile, however, the *Sawfish*, our battleship, was decelerating to approach the battle region from the front, and the carrier *HC* was accelerating at her maximum gee to get within drone range from the rear, accompanied by our second cruiser, the *Brooksville*. Our pincers were closing. I really had to admire Emerald's strategy; it was working exactly as she had outlined it to us. Soon we would enclose the enemy destroyers and go after their backup cruiser, which was now approaching in order to take on ours. Our trap was slamming shut on the pirates.

But the best-laid plans, as it has been said, can go astray. A destroyer made a lucky hit on the *Inverness* and knocked out her communications turret, and perhaps more. Her radio contact with us ceased and so did her acceleration. She had not been holed, but she was in trouble. She would be a sitting target for the enemy ships if she didn't get her drive back soon. Free-fall is for traveling, not for battling.

"Damn!" Emerald swore. "It'll be too long before our wings close; we'll lose her!" She bit her lip fretfully.

I realized that her inexperience had betrayed us. A veteran strategist would have a backup plan in case of the unexpected. Emerald's strategy had been good—good enough to win the battle—but she had not allowed sufficiently for chance. I wondered if the Egyptian king, of the Kadesh battle, had suffered similarly.

"We've got to help the *Inverness!*" Mondy said.

"We aren't supposed to get into the action," I said, as if I were not the commander.

"If they take out that cruiser," Mondy pointed out, "we'll be next."

I had to agree. "Unless we outrun them."

Emerald nodded. "Can't risk the Expedition Commander," she said without irony. The commander is generally considered more valuable than any single ship, and, of course, our strategist and intelligence officer were also at risk. If the Task Force were considered as an organism, we represented its brain. I had been foolish to permit such a grouping of key personnel to occur at the battle site. In addition, Emerald and I both knew that Mondy, with his susceptibility to battle stress, was now a risk to himself and this ship. There was no way to predict how he might react.

But we had misjudged him. "We barely have the force to do our job now," he said. "Without the *Inverness* we'll be so short we'll have to send for a replacement ship, and that will take too long." He seemed less nervous now, oddly.

"Way too long," I agreed. What was he getting at? I had always read the deep disquiet in him before; now I sensed a strange purpose.

"This is a fighting ship; let's use it," he said.

I exchanged a glance with Emerald. She was as surprised as I was.

Mondy grinned, now at ease. "Give the order, and I'll explain."

Emerald shrugged. "Sure thing, Peat Bog. We do need that cruiser."

"Captain," I said into the ship's intercom. I was not, of course, commanding this ship; I commanded the Task Force, a different matter. Captain was my rank, but the one who commands a particular ship is captain of that ship, whatever his rank, and he has final authority on that ship.

"Sir," he responded.

"We are joining the battle. Act in the manner you deem best to protect the *Inverness,* subject to the overriding directives of Commander Sheller."

"Yes, sir." There was a pause, then: "Secure for hi-gee."

We felt the change immediately. We were pacing the frigate; now our acceleration jumped to about two gee as the ship sought to close on the cruiser. The *Discovered Check* was turning, too, despite the spin; we felt the sheer. Our acceleration couches shifted position, their clamps holding us secure, as the gee of the thrust exceeded that of the spin.

Even at double-gee, a maneuver takes time. We had to wait, watching the slow change on our screens. It wasn't comfortable in either the physical or the emotional sense, but we were in shape for it—and so, it seemed, was Mondy. I realized now that his original potbelly had slimmed down; he was more fit physically than I had pictured him. "If it is not indiscreet to ask," I said cautiously, resisting the gee pressure, "how is it that you are having no more trouble now than we are?"

"This is reality," he said. "Here I have some personal control over my destiny. In my dreams I don't."

"That's not enough, Peat," Emerald said. "I've got more control here than you do, because I can dictate to the captain of this ship, in the name of tactics. But there's a hand squeezing my heart. There's none squeezing yours at the moment."

Mondy smiled. "I saw action in the Saturn Incident," he said, speaking in brief bursts as the gee squeezed more than our hearts. "We were behind enemy lines and short of rations, especially oxygen; we could not afford to take prisoners. Our lasers were low, so we used knives. We infiltrated an observation bubble, knifed their communication operators, and planted timed bombs. That was our job. After we vacated the bubble, the bombs would detonate, killing the remaining personnel. It went like clockwork; we took out five different bubbles that way and watched each blow behind us. 'Lovely!' I exclaimed. Then I realized that it wasn't lovely; it was awful. Those people were fighting to defend their system, just as we were; they were decent, hardworking people who just happened to speak a different language. Their blood was on my hands, some of it literally. I remembered how one of them had been a young woman; her blood had flowed over my knife as she dropped, and onto my fingers. Somehow it hadn't bothered me at the time, but in retrospect that blood was horrible, so hot and thick, her life spilled across my hand. My associates thought it was humorous. 'You really got it into her!' one quipped. He liked it, liked the killing, the gore of it, the sexual analogy: to ram a thing into the warm body of a woman, drawing blood. And suddenly I realized that I didn't like it—but it was too late. I was already responsible for the deaths of over a hundred human beings.

"When we reported back to base, I got a commendation and a promotion: my reward for murdering all those people. And yet in the end, we withdrew from Saturn and the other side took over; all our killing had accomplished nothing. I was left with no justification at all. And since then, I have relived those murders I committed, especially of that young woman—a woman very like you." He turned his head briefly toward Emerald, the gee drawing down his jowls, making him artificially haggard. "Sometimes in my dreams I think she's alive again, that all of them are alive, that perhaps I meet her living, and love her, for love was what she deserved, not that cruel knife. But I know it isn't so, and I can't face it, and I scream."

Now he turned to me. "You assumed I was afraid of action, but it is myself I fear. I don't want to murder anyone else, though I do it again every night. But this—" He paused again. "My companion of the quip, who liked killing, he couldn't get enough of it in the Navy when peace came, so he deserted and became a pirate. I know what pirates do. Them I can kill. They are like the sinister aspect of myself; they need to be extirpated. I cannot undo what I have done, but I can, to a certain extent, atone for it by abolishing the other killers. Only when I am actively atoning does my conscience feel at ease."

"I understand," I said. "I also killed—"

"Pirates," he finished for me. "And children. And a young woman you loved. I know you understand, but your guilt is less than mine, and your strength is greater. Your system protects your sanity, as it protects you from hallucinogens."

I had never thought of it that way. Could there be antibodies against destructive emotion? Surely I had suffered events that drove others mad, but I survived—and so did

Spirit, who was of my blood. We felt the impact at first but learned to cope, exactly as I had with the hallucinogen. Mondy had provided me another insight into myself. "Yes," I agreed.

"But now the *Inverness* is in trouble. If I don't act, many good lives will be lost. So I must act, to pay another installment on my debt."

And now, for the time being, he was at ease and fully competent. I had thought I understood him before, but my judgment had been imperfect because I had not allowed for the potential change in him brought about by circumstance.

Emerald, too, was looking at Mondy, her husband. She had suffered, taking care of him. Perhaps she had felt contempt for him. This was no longer the case. His insights into the nature of the Navy had brought us all promotion and success, and now his very suffering spoke eloquently for the state of his conscience. He had never accepted or forgotten the evil he had done. She had married me and then him; I had left evil behind me and had left her when it was expedient to do so. Mondy would never do either. I could almost see the wheels clicking to new settings in her head. What woman, granted the choice, would choose a truly independent man instead of a dependent one? Only a foolish woman . . .

We watched the action on our screens while Emerald continued to direct the overall battle. I now appreciated much better the distinction between strategy and tactics. We were now immersed in tactics. We veered abruptly to orient on an enemy destroyer. The change hardly showed on the screen, for our actual shift was small; but the gee was awful, triple normal, and our couches swung about like carnival carriages. At our velocity the slightest deviation from straight-line-forward translated to considerable actual shift, and the acceleration itself was fierce. Slowly we closed on the enemy craft. We could not fire at it, and it could not fire at us; one of us had to turn our guns on the other.

We took the chance. We cut acceleration, damped our spin, and used our attitude jets to rotate in space. This took several minutes, but soon we would be able to launch a torpedo at the other. We resumed spin, stabilizing ourselves. . . .

And the Caroline cruiser, alert to the pressure of a sitting duck, made a beautiful, or lucky, long-range shot and scored glancingly on our nose. Our torpedo tubes were jammed, and we were knocked out of attitude, our precession causing us to rotate slowly in space, end over end. Our hull was tight, but we did not dare use our acceleration jet until we recovered stability. We were, for the moment, effectively dead in space.

"Guide jets damaged," a technician reported. "Unable to correct."

Worse yet. We would have to have a repair crew work on the hull, and that was treacherous in battle.

There was a flare of light on the screen. For an instant I thought another shell had scored on us, but that was not so; an enemy destroyer had blown up. One of our ships had taken it out. The battle was continuing, but we ourselves could no longer fight.

Now the enemy destroyers were reorienting. "They're going to hole us," Emerald said grimly. Her face was drawn; she had never been in true battle before. There were tears of fear or frustration on her face. I think she feared death less than she feared the disaster this represented to her career. This was the stuff from which future nightmares were made.

But Mondy was unaffected. "No," he said. "They're going to board us."

"How do you know?" she demanded sharply.

"That is the nature of pirates. They're looters. They want this ship, and if they can't salvage it, they'll pillage it, rape the women, and maybe take them as slaves."

All true, as I well knew. We had many young female personnel in our fleet and on this ship, and Emerald herself was one. There was ugly business coming, but Mondy and I would probably not live to see much of it.

"See, they're not shooting at the *Inverness* anymore, either," Mondy said. "That would be a real prize for them."

"They can't hope to take over a cruiser!" Emerald protested.

"Certainly they can," he said. "They've got pacifiers."

Pacifiers: the electronic devices that caused all unprotected people in their range to lose personal volition. I had had devastating experience with one, as a refugee. "But we're protected from that," I said.

Mondy smiled grimly. "Of course. But they don't know that. I saw to it that accurate information did not get out. I believe our best strategy is to play dead—rather, to play pacified—and then take over their ship. Our men are well prepared for hand-to-hand combat."

"I don't like this," Emerald said. "Nobody ever tried to rape me before." Indeed, she was as pale as her dark skin permitted.

"It will not come to that, my dear," he assured her. "I have been in this type of situation before. We shall surprise them."

"You've had dreams about it!" she said. "You scream in the night! I've had to hold your hand! How can you fight them, even if you nullify the pacifier?"

"As I mentioned, reality is less severe than my dreams. My conscience is clear, for this. This time I am on the side of the victim." He turned to me. "Captain, I suggest we plan our strategy in the few minutes remaining before they board us."

"Agreed." I spoke to the *Discovered Check*'s captain, and we entered a four-person dialogue and set our new trap. This ship was aptly named for this ploy!

The ship shuddered as the pirate came into contact. A warning light signaled the presence of a pacifier field. We all had pacifier null-units in our uniforms; our staff had agreed this was essential equipment. But we all slowed our paces, as if caught by surprise, playing the game. The three of us had gone to the ship's main hall, hoping to serve as a preliminary distraction for the pirates, so that they would not be too careful. We wanted as many as possible to board before we acted. The two ships were now in free-fall, neither accelerating nor spinning; the pirate's contact had served to steady us.

The pirates operated the linked airlocks and entered. The first three were big, dirty bruisers, exactly the way we had imagined them. They carried hand-lasers and were alert for trouble, but when they saw Emerald floating there, they relaxed.

"Look at the braid on that black doll!" the party leader exclaimed. "A light commander—that's pretty high!"

"Come here, Commander Doll," the second ordered.

Emerald slowly looked at them, then caught a handhold and hauled herself toward the one who had called her. The pacifier field did not make people dim-witted or physically slow, it merely robbed them of volition. Emerald obeyed the direct order she had been given; Mondy and I remained where we were, supposedly lacking the initiative to act. Such inaction may seem incredible to people who have not experienced the pacifier's effect, but a pacifier had caused me to watch passively while my father was brutally slain.

"Hey, this one's full captain!" the first pirate cried, as more of them crowded in from the airlock. "He must be the big boss! What a find!"

"What's he doing in this little ship?"

"Ask him, dodo!"

So the second pirate asked me: "Who are you, Navy man? Why are you here?"

"I am Captain Hubris, Commander of this task force," I said carefully. The field tended to interfere somewhat with speech, so I spoke slowly and with seeming concentration, though I was in fact unaffected. "I wanted to be close to the battle."

He laughed coarsely. "You sure got your wish, Navy man! Now you're our prisoner. You'll fetch a good ransom!"

Emerald arrived before him. Eagerly the man grabbed her. "I never had a Navy officer before," he said, hauling her in for a rough kiss. She did not resist, and still Mondy and I did nothing; we were waiting for the other pirates to board.

"Who gave *you* the rights to her?" the pirate leader demanded. "Chick like that's for the top man!"

"You got your own woman," the second protested.

"So? I got a share of any I want—and I never had a Navy officer gal either, 'specially not a young, sleek creature like this. How old are you, doll?"

"Twenty-eight," Emerald replied. That reminded me that we had both been twenty-two when we met; how fast six years had passed!

The second pirate had to compromise. "Not as young as I thought. So we'll share her. Let's strip her first."

They went at it, yanking Emerald's sturdy uniform off piece by piece, cutting it where it snagged. The others gathered around to watch. Soon there were thirty of them crowding the chamber, apparently all that were going to board. We waited, making sure, while Emerald was stripped. All the pirates were running their hands over her exposed body, delighting in her healthy flesh. Mondy did not react overtly; we both knew that Emerald was not sensitive about exposure, and that she was buying time.

But there was no need to acquiesce to rape. I reached slowly into a pocket and brought out a small device with a bulb. It was a light grenade.

I snapped my fingers. Emerald and Mondy—and the hidden personnel we had placed—closed their eyes tightly. I closed mine and activated the grenade.

The flash was so bright it seemed to burn right through my flesh. It was gone in an instant, but it took a moment for my protected eyes to recover. Slowly I opened them.

There was chaos in the chamber. All the pirates had been temporarily blinded. It did not matter which way they had been facing when the grenade went off; the reflections sufficed.

"Get out of there, Emerald!" I called. But she was already moving, floating for the center passage, getting out of the line of fire. Mondy and I retreated similarly, putting metal between us and the floating pirates.

Sure enough, one of them drew his laser and fired. The beam scorched into the side of another, causing him to scream with pain. Believing they were under attack, several more pirates drew and fired, randomly.

The carnage was terrible. The pirates were destroying each other, because of their blindness, suspicion, and panic. In moments only four were functional, and as they caught on to what had happened, we took them out with stunners.

"Now we move on their ship," I said.

"I'll do it, sir," Heller said. I had kept him clear of the prior action, but now he was back bodyguarding. He carried a gas bomb. He launched for the lock, hurled the bomb through, and slammed the panel closed.

We waited fifteen minutes, meanwhile sending out our repair crew to work on our own hull. Emerald borrowed a uniform and dressed herself, unself-consciously. Then we opened the lock. The gas had dissipated and neutralized itself as it was designed to do, and the pirate ship was silent.

"Let's see whether we can crew this thing and use it ourselves," Emerald said. She was evidently somewhat shaken by the slaughter among the pirates but was in control. Certainly her understanding of what Mondy and I had been through in the past had broadened.

Captain Undermeyer of the *Discovered Check* joined us, as he was more savvy about destroyers than we were. He glanced about dispassionately as we entered the pirate ship. "She's been sloppily treated, but she's spaceworthy," he said. "Let's see what the bridge is like."

There were pirates scattered about their stations; all were unconscious. Our gas bombs were effective, the gas being odorless and invisible as it diffused; our strategy and drill were paying off. We had successfully reversed the pirates' boarding attempt and had a number of captives and a serviceable ship for our effort. Emerald had done much to make it possible, by allowing her attractive body to serve as a distraction while the trap fell into place.

We came to the bulkhead sealing off the bridge. Captain Undermeyer opened it and stepped through, and into the arms of a husky pirate. "Hold it there, men," the pirate said. "This brass is hostage."

"Fool!" Emerald cursed. "Why didn't I think of that?"

"You? It was *my* business to anticipate this," Mondy said.

"Not to mention mine," I agreed ruefully. I had encountered such a trap before, when rescuing Spirit. We had all become as overconfident as the pirates.

"Get in here," the pirate snapped. "Drop your weapons."

We started to move, and Captain Undermeyer elbowed the pirate. The pirate's laser fired, Undermeyer cried out, and Sergeant Heller launched himself through the air as the pirate brought his weapon around for a shot at me. The laser beam burned past his head as I flung myself aside; then Heller was on the pirate, pulping his face with several blows of his right fist as he grasped the man's jacket with his left hand.

All of us dived for our discarded weapons—they had, of course, not dropped but floated free—but there were no other active pirates. This one, perhaps the captain, had been lucky enough to avoid the gas until it nullified itself, so had been alert. We should have been on guard.

"You're a good bodyguard," I told Heller.

"I haven't saved your life yet, Cap'n," he said. "You got out of the way of that beam on your own."

Still, he had tried. My decision in giving him the position seemed justified.

Captain Undermeyer was not as fortunate. The beam had seared across his neck and the side of his face, nicking a vein; now he held his hand on the raw gouge to slow the bleeding. Already a medic was arriving, but I knew the good man would be in sick bay awhile. No chance now to activate the pirate ship; I was no pilot, and neither were Mondy or Emerald. But we would hold the ship for future use. We returned to the *Discovered Check*.

The situation had changed in the larger battle. The pirates' delay to plunder ships had given the *Sawfish* time to come on the scene at one side, and the *Hempstone Crater* on the other; already a number of drones from the carrier were aloft, chasing down pirate ships. Our pincers-trap had closed and all that remained was mopping up.

We had won our first battle, but had almost flubbed it by losing our top personnel, and two of our destroyers and a corvette were gone. We had gained back one destroyer, but that was only a ship and could not make up for the trained personnel who had died in the others.

"Sir, you can have my resignation," Emerald said to me.

"Take this woman away and talk to her," I told Mondy. He smiled; in the aftermath of battle, he retained his positive outlook. Emerald's inexperience had allowed us to be drawn into peril, but this first blood would toughen her and help her to become the strategist she could be. I knew Mondy would make her understand. He was a good officer and a good man, and now his qualities were showing. He had not lost competence under stress, he had gained it.

We advanced on the Caroline base, and it surrendered without resistance. One of the six major pirate bands had been dealt with.

But it wasn't quite over. There was one chore the Commander had to perform, and I did not feel free to delegate it to any subordinate, though I did not relish it myself. This was notifying the kin of our dead.

We organized our lists, I reviewed the backgrounds, and Juana started placing my calls. It is too painful for me to go into detail here, so I will provide a nightmare interview.

"Mrs. X? I am Captain Hubris, of the Jupiter Navy Task Force on a mission to the Asteroid Belt. I regret to inform—"

"Oh, no! Something's happened to Jonathan!"

"He died in honorable performance of his duty, and—"

"No! It can't be! He was such a good boy!"

"We regret that we are unable to return his remains to you, because—"

But the rest is drowned out by her screaming.

In actuality it was my own screaming; Spirit was holding my hand when I woke. As I said, this was a nightmare; no such interview occurred in reality. We were in the Belt, about thirty light minutes from Jupiter; a true exchange would take an hour between sentences. So I simply sent messages of condolence; my imagination provided the rest. Still it hurt.

"I was on similar duty when I started," Commander Repro said.

When he started on the drug. Now I could understand

that, too! I longed to deaden my mind to the horror of these notices but could not, for my system would soon throw off the drug. In any event, I *would* not. I understood too well the suffering of family loss; I had to suffer with these families, for the fleet and all its personnel were my responsibility.

We glory in war, in the shedding of human blood. What fools we are!

Chapter 9

SURRENDER

We wasted no time organizing for our encounter with the next pirate band, for those pirates were considerably stronger than the Carolines, and we did not want to give them much time to prepare. They were the Solomons, whose specialty was gambling. Their leader had adopted the name Straight, evidently relating to one of the winning configurations of the card game of poker, but he had the reputation of being straight in his dealings, too. This was essential for his business, for the gamblers had to have the trust of their clients, and the violation of understandings was not conducive to that. Straight was a pirate, and he had killed ruthlessly in the defense of his turf, but he kept his word. Mondy's research indicated that though the Solomons were one of the weaker bands in terms of hardware, they were perhaps the most competently led.

"Damn, I feel him," Emerald muttered. "I feel Straight taking my measure, and I don't mean my bust line! He's getting set to make a real fool of me in battle. I've got to come up with something good!"

"He shouldn't know it's you he's dealing with," I said. "I'm the Task Force Commander, and there's no hint of strategic or tactical genius in my evaluation. He should hold my ability in righteous contempt, especially since that last battle seemed like sheer chance."

Emerald bit her lip. "More truth to that last than I like! One thing's sure: I'm not going to put us in a ship in the battle! In fact, I'm not going to risk any ships if I can help it."

How nice it would be to win a battle and not have to notify the families of our losses! "How can you fight a battle without ships?" I asked.

"With drones," she said firmly. "They are the space-age analogue of the ancient airplanes, and in many respects their operation is similar. They are short range, so must have either a planetary base—better, a planetoid base, to avoid a punishing gravity well—or a carrier ship. But given that base, their effect can be devastating. In fact, a sufficient force of drones can dominate a given sector of space."

"There's our answer," I suggested. "Send in the *HC* and wipe the Solomons out." I knew it couldn't be that simple, but I was curious what she planned. That prior battle had made me nervous. We could have taken much worse losses than we had, thanks to mischance—and mischance is part of war.

"Unh-uh! They've got drones, too—more than we do. We've got to nullify them so we can bring our ships into play, and they've got almost as many ships as we do."

"But you have a notion," I prompted her. I was familiar with her mannerisms, as with her body.

"I have a notion," she agreed. "If it works, we'll wipe them out. But if they catch on, it'll be an even battle."

"We can't afford an even battle," I reminded her. "We have four more bands to snap after this one."

"Don't I know it! That resupply fleet better not be late!" She referred to the converted tanker coming from Jupiter on a secret schedule. It would bring food, ammunition, and CT fuel to restock what we had used. Supplies, as Commander Phist assured us, were the lifeline of a fleet in space. If anything happened to that ship, we would soon be hurting. In the bad old days of planetbound Earth, marching armies lived off the land, meaning they plundered the countryside. Sometimes they were more trouble to their friends than to their enemies. The Jupiter Navy paid its own way, as a matter of policy. But that meant we were dependent on our supply ships. The moment that tanker arrived, we would proceed to the battle with the Solomons.

Meanwhile, we checked the situation in the Caroline notch of the Belt. The pirates had ruled it, but they were not the only residents. There were regular settlers who farmed and mined and worked, staking out individual planetoids, some no larger than boulders. A colonist would set up a bubble-tent for air and a solar-focusing lens for energy—and presto: That boulder was halfway terraformed. Of course, it was a rough and ready and lonely frontier life with a relatively high rate of attrition; Belt colonists might not be physically impressive, but emotionally they were metal-hard. For a time, several planets had exiled their criminals to the Belt; it had been a handy way to get rid of them without having to go through the social awkwardness of killing them. Unfortunately those criminals had prospered and become the pirates that I was now attempting to eradicate.

If I speak of the Belt as if it is crowded with rocks, that is only relative; it would generally require a good telescope even to see the nearest neighboring rock from any one fragment. But though the Belt was actually a monstrous torus including more actual space than existed in all the Solar System inside the orbit of Mars, so that its thousands of planetoids and hundreds of thousands of motes were thinly spaced, they seemed much thicker to ships traveling at interplanetary velocities. A pirate ship could spring out from any one of them. Any rock at all is a nuisance to a spaceship, even if it's twenty light-seconds away, for it just might be on collision course.

The main base of the Carolines was a small city-bubble named Bright Hope. Perhaps that had been literal, at its founding; it had long since become cruel irony. The people there met us with fear, not joy of deliverance from the pirate yoke, and this perplexed me. Why should the sight of a Naval uniform cause them to retreat into tight-lipped silence?

At first we assumed they were afraid of reprisals, despite our reassurance. But ones we knew were victims of the pirates were the same. They did whatever we asked but would not speak. Impatient with this, I dressed in civilian clothes and took Isobel Brinker to the local free tavern.

The "free" did not refer to the beverages served; they were expensive. It referred to the human interactions. Anyone could speak freely here without consequence. It did not matter what he said, or whether it was true or false, serious or humorous, consequential or irrelevant; he had a right to utter it. No one had to listen, but no one had the right to bar him from talking or deliberately drown him out. People were armed but only with stunners. It was all right to take offense and to challenge a person to a duel, and victory with the stunner was considered vindication. But information presented in the free zone was privileged; a person could not carry a grudge or insult beyond this region. I realize this may sound ludicrous to a planetary person who has not seen it in action, and certainly there were violations, but it was a surprisingly effective system for the widely divergent personalities and cultures of the Belt. We had a variant of it in the Navy where enlisted personnel could let off steam by talking, bragging, or cussing out officers, and on occasion the officers were there and cussed them back, but it was all "off the record." Here among pirates it tended to be more violent, but we of the Navy were familiar with the principle. I knew this was the one place I could learn what I wanted. Here, people would talk without fear.

I took Brinker, the former pirate captain, because I needed a bodyguard. I was, after all, a potential target, and some pirates were less honorable than others. I also needed a woman. Not for sex; my interest in this older woman was hardly of that nature, and I had indeed seen to it that no man touched her. It was for appearance, so that I would not be solicited by local women for sex or by men for companionship. I wanted simply to talk and listen, without being unduly vulnerable. Brinker had agreed to serve me, and she was doing so; she had proved herself to be an extremely efficient computer technician and an intelligent woman. I still did not like her personally and had not forgiven her for the deaths of my refugee companions fourteen years before, but I respected her nature. She had blinding speed and unerring aim with laser or stunner—that was the bodyguard aspect—without seeming to be a bodyguard. She also was conversant with pirate ways, and that was important; I had such an inherent antipathy to pirates that I risked a blunder and needed spot advice. And as it happened, I did want to talk to her about a certain matter.

We took a shuttle to the dome of Bright Hope. It was anchored to a stone fragment hardly larger than itself, but, of course, far more massive. The planetoid spun, and the dome bestrode its axis. Thus this was a circular settlement, like those of Leda; the city floor was a band around its hull where centrifugal force was one gee. The dome was oriented on the sun, leaving the planetoid in shadow. Thus, inside, the focused sunlight came always from the seeming horizon, and there was no night. The residents simply shut off the light from their houses when it was time for night, and slept while the light continued to charge their home-energy reservoirs. It was a primitive system, but effective.

Sergeant Heller accompanied us but remained with the shuttle. I would signal if I needed him. Brinker and I walked to the tavern. She was in a dress that enhanced her spare figure appropriately, while I wore Jupiter civvies—hardly more anonymous here than my captain's uniform. Anonymity was not the point; no stranger could be anonymous here. I was merely signaling that this was not an official trip.

The tavern was surprisingly large, and there were perhaps a hundred men and women in it. Evidently this was the main social nexus of Bright Hope. We showed our stunners to the clerk at the entry, whose eyes widened as he recognized me. "You know what you're getting into, Cap'n?" he asked.

I nodded, accepted back my stunner, and waited while he checked Brinker's. The point of the check was not to disarm customers but to make sure that their weapons could not harm the premises or precipitate blood feuds on the premises. Then we entered and found seats at a central table.

I looked around. This place could have been taken from a page of thousand-year-past history. There was no automation in view; the crude wooden tables were served by human waitresses, or more correctly, bar girls. The customers were informally, even raggedly, garbed in simple trousers, shirts, and boots, the women in low- and high-cut dresses. The beverage of choice was ale, foaming in big pewter mugs.

I concealed my reaction. In the Juclip, wood was a precious commodity, because of the space and time it required to grow it, and home-brewed intoxicants hardly existed, since the commercial processors were so much more efficient. Here in the Belt the sunlight was more concentrated and anchorages for domes common, so farming of all types, including tree farming, was relatively simple. Thus wood was cheaper than artificial material, and it showed.

A waitress arrived with steins of ale for us. We hadn't ordered; it seemed this was standard. We paid, and Brinker reminded me to pay a little extra; this was a "tip," a gratuity to the waitress for her service. I had heard of such a thing but never before experienced it; Brinker was already helping me.

The floor show commenced: dusky-skinned young women with full breasts and skirts formed of grass. Grass! Nowhere in the Juclip did grass like that grow! The girls were of Melanesian stock, as were many folk in the Belt, and they did their best to preserve fragments of the historical culture they identified with. Watching them move their bodies, I mentally applauded their cultural effort. I suppose the commander of a Jupiter Task Force is supposed to be above noticing such an elementary thing as sex appeal in natives, but I was between marriages and quite tired of the Tail. These local women were of course off limits to Navy personnel, by my own order, because venereal disease did indeed exist in this undisciplined region of space. But psychologically this made them forbidden fruit, and in any event there is something about a well-moved grass skirt. . . .

I forced my attention, if not my eyes, to business. "As you know," I murmured to Brinker, "we have gained a ship."

"And lost two," she said. "You're lucky you didn't wipe yourself out."

"Yes. Inexperience was very nearly disastrous. I need an experienced captain for the new ship—one I can trust."

She gazed at me. "You are asking for a recommendation?"

"No. Can I trust you with such a ship?"

"I am a pirate. You know that."

"My staff advised me to be open-minded about pirates," I said. "It is not easy. I did not want to hire you, but you have served well. You could serve better. I am prepared to provide you with the means to escape my command and revert to your old ways—if you undertake not to do so. Will you serve me as the captain of a fighting ship?"

Brinker was a hard, controlled woman, but now her eyes shone with tears. "Yes," she said. "For such a command—body, mind, and soul."

That, from this particular person, was the ultimate commitment. "I will settle for loyalty," I said. "The Navy way. Discipline by the book."

"Yes."

"And it ends when the mission does, without record. You are, after all, a civilian, without security clearance."

"Yes." Her secret past remained secret, officially.

"I will see to the assignment," I said.

She shook her head ruefully. "I think this is the first time in my life I have said yes to any man three times in succession."

"It is the first time I have given a fighting ship to a pirate." But my talent told me this was the proper gesture. It was command that lured Brinker, not piracy. And I knew she could do the job. This assignment could save many lives.

A tall, elegant man of about forty approached our table, trailing a woman and a girl. He paused, glancing at me. "May we join you, stranger?" he inquired politely in English.

"Happy to have you, stranger," I responded, aware that in this region *stranger* was equivalent to *mister* or *sir*. "If you don't find it crowded."

"Cozy, not crowded," he said with a smile, fetching chairs from the nearby tables and fitting them around ours. He and his companions sat down. It was tight but feasible. "I thought you might like information, and I possess the best."

"Yes," I agreed. "Let me introduce myself. I am—"

"Let's keep it anonymous for the present," he interrupted with a smile. "Or at least on a first-name basis."

Already I was reading him. This was no casual encounter! He was a highly disciplined man who recognized me and had sought me out. "As you prefer, stranger. I am Hope, and my companion is Isobel."

"Charmed," he said. "I am Straight; this is my wife, Flush, and my daughter Roulette."

Straight! But I damped down my reaction. "How quaint," I said. "Your family is like mine, with symbolic names. I have sisters named Faith and Spirit."

Straight smiled pleasantly. "Indeed! I was certain we would get along."

The waitress arrived again. She glanced at Straight and almost dropped her tray of ale.

"At ease, wench!" Roulette snapped.

The waitress recovered herself and set down three new mugs. Straight paid her generously and with flair, as if long accustomed to this. Then he refocused on me. "I'm sure you have questions, Hope. Perhaps I can be of service."

Questions! An understatement! But still I kept it quiet. "As a matter of fact I do," I agreed. "I am concerned that the natives here seem hostile or fearful of the Navy, when it should be otherwise. But they won't say why."

"Elementary, Hope! The Navy is here only for a moment; the pirates are eternal. When the Navy departs, the pirates will return—and take reprisals against any colonists who collaborated with the enemy."

I knocked my forehead with the heel of my hand. "Of course! Why didn't I think of that?"

"Because you are not a pirate, Captain."

I nodded. "And you are." Yes, we knew each other's identities!

"Piracy has a long tradition in the Belt, Hope," he said blandly. "The Carolines are famous for their coconut-toddy orgies—another tradition. There are other points of interest, such as the huge stone coins, or the ruins left by a mysterious alien civilization. Tradition is important, where law is not."

"Oh?" I asked, interested. "Nonhuman artifacts?" In the tavern, music was starting, and some couples were dancing.

"My daughter is fascinated by those ruins," he said. "Tell him about them, Rue."

"I'd as soon kiss a snake," Roulette said.

I looked at her more carefully. She was stunningly beautiful, like a female jaguar, with red hair and deep gray eyes and fine lines, and righteous anger fairly radiated from her as she glared at me. She was not pretending; she hated me, and her father knew it.

"You don't like him?" Straight inquired mildly of his daughter. "How can that be, when you don't even know him?" My question exactly!

She made a facial gesture as of spitting. "I know what he is!"

"I doubt it," Straight said. "Ask him to dance with you."

"That isn't necessary," I said quickly.

"Ah, but it is," Straight said. "It is never wise to judge a person without proper knowledge of him. My daughter obeys me until another man breaks her will." He looked at Roulette, and his face hardened abruptly.

Roulette flushed. She jumped up, her chair crashing to the floor behind her, her right hand flashing into her blouse and emerging with a small stunner. Then she froze, for Brinker's stunner was pointed at Roulette's left eye. None of the rest of us had moved.

Roulette's flush receded. Slowly she put away her weapon; it seemed she had a holster under her left armpit. "Would you care to dance, stranger?" she asked me.

Now I was thoroughly intrigued. "Certainly, Roulette," I agreed, standing. I knew that Brinker would cover my rear, as it were; I have never seen a faster draw or more accurate aim than hers.

Roulette turned abruptly and walked with me to the dance area. She was graceful indeed, in motion. Behind, I heard Straight say: "You did not learn that move in the Navy, Isobel."

"Perhaps not," Brinker agreed wryly.

We reached the dance floor, and Roulette turned to enter my arms. Her figure was like that of the proverbial hourglass, with a remarkably generous bosom and a waist so tiny I wondered whether she constricted it with a corset. But when I put my hand on it, her flesh was soft, not rigid, and her waist was supple. Her shape was genuine.

The so-called ballroom dancing was one of the arts I had mastered in Basic Training; the Navy did not leave such things to chance. I was familiar with the moves, and my talent enabled me to pick up her variations, but I hardly needed to, for she was skilled and light on her feet. I had danced with many women but none like this. She was caviar.

"Why do you hate me?" I asked into her fragrant hair.

"Because you come to destroy my father," she answered, her body tensing.

"Why, then, does he seek me out?"

"He is a clever man. He always understands his enemies."

More interesting yet! "Why does he throw us together?"

"That is too horrible to contemplate!" Again she tensed; she meant it.

"What horror is this?"

Her dance step did not falter, but she turned her lovely face to gaze into my eyes with such muted yet intense rage that I was daunted. Truly she hated me! "Your very touch appalls me," she murmured.

"I have no designs on you," I said. "We do not mix with the natives in that manner."

"I have killed two men who tried to, as you so quaintly put it, mix."

What continued to bother me was that she was serious. She spoke of murder as if it were justified, and she felt justified. "They tried to force it?" I asked.

"One thought I was bluffing; I gutted him with my knife. The other thought I was unconscious; I severed his spinal column at the neck."

"I saw my older sister raped," I said. "When she was as old as you are now. She was beautiful, as you are—not as pronounced of figure, but of a lovely face and an innocent mind. If I had had a knife, I would have done as you did. But the pirates had disarmed me and tied me. As it was, I swore to extirpate piracy from the system."

Her reaction surprised me. "Where was her own knife?"

"She didn't carry one. She regarded weapons as unfeminine. They held her down and did it."

She stiffened again. Her whole body reflected the swift passions of her mind. "Several? Who?"

"Pirates of the Juclip. Their leader was known as the Horse."

"Where is he now?"

"Dead, I believe. My younger sister blinded and castrated him, and probably his own men killed him. We set them adrift in space."

"I like your little sister." Then she shifted moods again, mercurially. Her left hand came up and clubbed me on the side of the head. Reading her blow, I shifted away from it, so the impact was less than it seemed.

"Damn you!" she cried as she struck. Then she tore away and strode back to the table.

There was a smattering of applause from the adjacent tables. "I saw you didn't goose her," a man said. "So it must've been what you whispered in her ear. What's your secret?"

"I have a certain way with words," I said wryly, and walked to the table. Roulette was strange indeed! She had killed men who had assaulted her, and approved my sister's mode of vengeance against a rapist. She had just begun to soften toward me, then reacted savagely, as angry at herself as at me.

Ah, there was the key! She didn't *want* to like me, or anything relating to me! She wanted to maintain her original hatred, and I had made that difficult. Her father was a pirate, and she hated all who opposed him. Yet her father evinced none of this emotion himself; to him, it was more like playing a game of skill with a respected opponent.

Ironically, I now understood Roulette's attitude well

enough. I felt the same way—about pirates. My situation, and my advisers, were requiring me to modify my rage against the breed, and I didn't like that. A prejudice is always most comfortable when undisturbed.

"I regret I upset your daughter," I said as I resumed my seat.

Straight smiled. "Few men stir Rue's emotion as you have."

"And the others are dead," I agreed.

"They were not worthy of her."

"So it seems." I changed the subject. "May we exchange introductions now?"

"By all means. I am the leader of the Solomons."

The pirate band we planned to tackle next. "And I am the Commander of the Jupiter Naval Task Force, whose mission it is to eliminate the piracy of the Belt."

"Not merely the incursion of the Marianas?"

"As you point out, a temporary presence at one location does not eliminate the threat to it. To protect Jupiter's long-term interests I must destroy all piracy here."

"So it seems we must do battle," Straight said. "I really prefer to conduct my business in peace."

"It is an illegal business."

"True. But that is because interplanetary law is not always responsive to the needs of the people. My organization serves such a need, and serves it well. We are, in fact, a legitimate business in every respect except for the technicality of an outdated law. Many of our clients are important figures in their governments, and few have cause to complain."

"Unfortunately, another band overstepped the bounds of interplanetary propriety," I pointed out. "It is foolish to spit in the face of the Colossus."

"Agreed. But that is the Marianas band, noted for arrogance and indiscretion. That band and its kindred perhaps require disciplining. But why move against others who have not overstepped and are not likely to do so?"

He was making uncomfortable sense. "Jupiter does not distinguish between pirates. Too often before, Jupiter has dealt with specific annoyances when, in fact, they were but symptoms of a larger malady. This time we propose to deal with the malady, though it may require the excision of some healthy flesh as well as the diseased."

"I perceive the logic." He shrugged regretfully. "Can you be sure that you are not placing your mission in peril by tackling more than you may need to? I do not seek this battle."

"You are too competent to leave at my rear," I said.

"Shall we then establish reasonable terms of encounter? There is no sense harming more people or wasting more hardware than necessary."

"I agree. How about a region of space outside the inhabited Belt, off the Solar Ecliptic, so that no settlements are affected?"

"Excellent. Two fleets in space, alone. Shall we say in forty-eight hours?"

"Agreed."

Straight glanced at his silent wife. I saw now that though she was more heavyset than her daughter, she had similar bones. She would have been a phenomenal figure, in her prime, but twenty years of comfortable living had fleshed her out too much. That offered an insight into Straight's family life. "Shall we go home, my dear? Our business here seems to have been concluded."

They departed. "That man is dangerous," Brinker said.

"So is his daughter! We'd better get back to the ship ourselves."

We did so. As we traveled, Brinker briefed me on another aspect of pirate diplomacy. "Straight is trying to vamp you with his daughter."

"I noticed. And she is having none of it."

"Not necessarily. You have to appreciate the pirate mode of courtship."

"Courtship? That girl hates men!"

"No. She is strongly attracted to you. She hates herself for it, because she perceives love as a weakness, a submission. Pirate men don't love, they rape; pirate women don't seduce, they fight. Sex is a battlefield."

"You are in a position to know," I said doubtfully. "Is that what turned you off it?"

She grimaced. "Partly. But mainly, my love of command

was greater than my interest in sex or romance. It remains so."

"What are the details of pirate courtship?"

"The groom kidnaps the bride and rapes her. She is given a knife. If she doesn't kill him then, she is his. That's the essence. The details differ from clan to clan."

"Roulette says she has killed two suitors."

"Surely she has. That girl's a hellion."

"Why, then, would her father introduce her to me? I'm not going to kidnap her and rape her!"

"The courtship convention is often honored more in the forms than in the reality. If you defeat Straight in battle, his daughter might be worth a considerable price."

"I wouldn't buy her either!"

"But if you wanted her, you wouldn't kill her father. A pirate would, but not a Navy man. She's his life insurance."

"But I don't want her!"

She glanced sidelong at me. "Don't you?"

I reconsidered. "Damn it, I *do* want her. Sexually, at any rate. I never saw a better-formed woman, and I'm sick of the Tail. But that doesn't mean I'd let that affect my campaign strategy."

"Straight evidently is gambling that it will. Also, he may feel you are a good match for her. He doesn't want war, he wants legitimacy. Many pirates are similar. *I* am. He's covering all his bets."

I shook my head. "I don't like being covered."

"I know the feeling."

I was troubled, but at the moment I had pressing other matters to attend to. Soon we were consulting with my staff. "Brinker will command the captured pirate destroyer on a de facto basis," I told Sergeant Smith. "Cobble together a competent crew in a hurry."

"Yes, sir." He got on it, taking Brinker with him.

"We're going to meet the Solomons in battle in deep space in forty-eight hours," I said to the others. "Make the preparations." Actually, two days would not get us out of the Belt, but the principle of avoiding a settled region remained.

"But our supply ship arrives in thirty-six hours," Spirit protested. "That won't give us enough time to organize."

"We'll locate a vacant planetoid and use it as a temporary supply base," Emerald said. Obviously she had a specific planetoid in mind, as such things were not to be found just like that. If I seem to suggest that things fell into place for us conveniently, that is only because my staff arranged it so. "Our lesser ships will be able to protect that with the pincushion defense." She turned to me. "You agree, sir?"

I grasped for an answer, as I hadn't been paying full attention. "I suppose so."

"You have something more important on your mind, *sir?*"

"No," I said, embarrassed.

"A woman?"

"Ridiculous!"

"Tell us about her," Emerald urged mischievously. "You haven't had a really good woman since you had me."

I saw Juana smile obliquely at that, but she said nothing.

I sighed. "It seems a pirate chief is trying to fix me up with his daughter, for political reasons. Covering his bets."

"A pirate wench?" Spirit asked. "Is she clean?"

"This one would be," I said. Then I reacted against the mere supposition. "It's ludicrous! She has killed two men who wanted her."

"That fatal appeal," Emerald said. "I must remember it."

"Not *this* marriage!" Mondy objected, and they laughed. The two of them had grown closer in the past few days.

They returned to the details of strategy while I tried to shake off my own foolishness. So Roulette had a body of amazing proportions; why should that matter to me? Juana was as pretty as anyone, and—but that wasn't the point. Juana was no longer supposed to be of interest to me in that way, and neither was Emerald. I was looking for novelty; and that, indeed, Roulette was. Novelty and forbidden fruit. A pirate wench was certainly not for a Navy captain!

Sergeant Smith returned with Brinker. "I have set it up, sir. If you will just sign this waiver—"

"Waiver?"

"She's a civilian employee, sir. For her to command a Navy ship—it's irregular."

"She will not command a Navy ship," I pointed out. "It is a captured pirate vessel; and anyway, this is to be mostly off the record." Nevertheless, I signed the waiver. If trouble came of this, the blame should be mine, not his.

Brinker started to go, but I stopped her. "Sit in on the strategy session, Captain. You may have input."

"Yes, sir," she said gratefully.

Emerald leaned toward her. "What does she look like?"

Brinker was startled, glancing at me. "My staff has will and mischief of its own, Little Foot," I said with resignation. That was Brinker's song-nickname: the foot with no man to shoe it. "Satisfy their curiosity, so we can get on with business."

Brinker nodded. Then she made a gesture with her two hands, the classic hourglass shape. "Eighteen. Fire-hair. Face would launch a thousand ships. Imperious. Deadly."

There was appreciative laughter. "No wonder he wants her!" Mondy exclaimed. "There's nothing like that in this task force!"

Emerald slammed a backhand into his chest. It was her way of showing affection. She was not ashamed to show it, now.

We met the Solomon fleet at the designated spot in space. Emerald had planned carefully, protecting each major ship with several escorts. She knew from Mondy's research that the Solomons had three cruisers and a carrier with fifty drones, and a number of support ships; unless we used our battleship, we would be overmatched. But their ships were old, not as fast as ours, and their observation equipment was obsolete; at any reasonable distance, they would be able to detect our ships only as shapeless blips. Since we were doing battle in open space, this seemed to be no disadvantage; they did not need to track from any distance or to distinguish ships from possible

Belt fragments; they could use visual identification up close. With their superior force of drones, they could saturate our defense and put us in immediate difficulty. Yet Emerald, instead of concentrating our force to overpower them, split it in two. She sent one cruiser, three destroyers, the carrier, and all six of our tugs to meet the enemy fleet, keeping the rest of our fleet back.

I did not want to interfere, but I could not make sense of this. "Why split the fleet?" I demanded.

"The supply convoy is late," she explained. "That leaves us all right on food and fuel, since the battle with the Carolines was brief and there was not much maneuvering. But after this battle we'll be low on ammunition, so—"

"Low on ammunition? We should have plenty!"

"Not after double-loading the drones. So we'll have to establish a defensive base for them, where the supply tanker comes."

"Double-loading the drones? They'll be too heavy to accelerate properly!"

"Yes. That's why we're clustering them with the tugs. The tugs can goose them up to speed."

"Clustered? Those drones can only fire straight forward! If you cluster five of them together, they'll fire five shots at the same target when one is enough! No wonder we'll run short of ammunition! And what of the tugs? They aren't fighting ships! The enemy drones will come up on them and destroy them the moment our drones leave them behind."

"I don't think so," she said with a smile. "They'll be boosting our drones backward, so ours will be able to cover what's behind."

"Backward! Are you sure you know what you're doing?"

"I'd better," she said wryly. "Your career depends on it."

I turned away, ill at ease. I was no strategist, which was why she had the job, but this certainly seemed like nonsense to me. Nevertheless, I shut my mouth and watched my screen. The *Sawfish* had set course for the projected supply-base planetoid; we would arrive there soon after the battle commenced. The supply ship, behind schedule—

such delays were endemic in the Navy!—would arrive twelve hours later. I hoped our backward drones had not been blasted out of space by then, and the *Hempstone Crater* with them. I had never heard of a battle order as strange as this!

The Solomons' fleet was ready, but evidently Straight was as perplexed as I about the lineup. The pirates seemed to hesitate; then their fleet, too, divided, half of it going to meet ours, the other half moving slowly to intercept our battleship where they perceived it to be heading, beyond the planetoid. "Good enough," Emerald remarked.

"But if we land on that deserted rock while they remain in space," I said, "we'll be unable to get spaceborne without getting blasted!" Now I wished we had arranged to do battle in true deep space, a few light-days out of the Belt.

"But they will be unable to come in after us there," she said. "The pincushion is virtually impregnable when the fleets are nearly even."

I retreated to silence again. Emerald was supposed to be a strategic genius, but little of that had shown so far, and this arrangement seemed nonsensical. Why allow ourselves to be pinned on a planetoid? It was like a position in the game of checkers, with one king pinning the enemy's king to the edge of the board; the pinned king was indeed impregnable in its bastion, but it could not escape it. It was better to be in the center of the board with free movement; this was elementary.

But I had not paid proper attention to the strategy discussion and did not want to ask too many ignorant questions. The rest of the staff seemed high on this plan, so there had to be something to it. I was, in effect, a casualty of the pirate's daughter Roulette; I had been distracted by foolish thoughts of her when I should have been paying individual, undivided attention to the staff meeting. If I had been planning strategy myself, my fleet would be in a bad situation now, and it did not please me to realize that the cunning pirate Straight had probably planned it exactly that way. Damn that divinely shaped girl! And damn me for being distracted by that shape. I had been too long between wives.

Now the pirate half-fleet swerved at low velocity, coming around behind our fleet. Good God, we were already giving them the advantage of position! The cruisers could fire in any direction, but the drones were far more limited. The drones were now taking off in clusters, angling out from the carrier, and the superior force of drones from the larger pirate carrier was starting in pursuit. What did Emerald think she was doing?

The essence of the problem was this: Drones and small ships, destroyers included, had to fire forward, for their drive jets were in the rear, and their stabilizing spin prevented side firing. So in order to fire at a craft coming up from behind, a drone had to cut its acceleration, damp its spin, rotate in place, point backward, resume its stabilizing spin, resume its acceleration, and fire. The process required several minutes, and, of course, it made the ship a sitting duck for that period. That had been our problem in the *Discovered Check*, during the last battle. Our drones, double loaded, would be clumsier, and take longer to turn. So they would have to flee instead, and once they were well away from the rest of the fleet, the enemy drones could perform their own turning maneuver and orient directly on our fleet.

This, too, about drones: They were remote controlled. They were expendable. So they could be sent charging in to swamp a ship's defenses. Half of them might be shot down, but if just one of them scored on a cruiser, the pirates would be ahead, for a hundred drones were not worth more than one cruiser. The cruiser was crewed with living, trained people, while the drones were merely machines, operated by trained personnel in the carrier, one to a drone. To the operator, it was like being aboard the drone; his control was immediate, but when the drone was destroyed, the operator survived. Thus drones were very popular battle instruments, but they used a lot of fuel and required a lot of upkeep, so the Navy used them sparingly. Carriers were vulnerable when their drones were lost, so had to have strong escort fleets. And if a carrier was taken out, all its drones went dead in space. One lucky shot could completely reverse the progress of a battle. So the fact was, the age of carriers was passing as planet-sited missiles became more sophisticated; the Navy just didn't feel it expedient to recognize that yet. The old order of "carrier admirals" remained in power but perhaps not for much longer.

However, for this limited action against the pirate band, the drones of a carrier were a potent force, if properly managed. Things were suitably primitive in the Belt.

Still, Emerald's effort worried me. If the enemy took our drones out of commission, our whole fleet would be in trouble.

The pirates closed on our drones from behind, accelerating at higher gee, coming near firing range. I winced. "Now," I heard Emerald murmur.

Then our drone clusters separated into their component drones and leaped backward at the enemy drones. Abruptly, the region blossomed with explosions: The enemy drones were being blasted out of space.

Then I remembered: those tugs, accelerating our clusters *backward*. When our drones separated and accelerated on their own, they were already aimed at the enemy. No delay for turning. Suddenly it all made sense.

"Sixty percent casualty to enemy craft, estimated," a technician reported.

Spirit stood, stretching her arms. "Congratulations, Emerald; you've done it. We now have a sufficient advantage in drones."

Emerald was obviously pleased but suppressed it. "The battle is not yet over."

Maybe not, but the Solomons' striking arm had been truncated. Their fifty drones had been reduced to twenty without loss of any of our twenty-eight. We could now go after their carrier and quite possibly take it out before their remaining drones could turn and return.

Juana arrived. "News, sir."

"What is it?" I asked.

"New pirate fleet has been sighted. Estimated time of arrival: 2200 hours."

"Another fleet?" I demanded. "Whose?"

"Fiji. Two cruisers, ten destroyers."

"No carrier?"

"No carrier, sir. It appears to be a fast-moving raider force."

I pondered. We had more large ships but fewer destroyers. We could probably stop the Fiji pirate raid, but not while we were locked in battle with the Solomons. As it was, this new fleet meant disaster.

I consulted hastily with Emerald. "Damn!" she swore. "We can't handle two fleets together! We'll have to go into the pincushion defense with our whole fleet. That's the only way we can hold them off."

"Do it, then," I agreed. First we had to save our hides, then tackle new pirates.

As it happened, we were already headed for the planetoid, and so were our drones. We could complete our landing on it before the Solomons could prevent us.

But Straight, canny tactician that he was, found a way to nullify part of our effort. He diverted part of his force to intercept our incoming supply ship. We couldn't go to its rescue without becoming vulnerable to the Fiji fleet approaching from the other direction.

The supply ship and its escorts decelerated, staying clear; the pirates couldn't catch it without exposing their flank to us, but they had effectively balked its rendezvous with the planetoid. It was a kind of impasse.

We held a hasty staff meeting to consider the new situation. "We need those supplies," Commander Phist said, concerned. "We're low on ammunition and fuel now."

"We can't get them," Emerald said. "I had something in mind for the Solomons, but we aren't set up to deal with a fleet at our rear."

"You're making what may be an unwarranted assumption," Commander Repro said. "How do you know the Fijis are coming to help the Solomons?"

Mondy's eyes widened. "You're right! The Fijis are the scum of the Belt; they don't ally to anyone! They come in to pick up the pieces."

Now Emerald came alive. "Of course! They saw us gearing for battle with the Solomons, so they figure whoever wins will be so weakened that they can mop up the remainder. They're probably right."

Repro turned to me. "Sir, we have a difficult decision. I believe it would facilitate our discussion if you would let us thrash it out alone."

Startled, I glanced around at the others. "You don't want me participating?"

"You high again?" Emerald demanded of Repro. "You don't just kick the Task Force Commander out of a staff meeting!"

Repro waved a hand. "My mind is sharp enough at the moment, thank you, Rising Moon." He turned to me. "Indulge me, sir, if you will."

He was up to something. He was the one who had literally dreamed up this present organization; behind the addiction he retained a devious and penetrating mind. He understood people as well as I did, albeit in a different fashion. "I shall return in half an hour," I said, rising and departing.

I was curious what was afoot, but it was my policy to allow my officers to function in their own manner whenever possible. I knew I was no genius in any of their specialties; if they could plan a campaign better without me, so be it. I trusted them to do what they honestly deemed appropriate. Yet I wondered what insight Repro, a psychologist and propagandist, could have on a battle in space.

I made a routine inspection of the ship, verifying that things were in order. I like to think that my seeming unconcern lent confidence to the personnel; they knew that something was going on but could not believe it was serious when I wasn't bothering with the staff meeting. I wondered whether that could have been what Repro had in mind; he was, after all, also the Morale Officer. I decided that could not be it; why have a staff meeting at all, if reassurance was the only purpose? Beautiful Dreamer had something specific to present.

Meanwhile, we were rendezvousing with the planetoid, decelerating for our landing. A ship the mass of the *Sawfish* could not land on a true planet; the stress of gee would break it up. But a planetoid like this had so little gee that we would have to anchor our ships to it. The pirates would not dare approach until they got into a solid formation, and by that time we'd have our landing. The pincushion was what it sounded like: a ball of rock with ships sticking out all around like pins, able to fire in every direction. Enemy approach was almost impossible because of the massed firepower of the anchored ships.

But that cutoff of our supply ship was worrisome indeed. The waging of war in space requires enormous amounts of CT fuel; the drones are especially demanding in that respect, because of their high acceleration. We could finish the battle we were in, but the Fiji fleet would find us virtually dead in space. Our lifeline had been cut. I couldn't really blame Emerald for this; no one could have predicted the intervention of a third fleet at this time, though it certainly made piratical sense in retrospect. There were sharks out here in the Belt, feeding on each other's wounded carcasses. We were suddenly in trouble, and I didn't like it at all. This was, after all, no practice exercise with rubber knives; our lives were on the line, not to mention our pride. We could be about to suffer the very fate projected for us by the politicians of Jupiter.

I returned to the staff meeting when my uneasy half-hour exile expired. "Have you worked everything out?" I inquired somewhat wryly.

They were serious and somewhat nervous; I picked up the emanations. It was as though they were the members of a jury about to deliver a verdict of guilty, and not easy about it. Strange indeed!

"Sir, we have thrashed this out," Spirit said, speaking with atypical formality. "We have concluded that our best course is to proffer our surrender to the Solomons' fleet."

I felt faint. I found my gee-couch and sank into it. "Please say again?"

"Straight is a halfway decent man," Spirit continued. "He generally keeps his word, and he's not bloodthirsty. Go to him under flag of truce and present our situation. We could hold out here with the pincushion, leaving the Solomons to meet the Fiji fleet alone. If he will give us safe passage to our supply ship, we will vacate this base, which is the only usable one in this region, and allow him to take it. He will then be able to use the pincushion himself to hold off the Fijis, while we can return to Jupiter, having failed our mission. We'll have to provide him hostages, of course; he can choose among us for them, and ransom us back to Jupiter in due course."

I found my voice. "How can you recommend such a thing! We aren't even in serious trouble, as long as we hold this rock!"

Mondy spoke. "Sir, we have analyzed this to our satisfaction. We are not set up to withstand an extended siege, which is what we'll face after the Fijis drive the Solomons away. In the end we'll have to capitulate from hunger and power depletion, unless we can get our supplies, and it is much, much better to deal with Straight. We are being realistic. We can save all our lives and equipment this way."

At the expense of the mission! I looked at each in turn. All of them were serious, yet there was something they were concealing from me. "Now look," I said. "I'm not going to proffer surrender while you lay a trap! I don't like this notion at all, but I won't deal in dishonor."

"No trap, sir," Emerald said. "Commander Repro has made an excellent if unusual case, and we agree. You must go to Straight with our offer."

Again I looked at them. There was no banter, no nicknaming. I had never seen them, as a group, so nervous yet united. They definitely were not giving up, yet they really did want me to surrender to the pirate.

I had assembled this excellent staff, under Repro's guidance, and Repro himself was the agent here. I trusted his judgment of these officers. They knew better than I did what was required. I could overrule them, for I was the Commander; the final responsibility was mine. But I was reluctant to do that. "You won't explain?" I asked.

"After this crisis passes, sir, we will explain," Spirit said.

I sighed. "I hope you have not lost your collective wits! All of us will be court-martialed for pusillanimity when we are ransomed back to Jupiter. All of our careers will be finished."

"But we will suffer no further losses," Emerald said. "We are thinking not of pride but of the greatest good."

I turned away, unwilling to believe it. My staff—united in defeat when we had won the first part of the engagement? I had sworn to extirpate piracy from the face of the System; how could they expect me to capitulate? My whole will was toward the destruction of the pirate power—or death in the attempt. Simple surrender the moment the going got tough? *Surrender?!* There would not only be a court-martial, there would be a scandal; and I would be the leading witness for the prosecution.

Yet I had to do it. I could not go against their collective judgment without violating my belief in my own talent, and I knew my sister would not betray me. She, like the others, sincerely believed this was the best course. But I was angry and perplexed. This made no sense I could see.

I signaled the Solomons' command cruiser. "Captain Hubris requests clearance for one ship for personal parley."

There was some dickering with intermediaries, then Straight himself came onscreen. He was dressed informally, as if on vacation; I would not have figured him for either pirate or military commander if I had not encountered him before. "Parley, Captain?"

I was not going to do this thing on the air! "I will come to you under white flag. Just don't shoot my transport vessel out of space."

He considered briefly. "I'll send a ship to pick you up."

Smart counter! His own ship would not be booby-trapped. A pirate had to consider pirate devices. "Agreed."

I gave the order, so that our gunners would let his ship pass. It turned out to be a mere gunboat, hardly enough to threaten our battleship but surely a terror against farmers on the rock fragments of the Belt. I boarded alone; a bodyguard would have been pointless here.

In due course I arrived at the pirate cruiser. It was elaborate inside but not in the manner of a fighting ship. It was a gambling den with lush carpets and fancy lounges and games of chance of many kinds. It wouldn't be much use in battle, especially not against a competent Navy cruiser.

The Solomons were not in as strong a position as it had seemed.

And my staff wanted me to surrender.

I was conducted to the gambler's office. "Parley?" Straight repeated.

I came immediately to the point. "My staff advises me that I must bargain with you on terms of surrender."

He smiled. "Captain, you pulled a very nice maneuver there with the drones. But we are hardly ready to surrender."

"Not you. Us."

An eyebrow elevated. "You—to me?"

"We're low on fuel and ammunition. You have blocked off our resupply ship. The Fiji fleet is approaching. We prefer to surrender to you, rather than be starved out by them. All we ask is safe passage for our ships through your line so they can return to Jupiter without losses."

He shook his head. "Surely you don't expect me to accept that at face value."

I grimaced. "I hardly accept it myself. But I trust my staff, and my staff informs me that this is the best way out of an untenable situation. If we do further battle, the Fijis will wipe out our remnants, and that would not be good for either of our fleets."

"True. But we could separate without fighting. I never sought this battle."

"If we could trust each other," I said. "My staff evidently feels we can't."

Straight shook his head. "There is little honor among pirates. If I lost power, the Solomons would quickly fragment, until some other leader arose, probably after a good deal of violence. And I would lose power if I made a suspicious deal with the Jupiter Navy. I can't retreat; the wolves I face in the Belt are worse than those of the Navy."

"My staff probably understands that." I made a gesture of impotence. "So it seems I must surrender. It is not of my choosing or liking. It means the end of my career, and the abrogation of my oath." I spoke bitterly; how could my staff do this to me?

Straight nodded. "I understand that. I think I would

have preferred to finish our battle. You realize we would
have to take hostages: you and your leading officers."

"Yes. And ransom us back to Jupiter."

"We could use the leverage of the hostages to force complete surrender of your ships."

"Would such honor as you have permit that?"

It was his turn to grimace. "No. I am regarded as a fool
in some quarters. I am a businessman, and my business depends on the validity of my word. Otherwise my wealthy
clients would desert me."

"So it is feasible for us to surrender to you, rather than
to another band. I would have preferred some other
course."

He looked at the ceiling. "I remember courting Flush.
She was the most beautiful wench in the Belt in those
days. I raided her dome and carried her away and raped
her that night. Oh, how she fought! I bear the scars of her
nails and teeth yet." He showed his forearm where indeed
there were scars.

I looked at him, startled. What had this to do with the
subject of surrender?

"My aunt, who never liked me, gave her a blade," he
continued. "But when Flush had it at my throat, she did
not use it. And so she was mine, in the pirate fashion, and I
have trusted her with my life ever since."

"She had the knife, but surrendered to you," I said, not
certain I had made the correct connection. He was definitely telling me something important, but I could not yet
fathom what.

"And her clan joined mine when they saw she was mine,
and they have been loyal throughout. I never raped her
again, never had to. Of course, we put out word that she
fought me for two years, in the bedroom, until she was
gravid with Rue, but that was a matter of protocol, so there
was no dishonor on her clan."

"You seem like a happy family," I said, somewhat taken
aback. This was not the sort of news one gave an enemy.

"As such things go. We honor the tradition."

I shook my head. "No offense intended, but that tradition is foreign to me."

"It is best to understand your enemy." He shrugged. "Give me a little time to ponder your offer. Roulette will entertain you in the interim."

"I don't gamble," I said.

"You are gambling now."

Touché! He smiled as he touched a button on his desk. In a moment his daughter appeared. She wore a bright red blouse and dark red skirt. The combination reminded me of fresh blood and old blood. Yet she was as strikingly beautiful as ever, and though I condemned my masculine foolishness, I knew I wanted her. "Entertain our guest for a while," Straight told her.

Roulette fired a glance of anger at me but indicated the door. I followed her out, my emotions mixed. Again, Straight was putting me with his daughter, again against her will. But to what point? He no longer needed to dangle such bait or to evoke my interest in her to protect his situation. There could be no future in our relationship. The situation had already given Straight victory.

She led me to a game room. It was filled with gambling machines of every type. Some were old-fashioned pinballs, a staple for centuries, in which a ball rolled and bounced around in a chamber, causing ascending numeric scores. Others were the historical one-armed bandits, whose windows showed simple designs of fruits and objects; the correct combination resulted in a payoff of coins. Still others were electronic video games, with all manner of trick devices of animation and challenge. We took one that showed two space fleets about to engage in battle. Roulette took one fleet, I the other. The fleets charged each other, under our control, and the dexterity and strategy of the players determined their success.

Sad to say, Roulette tromped me. "You must have been practicing this!" I protested.

"Haven't you?" she asked acerbically.

That stopped me. I was a Naval fleet commander; couldn't I manage my mock fleet adequately? Yet I was here to surrender; perhaps that was answer enough.

"The truth is, I am not expert in tactics," I said. "It is my position to command the officers who *are* expert, so that we form an efficient team. I'm really a figurehead."

She gazed at me with mixed surprise and contempt. "My father's no figurehead! He *is* our team. He directs the battle. He supervises everything. And he has trained me to do it, too."

Now I was surprised. "You can direct a fleet in battle—a real fleet, not just a game fleet?"

"I was directing our fleet when our drones met yours." She grimaced. "You decimated us. Who directed that ploy?"

"Her name is Lieutenant Commander Emerald Sheller. She—"

"She?"

"Yes. She is our strategist, my former wife."

"You use women in positions of power?"

"Of course. We go by qualification and competence, not sex."

"Not sex? But you cast her aside when you tired of her."

"No. The situation separated us. We remain friends."

Something changed in her. "I'd like to meet her."

"You will. Your father will surely select her as a hostage."

"A hostage." She considered a moment, then turned on me a look of absolute fury as sudden and inexplicable as the one she had made the last time we met. I could read emotions but not always the causes of them. "God, I should kill you now!"

Anyone would have been surprised by this. She was sincere. She did not strike me as emotionally unbalanced, though she was certainly volatile. She believed she had reason to hate me.

So I inquired, as I usually do. "Why?"

She strode off without answer. I followed, covertly admiring her figure and her movements. Intellectually I knew it was ridiculous to desire this fiery creature, eleven years my junior, but intellect was not the motivating force.

Straight met us at his office door. "I have decided," he said. "We shall not accept your surrender."

"You insist on fighting? It is pointless while the Fijis—"

"As is flight; they would merely pursue, knowing us to be in a weakened state because of the decimation of our drones. It is necessary to deal with the Fijis firmly." His lips twitched, and I knew he was thinking of the manner he dealt with all things. "Firm" could mean anything from an admonition to destruction in space. "So we shall surrender to you."

"What?"

"You lack fuel and ammunition, but your supply ship is bringing those. We lack ammunition and food; we were not able to supply our fleet on short notice for an extended campaign. Feed us, and we'll surrender."

"No food?" I asked, bemused.

"I'll send my daughter with you as the first hostage. You may select others in due course. Just so long as we get it done before the Fijis arrive."

"But—why?"

"You have honor," Straight said. "We can trust you not to murder us. That's a good deal more than we can say for the Fijis."

"But you wouldn't have to face them if—"

"If we had your surrender? No, as I explained, we cannot retreat, and we don't have enough power at the moment to defeat them. We might get the supplies we need from you, but we could not use your hardware against them; your surrender is basically a device for safe conduct, not a commitment to fight a battle for a pirate band. But if the authority is yours, you will fight them, and we may be able to save our skins."

"I—I'll have to consult my staff," I said.

"By all means. Our boat will take you and Rue back now. But I'm sure your staff already knows."

I had never felt this stupid before. "They knew?"

"That's why they sent you. They knew I would not yield to any demand for surrender, so they reversed it, forcing my hand. They didn't tell you, because it had to be an honest offer; I can tell the difference. They outplayed me, just as they outplayed my daughter on the drone encounter. You must have one hell of a team, and one hell of a psychologist among them."

I looked at Roulette. "You knew!" I said, almost accusingly. "That's why you were so angry!"

"I guessed," she said grimly. "I can read signals, too, and I know my father. He'd never let surrender interfere with his larger plans." She shrugged beautifully. "Well, come on, Captain; the damned thing's done and I'm hoist."

And so the surrender was arranged, and a mind-bendingly beautiful girl came into my power.

Chapter 10

RAPE

Rue behaved like a confined jaguar on the trip back. She remained hostile but seemed to accept her fate. I did not try to talk to her, though I was highly conscious of her presence. Yet again I wondered: Why had her father put her into my hands? He had to be aware of the effect she had on me, for he was a shrewd judge of character and she was a figure to dazzle any man. The Solomons had not had to surrender; that had come entirely too readily, though I knew it was genuine. The Fiji threat had been only a pretext to justify an action I now realized Straight had contemplated from the outset. It was almost as if he were collaborating with my staff to unify our forces. But his daughter was irrelevant to that.

We connected with the *Sawfish*. My sister met us just inside the lock. For a moment the two women studied each other, Roulette's gaze flicking down to Spirit's four-fingered left hand. I knew she was thinking of what I had told her about Spirit's experience with pirates, and the vengeance she had taken against them. And, before a word was spoken, Roulette's attitude modified subtly. She might hate me, but she did not hate Spirit.

"This is Roulette—our hostage for the Solomons' surrender," I said somewhat lamely.

Spirit didn't even seem surprised. "I recognized the figure. I'll see her to a cabin."

"You knew," I said.

"We thought it likely," she agreed. "We showed Straight our power, and he responded."

"The game is not over yet," Roulette said.

I nodded ruefully—which term may be appropriate in more than one sense. I had served as an ignorant messen-

ger between two maneuvering forces. My staff had sent a
message of surrender, and Straight had responded with
his daughter as hostage. Move and countermove, neither
what it seemed. I felt like a pawn in the middle of the
board, watching while one side proffered the sacrifice of a
knight and the other countered with the sacrifice of a
bishop. The true significance lay not in what was done but
in what was declined.

"Arrange for rendezvous with our supply ship and for
transfer of food to the Solomons fleet," I said. "Establish liaison for working out the fine print of the surrender. And
quickly; the Fijis—"

"I can help," Roulette said. "I know the personnel to
contact in our fleet, and what they need."

There was one reason Straight had sent her! Her cooperation would greatly facilitate the process.

Spirit glanced at her appraisingly. "You have practical
training?"

"I'm my father's S-3." S-3 is the Operations section, vital.

"At your age?"

Rue smiled. "Pirates aren't subject to Naval regulations. I've been an officer since birth. It's a family corporation."

"We shall test you." Spirit took Rue away with her.

I watched them go. I remained amazed at recent developments. I was a virtual spectator of a game of strategy I
could not quite comprehend. I saw that Spirit and Roulette
understood it, though. I wish I could present what follows
in this narrative as a brilliant and successful ploy on my
part, but really it wasn't. I was merely a pawn in the guise
of a king. Or perhaps I was the king—but in chess, the king
is the most restricted and protected of pieces, though he is
the focus of the game. My sole power was in the judgment
of people and the delegation of power to them. Now they
were using that power.

I went to the bridge to discover what was going on in
space. The Fiji fleet was bearing down, heedless of the
Navy-Solomons negotiations; we were not going to be able
to rendezvous with our supply ship, organize our supervi-

sion of the Solomons, and establish our pincushion defense on the planetoid before the new enemy arrived.

"We'll vacate the base," Emerald said. "The supplies are more important."

"But we can't set up for battle in space in time," I protested. "The Fijis are in formation, while we're caught in maneuvers."

"Bad luck for us," she said with a smile.

"There's something you're not telling me," I accused her.

She turned a wide-eyed mock-innocent gaze on me. "Why, sir! Don't you trust me? Has any part of me ever been secret from you? I am but the rising moon; you are the sun."

I was annoyed but played along. "Just see that my trust is not misplaced. You supposedly subordinate officers have been very free with my command and career recently."

"We only want what's best for you, sir," she said contritely.

We vacated the planetoid, though I could see that in our haste we had to sacrifice some equipment and precious ammunition that had been in transfer between anchored ships. Reloading in a vacuum is not a rapid thing, because of the limitation of airlocks. Much better to establish temporary pressurized tents on the base. Already the Fijis were gaining booty!

Meanwhile Spirit and Roulette handled the ongoing negotiations with the Solomons. Rue was as good as her word; she knew every officer of their fleet by name, and when she spoke, they jumped. Spirit simply named the ship she wanted to contact, and Rue did the rest.

"This is Roulette, hostage aboard the Navy flagship," she said to the screen as we addressed one ship. "They have food for us, and time is short. Get me Cap'n Snake-eyes on the double." The pirate ship captain appeared in seconds. "Snake-eyes, clear a channel through our fleet for the Navy supply ship, and detach a tug to pick up their pod as they pass. What your ship needs has already been allocated. Then stand by for further orders from this ship. Commander Spirit Hubris will contact you, and you will obey her implicitly."

"Yes, sir," Snake-eyes agreed nervously.

"And relieve Seven-up of command of your forward battery. If that trigger-happy bastard fires one shot during this maneuver, my father will fire a shot at you."

Evidently that threat had meaning, for Snake-eyes blanched.

So it went. Spirit turned her head to look at me behind Rue's head, nodding affirmatively. The pirate wench was testing out competent.

Then Rue herself turned her head and shot me another glare of hate. I turned away, ashamed of myself for not being able to face her down. She was doing the job her father had dictated; none of this was for my pleasure.

What was it about her that so unmanned me? She was a striking figure of a woman, true—but so were others I had known, if to lesser degrees. Mere physical appearance was not overwhelmingly important to me. She was young; but again, I could have youth in the Officers' Tail anytime I felt the inclination, and generally I preferred to associate with women my own age. She was fiery, but so was Emerald; there was no longer much novelty in that.

"Forbidden fruit, sir."

I jumped. I was in the passage, and Juana was coming up behind me, evidently on some mission for another officer. She was my secretary but had become common property in this crisis. "What?"

"She's a pirate wench, sir. You're a Navy officer. You always did prefer forbidden fruit. You know you can't have her, so you want her. It's perfectly natural."

She was surely correct. I was having difficulty perceiving such things for myself because my own emotion was involved, nullifying much of my objectivity. As I gazed at Juana, the melody of her song passed through my mind. *O don't deceive me, O never leave me, how could you use a poor maiden so?* A lovely and sad refrain, of love no longer requited. Juana had a roommate but only to avoid the Tail; she had formed no close attachment since I deserted her by becoming an officer. She knew about the desire for the forbidden.

I glanced about. We were alone for the moment. "Anybody looking?"

"No, sir. We're all pretty busy now."

I grabbed her and kissed her. Juana wasn't even surprised; she knew me of old. She clung to me, showing more passion than she ever had when we were roommates. She remained a marvelous person. I remembered how she had taken me in hand, so to speak, during the drug episode. She did not love sex, but perhaps she loved me.

I drew back. "You're right. Forbidden fruit is best."

Her eyes were moist. "God, I miss you. Sir."

"You could go to Officer's School." If she became an officer, I could room with her again.

She smiled, shifting the mood. "I don't miss you *that* much!"

I had to laugh. "Thank you."

She started on down the passage. "You're welcome, sir."

I stood and watched her go, experiencing that special poignancy of remembrance. We had seldom been separated in the physical sense; she missed our original camaraderie as equals. Juana and I—we had been the first, for each other, in the Navy fashion, and that private bond would always remain. I had her secretarial competence, her understanding, and her friendship, but as an officer I was in a different world, and there was a certain pain in that.

And she was right. I had perhaps become somewhat jaded over the years, since I could have almost any woman I chose, through channels. The girls of the Officers' Tail were commissioned but never served as officers beyond the Tail; it was an arranged thing, and enlisted women could volunteer for that commission, bypassing Officer's Training. Some tried it for a while, then chose to revert to regular enlisted status. The same was true for enlisted men; if a female officer had a hankering for a sergeant, and he was interested, this was the route.

So I had had a fair variety of women in the Tail but had loved none of them. Love was only for Helse, my dead fiancée. But I could be attracted, and Roulette was indeed the most forbidden of creatures, for I could not truly accept any pirate. Only Spirit's wish and Repro's intercession had enabled me to hire Brinker, right as that decision had turned out to be, because I had known her as a pirate. Sex appeal in a pirate: That did indeed set an internal conflict going. That understanding relieved me; now I could handle my mixed feeling for Rue.

But the mystery of her antipathy to me remained. I intended Rue no harm, and she knew that. Her father had thrown us together, and perhaps she had cause to resent that, but I would hardly force my attentions on her. Yet she acted as if I offended her in some unforgivable manner. As if my mere existence was an affront to her.

I shrugged and moved on. All would come clear in due course. Meanwhile we had a maneuver to complete.

We completed it, getting clear of the base and conveying pods of food to the hungry pirates and restocking our own supplies of fuel and ammunition. But the Fijis, perceiving that we were not after all locked in battle with the Solomons, hesitated, then pounced on our abandoned planetoid base. Now they could scavenge among our leavings, and with their pincushion defense, we would not be able to touch them once we got our fighting formation back in order.

"Call them, sir," Spirit told me. "Give the Fijis an ultimatum of immediate surrender—or destruction."

"But that would be foolish!" I protested. "We have no—"

"Or delegate someone to do it."

"But—"

"Roulette, maybe. She'll enjoy this."

I spread my hands. *"You* delegate it."

She smiled knowingly. "Rue, would you like to deliver the Navy's ultimatum to the Fijis?"

Roulette came over to the screen. "I hate the Fijis almost as bad as I hate the Navy. But a bluff's no good. They're smugglers, and lying is their pride. Bloodstone would laugh in my face."

"Is there any redeeming quality about the Fiji?" Spirit inquired.

"You ask a pirate that? No, the colonists and settlers are decent, but Bloodstone's a brute. We Solomons are in business and we honor our given word, but the Fiji pirates honor nothing but power. They don't kill for victory, they kill for pleasure—an inch at a time. They captured one of our parties once, and sent us back their hands, one finger at a time, each one flayed. Our biolab said the skin had been pulled off while the fingers were still attached and alive."

I stiffened, and so did Spirit. Slowly, Spirit raised her left hand, showing her missing finger. "We have met that kind," she said. "The Horse didn't flay my flesh, though."

"I noticed. But you settled the score." Roulette settled herself before the screen. "Is this a bluff?"

"No," Spirit said.

"Then I'll do it." She went to work, and in a moment she was in touch with the Fiji operator. "Get me Bloodstone," she snapped imperiously.

"Who the hell wants Bloodstone?" the man demanded.

"Roulette."

Another face came on: grizzled, grim, with earrings in the classic pirate style. "What you want, you luscious tart?"

"Surrender this instant, or be destroyed."

Bloodstone bellowed out his laughter. "Listen, you juvenile slut, when I clean up Straight's mess I'll screw you to the damn bulkhead. You never had a real man before."

"I never had a man at all," she responded. "Only with my knife."

"Yeah, I heard. You don't rate a knife with me. I'll cut your tongue out before I take you; then each of my men'll take a finger or toe as a memento when they have you. After that we'll get serious. So powder up your plush a—"

"You have one minute to surrender to the Jupiter Navy," Roulette said evenly.

Bloodstone laughed again. "The Jupe Navy! Go stick it up your puckered, rosy red—"

"Thirty seconds."

"God, I'll enjoy plunging you, wench! Right before I plug your ma and bugger your—"

"You won't surrender?"

Bloodstone just laughed coarsely, making obscene gestures with his hands.

The minute finished. Spirit signaled a technician.

The planetoid exploded.

I gaped. "What?"

"We mined it," Spirit said. "We had expected the Solomons to take it over, but after the surrender, this seemed better."

Roulette watched the expanding ring of debris in the screen. "Beautiful," she murmured, licking her red lips. "You really don't bluff, do you!"

"No," Spirit agreed.

I was horrified. "But the whole fleet—"

"They aren't all dead, of course," Spirit said. "You don't kill ships simply by propelling them through space. We'll have to round them up and administer first aid."

Rue snorted, a sound that surprised me. "Some first aid! Their casualties will be thirty percent, and the rest you'll be able to lead about by the hand."

"But better than the carnage of a battle," Spirit said.

"I'd have chosen battle," Roulette said. "But it was a nice ploy. My father wouldn't have fallen for it, but Bloodstone's a sucker. Look, before I get locked up, may I meet your strategist?"

"This way," Spirit said, leading her toward Emerald's site. I could see that Rue had developed quick respect and even some awe of my sister.

It followed as Spirit had said: We chased down the semiderelict Fiji ships and made them captive without resistance. Bloodstone was dead, one of the unlucky percentage, though perhaps it made no difference, since we would have executed him, anyway.

We put the survivors on trial. We lacked time or facilities for a full-blown legal process, but we were as fair as was feasible in military doctrine. Each pirate was interviewed separately by a legal specialist from Spirit's S-1 Adjutant staff, since that was concerned with personnel, and allowed to present his case before the panel of judges with the help of the specialist. This process can take months or years in the civilian society; it was jammed into days or even hours here, very much the assembly line. But we did try to be fair as we performed our triage. The established criminals were summarily executed; Spirit supervised that aspect, as it was a function of her office and I lacked the stomach for it despite my hatred of piracy. My sister had always been tougher than I was; now it showed. The doubtful cases were put aboard a patched pirate ship and sent home under suspended sentence; if we ever encountered them active in space again, they would be executed without trial. We branded them, literally, for future identification. I suffered a qualm about this, too; in fact, my antipathy toward pirates was suffering some attrition, as it came to the cruel mechanics of implementing it. I realized I had been unrealistic; I had wanted to abolish piracy without actually hurting any pirates. But we were far from Jupiter now, and reality was stern.

The third group of processed pirates concerned me directly. Spirit sent me a number of men who were prospects for induction into the Navy. I discovered I did not like this, either. But Commander Repro braced me on this subject, and he was again correct. We did need to salvage what we could, and that included men as well as equipment. Otherwise we would find ourselves with a number of ships we could not properly man. So I girded myself to these necessary chores of attitude and interviewed the prospects, using my talent to separate the sheep from the goats. The goats were shipped out, unbranded; these were noncriminal pirates. I proffered employment to the sheep, provided they would swear allegiance to the Jupiter Navy. Some would and some would not; we kept the first and shipped the second.

With one exception: Shrapnel. He was a tough, smart man of about my own age, an experienced commander of men. His dossier informed me he had served in the military force of one of the Uranian nations and deserted when lured by the wife of a superior. He had turned her down, and the vengeful female had accused him of what she had tempted him with, forcing him to flee the wrath of the prospective cuckold. Shrapnel was an honest man, forced to piracy by circumstance; there was a price on his head on

Uranus, and any legitimate government would have extradited him to Uranus. He had acted with honor, even in the Fiji band, holding his place there because of his competence and the fact that Bloodstone trusted him as a lieutenant. Bloodstone had not liked him but had known Shrapnel would not betray him, which was more than could be said for most Fiji pirates. The men of Shrapnel's command had not raped or pillaged wantonly, in sharp contrast to the Fiji norm. I knew that if Shrapnel swore allegiance to me, he would be an excellent officer. We needed him, for now we had several new ships to fill.

But he would not so swear. The Fijis had been defeated, and Shrapnel had been injured and unconscious when captured, but he had not yielded. He came before me in chains, for he was a powerful man, and versed in martial arts; he had tried to make a break for it as soon as he recovered consciousness.

"I can offer you security for the duration of this campaign," I told him. "I can release you to a region of your choice when we return to Jupiter. All I ask is that you serve me for this campaign."

"I serve Bloodstone," he said firmly.

"Bloodstone is dead."

"Then I serve the current leader of the Fiji."

"The Fiji band has been destroyed."

"Then I serve whatever band takes over the Fiji territory."

I smiled. "That will probably be the Solomons. They have surrendered to us, and we are freeing them provided they no longer oppose us and stay within interplanetary law in all matters except the technicality of gambling. No murders, no raids on innocent ships, just business with voluntary clients."

"Straight has always been that way," Shrapnel said. "If he moves in, I will serve him. But you are the representative of a planetary navy, the kind that honors extradition. I will not serve you."

I sighed. I wanted this man, pirate though he was, but that same quality of honor that made him worthwhile also barred him from the Navy. "Swear, then, that if I free you,

you will practice no piracy and will not oppose the Jupiter Navy."

He stood silent, refusing. "Then I cannot free you," I said regretfully. "You are too competent to set loose. It seems a waste."

"That's war."

I thought of another angle. "Will you accept hostage status and obey the officer's code as a prisoner?"

He considered. This code granted a high-ranking prisoner freedom of person, on his bond not to abuse the privilege. It allowed the prevailing power to treat honorable prisoners as hostages rather than felons. Roulette had that status and was honoring it; she had not been "locked up." It was a considerable convenience for both victor and vanquished.

"Does that permit extradition?"

"No extradition for hostages," I said.

"Then I will accept it."

I turned to Spirit. "Free this man on his own recognizance. Assign him a hammock and an officer's pass for facilities."

She nodded. This was an expedient compromise, and it offered a lot: lodging, meals, courtesy, and use of the Tail.

Even in active war, there are periods of inertia. The processing of pirates, rushed as it was, still took time. Unfortunately, this also gave the other pirate bands a chance to analyze what had happened and to make their plans and build up their forces for defense. The next band we planned to tackle was the Marianas, the strongest in the Belt, the pirates who had taken over the Jupiter base. They dealt in human slavery, and they were absolutely ruthless. They had no intention of being wiped out by my task force. They had three battleships and a good support fleet, and they knew how to use them. The plain fact was that the Marianas were stronger than we were, despite our acquisition of a number of new ships.

About the time this came clear, we suffered another blow. Somehow, someone had pulled a string and gotten our mission reduced in importance. Spirit was first to learn of this. She came to me in such a fury as I had not seen in her since our childhood years. "Those black-hole admirals!" she swore. "They cut off our supplies!"

"They what?" I tend to react somewhat inadequately when surprised, which is one reason I don't enjoy being surprised.

"They couldn't recall our task force, because that would suggest the Jupe Navy was giving up," she explained. "But we haven't performed the way they anticipated—"

"We've been winning, not losing," I filled in.

"Precisely. So they have deleted the authorization for supply convoys on the pretext of cost-cutting. We're supposed to make do with what we have."

"What we have will disappear in the first battle!"

"Which will force us to close shop and come home before we starve, even if we win."

We held a council-of-war staff meeting. All our officers were angry, but it was Emerald who had most positive suggestion. "We can forage from the land. The real Carolines and Solomons and Fijis are not pirates; they are decent, hardworking colonists. We can get what we need from them."

"That sort of thing alienates the populace," Mondy warned. "We can't afford to act like pirates ourselves."

"We don't have to act like pirates," Phist pointed out. "We can pay for our purchases."

"Up to a point," Spirit said. "We don't have surplus funds for an extended stay."

"Unless we borrow from the payroll," he said.

There was a pause. Tampering with the payroll was extremely irregular business.

"If the men authorized it—" Spirit said.

We put it to the men, i.e., the enlisted personnel, male and female, and allowed three days to debate the issue. Abort the Belt mission or borrow from their pay in order to extend the mission. Victory over the Belt pirates would lead to some legitimate plunder that would be used to reimburse the payroll in kind. It was awkward and risky but feasible in theory. It was also un-Navy.

They hashed it out and voted, and decided by a clear if not overwhelming majority to extend the mission.

But this did tighten our time. We had to meet and defeat the Marianas soon, and we still lacked the fleet strength to defeat them, unless Emerald could come up with some phenomenal ploy.

"Mohi Heath," she said. "The Mongol commander Subedei was outmanned and far from home in 1241, but he used a daring tactic to overwhelm the Europeans. I think it would work for us. But it's risky. We really need more ships."

"Jupiter won't send more," Spirit said. She remained angry.

"We could get more," Mondy said.

"How?"

"The Solomons."

"The Solomons won't fight for us," Spirit said. "They won't fight *against* us, because Straight surrendered and we retain their hostages, but they certainly aren't *with* us."

"But that would change," Mondy said, "if we took the proper step."

Emerald's eyes seemed to develop an internal glow. "You conniving bastard! Are you planning what I think you're planning?"

"Just moving up the schedule a little, on the inevitable."

Now Spirit caught on. "Would it work, so soon?"

"What are you talking about?" I demanded.

Juana, the ever-present secretary, was standing beside Spirit. "Don't ask, sir."

"Fetch Brinker; she'll know," Emerald said smugly.

"When you girls start acting mysterious," Phist said, his voice carrying the same baffled annoyance I felt, "it's time for us men to beware."

Juana hurried out to fetch Brinker. "I think Straight had this in mind from the outset," Emerald said. "It was tacit in the surrender. He knew all along it would come to this."

"Knew what?" I asked.

Emerald exchanged a dark glance with Spirit. Both smiled. Neither answered me.

Brinker arrived with Juana. Ordinarily Brinker would have been aboard her own ship, the destroyer we had captured from the Carolines, but she was on the *Sawfish* now to help interview pirates and ascertain their competencies. As a former pirate herself, she had excellent insight in this regard. Now she was smiling grimly; evidently Juana had told her what was up.

"Will it work, Little Foot?" Emerald asked.

"It should, Rising Moon," Brinker agreed. "That's the pirate psychology."

"Of course it is," Repro said. "But there's one problem you vixens may not have considered."

"Peat Bog's no vixen!" Emerald retorted, reaching across to take Mondy's hand affectionately. "He's as cunning, underhanded, sinister, devious, and scheming as any of us."

"Haven't you been playing keep-away long enough?" Phist asked.

"Must have," Emerald agreed. "Who's going to tell him?"

Now the women were serious. None of them wanted to tell.

"I'll do it," Mondy said. He faced me formally. "Sir, if the men must sacrifice their pay, you must sacrifice also. You will have to marry the pirate wench."

"What?" I believe I have mentioned my stupidity when surprised.

"Roulette," he clarified, as if I didn't know. "Straight's hourglass daughter. The creature you've had your eye on. Now you can have her."

I remained baffled. "Why?"

"Because, sir, the pirates will only follow one of their own. Marry her, and the Solomons will form an alliance with us and help us fight the Marianas. With the Solomons actively on our side, our force will be equivalent to that of the enemy. And if the enemy doesn't know about that alliance, the element of surprise could be our crucial advantage."

"I'll say!" Emerald agreed. "We need them, sir."

"But Roulette hates me!" I protested weakly.

"That depends on how you look at it, Worry," Emerald said. "She knows her father intends her for you. She hates the idea of submitting, especially the way it has to happen."

"The way—"

"The one small problem," Repro said with heavy irony.

"You will have to rape her, sir," Mondy explained.

"I what?"

"That is the pirate way," Repro said. "These forms are important; they must be honored."

Appalled, I looked at the women, as different from each other as they could be: Emerald, Spirit, Juana, and Brinker. Surely they could not approve—

Slowly, in unison, all four nodded affirmatively.

"But I wouldn't—" I protested faintly. "I *couldn't*—"

"We shall just have to teach you how, sir," Emerald said with a metallically brilliant smile.

Now, at last, the reason for Rue's rage toward me was clear. She had known. She had cause.

Yet the cold equations of this situation were also clear. This was, indeed, a thing I had to do. I could not escape it.

They taught me with a certain vicious pleasure. Commander Phist, a genuinely decent man, absented himself from the proceedings, and Isobel Brinker pleaded the press of other business, but the others pitched in with what I felt was a bit more enthusiasm than was strictly warranted. They required Brinker to write out a summary of the pirate marriage convention before she departed, and this helped clarify what Straight had said about his marriage to Flush, and why he had told me that.

It seemed it was not mere abduction and rape; it was an intricately structured program, almost a play, with the words and actions virtually choreographed. The groom raided the bride's ship—in theory, pirates always lived aboard their ships, even when comfortable planetoid facilities were available—carried her away bound and gagged so that her screams would not alert her male relations, and brought her to his own ship. Obviously, today, this had to occur with the tacit cooperation of the bride's family, as it was just about impossible for an enemy to infiltrate a ship undiscovered unless he used a gas bomb. He would have to wear a space suit and put her in one, making the business immensely awkward. So in practice the bride was generally turned over to the groom's ship peaceably, and the abduction occurred from her private chamber. Terrified, she was not supposed to resist effectively. But later, when she realized what her fate was to be—

We rehearsed it. Juana served in lieu of the bride, for this stage. We set her up in the stateroom, and it was my task to carry her to the far end of the ship, the groom's quarters. I dressed in combat fatigues, armed, with a laser-proof vest, and sneaked up on her door. I felt like a thief—or worse, a rapist. The others of my staff would move about the passages randomly; all lesser personnel had been cleared from the region, as we did not want news of this program to become fleet gossip. My bodyguard Heller remained at the border of the groom's territory; once I passed him, I was through the first stage.

I tried the door panel. It was locked. Naturally someone had thought to include this unnecessary trifle of realism! I had to use my Captain's key to release it—never mind how a raider from another ship would have accomplished that!—and there was a little sound. That "woke" Juana; as I entered, she sat up with alarm, turning on her hammock-side light.

She was in a low-bodiced pink nightie that revealed rather more of her lush torso than I was entitled to see, and the light was behind her, making much of the material become translucent. Juana had always been a fine figure of a woman, and I had always liked her, and we had some intimate mutual memories; the sight of her this way really did excite me. I realized that my loyal staff had its fiendishly apt hand in this; they had presented me with a model who was guaranteed to turn me on, while being forbidden. Realism—ah, yes. Probably this particular touch was Emerald's doing; she had a pointed sense of humor. But so did Spirit. Women tend to think that a man's easily stimulated reactions to flesh and setting are amusing; I was not amused.

"Who's there?" Juana asked, alarmed, leaning forward.

I wish she hadn't done that; her exposed breasts were true marvels of shadowed rondure. I had always been partial to breasts like that, ever since Helse had unbound—

That brought me back to business. I drew my rubber knife and menaced her with it as I approached. "One peep and I'll gut you, wench!" I hissed.

Juana gazed at me wide-eyed. She began to quiver with laughter. That did more things to her exposed bosom. God forgive me, I wanted to dive into that hammock and take her right then and there, though she was in no sense mine to take, and hammocks are terrible locales for sex; the Tail uses bunks. I was turgid for her, and surely she knew it; we still liked each other more than military propriety condoned, and I think women adapt less readily than do men to the sexual and social requirements of the Navy. She had me, at this moment, pretty much where she wanted me: hot with desire and unable to implement.

I grabbed her by one arm and hauled her out of the hammock. The covering sheet fell away, exposing her fine legs. She was in a shortie-nightie with nothing beneath—the kind of outfit correctly calculated to madden men's minds. I could almost hear Emerald laughing, and as I hauled Juana in to me and picked her up by the shoulders and legs, I knew she was laughing, too. First she took the rubber knife out of my hand, so it wouldn't get in the way; then she put her right arm around my neck, holding herself close, making it easier to carry her. My left hand came around, almost touching her left breast, while my right hand lay against her left thigh. Her nightie, naturally, slid up to bunch at her hips; she might as well have been naked. She tried ineffectively to draw it back down with the point of the rubber knife. She surely had not selected that outfit herself; she was not that kind. But she was enjoying it now.

I carried her out into the passage and down toward the groom's quarters. Suddenly she perked up, remembering something. "I'm supposed to try one scream," she whispered.

Well, conventions differed on that. "Scream, and I'll gut you!" I said through clenched teeth.

"How?" she inquired, delicately chewing on the rubber blade.

She had a point, literally. My error! "I should have gagged you," I said sheepishly.

"Too bad!" She inflated, getting ready to scream a good scream. I had to stop her, though well-nigh dazzled by the sight, for I was still in bride territory. Hastily I clenched her in to me and reached my head around to meet hers. She met me halfway, and we kissed—deeply and long. But meanwhile I kept moving down the hall.

In due course she broke, having to expel her chestful of air. "That wasn't fair," she whispered.

"All's fair in love and war," I reminded her smugly.

She offered no further resistance, and in due course we made it to Heller's checkpoint. His eyes rounded, then narrowed appreciatively as he spied Juana's dishabille. "With that in your arms, what do you want with any pirate wench, sir?" he inquired.

"Officers don't rape enlisted personnel," I answered gruffly, averting my eyes. "She's just a stand-in, a dummy."

Juana forced a frown. "A dummy? I'll have you know I'm just as smart as the next abducted preravished innocent maiden!"

Repro appeared. "Very good so far, sir," he said. "But you made several errors—"

"Damn it, no one told me she was going to be dressed like this!" I exploded, carefully setting her down. Gravely she returned my knife to me, while Repro frowned.

"Roulette will be dressed like that," he pointed out. "If you allow her body to distract you prematurely, you're dead."

"Point taken," I agreed grudgingly. "I'll gag her."

"And tie her wrists and ankles," he advised. "That pirate lass would use her legs to put you in a headlock."

"In this sort of outfit?" I demanded, indicating Juana.

"I'd like to see that headlock!" Heller chortled. I glanced at him, and he added: "Sir." Which hadn't been the point, as he knew.

Repro nodded. "She surely knows all the tricks, sir, and will use them." He glanced on down the hall. "Very well, let's get on to the hard part. According to the script, a female relative of the groom sneaks the bride a knife—"

"That's after the rape," I said.

"No, the Solomons do it the hard way. She has the knife during the rape."

"She'll cut my heart out!"

"Not your heart, precisely; there will be a more accessible target," Repro said. That did not encourage me. "You must disarm her, of course, for the act. Afterward, you return the knife to her, and if she remains upset—"

I changed the subject. "Which relative gives her the—"

Spirit appeared. "I am the one. Hope, give me that weapon."

I handed the rubber knife to her. She turned. "Emerald, take over."

"Emerald?" I asked.

Emerald appeared. "You didn't think we'd let you rape a nice girl like Juana, did you? I'll handle this chore."

"I think I'd be better off with the pirate wench," I said.

Spirit slipped the knife to Emerald. "You poor, innocent damsel," she said in honey-drip tone. "I cannot stop my evil brother from this cruel assault, for I am only a woman, but at least I can give you some chance to defend your treasure."

"Bless you, sister," Emerald said, smiling maliciously. "I'll disembowel him!"

"Hey!" I protested.

"Roulette will," Spirit reminded me. "Don't trust her for a moment, Hope; that's how she got her other two suitors. She's your enemy—until you conquer her."

"And thereafter," I muttered.

"Not so," Repro said. "She'll love you, in her fashion, once you prove you're worthy of her. That's the pirate way. But you must indeed prove it, the hard way."

The hard way—in a double sense. But now I was soft, in the same sense. The reality behind this game was anathema.

We went to the groom's chamber. Emerald sat on the bunk—no hammock for this scene!—knife in hand. She was dressed in a tan wet suit, normally used for planetary water action. She might as well have been nude, for the suit cleaved to every intimate contour of her body; perhaps that was the point. She had been slender to the point of lankiness when I had first met her; in seven years she had fleshed out somewhat in breast and thigh and was, if anything, more seductive than before. She was a married woman, and the suit protected her sanctity; it was literally impossible to rape her without first removing it, and, of course, I would not do that. But she *looked* vulnerable. She was not as lush as Juana, but she was definitely healthy and female—and for her, too, I retained the masculine hankering, remembering the joys of her nocturnal athleticism. It is said in the Navy Book that sex and love are things apart, independent of each other, but for me the separation has never been perfect. I have loved no woman entirely since Helse; but I have loved each sexual partner a little, even those anonymous professionals of the Tail. I knew that Emerald, like Juana, had not forgotten our private shared experience and had perhaps not forgiven its termination.

I shed my outer apparel and stood in brief trunks with an armored crotch. If Emerald scored there with knife or knee, I lost, but this was, after all, only a rehearsal. For the real event I would have to be naked. Perhaps it is fitting that a man bent on rape must leave himself vulnerable to this type of injury.

"Remember," Repro warned. "In the normal pirate course, the bride offers only token resistance, just enough to whet the groom's appetite. But there are degrees, and sometimes she really does fight. Roulette is of the old school; she will be savage. So, to be safe, you will have to knock her out first. Make sure she isn't faking unconsciousness, too. In fact, bind her arms together and her legs apart. But for this practice session—"

"Faking will do," Emerald finished. "Mondy will call the points."

Nothing like having her husband on hand for rape! "Let's get it over," I said, freshly disquieted.

I came at her weaponless. Theoretically I was here for love, not war; this was the nuptial night. The bride was supposed to be attractively garbed, ready for the conclusion, but under her gown she carried the secret knife, her last defense against the indignity of rape. Theoretically the groom did not know this, but, of course, he did, because it was scripted. Still, some prospective grooms did die, and when that happened, the relative who had provided the knife was required to conduct the ex-bride safely back to her own people. There was no penalty for a woman defending herself from rape; the crime was the man's, for failing to accomplish his mission.

However, if through some mischance of violence the bride died, there could be war between clans. It was better to suffer the humiliation of an escaped bride than to kill her in the attempt.

Actually, I could appreciate aspects of this system. It did have its checks and balances, and it was a fair compromise between violence and cooperation. Pirates needed to preserve their image of barbarism, even when they were halfway civilized. It seemed that the women supported this system as much as the men.

"Stay away from me, you monster!" Emerald hissed with a fighting smile. She was enjoying this a good deal more than I was!

"Remember," Repro reminded me. "Don't fool with her. First knock her out. It's the only safe way. Pull your shot for this, of course; it will count."

"I don't like striking women," I said.

"That's a pirate with a knife aimed at your groin," he said. "Think of her as a panther who has killed twice and is going for three. This is an arena, man! It's you or her."

I understood all that, but still I hesitated. I came up to the bunk, hoping to catch her and pin her to it.

Emerald reacted the moment I touched her. One hand clawed at my face, and one knee came at my groin. I dodged aside, my military training serving me well, and she missed both shots. "No score," Mondy murmured from the far side of the bed. A referee for a rape!

I approached her again, more carefully. This time she brought out the rubber knife, making a vicious slash at my arm. It touched the skin as I jerked away. "First blood: bride," Mondy reported.

But already I was bringing my other hand about, catching her wrist. I exerted leverage, twisting her arm uncomfortably. Small leverage against a particular joint at the right angle can be immediately effective. She was at a disadvantage on the bed. In a moment I forced my wrist down, till she dropped the knife. "Bride disarmed," Mondy announced.

Emerald jackknifed, her feet coming up to strike at my face, but my continuing leverage on her arm prevented her from getting at me. I moved onto the bunk, getting on top of her, using my body to pin her upper body down. Her legs remained free but had no purchase; she could not escape. "Bride pinned," Mondy said dispassionately.

Pinned but not conquered. I could not rape her in this position. I tried to get my legs on hers but could not; I would have lost my leverage. It wasn't all that easy to rape a resistant woman!

Repro was right: I would have to knock her out. Half-measures just wouldn't do. I closed my right fist and struck at her head, pulling the blow so it wouldn't really hurt her. But she was ready for this and lifted her head as I moved to fall inside my swing. My forearm touched her ear instead of my fist. "No score," Mondy said.

She bared her teeth. Her own left arm was free now. She grabbed a handful of my hair and hauled my head down to hers. I feared her teeth and resisted, and in that distraction she got a knee into my side and shoved me away. But this gave me an opening; I flung myself on her, pinning her knee under me, getting between her legs at last.

"Oh, hell!" she whispered. Then she yanked my head down again, turning her face to meet mine; I no longer had the position to avoid her.

But I didn't need to. I had her in the rape position. I jammed my armored crotch against hers, to make the point.

Her mouth met mine and merged with a savage kiss. She was trying to distract me, but I refused to let my victory go that readily. I jammed at her nether section again, determined to receive credit for the point.

Her tongue came through our kiss to touch mine. Her hips moved against mine. Her hand let go of my hair and rested on my neck instead. I felt the softness of her breasts pressing against me as she breathed. Again I remembered how she had been in the days of our marriage. Often our lovemaking had been violent, like this, and always exciting.

I am not sure by what stages our struggle converted from opposition to love, but the rest of the universe tuned out and we found ourselves thrusting desperately against each other, our tongues performing what our torsos could not. We rolled on the bunk, her legs twined about mine, our arms clasping each other. Our breathing became savage, but our lips did not separate. For a moment it was like mutual resuscitation: I breathed into her lungs, and she breathed into mine. Then we shifted; obviously, God gave man a nose so he would not have to break a kiss to breathe. Then my urgency overwhelmed me, and she shuddered in my embrace, and our mouths pressed together so hard there was sharp pain on our lips. For a timeless instant we remained in a tension of passion, saliva squeezing past our lips to smear our faces. Then slowly, we relaxed.

I realized that I had climaxed in my steel crotch-guard, and she in her wet suit. We had not touched, physically, technically, anywhere but at face and hands, but we had in fact made love.

My recovering gaze traveled past Emerald's head to spy Spirit and Mondy standing silently beside the bunk. Did they know? They had to!

"I told you I'd get even," Emerald said, and I realized she was addressing Spirit, not me. But I was too preoccupied with my own embarrassment to analyze that. I just wanted to get out of my trunks and take a shower.

In this manner I trained for my wedding night. But though I perfected the mechanics of it, my mind and emotion did not proceed apace. "I'm just not constituted to rape anyone in reality!" I protested.

They tried to reason with me. "It is necessary," Phist

pointed out. "We must have the resources of the Solomons, both human and material, if we are to conclude the Belt campaign successfully. I assure you that without replacement for our supplies from Jupiter, we cannot prevail. With the money Straight is prepared to provide—"

"Money?" I asked.

"We need it to continue purchasing food from the colonists. Straight deals in money; he has huge amounts. What he lacks is legitimacy, and a formal alliance with us would give him that."

"It's his daughter I'm raping!" I exclaimed. "How can he give us money?" I was talking foolishly, trying to cover my inadequacy, but Phist was answering seriously.

"I have talked with him and with his Logistics officer. The understanding is as I have described. This is the way the Bands of the Belt make alliances: not by treaty but by marriage. This is his desire."

"Shoving his daughter at me!" I snapped.

"It was necessary to show you what he had to offer, just as you did when you sent your sister to me. This is not so different from what our unit has been practicing, sir."

Damn his logic! Of course he was correct.

"It's a good offer, sir," he continued. "She is esthetically desirable—I doubt there is a prettier woman in the Belt— and a good officer despite her age. You will have to appoint her S-3, of course—"

"What!?"

"Sir, we have a vacancy at Operations, and she is qualified. Sergeant Smith is competent, but an enlisted man can never officially assume the office. Straight saw immediately that the position was open. . . ."

I am so accustomed to my talent that I tend to forget that others have talents of their own. Obviously Straight had a fine eye for the exploitation of potentially profitable situations and was willing to gamble for gain. He had noted the authority of women in my unit, so had played his trump card early, and I, perhaps dazzled by the stunning body and fierce temperament of the girl, had not realized.

"But she hates me," I objected weakly, knowing that this argument would be shot down as effortlessly as before.

It was. "Talk again with Repro. He says hate is akin to love. But you have to win her *her* way."

"How could I trust her as an officer?"

"Marry her and she's yours," he assured me. "She will be as loyal to you as she has been to her father, even if she hates you. Accept the judgment of those of us whose talents are not blocked by private emotion: She can be trusted in this respect. She is well worth your effort."

"But rape—it's just not my way! I saw—"

"One moment, sir, while we switch specialty teams." And in a moment Phist was gone and Repro was present. "You were saying?"

"I saw my older sister Faith gang-raped," I said. "At the time she was beautiful and just eighteen—" I broke off. "My God! *Rue* is beautiful and eighteen!"

"Yes, of course," he agreed smoothly. "Naturally you do not wish to put yourself in the position of raping your sister."

"Roulette isn't my sister!" I protested.

"But she is, as you pointed out, virtually the same—"

"No! She's entirely different! She's Saxon!"

"You have prejudice against Saxons?"

"No! But Roulette's fiery; Faith was quiet. And Faith was no—"

"Go on," he said calmly.

"No pirate," I finished somewhat lamely, realizing that I was wading into a quagmire.

"So the situations are reversed," Repro said. "The pirate is not raping the innocent; the innocent is raping the pirate."

"Damn you!" I exclaimed.

"Why don't we explore the implications?" he suggested in his best psychiatric manner. The bastard was competent! "Pirates wronged you by raping your sister. Isn't it only fair that—"

"No!"

"But a long-standing grievance could be—"

"Rape is evil! I never want to be part of it!"

He frowned. "Would you want to be part of an affair with another man's wife?"

Ouch! "Rising Moon! I never intended to—"

"Of course. It was merely a rehearsal for your coming marriage to the woman for which Rising Moon stood in lieu. Peat Bog understands that."

"Damn you!" I repeated. "You're saying I have to follow through with this rape, or—"

Repro spread his hands. "I'm not saying anything, sir."

For sure! I was accusing myself. How could I face Mondy? I should never have let that rehearsal get out of hand! What I had done—*was* it any better than rape?

Someone cleared his throat. I looked up, startled. There was the one I dreaded: small, middle-aged, brilliant Mondy. How could I even apologize to him?

"Something I must tell you, sir," he said.

I tried to speak and could not.

"You gave her up to bring me into the unit," he said. "It was understood at the outset. I was the interloper—"

"No! A deal's a deal!"

"Yes. And you honored it, sir. Never once did you reproach me in any oblique manner for sleeping with your woman."

"She's not my woman!"

"She was, sir. She loved you—"

"There was no love!"

"And so, for you, she gave you up. And for the good of the unit. I was more selfish; I took payment in flesh for coming in. As time passed, I regretted that increasingly. I knew this unit was where I belonged, where I had always belonged. It is, as you promised, a family. I thought at first that the singing was foolish, but now my song gives me a sense of identity within the community I never had before. The unit has become my life; the nightmares are gone. I can no longer justify keeping Rising Moon; her purpose has been served. I was seeking the courage to do what was right, to return her to you—"

"No, Peat Bog! She—"

"She loved you. She gave me all I asked, more than any woman before, and I loved her from the outset, but I knew the sacrifice she was making. It was wrong of me to use her. But I was addicted to her. I couldn't give her up. I could not afford the luxury of generosity the way you could. I—"

I shook my head. "Damn it, Mondy, you've got it all wrong! I never loved her with my heart, only with my body. I never really loved any woman since my beloved died. I used Rising Moon myself; that's how I brought *her* into the unit. Because I needed her strategic skill. I bought her—and then I sold her. To you, for your skill."

"But after the rehearsal," he continued without seeming to hear me, "something changed. She had thought of you, even in my arms; this time she—"

"Damn it, Mondy, I'm sorry! I had no right to—"

"She had you, as she had in the old days. And"—he shrugged—"this time it changed. Maybe she felt guilty. She came to me contrite, and for the first time in our relationship, I *had* her, body and soul." He smiled wistfully. "I'd have given my life for that, for the reality instead of the courtesy—and instead you gave it to me free. She's mine now. She just had to try it again with you, to discover that. She's a good woman once she knows her mind."

"Yes," I said, relieved and amazed.

He smiled. "So go get your own woman, sir." He turned and went to the door, and Emerald entered, passing him with a quick kiss.

"I suppose I knew it when we were in trouble in the *Discovered Check*," she said, coming to me. "But now I am sure of it. He truly understands me, as you never did, sir."

I nodded affirmatively; evidently it was so.

"Now you've got a woman of your own to catch. You can't treat her the way you did me. She'll use her teeth, for one thing; don't even try to kiss her. And she's fast with that knife; she'll make a feint at your face, then cut out your crotch. Don't fool with her at all, sir; first foil that blade, then club her on the head. Make sure she's out, then do it, fast and furious and hard. Bruise her inside. When she wakes and knows you've been into her, she'll have to yield. She won't use the knife, because it'll be too late; her treasure will be gone. Next time you take her, she'll fight, of course, but she won't have the knife and she won't try to kill or maim; it'll be much easier for you to rape her and easier yet each succeeding time until she can drop the pretense."

"Each time I—!" I protested.

She flashed her metallic smile again. "Pirates always rape. Their wenches expect it. It'll be long before you tame her in bed. But in public she'll serve you loyally, and that's what counts. The alliance. But on the wedding night, don't take any chances at all. This bitch is deadly!"

"Emerald, I couldn't bring myself to rape anyone!"

"Oh, come on, Worry! What do you think you did to me?"

"But you—"

"I responded—after you pinned me. That's the way it is. A girl fights as long as she can; then she relaxes and enjoys it."

"I don't believe that!"

She laughed. "I'm speaking mythically, you idiot! Of course it's male propaganda! But with the pirates, it's more than a myth. *They* believe it. Roulette will fight you tooth and nail, literally, until you conquer her; then she'll accept you, exactly as her mother did her father. It's in their culture, Hope; you've got to play the game their way."

"I don't think I could even get an—"

"Next to a shape like hers? Who you kidding, sir! You'll be bursting to get into her."

"Thanks for the encouragement," I said wanly.

"Same's it was with me. You never intended to do me; in fact, you didn't think it was possible, with the crotch-guard and wet suit. But you got into the spirit of it, and—" She broke off. "Spirit, that's right. I'm overstaying my turn. Good luck, sir." And she was gone.

Spirit entered. "All right, Hope, it's all set. I slipped her the knife this morning, and the news about the S-3 slot. So now she knows what she'll lose if she kills you."

"But—"

"Repro advised me on that. Rue is tough; she really will fight you. None of this token stuff. But after you take her, and she wakes and has the knife—she's allowed her strike then, and you can't resist; that's when this will weaken her resolve. She knows her father wants this alliance, wants legitimacy more than anything else, and what she personally will gain from it—much more than the average pirate bride—and that you keep your word. She has a good life coming up if she spares you in the aftermath. I think she will. But first you have to beat her and take her maidenhead; there'll be no gift there! Tonight."

"Tonight! I'm not ready!"

"Repro said it had to be soon, before you lost your nerve."

"I never got up my nerve for this! Spirit, do you realize what this is? You saw Faith raped!"

"And I saw how Faith recovered from it, too. But this isn't the same, Hope. Roulette is a *pirate*. This is the only way she'll ever marry, and she knows it, and wouldn't have it otherwise. She likes you—"

"She hates me!"

"I think we've been over that before. She hates you to protect herself from loving you before it is time. All that emotion will flip 180 degrees once you take her. Once you savage her. And she's a lot of young woman, Hope; don't sell her short. Her father raised her for this from birth: to be too much for any ordinary pirate to take. I think we've set up a pretty good bride for you, and she does have a body you'll enjoy." She smiled knowingly, and in that instant I saw her as she had been as a child of twelve, not exactly a child even then.

"You know I believe in gentle love," I said weakly.

She put one arm about my shoulders and squeezed. "I know, Hope. But think of this as a battle. A competition. If you win, you both win; if she wins, you both lose. You both know it. She may even help you unconsciously; she may not slash as hard as she can, or she may give you an opening to knock her out. Take it, Hope! Knock her out, rape her, and be done with it. We'll have the cameras on you, of course—"

"The what?"

"In case something goes wrong. A complete record of the proceedings, EMPTY HAND style. So everyone can see she has the knife, that you're naked and unarmed, and that she fights for her honor and you rape her fair and square.

Her father may want to review that tape before he recognizes the marriage."

"Her father!"

"And we of the staff will be present personally—"

"What?"

She smiled. "It's the pirate way, Hope. The groom's clan has to witness the victory, so that no one can claim he didn't perform. And if anything happens to the bride, I will be obliged to seek revenge—"

"You?" My staff had ganged up on me, hitting me with point after point; now my sister was putting me away.

"I gave her the knife, Hope. It's real; no rubber one this time. I'm responsible for her until you win her. So whatever you do, don't kill her, because if she dies and I don't kill you, her clan will be honor-bound to do it, and—"

I stared at her, suddenly knowing that she would do it. She would kill when she had to, to honor whatever commitment she had, even if she had to kill me. She had survived among pirates; she was made of sterner stuff than I was. There was no one she loved more than me, but she would do it. And then probably kill herself. I *had* to perform.

I forced my voice to be calm. "I see the complication. I have no intention of killing her. Or of hurting her. Spirit, I just can't do this thing, no matter how all of you insist on sugar-coating it! It's primitive, it's brutal—"

"Hope, you've got to. We need that alliance just as much as Straight does, and you need that woman. You've been too long on the Tail. Just pretend she's a warrior, trying to kill you—because sure as hell she is! It's you or her, and there's only one way to beat her. Focus on that and everything else will fall into place. This is the way it has to be, Hope. If I could rape her for you, I would. But I can't."

The way it had to be. Yes, I understood that, intellectually, not emotionally. What I understood emotionally was that my sister was requiring this of me. Anything else that I could not handle, she would handle for me, such as the overseeing of the necessary executions, but this I had to do myself.

I realized that it would be easier to perform the rape than to balk Spirit.

The dreadful nuptial was scheduled for the evening. Already they were setting up the gallery and cameras. I had several hours to prepare myself, and I knew it wasn't enough. Eternity would not be enough! How could I school myself to rape a lovely eighteen-year-old girl?

I struggled like a fish on the hook, in the lake of a fishing-resort bubble, only I was not the fish but the fisherman, and the line was pulling me in and I was drowning. I was committed, yet I flopped on the ground as if seeking escape.

I talked to Isobel Brinker, she of the unshoed Little Foot who needed no man, but she did not support me. "Were I in your place, I would do it," she said.

"That's what Spirit said. But how can you, a woman—"

"I am also a pirate. I share the culture."

"If you married, you would expect to be raped?"

She laughed. "He'd damn well *have* to rape me!"

"But you masqueraded as a man, avoiding that."

"And would again, if I returned to piracy."

"I see more merit in your position than I once did."

"Oh, I approve of the system. I just don't happen to like the role."

"Neither do I!"

"I never enjoyed killing, either, but I did what was necessary—as did you."

Yes, I had probably killed more people than she had. But never dispassionately. Rape was more personal, and more ugly, to me. It was the brutalization of the act of love. Helse had taught me the true nature of sex as a function of love, and I did not see how I could go against that.

"You keep thinking of her as a pretty girl," Brinker said. "She's not. She's a pirate. She can kill as readily as I can. If you don't get that straight in your head, she'll kill *you*—and all that you have worked for will be lost."

Brinker was a pirate, telling me my business. Of course, she was correct. I knew and yet still could not accept it.

The abhorrence of rape was as deep in me as anything. I would not be the person I am, were this not so.

I called Straight, half-expecting him to refuse my call, but he accepted. "You know what I contemplate?"

"Certainly, Captain. It is scheduled for tonight, your time. Do you want my advice?"

The victim's father—proferring advice! "Yes."

"Strike swiftly and hard. Parry the knife, score on the jaw. Grab her hair and lock her head down so she can't slip free. Don't let it drag out. If you don't succeed in the first minute, back off and send her back to me; that's the only safe course. Don't delude yourself with any notion of fair play; that will only make you the third notch on her blade."

I remained amazed that he could speak this way of his daughter. "If I backed off, would there be a treaty then?"

"No. My men would not serve. My power exists only so long as I honor the necessary conventions."

I shook my head. "You actually *want* this to happen to your child?"

"What I might want, in a more civilized situation, is beside the point. It has to happen, Hubris. I want my daughter to be well married; I have exerted my influence only to select the proper man, after making two mistakes."

"What of your wife? Does she approve?"

"Ask her." The screen divided to include Flush's face.

"I never would have respected Straight if he hadn't tamed me," Flush said.

"But rape—"

"Do you think he would have respected me if I'd submitted without struggle? What man wants an easy woman?"

"I—suppose that's true," I mumbled.

"And what would my clan have thought?" she demanded, making her point. "I want my daughter to have the same respect I have had. Only one man ever touched me, and *he* had to fight."

Defeated again, I cut the connection. I sought out Shrapnel, the Fiji prisoner who refused allegiance. "A question, if you would," I said.

"It's your time, Cap'n."

"Have you ever married?"

He was surprised. "Sure—once. Didn't last, though."

"And you raped her?"

"Of course. She liked that. But six months later she found a rougher man."

"She left you for a more violent pirate?" I asked, amazed again.

"That's right. I retained some of those old civilized ways, and they turned her off. She didn't respect me. She didn't have a mark on her when she left. I like it better now, with your Tail; they don't mind if it's not violent."

"Thank you," I said dispiritedly. I turned away. There was simply no getting away from it. I was the only one who wasn't in step.

"Cap'n," he said.

I turned back. "Yes?"

"I know this isn't much, but Miss Roulette's a pirate. I would serve her."

"Even if she became our Navy S-3?"

He spread his hands. "A man's got to compromise a little, sometimes. I'd give her something special for a wedding present."

"Thank you," I said, and turned away again.

I returned to my chamber and lay in my hammock, seeking sleep or inspiration or a new outlook. None came. I stared at the ceiling. It was blank. I tried to think of a better approach. None offered. I was stuck with a job I knew I would botch, perhaps at the cost of my life and mission.

Someone entered. "Go away," I said, my eyes closed.

The intruder ignored that. A hand touched my shoulder. I shook it off, opening my eyes. I saw a boy of about fifteen, in civilian clothes; by his complexion I judged him to be Hispanic. What was he doing here?

"I think you need me, Hope," he said. His voice was adolescently high and somehow familiar.

"Do I know you?" I asked.

"I think so," he said with a smile. "You were going to marry me."

Startled, I looked at him more carefully. He wore a close cap that concealed most of his hair, and his face was smooth and without beard or blemish. His arms were thin; he had not graduated from any military training program.

I reached up and took hold of his cap, drawing it loose. His brown hair fell out, flowing to his shoulders.

His? *Her* shoulders. "Helse!" I cried.

My beloved smiled. "When you call, Hope, I am here."

"But you're dead!"

"For a time, yes. But I will live for you when you ask me to."

"Oh, Helse, I love you, but I can't believe in you!"

"I know." She removed her masculine shirt, showing the binding about her chest that masked her bosom. She unwound that, letting her breasts free. They were not the splendors that Juana or Roulette possessed, but they were the first I had loved. Helse was, after all, only sixteen, still maturing.

"You're lovely," I told her.

"I know." She stripped down her trousers and panties and stood naked for a moment, appraising herself. Then she joined me in the hammock. It was a squeeze, but I welcomed it.

Hungrily I kissed her. But then I paused. "The last time I was with you, Helse, it turned out to be—"

"But I can't come to you in my own body, Hope," she protested.

"I can't love you through a substitute!"

"Yes you can. Megan—"

Megan, the girl of the picture who had looked so much like Helse. The scientist's niece. The one QYV had promised me for the key. For an instant I was tempted; then I rebelled. "No! I want you—only you!"

"You wouldn't like me now, Hope," she warned.

"Yes, I would!" I insisted foolishly. It was as if I were a boy of fifteen again, heedless of reality in the flush of first love.

She sighed. "I must do what you want." She began to change. Her clear complexion became rough; then her skin flaked away. Her hair came out in tufts. Her lovely breasts shrank like dehydrating fruits and fell off. Soon there was no more than an ancient corpse beside me, with the bones beginning to show.

I realized I had been a fool. Of course this was her physical nature now; she had died fourteen years ago. "Oh, Helse! I'm sorry!"

"But you will join me," the awful skull said. "When the pirate wench slays you." She tried to laugh but lacked the wind for it.

I woke, shuddering. I was alone in the hammock. Neither living nor dead flesh had visited me physically; it had been a vision.

In my visions I can believe almost anything, but in the waking state I am more cynical. I did not believe that my death would bring me to Helse; it would only extinguish me. I would be absolutely foolish to let myself be killed.

Which perhaps was Helse's point. She had always known when my feelings were going astray.

"Thank you, Helse," I said to the empty room.

It was the hour of decision. I went to Roulette's chamber. For this I was dressed, and I had a knife.

I stood before the door panel. Something nagged me, and I paused until I had it. This was a play, of course, a choreographed ritual, but aspects were real. The pirate wench knew I was coming, and she was pledged to fight me; would she simply remain in her hammock?

I tried one of the oldest tricks in the business. I removed my shirt, opened the door, and tossed the shirt into the darkened room. It flared, ballooning in the breeze of its motion before falling to the floor.

Something leaped at it. Immediately I jumped in, catching her from behind. She had stabbed the shirt. I put her in a neck strangle, expertly squeezing so that her carotid arteries were constricted in their deep locations. In five seconds she was unconscious, because the blood flow to her brain had been cut off. She never had a chance, because she had been too eager to strike and had fallen for my countertrap.

Quickly I laid her down and used my shirt to bind her wrists, and the sheet from the hammock to secure her legs.

I had not forgotten the lessons of the rehearsal! I tore off a section of sheet to gag her, then picked her up and draped her over my shoulder. The abduction was in progress.

I carried her to the groom's chamber—actually, for this special occasion, a converted recreation room—and laid her on the bed.

The groom's team was present, seated in chairs near the walls. Repro, Phist, Mondy, Emerald, and Spirit. Brinker operated the video camera, and Juana was in a corner making shorthand notes. Seven people in the gallery. It was time for the second act. I remained uncertain I was up to it.

I stripped until I was naked, disposing of clothing and knife, preparing for the nuptial rape. At the same time, Spirit untied Roulette, who had, of course, recovered consciousness; a proper blood strangle puts the victim out only briefly. Had I not tied the bride, she would have come suddenly alive at the least convenient moment. Now she was ready for me.

She wore a pale blue negligee that offset her red hair dramatically. Her tresses were artfully wild, making her resemble in my mind a waiting jaguar. Her eyes blazed out at me defiantly. Perhaps it was her striking beauty and softness of form, merged with her evident readiness to explode with tooth and claw that enhanced the feline impression; or maybe it was a carryover from my drug-vision of some time back. Whichever, I found this alarmingly sexy.

Sexy? Well, that was, after all, what I was here for.

I was naked now, and Roulette was clothed. It didn't help that three men and four women were watching, and that I had had sexual relations with two or three of those women. The moment I experienced the masculine reaction, fourteen eyes would be on it in addition to those of the bride; that daunted me. If I did not experience that reaction, I could not complete my mission. What ignominy it would be to render her helpless and then be unable to complete the act.

It is said that a watched pot never boils, and that the main cause of impotence is the fear of impotence. That seemed to be true. I was defeated before I started.

Roulette stared at my face with her blazing hate. Then her eyes traveled down my torso, and she smirked.

That was a tactical error on her part. Shame converts readily enough to anger, and it was so with me. The audience faded somewhat from my awareness, as if fogged out by technical means to enhance the foreground. Flushed with reaction, I advanced on her. I was supposed to brutalize her; that much I could do!

And with that realization I felt a tug at my groin. Ouch! The thought of hurting a beautiful young woman gave me a sexual reaction! I *was*, to some extent, a pirate!

That, in turn, cooled me. But now I was at the bed, and I had to act or retreat. I almost retreated, but then she made her second error. She struck at me, swinging her small fist at my groin. Automatically I blocked her arm, and then her other hand swung out, bearing the knife, the blade driving directly at my face.

Now the battle was joined, truly! My head moved aside before I even realized, consciously, the nature of the thrust. Her hand passed by my ear, and in that moment she was vulnerable. There are ways in which a weapon handicaps a person, for it limits the variety of attack. I knew how to handle a knife-fighter. Before she could bring her blade back, I had her arm in a pain lock.

"Oh!" she cried involuntarily. She tried to fight it but could not; I could readily have broken her elbow. She tried to retain her hold on her knife, but slowly I increased my pressure, and she had to let it drop.

She relaxed. "I guess you've got me, Captain," she said.

I let her go, and instantly she arched off that bed and leaped at me, claws and teeth flashing. A jaguar indeed! But I had not been deceived; I caught her by her shoulder and thigh and lifted her as I might a mannequin, and flung her down onto the bed. It was a hard fall she took, and part of the air of her lungs whooshed out. I dropped with her, pinning her with a judo hold down, my right wrist angled to press at the back of her neck, my head close to hers. She struggled, but when she did, the cutting edge of my wrist brought pain that forced her to desist. That is part of the technique of a hold down; it is not strength or weight alone that makes it effective. A midget could have pinned a giant with this one.

I murmured almost in her ear: "The wife of an officer of the Jupiter Navy is exempt from civilian prosecution. She can travel with him anywhere in the Jupiter Sphere. Wherever she goes, she will be treated with the deference due her husband's position. She must, of course, entertain visiting officers in a formal manner, but she has a maid for the busywork. She dresses prettily and listens politely to their droll stories, while their wives eye her jealously. I can't say it's much of a life for a women as lovely and talented as you, yet perhaps it has its appeal."

I let her go. Again she sprang up like a released steel spring, grabbing for my hair while her two knees came up. Had her move been successful, she could have caved in my face with those knees. But, ready for this, I simply lifted my head clear, caught her rising right leg, and gripped her right buttock through the negligee. With that leverage I turned her over. Before she could react, I caught her negligee and hauled it up toward her head. Then I grabbed for her nightgown beneath it and hauled it up likewise, exposing her classic bottom. I spanked it smartly.

She seemed virtually to spin in air, outraged. But her elevated skirts hampered her, and the material started to tear. I grabbed it again and swept it over her head, stifling her with two layers of cloth while her body was exposed to the breasts.

She was helpless again for the moment, head and arms entangled. I stared at those perfect breasts; half-dazed, I had never seen a better pair of structures in my life. Now I had the male response. Suddenly I wanted to fling myself on her and do what I had come to do. But caution prevailed.

I gazed and spoke to her again. "There are sights to be seen in the Jupiter System that few pirates are privileged to experience," I told her covered face. "One day I mean to see them myself. The great city-bubbles, some of the largest in the Solar System, floating the massive atmospheric currents of the Colossus, laid out with streets and parks and small lakes. I understand the freshwater fishing-bubbles are fun for the honeymooners; the water is in a channel-river that makes a spiral loop several times around the bubble before reaching the lake at the equator. Couples float down it in canoes and keep any fish they catch. I think that would be fun, especially with the right company."

She finally burst out of her confinement. "You can stare at my naked body and talk of fish?" she demanded. "You're supposed to be ravishing me!"

"But I don't believe in rape," I said innocently.

She wrenched about, striking at my face with her fists. I swung clear of her blows, and she sat up and pushed me farther away, causing me to lose my balance and fall on the bed. Her knees came up; I jerked my head up, and she spread her legs and caught me in a head-scissors. My error; I had been warned about this very thing. I knew I should have knocked her out when I had her entangled. A head-scissors is not the most serious situation, but it can be awkward to break, because the legs have more power than the neck. She had me pinned, and my arms could not pry her knees apart.

Furthermore, I was facing into her naked split. Supposedly this is a position to inflame a man's passion. Actually, I don't regard the genital region as the most esthetic part of a man or woman, and I was desperate to free my head before she found some more deadly way to capitalize on her advantage, but every part of Rue was a marvel of rondure and symmetry, and I was indeed impressed by what I saw.

She shifted position, and I gained leverage, and got my arm between her thighs. There are nerve complexes there, and I jammed my thumb into one, and the sudden pain forced her legs apart. I yanked my head out, sat up, and discovered that she was reaching to the floor to recover her knife.

I grabbed for her arm, but it was too late; she had the knife. She blocked my hand with her left arm while her right hand raised the blade.

I disengaged and threw myself to the floor as the knife plunged forward. I wasn't quite fast enough, and she grazed my leg. I felt it only as sensation, not pain, but the blood was welling out of my calf. That knife was sharp!

I paused, but she knew better than to pursue me. The bed was her bastion. She awaited my next attack, her blade poised. She might not be expert at unarmed combat, but she did know how to use that knife.

A portion of her negligee trailed over the side of the bunk. I dived and caught it, feinting at her knife hand as I did so, to conceal my purpose. Then I stood back and yanked on the material.

No good; it simply tore loose, leaving her with a ragged but sufficient covering. But I realized I had a device here; she could not protect both her knife and her clothing. I made another pass at the knife and got another handful of cloth. I tore it free. After several such sallies, I had her halfway naked; after several more, I had stripped the rest of her.

I had thought this would at least disgruntle her. It did not. She remained poised, her blade awaiting its opening. She had come close to scoring on me again as I tore away her apparel, and now none remained to distract her. She was one lovely, firm-fleshed young woman, and knew it; it was harder than ever to concentrate on what I was doing.

What *was* I doing? I should be trying to knock her out so I could rape her in peace, and my own weapon was hardly ready. It was dangerous to let this drag on like this; sooner or later she would score with her blade. Every adviser, including her own father, had told me to finish it quickly.

But now, having suffered first blood, I knew emotionally as well as intellectually that this was a serious fight. She would stab me if I didn't stab her. Yet still I clung to my idiotic notion that she would somehow submit without violence, once she saw the light, so that it wouldn't be rape. I knew better, but it prevented me from undertaking the brutality I was supposed to practice.

"An Operations officer has status in her own right," I said. "She does not have to play hostess for her husband if she chooses not to. She exerts significant power, organizing the operation of the command, answering only to the commander himself. She salutes only him. This is not ordinarily a prerogative of marriage to the commander, but in this case the marriage is required for legitimacy, and the office can only be assumed while this mission exists. But for that limited period, it's about as much power as any woman can have." I knew, now, that she craved legitimacy and power beyond all else, as some women do. Her father had encouraged this attitude in her, making her his heir in nature as well as in office.

"Damn you!" she flared. "Shut your mouth!"

"Just thought you'd be interested," I remarked innocently. "You did very well when you organized the arrangements with the Solomons. I appreciate competence wherever I find it."

"You're not fighting fair!" she protested.

"Well, as they say, all's fair in love and—"

"Next you'll tell me you love me!" she cried indignantly.

"No. I could never love a pirate. I merely want to use you."

"Well, get on with it, then! You won't use me by talking at me!"

All too true. Her knife had never wavered. There was no easy way to conquer this hellion, certainly not by words.

I became aware again of the audience sitting around the chamber, making no sound or motion. I certainly wasn't following their advice. It was evident to all that I simply wasn't ready, physically or emotionally, to finish this business. Even the victim was getting disgusted. Probably I should retreat, giving up the effort. No rape, no marriage, no loss of life. But also no alliance, and no continuation of my mission in the Belt. That was no good, either.

I studied Roulette, trying to fathom an opening so I could disarm her again. Once I got the knife away and held her struggling body close, I thought I could do the rest. But I wasn't sure. If I still couldn't perform—

I looked into her eyes. Was there a pleading there? She knew what I had to do, and why, and knew what it would mean for her. She knew that if she killed me, or even escaped me, all would come to naught. If ever a woman could be said to want to be raped, this would be the occasion. I knew I had to do it, and she knew she had to be the victim, but neither of us was able to overcome our aversion to it. I could not force her, and she could not accede without violence, however much we both might desire the consummation. An impasse of a sort, like that Juana and I had suffered in the Tail, and I did not know the solution. We were locked in a situation neither of us wanted.

Then I looked through her eyes, and her face changed. The jaguar aura faded, and her features became rounder, older, and beautiful in a different way. Her naked body became less pronounced but just as feminine. And—I loved her.

"Helse," I whispered.

"No," she said.

"Who, then?" For now I saw that she was not precisely Helse, who was dead, but another woman very like her in appearance, though older. The woman Helse might have become, had she lived to her thirties. Had she been Saxon.

"Megan," she said.

And so she was. The one other woman I could love, perhaps, though I had never met her. I stepped toward her. "I hardly know you," I said. "Only through your picture, that I glimpsed with my beloved."

"I am older than you," she said.

"I know. I could never love a younger woman." I moved in to kiss her. A part of me was surprised to see this ready acceptance of a woman I had never met, yet I also knew she was as close to Helse as I could ever come. For even the suggestion of Helse, I would give up virtually everything else I valued.

She met me partway. I felt a sting at my left shoulder; I shrugged it off. There was another. I ignored it and brought my lips to hers. The kiss was sharp, almost painful, but wonderfully sweet. I felt her body tight against mine, gradually relaxing. What a woman she was!

We drew apart, a little. She gazed at me wide-eyed. "Oh, Hope, I'm sorry!" she said.

"Sorry?" I asked, surprised.

Then her lovely features clouded and changed and reformed to those of the jaguar maiden. A smear of bright red was on her chin. My lower lip hurt; I brought my left hand up to check it, and discovered I was wounded in the shoulder. Pain stabbed through me, and I saw there was blood down along my arm from two deep knife wounds. An artery had been punctured.

"You stabbed me!" I exclaimed. "And you bit me!"

"Well, you hugged and kissed me!" she retorted.

"And you're not Megan." That, more than anything else, I could not forgive her.

"Who the hell is Megan?"

I struck her, a slashing openhanded blow across the side of the head. Her head rocked back, her mouth open, but I caught her again on the other side with my backhand. She fell on the bed, blinking. "Who the hell are *you?*" I demanded.

Her right hand swung up, bearing the blood-tipped knife. My own right hand moved so quickly my eyes did not follow it and caught her wrist. I stared into her eyes as I brought her knife hand down to her own face. Strength for strength, she could not compete with me. "You prefer sadism?" I inquired. "Shall I make you slit your nose? Men would not find you so pretty, then."

She fought, but she could not budge the knife except by letting it go. She did so, and it fell flat across her mouth, not cutting her, and slid to the bed. "I never saw you like this!" she gasped.

"You never saw me at all, you arrogant bitch!" I snapped. "You like me better now?" I jerked my right hand and forced her right hand to strike her face. "Suppose you chew off your finger while I watch?"

"You brute!" But it was neither fear nor horror that governed her now. Her tone was one of discovery and admiration. "Kiss me again, I won't bite!"

I released her hand, moved my face close to hers, and spat in it. Blood and saliva splatted against her cheek. "I'd as soon kiss a snake!"

She shuddered, not with anger but with rapture. She spread her arms and her legs. "Do it now!" she breathed. "I can't fight you when you're like this! You're a real man after all!"

I drew away from her and stood by the bunk. "Look at me," I said. "I don't want you. You're not Helse, you're not Megan. What good are you?"

"Revile me!" she whispered. "Hit me! Make me scream!"

"You aren't paying attention, you pirate slut," I said. "Look at my member. You don't turn me on at all."

Now she looked. She saw I was not bluffing.

"I can't believe it. You brutalized me; you must want me."

"You have failed as a woman," I told her.

She snatched the knife from the bed beside her. She pointed it at my groin. "I'll cut it off!"

"Go ahead." I raised my arms and set my hands behind my head, not retreating from her.

She thrust and aborted, making a feint. I did not budge. I had called her bluff. She knew that if she castrated me she would lose the only man who had broken her will.

Slowly she brought the blade to her own throat. "If you won't have me, no one will," she said.

"Spirit," I said.

My sister rose from her chair. "Yes, Hope."

"If she dies, you are bound by honor to kill me."

Spirit hesitated. I had been in awe of her before; she was in awe of me now. "Yes," she whispered.

"I can't hear you," I said.

"Yes!" she screamed.

"Set the laser."

Slowly she brought out her laser pistol, adjusted it, and aimed it at my face.

My eyes had never left Rue's. "You see we honor the pirate convention. Do you believe Spirit will kill me?"

Roulette turned her head a moment to gaze at Spirit's face. "Yes," she breathed. "She doesn't bluff."

"So you may safely kill yourself," I continued. "You know you will be immediately avenged, and there will be no onus for your father to bear, no embarrassment to your clan."

Roulette flung the knife away. "You bastard, you have mastered me! Finish it!"

"Why should I?" I demanded cruelly as Spirit lowered the laser and returned to her chair.

Rue considered momentarily. "May I touch you?"

"You may do what you like with me."

She leaned forward and reached for my member, but she was inexperienced and did not know how to force a reaction. Observing her defeat, she dropped to her knees before me, flung her arms about my legs, and pressed her face to my torso. I felt the moisture of her hot tears, and that brought on the masculine reaction. In humiliation she had won what she had lost in her arrogance.

She returned to the bed and lay back, legs spread. "Now do it!"

I stood still, in two senses. "Do what?"

"You know what!" she flared.

"Why?"

"Oh, God—must I beg for it?"

"Yes."

She stiffened, then forced herself to relax. "Please."

"I can't hear you."

"Please!" she cried.

"Address the camera," I said.

She faced the camera. "Please rape me! I beg you!"

I glanced at the audience. All of their eyes were glowing, and their jaws were set. They were embarrassed and angry. There are reasonable limits to all things, even sadism. I realized that I did not like what had been evoked in me.

I looked back at Roulette. She lay there, spread, waiting. Her bosom was heaving, and her face and neck were flushed.

It had to be violent; that was important. I owed her that.

I got on her, and as my member touched her flesh, I felt the climax on its way. I thrust savagely, not to hurt her but because I had only about three quarters of a second to get into her before exploding.

She clung to me, relishing it, climaxing instantly as I tore through her virgin membrane. She kissed me passionately. My blood was on her lips, her blood on my member. My essence pumped into her with the most urgent pleasure I have experienced.

"Promise me one thing," she whispered as it subsided.

"One thing," I agreed into her soft, fragrant hair.

"Never make me beg again."

"I promise." I had raped her spirit rather than her body;
I would never again need to humiliate her like that.

Chapter 11

PRISONER

She had stabbed me twice in the left shoulder, severing an artery, but in my vision-trance I had exerted control over the autonomic system and closed the wounds with minumum loss of blood. She had bitten right through my lip, but again I had sealed it off. The holo-tape showed it perfectly. That was what had cowed her: I had seemed like other than a man, a creature she could neither hurt nor resist. At that point it had become psychologically necessary for her to prove I *was* a man and that she could make me respond to her appeal. That she was a woman. The more I demurred, the more important it became for her.

The rest was routine. I took her back to her father's ship. The holo of the proceedings was not necessary; indeed, Roulette insisted that it not be shown, and that none of the witnesses speak of the nuptial night in any except the most general terms. As far as outsiders were concerned, I had charged in, gotten stabbed, disarmed her, knocked her semiconscious, and raped her while she bit through my lip: exactly the way it should be. Now she was mine, and she stayed close by my side and limped a little and obeyed my every word without protest, demonstrating the extent to which she had been tamed. It was a matter of pride for her to do this, to make it absolutely clear. Her father glanced at her and nodded, satisfied. He glanced at my bandaged shoulder and swollen lip and nodded again. Obviously it had been a good fight. . . .

Now the alliance was made. It had, in fact, been sealed the instant I penetrated Roulette. The fleet of the Solomons became a division of ours, their stores of money became ours, and their men saluted our officers. We could now afford to purchase all the supplies we needed, without holding back on our pay roster. We integrated our commands, and I interviewed key Solomons personnel, making sure there were none who would betray our effort. There were none; whatever their nature, they were loyal to Straight—and to his daughter. Roulette was now our S-3 Operations officer and my wife, and that was good enough. And the Navy made no further issue of the Solomons' business interests. Straight had his legitimacy. I realize this may appear to be an accommodation with mischief, but my objection was not to gambling but to criminal activity. In the real world, such distinctions and compromises have to be made.

It took time, of course, for fleets are not integrated in a day. Or in a week. But we now had time, thanks to this alliance. We organized our forces, trained them—Sergeant Smith had his work cut out!—and prepared for the next battle. We had our Navy fleet, the Solomons fleet, and the remnants of the Fiji fleet, but our next encounter was to be with the Marianas, the most formidable of the pirate bands, and they were organizing, too. The fate of the Belt would hinge on this next battle.

There was one gratifying consequence of the marriage in another respect. My staff had been debating what song to give Roulette when she joined us, and factions were forming in support of one song or another. Spirit favored "Wheel of Fortune," which describes a man's glimpse at the body of a fabulously beautiful young woman and his dazzlement thereof, while Emerald preferred something relating to the ravishing of maidens. Our community was split; they referred to Roulette as "The Ravished" while humming "Wheel of Fortune." We needed to settle this, but neither Spirit nor Emerald would yield, their rivalry finding expression in the naming of a new officer.

Shrapnel, our hostage-status pirate, made petition to address my staff. I granted it immediately, knowing what was on his mind. He stood before us and spoke his piece:

"I hereby offer my service and my loyalty to Rue, if she accepts."

Roulette, annoyed by this familiar use of her name, frowned. "Why the hell should I want it, Fiji?"

Oops! I tried to catch her eye, but she arranged not to let it be caught. She remained imperious in little ways.

"I bring a gift that will please you," Shrapnel said.

"I need nothing from you!"

"Um, Rue . . ." Spirit murmured.

"Oh, all right," Roulette snapped. "You think you can please me, Shrap? Show me your power."

For answer, Shrapnel began singing. We listened, amazed, for he had the finest tenor voice any of us had heard, and complete control. Obviously he had had training in this, somewhere along the way; there was magic in his delivery.

Come all ye fair and tender maids
Who flourish in your prime, prime:
Beware, beware! Make your garden fair
Let no man steal your thyme, thyme—
Let no man steal your thyme.

For when your thyme is past and gone
He'll care no more for you, you;
And every day that your garden is waste
Will spread all o'er with rue, rue—
Will spread all o'er with rue.

A woman is a branching tree
A man a singing wynd, wynd;
And from her branches, carelessly,
He'll take what he can find, find—
He'll take what he can find.

It was the loveliest, saddest song I had ever heard, and the feeling came through with an impact that smote us all. The allegory was potent: a woman like a garden, with fragrant herbs growing, like thyme, that would be replaced by the bitter medicinal plant rue, if not properly kept up. But thyme is pronounced "time" and rue is also regret, and wynd is wind; when the wind carelessly plucks what it wishes and departs, the garden may be destroyed. For a woman to leave herself open to that is to invite heart-break.

And the name of the song was "Rue."

Emerald and Spirit exchanged a glance and nodded. Rue sat stricken, not moving at all. The song was apt in so many ways, and so beautiful; there was no question it was hers. Shrapnel had done more than show her his power; he had named her. And her name was Rue.

Now Shrapnel saluted, sharply and cleanly, and held it until Rue, moving as in a trance, returned it. "Welcome to the S-3 staff, Shrapnel," I said.

In an hour the song was all over the fleet. But no one could lead it but Rue. She had to go from ship to ship, to sing it for each company; it was, in fact, her initiation.

In due course we arrived at the Marianas' segment of the Belt. My Navy fleet led the way with the Solomons auxiliary taking an alternate route through a channel in the Belt debris. We were to rendezvous at the Marianas capital region; then we would tackle the main pirate force in one definitive battle.

"I'm using the Mongol strategy for this one," Emerald said at our staff meeting. "I trust you all are familiar with it?"

Phist coughed. Spirit smiled. Naturally none of us were familiar with it. "I'm just a ravished pirate wench," Rue said. "What do I know of history?"

"Pirates do not study history?" Emerald inquired.

"We're too busy with the present."

"The Marianas won't be familiar with the tactics of the ancient Earthly Mongols, then?"

"What the hell do the Mongols have to do with us?" Rue demanded. "Of course, they don't know about that stuff."

"That's what I thought. Those who will not heed history are doomed to repeat it. Perhaps you would be willing to play the devil's advocate here."

"The what?"

"I'll do it," I said quickly. I had learned already that Roulette had a prickly temper, especially where her areas of ignorance were concerned.

"Good enough," Emerald said. "You'll play the part of King Bela of Hungary. You have a force equivalent to that of the invading Mongols, and you are established west of the River Danube, while the Mongols, having destroyed Russia, are advancing southwestward toward you. What do you do?"

"Hold on, Rising Moon!" I protested. "I've got to know more than that! What kind of armament do the Mongols have? How does it compare to mine? Whose side are the natives on? What about supply lines?"

She smiled. "You're learning, sir. The Mongols are a real terror. The force they send against you is a spin-off from the greatest land empire ever conquered, but now their supply lines are so extended they must forage from the land. They are lightly armed horsemen, highly mobile, who tend to attack swiftly and retreat, then attack again. They have destroyed all enemies so far, including your associates, who underestimated them. But you are on your home territory, and the local people support you. In addition, it is winter, with deep snow all about, hindering their mobility and making it impossible for them to steal or destroy your crops. You have your secure bases, with ample supplies, while they are traveling in the open, lean and hungry. They're coming fast."

"Well, then, I'll just sit tight and wait for them," I decided. "And I'll attack them as soon as they cross the Danube, catching them with their formations unformed and their backs to the river, while they're tired from traveling. I'll probably pulverize them."

"One branch of their force splits off, attacking your allies to the north," Emerald continued. "The Mongols are successful, so you can't depend on help from your allies, but it is plain that this side campaign will prevent that smaller Mongol force from rejoining their main force in time to fight you. So in that respect their diversion seems to have backfired; you now face a slightly inferior force."

"I'll polish them off before their other unit gets here ," I said. "It's my golden opportunity." I paused. "Unless they have a secret weapon?"

"Nothing physical," she assured me. "But strategically they're sharp."

"Like boosting drones backward," Roulette muttered. "Or mining their own bases." The other officers chuckled. The Solomons had been able to replenish their lost drones from the Fiji reserve force that had not come against us, but it had been an effective lesson.

"Well, you won't catch me with any of those cheap tricks!" I said, enjoying this. "I'm canny old King Bela, and I know my troops and my territory, and I'll follow sound strategic and tactical principles. The Mongols can't budge me by anything less than a full-scale attack, and I'm well prepared for that."

Rue cocked her head at Emerald. "Those Hungarians look pretty secure to me. How *are* the Mongols going to take them?"

"I think this is useful," Repro interposed. "Captain Hubris makes a good enemy commander. Why don't we continue him in that role, so he can provide an insight into the most likely course of the Marianas?"

Rue clapped her hands in a girlish gesture that startled me. She was, indeed, still young. "He'll make a great enemy! He's already a rapist! I won't tell him a thing, no matter how hard he beats me!"

She certainly loved that wife-brutalizing image! I had, of course, made love to her again, since the first night, but she had insisted on being violenced. This tended to put me off; I had risen somehow to the occasion the first time, but despite Repro's warning, I had hoped for the more normal, gentle procedure thereafter. This woman, it seemed, actually wanted to be sexually savaged. She referred to my rape of her not with horror but with pride. But that was another matter; right now I had to decide whether to remove myself from the strategy of this important upcoming battle. "Very well, I'll try it this time," I agreed. "You have made me play the role of a rapist; the role of an ancient king can't be worse than that. I hope I don't regret it." Little did I know!

"It will be your finest campaign, sir!" Emerald promised me, her eyes assuming that dangerous glitter.

And so I removed myself from the active planning of our strategy, becoming instead the enemy commander. For obvious reasons we never publicized this aspect; on the record I was the man in charge throughout. As a figurehead I was a success.

We crossed the river some distance from the main Marianas base. I must clarify this, lest the narrative become confused. The Mongol/Hungarian battle of 1241 had occurred on the land mass of the Eurasian continent on Earth, with the flowing water of great rivers representing significant barriers to the passage of armies, especially when those rivers were guarded by enemy forces. The Marianas from which the pirates took their name were a chain of islands in Earth's huge Pacific ocean. There the barriers were not water but land, often in the form of submerged reefs, limiting the passage of sea-traveling ships. But here in space there was neither land nor water, neither ocean nor reef. Yet the analogy held, for there were indeed rivers and islands. The islands were the countless planetoids, few of which were large enough to anchor a ship, but many of which presented problems for navigation at cruising velocities. In some regions there were extended bands of dust and sand that stretched interminably through the Belt, almost invisible from a distance, but highly abrasive and awkward for passing ships. A single particle of spaceborne sand could not significantly damage a ship, but a thousand particles could wear down the finish and weaken the metal, and a million could make that ship unreliable for extended use. In a river of sand there were many millions of particles, and their force could be felt beating against the hull, scouring it. No ship's captain could feel easy about that, so unless it was an emergency, he would not trust his ship in it. Certainly we did not; we sent drones out to scout the river in detail, recording all details of its curvature and thickness and density. Then we fumbled through a ford, a narrow section of the river that was relatively free of sand. Such fords were not necessarily obvious, as they slanted and twisted through the convoluted rivers, impossible to spy from afar, but this one was large and clear. It was evidently in common use, for it was marked by radio buoys. The enemy had not even thought to set a guard on it, perhaps because it was several days' travel from the base. So what could have been a delay for us was not; we hardly slowed our progress, since we had spaced our formations to provide sequential access to the ford. Mongols were smart about travel arrangements.

We proceeded at reduced velocity toward the Marianas. We were now in their territory, but there were few planetoids and there was no resistance. As the "Enemy King" I could appreciate why; all my forces had been gathered in to the central fleet, where they would be most effective. It would have been pointless to put up token resistance to the might of the onrushing Mongol horde. Even unimpeded, our journey took several more days, for space is vast.

By day Roulette shared the ongoing preparations for the encounter. I knew she had extensive knowledge of pirate ways, and that she was sharing her information with the other officers; she was invaluable in this respect. Shrapnel, too, was working with Sergeant Smith to train special forces; the two got along well together, and there was a lot to do. One good man can be worth as much as a cruiser! Like the Mongols, we were alert to the ways of the enemy. My use of the term *horde* above is, in part, facetious; we were no horde, and neither were the original Mongols. We were a disciplined, potent fighting machine, as they had been. Battles are seldom won by hordes.

By night Rue was mine, in her fashion. I have stressed that emotional love was no part of my military experience, yet to the extent I was able, I was smitten by her. It was not merely that she was the loveliest creature I had encountered, in every physical way the personification of beauty and sex appeal, though that was certainly a significant part of it. It was not that she was intelligent and spirited, though I liked that, too. It was no longer that she was forbidden fruit; now that fruit was in my possession. It was not that she was a nice person, for she was not; she was a tempestuous, strong-willed, sharp-tongued wench with redeeming qualities to balance it out. I think mainly it was the challenge that she represented; specifically, the emotional challenge. For if I did not love her, neither did she love me. She understood, as well as I did, the nature of this marriage; it was a necessary device to facilitate a necessary alliance. I had already made and broken one marriage for the benefit of the unit and might do so again; she had no absolute security. Yet I could not think of any man-woman relationship as purely political, not when it involved sex. Not when the woman was as vibrant and desirable as Rue. And I think she had some similar reservations.

She was in some ways a wild creature, controlled but not tamed. I wanted to tame her, specifically, in bed. I wanted sex *my* way. Gentle and loving and mutual. And she simply didn't understand. "You promised not to make me beg," she reproached me.

"Nonviolence is not begging!" I protested. "I want you to respond without humiliation or pain."

She looked at me as if I were uttering something disgusting. She had been raised to believe that rape was the natural order, and that a woman could only enjoy sex as an adjunct to some sort of distress. Anything else was obscene. She literally could not turn on unless treated roughly. If I refused to be rough, she simply lay there and tolerated me; her code did not permit her to resist me anymore, whatever she implied in public. The code varied from band to band and clan to clan, but she was true to her variant. Inevitably I found I had to strike her, or revile her verbally, to make her happy.

And so it seemed I had won the sexual battle, on the nuptial night, but lost the war. I had raped Roulette but could never share any other kind of sex with her. This promised to become a minor private hell, for I desperately wanted that other kind of relationship. I was a prisoner of her nature.

On one occasion, when we had come to an unsatisfactory culmination, I heard her singing faintly: "And every day that your garden is waste, / Will spread all o'er with rue, rue . . ." In a fury of embarrassment, I left the chamber. But on the next occasion, when she started the song, I struck her on the shoulder with what minimal roughness I could get away with, and she stopped, and it was better. She was training me.

Our fleet arrived at what we code-named the Danube: the larger, denser river of sand that sheltered the Marianas' base. We had split into three groups with the wings proceeding first, scouting the territory for resistance or ambush. When it turned out there was none, our center group accelerated at 1.5 gee and closed the gap rapidly. All three arrived at the Danube together, perfectly coordinated. My staff was competent about maneuvers.

But observing this in my role as King Bela of Hungary, I refused to be tempted by the seeming delay of the Mongol center. I remained safely ensconced beyond the river. Let the Mongols cross the single ford; I would mow them down while they were vulnerable, and if they did manage to cross, they would still be fighting with their backs to the river: an uncomfortable situation. The advantage was all mine, as long as I waited and forced them to come to me.

Indeed, my assessment was accurate, for the Marianas did not come out to meet us. Mondy's sources informed us that they had a fine and ready fleet, well disciplined and well supplied, probably able to defeat ours in open battle. But they were canny, waiting for us to commit ourselves, knowing that it would be ten or twelve days before our unit under Straight could join us, and that they could choose to attack us at any time before then. They could afford to wait while our supplies diminished.

I was of mixed emotions. I knew we had to beat the pirates and that Emerald had a strategy to do this that the others believed would work. But as King Bela I could not see how a Mongol victory was possible. The Mongols *had* to cross the Danube—and be vulnerable.

"I'm glad I'm not on your side," Rue remarked smugly. I whammed her on her delightful derriere, and things proceeded from there. I hated to admit it, but there was a certain pleasure in roughness. I had never had as intense an experience as the nuptial rape. Could her way be right?

Emerald muttered something about the situation being wrong and ordered a strategic retreat. The Mongols had made no effort to cross the Danube but went back the way they had come.

What? As King Bela I gaped, then realized that once the Mongols had realized that they faced a superior force in an impregnable position, they had known that combat would be disastrous. So they had to back off, stalling for time until their missing unit caught up.

Did I want them to do that? I decided that was not in King Bela's best interest. Cautiously I deployed some of my forces across the Danube, ready to back off if this turned out to be a ruse. But it wasn't; my advance only hastened the retreat of the Mongols, who were no longer in fighting formation. It hadn't occurred to them that I might advance at this stage; their horses were pointed the wrong way.

In space, my strategy was echoed by the Marianas. Suddenly our fleet was in genuine retreat. Whatever Emerald had planned had gone wrong; the Marianas had stuck to conventional strategy, refusing to be spooked or cowed, and it had paid off. Conventional ways are conventional because they are basically sound; one deviates from them at one's risk.

Emerald seemed disgruntled when I met her. "Well, it just didn't make sense to cross the Danube in the face of a prepared, alert enemy force," she said defensively. "So we moved back to give you some room; we can fight better in clear space, away from the river."

"But you can't turn a formation on a dime in space," I pointed out. "I'm coming out in forward-facing battle order, my van on your tail. If you pause to reform your formation, I'll tear you up. It's similar to the problem of a small ship trying to turn about in space, during pursuit."

"You won't follow that close," she said. "All we need is enough leeway to turn."

"I won't give you that leeway."

"You'll have to. We have faster ships than you do."

"Not all of them," I countered. "Any that lag will be lost, so you have to slow the main fleet to accommodate them. My own slower vessels can afford to trail; there's no foe behind *us*."

Grim-faced, she turned away.

I had my victory, but it tasted of ashes, for I was in real life the commander of the fleeing force. We would probably survive this debacle, for the Marianas could not force us to fight, but we certainly couldn't win a battle we never fought. Our reputation would suffer, and the remaining pirates of the Belt would hold us in contempt. Our fleet would be intact, but my mission would become impossible.

We accelerated but so did the Marianas fleet, keeping pace, nipping at our stragglers. My assessment was correct; our fleet velocity was limited not by the acceleration of our fastest ships, but by that of our slowest ships, while the enemy's pursuit was the opposite. Their fastest harrying our slowest; that was the awful reality of an extended retreat.

Our strategic one-day withdrawal became a nonstrategic flight in the second day, and a virtual rout in the third. There was no longer any pretense of orderliness; our destroyers hung back only to protect our rear, and in this position they weren't too effective at that. We held our losses to a minimum, but the retreat continued; there was simply no way to turn it. On into the fourth day it went, back along the route we had come. Disaster!

We were now closer to the other river we had crossed, dubbed the Sajo. Beyond that was the Mohi Heath, after which this historic rout had been named. I did not know the details of it, but I knew the Mongols had not gone on to destroy Earth's Europe, so the outcome was clear. How could Emerald have chosen this as a model!

If only Straight had wrapped up his side campaign earlier! But his diversion had been necessary, Emerald had explained, to protect our flank from attack by the pirates' allies. Also, it provided *our* pirate ally with some excellent opportunity for plunder; that had been a tacit understanding. He was to plunder only pirate resources and leave the colonists alone, and I trusted his commitment on that—but the delay had proved deadly for us!

And what would we do when we came up against the River Sajo? We could not turn south along it for several reasons. First, we could not make the turn without getting torn up by the spearhead of the Marianas, and if we did complete the turn, our right flank would be exposed to their continuing attack. And if we staved off that, where would we go? The Sajo was part of a tributary system to the Danube, joining it to the south. That was a cul-de-sac, a dead end. If we turned north we faced similar problems and would be heading into the mountains; in this case, the larger planetoids that we would have to maneuver around while under fire from the pirate van. No, our only choice was to funnel through the ford again, then try to prevent them from following. We could probably succeed in that, but it hardly mattered, for they would remain the clear victors in this embarrassing encounter.

"I'm glad I'm not a Mongol," I muttered with something like gallows humor.

"Get it out of your system," Rue advised, for we were in our chamber. "Rape me really hard."

The awful thing was, she meant it. To her way of thinking, a major function of a married woman was to alleviate her husband's distress of any nature by serving as the violent object of his rage. He could beat her up and vent his passions on her body and be at ease with himself, all tensions abated.

I looked at her, standing there in her translucent negligee. She was so stunningly beautiful! Oh, I wanted her, but not this way. "I almost liked it better when you hated me," I said.

She smiled sweetly. "I still hate you, Captain."

I shouldn't have been surprised or shocked, but I was. My illusions about the nature of this marriage had taken another jolt. Suddenly it was too much. I was in humiliating retreat on both the military and romantic fronts, and here was my ultimate defeat: her continuing antipathy.

Something crumbled inside me. I dropped facedown on the bed and sobbed.

Dimly I heard her disgusted voice. "What the hell's the matter with you? *No* man does that, not even when he's dying of a gut wound. Stop it this instant!"

But I was overwhelmed by defeat. I continued to cry into the pillow.

"You damned gutless wonder!" she swore. "Quit it!" And she struck me on the back with her petite fist. "I can't stand to see a man cry!"

I ignored her. She got on the bed, dug her hands into my side, and rolled me over. Through blurred eyes I saw her sitting beside me, absolutely helpless and furious. "You cursed baby!" she exclaimed. "What do I have to do to make you stop, treat you like a damned infant?"

"Yes," I blubbered.

"Shit!" she said.

But after a moment she reconsidered. "Okay, jellyfish! You want it, you got it. Come here, baby." And she lay down beside me, stripped her night clothing, and hauled my head roughly into her bare bosom. "That better, you sniveling weakling?"

I turned my head, and my cheek slid across her smooth, full breast. I closed my eyes, imagining it was Helse's breast. Suddenly I was at peace. "Yes."

"Oh, for God's sake!" she muttered, her efforts to shame me having failed. "I should smother you!" And she brought her free hand up to press her other breast at my mouth, preventing me from breathing through it.

I took her nipple into my mouth and sucked on it, a baby indeed.

"You bastard!" she swore, shuddering with outrage. "You spineless, ludicrous excuse for a man! That's disgusting! What the hell do you think I am?"

I closed my teeth, biting gently on her nipple. "Oh!" she exclaimed, but she did not draw away. "You're hurting me!"

Then she paused, evidently struck by a realization. "Do it again."

I bit her again, lightly. "You sadistic brute!" she murmured, and pressed her breast closer in to my face.

Then it was my turn to pause in realization. She did not have to be truly hurt or degraded; she only needed a pretext. We were playing at the game of "baby," and now she was getting into it. Perhaps we had found a compromise.

I held her close, and she held me close, and I worked on her divine breast. In due course she heated, physically, and became all soft and shivery against me. "Oh, God." she whispered. "Oh, God . . ."

And so, in our askew fashion, we made peaceful and mutually satisfying love for the first time. Out of defeat had come a kind of victory.

Our fleet did funnel through the ford. Emerald did a masterful job of integrating our dispositions so that the Marianas were unable to capitalize on our constriction. We shot through the river pass at relatively high velocity, decelerating, so that our ships would be in position to defend the ford. Here, at last, was where our six-day retreat ended.

The Marianas had to decelerate also, for they did not care to subject their ships to the rigors of the river of sand and were unable to use the ford while our ships guarded it. They had no other way to cross, so were at a loss. Balked, they drew up before the ford, ready but unable to attack. Almost, I shared their frustration; it was not pleasant to have the prey escape. What should have been a phenomenal victory for King Bela had been reduced to a mere advance, owing to the accident of terrain.

The *Sawfish,* facing back in order to decelerate, braked all the way to a halt, then proceeded back toward the ford. "What are you doing?" I demanded of Spirit, the first member of my staff I located.

"Attacking the enemy, sir," she said. "Now we have successfully re-formed; we can meet them face-to-face. What do you say to that?"

"I say I'll pulverize you!" I said as King Bela. "You're just as bad off here as you would have been at the Danube, and tired from a six-day flight, and shorter of supplies than ever."

"So you'll commit all your forces to wipe us out," she said.

"Of course. I'm certainly not going to back off now."

"Well, may the best fighting force win," she said.

She was up to something. But the Mongol course still seemed foolhardy to me. If they wanted to fight with their back to the river, they could have done that at the Danube.

Here, if they won the battle, they would have nothing to exploit, for this was an uninhabited region. By the time they reached and crossed the Danube, the Hungarians could organize another effective defense. But the Mongols were unlikely to win, trying to fight out from the cramped formation necessitated by the bottleneck of the ford.

But I kept my silence. Evidently Emerald and my staff knew something I didn't. Whatever it was, I hoped the Marianas didn't know it, either.

The *Sawfish* crossed the Sajo and emerged from the ford. There, ranged in full battle order before us, was the entire Marianas fleet: a battleship; two small carriers; and ten destroyers, buttressed by numerous escort ships. They were poised, waiting for us to get clear of the river, so that we could not conveniently retreat again. This time they intended to be sure of us.

Our lesser vessels spread out around us. Our own carrier, the *Hempstone Crater,* was beside us, protected by the big guns of the battleship. But against the plainly superior force of the Marianas, what use was this?

The gap between us closed. The guns of the *Sawfish* fired; the unequal battle was on. The enemy ships advanced, eager to finish this campaign. They certainly seemed to be unstoppable. We could put up a decent fight but could not win. There just was not time enough to get all our ships through the ford and into play before the first ones were overwhelmed.

Then from our right appeared another fleet of ships. Peripheral dust around the River Sajo had concealed their approach, but now they were too close to hide. "What's that?" I demanded, alarmed.

"That's Emerald," Spirit informed me blithely.

"But she's here on the *Sawfish!*"

"No. The Rising Moon transferred to the *Inverness* last night—she's a nocturnal person, you know—and led two-thirds of our force to the other ford."

"What other ford?"

"The one our scouts located when we crossed the Sajo the first time. It's a subtle passage, and it seems the Marianas don't know about it."

"Don't know about it!" I exclaimed. "Are they fools?"

She shrugged. "Dear brother, you're King Bela. Did you know about it?"

"No, but—"

"Did you even think of the possibility?"

"I had other things on my mind!"

"The prosecution rests."

"Is that what happened at the real battle of Mohi Heath?"

"You got it. Bela's soldiers panicked, finding themselves attacked on flank and rear. The Mongols left the Hungarians an avenue of escape, and mowed them down in pursuit. In three days, about two-thirds of them were killed. It was one of the Mongols' most convincing victories."

I shook my head. "Next time someone else can play the role of the enemy commander! I don't like losing battles."

Roulette came up beside me. "Oh, I don't know. I can think of one a couple of nights ago—"

"Bitch," I told her. I had learned the hard way how much she liked that sort of appellation. But there, as in the space battle, my retreat was over.

It was indeed a massacre. The discipline of the pirate fleet dissolved, and it was each ship for itself. I saw the wisdom of the Mongol strategy: Had the enemy been completely surrounded, the ships would have fought with the courage of desperation. But since they had a route to flee, they turned and fled, and our faster ships had no trouble running them down singly.

We did not destroy their ships unless we had to. We closed on the best prizes and forced their individual surrender and took them over for our fleet. Those that refused to surrender were infiltrated by our commandoes, using the technique we had drilled on and that I had used to fight Sergeant (then Corporal) Heller. Now this preparation paid off. We took some losses, of course; these are inevitable in battle. But these were offset by much greater gains.

Roulette and I amused ourselves by transferring to the carrier and piloting a pair of drones. This was really an adventurous minimal-risk pursuit, since we never left the

carrier. Each of us was ensconced in a framework of remote controls, the headsets feeding the drones' perceptions
directly to our eyes and ears, our hands and feet operating
the electronic directives. Both of us had had our prior practice in dronesmanship, of course, but never in a genuine
battle situation. Our assignment now was to scout out the
location and defenses of particular fleeing enemy ships, so
that our destroyers could zero in on them efficiently. Efficiency was the watchword; we wanted to nullify as many of
these ships as possible before they reached the Danube.
Thus all trained hands were pressed into service, ours included, so that the drones would operate in shifts.

It was easy to get into the feel of it. The moment my
drone was launched by the ship's catapult, its lenses became my eyes and its code signals my ears. It was almost
as if I had sprouted a jet and a cannon and was flying in
space—or riding a fine, fast horse across a plain. It was an
exhilarating experience; though I was bound to my ma-
chinery, I felt free in space.

Beside me was Drone number 18, the one my eighteen-
year-old bride had chosen. Though she was conversant
with the mechanism, she had not before handled a Navy
drone, so I would keep her in sight and advise her when
she needed it. It seemed as if we were radioing each other
in space, but the mechanism was simpler than that: Our
natural voices carried readily across the two-foot distance
separating our control sets. Soon we were singing in
space, ". . . takes a worried man . . ." ". . . make your garden
fair . . . ," making a kind of harmony where none belonged,
exactly as was the case with our marriage.

It would be nice if I could claim we accomplished some
heroic, or at least significant, deed. But we did not; we
were simply small elements in the massive salvage effort
made by our fleet. We spotted a handsome corvette and
covered it with our guns until one of our destroyers approached and forced its surrender. What was perhaps more
significant, as I view it in retrospect, was our conversation
while we waited for the destroyer to arrive.

"Hope?"

She seldom called me that! "Yes, Rue?"

"We have defeated the Marianas and soon will free your Jupiter base. Your mission to the Belt is accomplished. There will be no further need for the alliance between your fleet and the Solomons."

Now I grasped her concern. "And no further need of our marriage," I finished.

"Yes."

I sighed. "It was never my intent to hold you against your will, Rue. You have always been free to return to your father."

"A man is a singing wynd."

"But I do not take any marriage lightly," I said, nettled at the implication. "Many pirate and military marriages may be mainly matters of mutual convenience, and certainly ours has been, but I think you make an excellent S-3 officer and a fair wife. I don't want to lose you, Rue; I want the marriage to continue."

I half-expected an expletive of negation in response, but she was silent a moment. Then: "But you must return to Jupiter."

"I will take you with me, if you want to go," I said. "As a ranking officer I have certain privileges, among them the right to appoint whom I please to positions within my command, and to marry whom I please, in or out of the Navy. You are technically a civilian, but as long as you remain married to an officer of the Jupiter Navy, you will have status in the Navy. I remain ready to take you on a tour to Jupiter."

"You are not dumping me the moment my use to you is over?"

"That is not my way, Rue. I have made and broken a liaison and a marriage in the Service—but only for solid, mutually agreed reason. You are welcome to check with Juana and Emerald."

"The Used Maiden still loves you."

"So her song says. But does she say I wronged her?"

Rue sighed. "No. She speaks no evil of you."

"It's not a casual matter with me. I married you for the alliance with your father, but my commitment is not limited to the alliance. Not unless you wish it to be."

Again there was a pause. "What of Helse?"

"I did not promise you love. Your body delights me, but—"

"She's dead, Hope!"

"Yes. But I love her."

"What of Megan?"

"What do you know of Megan?"

"You called to her, just before you raped me."

"It was a vision. I do not know her."

"But she will be the next woman you love."

I was silent, and the conversation terminated there. It would be nice if all conversations led neatly to significant conclusions, but few do. Our lives are not so neatly organized. But I believe this interchange marked another turning point in our relationship. Roulette was coming to terms with my nature.

We wrapped up the drone mission, and our fleet wrapped up the capture of the enemy ships. Some Marianas did escape—the fastest ships—but the enemy losses were about seventy percent, as it had been with the Hungarians in the thirteenth century A.D. of Earth. The pirates, who had not heeded history, had indeed repeated it.

Roulette found pretexts to be with Emerald as much as possible. Her purpose was plainly positive: She was highly impressed with the strategic victories we had had, and wanted to learn at the feet of the master (mistress). Emerald was gruffly flattered; she liked having a disciple, especially one who was a subsequent wife of mine. Perhaps not all of what they discussed was military.

I found myself associating more with Mondy, who was busy interrogating new prisoners, seeking information on the remaining pirate forces. Since he could not necessarily trust what they told him, he had me interview the key ones. I informed him who was lying and who was telling the truth, and that enabled him to assemble reliable data. This was important, as Emerald's strategy was based on the nature of the enemy as defined by her husband. Mondy had informed her that the Marianas' chief was prone to go for the big play, eager to capture quality slaves; he would be conservative until he believed he had the advantage, then sweep in for the kill. Exactly as he had done. Her ploy of Mongol retreat would not have worked against the more canny Straight. But this routine work required several days, and by the time it was done, we had crossed the Danube and laid siege to the Marianas' home base.

At this point I had better dissolve what remains of the historical analogy. This was not medieval Europe, and not the twentieth-century Pacific; it was twenty-seventh-century space, with aspects unique to itself. In this day, winning a battle was not the whole story; it was the necessary prerequisite to the proper completion of our mission. Now we had to ascertain what damage the pirates had done to the Jupiter base and get that base functioning properly again. That could take some time.

Mondy, chronically paranoid about enemy activity, urged me not to go personally to the freed Jupiter base until his men had checked it out carefully. Ordinarily I would have heeded his caution, but events prevented. Another pirate band, the Society, whose business was fencing pirated goods to reputable markets, was approaching with three carriers. I knew we would be far better off if we secured our main base before engaging the Society band. For one thing, we had many thousands of prisoners that we needed to park under guard, and the base had facilities for this that our ships lacked. There also should be substantial supplies there, to restore our fleet vitality. So I had to rush it, against Mondy's better judgment.

We sent in pacification troops in the guise of a liberation force. They were welcomed as saviors by the base personnel. Spirit ran rosters of names through her computer section, checking them against those of the base's original complement of officers. They checked. Apparently, the base personnel had been treated with temperance by the occupying pirates—at least until the outcome of the campaign was known. Mondy remained suspicious but had to admit it seemed all right.

"Look," I told him. "If I go there, and nothing happens, then we'll know it's all right. I can serve as a lightning rod; I'm the mission figurehead. We only have a couple of days to settle this before we have to meet the Society; this is the only way to do it in time."

"Take adequate guards," he said grudgingly.

"An openly armed force is no good," I pointed out. "I must seem satisfied, relaxed, unsuspecting." The truth was, I was sure it was all right. The pirates knew they had no future at the base and could only invite retaliation if they pulled any tricks at this point. "I'll go there on recreation liberty with my beautiful bride. But I'll bring my routine bodyguard."

"Not enough," he objected. "At least take Brinker and Shrapnel. They know the pirate ways."

That made sense. Brinker, in a dress, looked innocent enough, and once Shrapnel had sworn allegiance to The Ravished, he had proved to be extremely useful. He did indeed know the ways and faces of the local pirates. In addition, a picked squad of sharpshooters was assigned to keep an eye on us at all times, just in case. But we planned to act as if we believed we were mostly unobserved.

The physical premises were impressive. Several good-sized devices were anchored to the planetoid, much as they were on the moon Leda, and indeed this complex was on a similar scale. One reason the pirates had not killed the regular personnel was that it would have been impossible for them to maintain it themselves; they had to rely on the trained base personnel, both military and civilian. They had, of course, confined the base commander and his officers but had otherwise been satisfied with benign enslavement of the working personnel. Ships had been looted and supplies rifled, of course, and the base was in a state of general disrepair. Most of the young women had been raped; in fact, they had been converted as a class to a gigantic Tail for the pleasure of the pirates. But military women know how to handle rape; it is part of their training; these ones survived their months of captivity—actually, it had been just about a year—with only a trace of the trauma experienced by civilian women. Mainly, they were angry, very angry. The men, conversely, had been denied sex; the pirates hadn't wanted any others impinging on their assumed prerogatives. That was the first thing the Base personnel asked for when we took over: resumption of legitimate sexual activity. Roulette, as Operations officer, arranged for that with the mischievous malice of a pirate: She assigned the captive pirate women to Tail duty for the initial rush.

The Belt was nearer the sun than was Jupiter, so the energy of the sun was easier to come by. Jupiter-scale lenses had been set up here, however, in a typical snafu, so that there was too much concentration, making the domes so hot that surplus heat had to be vented. Water was circulated through the bed of the planetoid, heating the rock as it cooled, and the planetoid thus served as a giant dissipator of energy.

This made for the warmest water in captivity. Our small party quickly deserted the housed area and went to the wilderness training area dome, where a band of sandy beach paralleled a torus-shaped lake pretty much as I had described the phenomenon to Rue during our wedding struggle. She was delighted. We admired the lush tropical vegetation that had survived the inattention of the pirates, then stripped naked and plunged into the warm water and splashed each other like children while our more conservative companions sat on the hot sand in the sun and chatted idly.

But as we got deeper in the water, Rue turned serious. "I don't know how to swim," she said. "I've never been in water over my head."

"I'll show you how," I volunteered. God, she was beautiful this way!

"No—you'd hold me under, drowning me until I submitted."

"Now there's a notion!" I agreed, grabbing for her.

She didn't scream; even in play, she wasn't the type. "But I don't want to drown!"

"Then submit, slut! I've never had a woman in water."

"But I know you won't really drown me," she protested in a typically female reversal.

I got hold of her. "Pretend, damn it!" I drew her luscious, slippery body into mine.

"Pretend?" She seemed genuinely baffled.

"It's a game," I explained. "Like the mock space-battle game on your father's ship: a representation of something that is, in fact, more serious. I'm the violent man, and you're the innocent maiden from the garden of thyme. I will drown you if you even hint at resistance. You must do whatever I say, and it is rape because you are coerced by the terror of drowning."

"I suppose so," she agreed uncertainly.

"Hug me, wench!" I commanded. "Or I'll hold your head under."

She embraced me. The water lapped around the contours of our touching chests.

"Kiss me," I said. "Or . . ."

She kissed me—and with real feeling. She had always been good at game playing; she just hadn't played this particular game before. I realized that this was a way to tame her for gentle love: making a game of it, the actual rape replaced by the mere threat of violence. This had real possibilities!

"Wrap your legs about my—" I began.

"Alert!" Heller cried on the beach.

I broke the posture reluctantly and looked toward shore. Six men were charging across the sand, waving huge curved swords.

Our three on the beach had their lasers out, but they were not firing. I realized that there was a suppressor field on; we had been effectively disarmed. We had indeed walked into a trap.

Heller turned toward me. "Swim away, sir!" he called. "We'll hold them until the troops arrive. Stay clear!"

But Rue couldn't swim, so would be left victim to the pirates. Also, I did not relish leaving three unarmed people to fight six sword-slashing men. I forged on out of the water, and Rue followed me. "Should have known!" she was muttering in disgust. "I let a man kiss me, and this happens!"

"You stay out of it!" I snapped back at her.

"Like hell!"

The first two pirates came at Heller and Shrapnel, their curved swords slicing violently down. But both my men were conversant with this sort of combat. Both dodged and dropped, blocking the pirates at knee level, sending them flying to the sand. But as I watched the action, not yet able to reach them, I saw that the two were now vulnerable to the following two pirates. The swords slashed down before our two men could get to their feet.

Now Rue and I were on the sand, running, but traveling in my imagination in slow motion. I saw Shrapnel rolling out of the way, avoiding the worst of the cut aimed at him; but Heller slipped in the sand and was caught, and the blade sliced into his back. I suffered *déjà vu*: watching my father cut by a pirate sword. As then, I could not prevent it.

Meanwhile, the two remaining pirates were converging on Brinker. She did not try to flee; she stepped into one with what seemed like an ineffective punch to his belly, but he groaned and dropped to the sand. She had knifed him! But the second caught her in his arms from behind, and her strength was no match for his.

At this point Rue and I arrived. Rue's shoulder crashed into the side of the pirate holding Brinker while I dived to wrest the sword away from the nearest fallen man. He hung on; I kneed him in the nose and he let go. Then I lifted the blade and clubbed him on the head with the hilt, knocking him out.

I looked up and saw that the other thrown pirate was on Rue, poking at her with his sword. Evidently her stunning figure had made him pause but not hold back entirely. She cried out as the edge sliced into her right arm.

Then it was as though a cloud formed around me—a cloud of horror and outrage. I saw the fallen body of Helse, crying to me, "Do it!" Helse—just before she died.

"Not again!" I cried.

Then the sword was singing in my hand. A pirate came at me, his own sword raised; I dodged it and jumped past him and whirled, my sword swishing in an arc that intersected the back of his neck. The blade hung up on his vertebrae, but it didn't matter. I could tell as I yanked it free that he was dead.

I dived at the pirate attacking Rue and skewered him from behind. My point entered his back and must have passed through his kidney; he dropped as I braced my bare foot against his buttock and hauled my weapon out.

I whirled to face the next, but he was already starting a two-handed chop at my head that I could not avoid.

Then he lost balance, and his stroke missed. Heller, supposedly dead, had reached out and grabbed his ankle and yanked it out. Now my own blade came around, slashing the pirate across the chest, and the blood welled out as he fell back.

One other pirate remained standing, and he was pawing at his face. Brinker, keeping her poise, had hurled sand in his eyes.

Now, at last, after these interminable few seconds, the security squad arrived. The sharpshooters had been caught by surprise by the nullification of their laser rifles. But now the pirates were done for. I picked up my shirt to wrap around Rue's cruelly wounded arm and staunch the flow of blood.

"You're a berserker!" she exclaimed faintly through pale lips. "You went crazy, tearing up those men!"

"I lost my bride to pirates once," I said. "I would not let that happen again."

"You did it to protect me?"

"Well, I value you; you know that," I said awkwardly, knowing she did not appreciate mushy sentiments.

She turned away. The security force took charge, and the brief, violent interlude was over.

Heller was dead. His last act in life must have been the one he took to save my life. He had fulfilled his vow, and I had no way to thank him. Except to leave him with a clean record and a commendation.

The pirate remnant had indeed set a trap for us. The six had been a suicide squad, hiding when the others vacated, waiting for the opportunity to catch us alone. They had intended to kill me or Rue or both of us, to deprive our force of its leadership and its basis for the alliance with the Solomons. The personnel of the base were innocent; they had known nothing of this.

Now we turned our attention to the Society fleet. Perhaps I should say that I turned my attention to it; my staff had been setting up for it all along. The Society band was not a strong one, but it had a lot of drones—twice as many as we could field at the moment. Mondy's information indicated that theirs was a suicide mission; they would send their drones at our ships and base without regard for their losses. In fact, their carriers were already decelerating, making ready to retreat; their drones would not even try to return to their bases.

This was awkward, because drones are hard to stop. They're small and fast, particularly when jammed up to top velocity, and they pack a considerable punch, and kamikaze drones have nothing to lose. We could try to shoot them all down, but probably they would loose their torpedoes the moment they came in range, and it is almost impossible to pick a traveling torpedo out of space. With targets as big as our battleship and the domes of the base itself, those torpedoes could hardly miss, and could wreak incalculable havoc.

This time I insisted on knowing Emerald's strategy. It was simple enough. "We've got to take out those drones before they fire, and that means sending ours out to intercept them."

"But they outnumber ours!" I protested. "Even if we trade off even, many of theirs will remain to attack us. They won't fall for the trick you used on the Solomons."

"Our drones will just have to take them all out," she said.

"We have how many drones now?" I asked.

"Thirty-three, on one and a half carriers."

"And they have?"

"Sixty-eight, on three carriers."

"And when drone meets drone in open space, what are the odds?"

"One drone can take out one drone in a given pass, if it shoots first and accurately. But the odds are about even which one wins, assuming the two are of equivalent sophistication."

"And is this the case here?"

"It is."

"Then how—?"

"I'm going to have ours fire on the bias."

"But drones can only fire directly forward."

"They fire in the direction they are pointed."

"Isn't that the same thing?"

"Not necessarily."

I gave it up; she was unable or unwilling to make her strategy comprehensible to me. But I made sure to watch, for though this was theoretically a minor engagement, the consequences of a loss would be horrendous. We *had* to stop those drones!

I watched our carriers go out. The "half" carrier was a damaged one captured from the Marianas; spot reconditioning had proceeded only to the point of allowing a dozen drones to be launched from it, and only eight were actually available. With more time we could have done much better, which was probably why the Society was making its play now.

The carriers went out to the sides, so as to launch their drones at right angles to the path of the enemy drones. The ideal, in drone versus drone combat, is to "cross the T"; that is, to fire at your enemy from the side, so that he can't fire back. In fact, a formation ranged in even rows would be highly vulnerable to multiply placed shots from the side. That was one way a few drones could indeed take out many. The type of loading made a difference, too; the Society drones carried heavy torpedoes, while ours were loaded with explosive shells. We could fire four shells for every one torpedo they fired. Of course, we couldn't take out their ships very well, but we didn't need to, for a carrier without drones is like a panther without teeth. Had we been able to go for their carriers before their drones got within torpedo range of our targets, that would have been worthwhile; but their tactic of launch and retreat had obviated that. So we had to deal directly with the drones.

A more popular analogy, perhaps, is to the planetary aircraft: Some are bombers, able to damage landscape, while others are fighters, able to damage other aircraft. It does make a difference. Theirs were bombers, ours fighters. We had a better chance than I had first thought. Still, I was uneasy.

The enemy drones came on in staggered wave formation, somewhat like nestled flying-goose Vees, so that crossing the T became ineffective for more than one or perhaps two ships at a time. This was a standard precaution, and a good one. Each drone stood behind and to the side of its neighbor, as it were; the overall effect was that of a huge flying arrowhead. Nine drones were in the leading wing, four trailing to each side of the point. Seven wings and a wedge of five filling out the tail section. Each was positioned so that it could launch its torpedoes forward without being blocked by the drones in front; the wings were also staggered vertically, to add another margin of safety from interference, and to broaden the coverage of the target. Sixty-eight deadly missiles, headed for our base!

The enemy was aware of our defensive formation, of course, but ignored it. The Society knew we would take out some of their drones but also knew that with only thirty-three of ours in service, and their staggered formation, the very best we could hope for was a kill total of thirty-three. That would leave thirty-five of theirs to charge the base, for there would not be time for more than one pass. Our drones could not decelerate, turn, and reaccelerate to catch theirs, which were already traveling at speed. Our base guns would take out perhaps half the remainder, but the odds against getting them all were prohibitive. And if even one drone got close enough to launch its torpedo, a base-dome would be holed, and that would finish it. The sudden holing of a dome is more disastrous than that of a ship, for a dome is not a space vessel. The explosive decompression tears it apart, and even those people inside who are fully suited and ready are unlikely to survive, because of the violence of the destruction. We could not afford to let that one torpedo get through.

Emerald had said she expected to solve the problem by firing on the bias. I still could make no sense of this. Our drones were now accelerating toward the enemy formation at right angles. They would intersect the Society drones just outside torpedo-launching range. Our formation would be as plain on their radar as it was on ours: a completely conventional array, incapable of taking out more than its own number of enemy drones.

Well, at least our fire would be accurate. Emerald had tied it to our master firing computer after our pilots had positioned their drones. That computer was now orienting each drone to place its shots in a specific pattern. This wasn't really too complicated, since all shots went in exactly the direction the drone was pointed; several would be fired in rapid order, their shells timed to explode at diminishing intervals, so that the detonations would occur simultaneously along the firing line. If there were six drones in that line, all could be hit. But, of course, there were only one or two in any line. That was the problem.

The intersection of drones could be tricky. Since it was an advantage to be the second drone on the spot, so as to be able to fire on the first and destroy it, drones were given to abrupt cessations of acceleration near the point of intersection, to change their moment of arrival and foil the timed shells. They could also increase acceleration, to leave the shells behind. Even with light-speed tracking, there was a brief delay in corrections, and the tolerance was narrow, so there was only about one chance in three that a computer-placed shot would score. This was normally compensated for by having the defensive drones (that is, the drone-fighting drones) fire in formation, placing three shots in a line before the enemy drone. If all the spots the enemy could be were covered by exploding shells, then the likelihood of destroying it became total. But that used up a lot of ammunition. Each of our drones carried six shells, so could take out only two enemy drones on that basis—if it had time to orient on two. And if the formation was correct, since it actually required three drones to place a line of shells in front of any enemy drone traveling at right angles. So, in the very best of circumstances, we could take out only sixty-six enemy drones, and the two remaining would have a clear shot at the base. Our best was not good enough.

The two fleets moved close together. On the radar screen the blips were on the verge of merging. The moment of decision was at hand. I dreaded it.

Suddenly the Society blips were obscured. All across the formation they were breaking up.

"One hundred percent, sir," a technician reported, interpreting the radar image.

Emerald relaxed. "That's it, then."

"They're gone?" I asked, bewildered. "But the flights didn't even intersect!"

She sighed, pleased. "Must I draw you a picture, sir?"

"That might help."

She grabbed a note pad. She drew a pattern of dots. "Here is the enemy's nestled V-formation," she explained. "Note how no two drones are on the same horizontal line."

"Yes, of course. So we couldn't—"

"Note how they happen to fall into bias lines, five ships per line."

"But that's no good to us," I protested. "We were proceeding at right angles."

"We were *coasting* at right angles," she said. "But the orientation of our drones changed. We oriented on their lines and fired—"

"On the bias!" I exclaimed, catching on at last. "Slantwise, early, so as to catch five ships per line!"

"Well, some of their lines are partial," she said. "But we caught them before they made their evasive acceleration, so they were sitting ducks. Some of our ships took out five, and some only took out one, but we were able to cover them all in a single sweep. The Society threat is over. Now all we have to do is round up their fleeing carriers for salvage."

"It's so obvious in retrospect," I said. "Why didn't they anticipate this?"

"Why didn't *you*, Worry?"

I shrugged. I had indeed been worrying! "I suppose I'm just a conventional thinker."

"Well, you'll have credit for one more brilliant victory, figurehead." There was no bitterness in this statement; she knew that scholars of this campaign would quickly catch on to the truth. The Rising Moon had proven herself—again.

But already we had to plan for another battle, for the Samoans, the drug dealers of the Belt, were organizing. We had eliminated, in order, the pornographers, the gamblers (well . . .), the smugglers, the slavers, and the fencers, but Commander Repro and I had personal reasons to get the druggers. In addition, we knew that if we did not destroy the last of the major bands, Samoa would simply move in and restore the prior order of piracy.

At this point I was satisfied to leave our strategy to Emerald. I had to plan for the time beyond that last battle, our departure from the Belt. We had fences to mend back at Jupiter. I discussed it with my wife.

"We shall have to leave soon, Rue," I said. "My task force was commissioned only to clean up this mess in the Belt; the moment that's done, I must bring the fleet home. Once again I must remind you that you are free to—"

"That game," she said. "The one in the water. I think I know how to play it better now."

"I'm sure you do," I agreed, putting off whatever she had in mind until I had established my position. "There are certain problems, either way. If you choose to come to Jupiter, you will have to leave your family and band, and it may be your father will need you here. The organization of the supplementary fleet we have developed from salvage will fall to him—"

"Just tell me you will drown me," she said.

"On the other hand, if you come with me, as you are welcome to do, you will always be dependent on me for your status, for you will have none of your own at Jupiter. You must remain married to an officer of my level. So you should consider very carefully whether—"

"Please don't drown me, sir!" she cried. "I'll do anything you say!" She flung her mass of red hair about fetchingly.

"And, too, you must appreciate that you can no longer be my Operations officer there. The assignment has force only during this mission, in my task force. So I really cannot offer you much—"

She clutched my shoulders, drew me in, and kissed me. If this was feigned passion, it was an excellent feign. "Okay, kiss me," I murmured after the fact.

She reached up and tore open her own blouse. "Oh, sir— please don't rape me violently! I'll submit peacefully!"

"But I don't like submission," I protested. "I prefer mutual—"

"I'll pretend! I'll pretend!" she cried, bearing me back upon the bed.

This was getting quite interesting! "How well can you feign it?"

"About as well as you feigned fighting for me, there on the beach when you berserked."

"Rue, I wasn't feigning tha—"

She shut me up with another kiss. I shrugged mentally and proceeded to it. She was, after all, an incandescently attractive young woman, and this was the closest yet she had come to the sort of passion I preferred.

But as the climactic moment approached, she paused, suddenly sober. "Hope—"

"Don't tell me!" I said. "I don't want to be reminded of the pretense. You're doing great!"

"Would you hit me, please."

For an instant I froze. Then I realized that this was the one pretext she still required—reduced to a token, but still necessary. I brought up my hand and slapped her cheek hard enough to sting but not to hurt her. "Bitch!" I murmured.

Then she was all mine, or I was all hers, and it was good indeed. There is at times great joy in young flesh. But I realized that this was about as far as she could go toward my type of love. I had to be thankful that she tried so hard to reach this point. She really did want to please me, and had met me more than halfway, and I was deeply flattered by her effort. She did indeed please me.

As we lay there in relaxed dishevelment, there was a knock on the door. That had to be one of my staff; only they sought personal contact at this hour.

"Go away!" Rue called languidly.

But the knock repeated. Angrily, she flounced off the bed and proceeded naked to the door. She flung it open. "Go away, creep! I'm getting raped!"

Gerald Phist stood there, somewhat abashed. "I regret—"

"You want to rape me, too?" Rue demanded, hands on hips.

"Not exactly, attractive as you are. Something has come up—"

I knew Phist wouldn't interrupt like this without solid reason. "What is it, Commander?" I called.

"Sir, I regret to inform you that orders from Jupiter—"

"Jupiter wants to rape somebody?" Rue demanded.

"I'm afraid so," Phist said, evidently embarrassed by more than her spectacular nudity. "I am directed by the duly constituted authority, in accordance with article—"

"What's the gist?" I interrupted, alarmed.

"Sir," he said miserably. "I must remove you from command of the Task Force, and—"

"What?" Rue cried, her breasts quivering with indignation.

"—place you under arrest," he finished.

"You can't do that!" Rue cried, outraged.

"He can do it, and he has to, or he wouldn't be here," I told her. Then, to Phist: "What pretext?"

"Insubordination, sir. Consorting with pirates. Cowardice in battle." He grimaced. "I want you to know, sir, I support none of these charges. But—"

"No, I understand, Gerald," I said. "Do your duty."

"I must confine you to quarters. And your sister."

"She's your wife, imbecile!" Roulette snapped.

"Yes," he said soberly. "And I must ground the fleet."

"But we have to fight the Samoans!" Rue said.

"No. The directive is most specific. No further combat."

"This close to finishing it?" she demanded. "I smell a—"

Phist nodded, agreeing. "But the directive is clear. I'm sorry, sir."

"May I make a call out?" I asked, numbed.

"No, sir. You are to be incommunicado."

They were closing the net suddenly and tight! Which was of course the way such dirt had to be done. "Roulette—surely she is permitted to call her father?"

Phist hesitated. "It is true she is not Navy."

"Go call your father," I told her. "Tell him I have been deposed and arrested, so must void our marriage."

"Void our marriage!" she exclaimed, shocked.

"You are better off now with your father."

"No," Phist said. "I cannot permit her to leave our custody. She is privy to too much Navy information. She may inform her father but cannot join him."

"But she's a civilian!" I protested.

"She is a pirate. She must be interned."

I sighed. "Go make your call, Rue."

"Like hell! None of this shit is—"

I lashed out with my hand, catching her cheek with a backhand blow. "You understand me, wench? *Tell your father!*"

She stared at me, rubbing her face. I had never before struck her that hard. "I—understand you, sir." She fetched her clothing and donned it while Phist waited, ill at ease.

"I wish you hadn't hit her," he muttered.

"I had to make my point." Of course, I hadn't liked doing it but had to show her that I was serious, pirate fashion. There was more to her message for her father than the spoken part.

In short order Roulette was ready and left with Phist to make her call. Phist would monitor it, of course, and cut off the call if she said anything more than was proper in the circumstance. He would follow the book precisely.

Rue turned briefly at the doorway and glanced back at me. Already a mark was beginning to show on her cheek. It was, ironically, the mark of my affection. Then she moved on out. Phist closed the panel behind them, and I heard the lock click. I was a prisoner.

Chapter 12

FINAL BATTLE

Gerald Phist was an honest man; he followed the directive to the letter. He proceeded to an efficient reorganization of all properties of the Task Force, preparatory to the voyage back to Jupiter, and disposed of all non-Navy equipment. We were permitted to monitor these preparations on the interfleet video system, since the directive covered only what we were allowed to communicate out, not what we received. Thus we knew what was going on without in any way affecting it.

Mondy and Emerald were allowed to visit me at will, and Spirit and Repro, for all were under similar arrest. Our section of the ship was simply cordoned off, and only service personnel on specific business were permitted to enter. Phist himself stayed clear, not even communicating with us; in no way could he be said to be in violation of any aspect whatever of the letter or spirit of the directive.

Rue, interned with us, seethed. "The bastard's mutinied!" she exclaimed. "He's taken over your command!"

"Commander Phist is a good man and a fine officer," I said. "He is doing his duty, nothing else, as he always has, regardless of personal considerations. I can't fault him."

"But he's torpedoing the whole mission! The Samoans will take over!"

Mondy smiled. On this occasion we were all seated around my chamber, which, as the Captain's quarters, was the largest and best furnished. "May I, sir?"

"By all means, Peat Bog," I agreed.

"Perhaps you have not paid proper attention to the incoming data, Roulette," he said. "It tells a story of probable success despite adversity."

"All I've seen are ships being mothballed and our plunder ditched," she said.

"The Jupiter Navy does not plunder," Mondy said. "The pirate ships we captured and recommissioned are being sold to the highest bidder, in accordance with regulations. The proceeds will be used to liquidate all outstanding Navy debts in this region."

"What about all the money you borrowed from my father to buy supplies?" she demanded.

"Precisely. That debt is in the process of being settled."

"And who the hell is buying these ships?" she continued. "Those aren't just scrap metal, you know! Those are functioning carriers and cruisers and destroyers; in fact, they now amount to more than half the fleet! Any pirate who gets hold of those ships can dominate the Belt, or whatever part of it the Samoans don't take over." She paused, alarmed at her own assessment. "Who is buying those ships?" she repeated.

"Your father."

That stopped her for a moment. "What does he want with a battle fleet? All he wants is a legitimate gambling empire."

"I believe he plans to engage the Samoans," Mondy said innocently.

"He can't! They have more hardware. The full Task Force could have tromped them, but not half of it, with no Navy crews and no genius strategy. It'll be suicide!"

"Those ships do have crews," Mondy said mildly. "The pirates who have joined us have been released, as there is no future for them at Jupiter, and they are not prisoners. There is no longer an alliance between the Navy and the Solomons band, so their allegiance devolves on Straight, the dominant pirate leader."

"No alliance? My father's a pirate, but he keeps his word!"

"He kept it," Mondy said. "The Navy broke off the alliance, with Captain Hubris's deposition and the voiding of your marriage."

"There's no voiding! I never agreed to that!"

"But you did relay Captain Hubris's message to your father."

"Yes. But my father knew that wasn't real."

"Why not?" Mondy asked, knowing the answer.

She touched her cheek, which showed a bruise. "Because Hope hit me. Hard enough to show. He never did that before, not since the wedding. My father saw that mark."

"And so your father knew that the Captain still laid claim to you," Mondy said. "Yet his message was that the marriage was voided. Didn't that seem strange to you?"

"It meant he still wants me as a concubine," Rue said, her lower lip trembling. "I'll settle for that."

I started to speak, but Mondy wasn't finished. "But without formal marriage," he pointed out, "the alliance between your two groups has no basis. Straight's on his own now, owing nothing to the Navy."

"And he's fool enough to fight the Samoans for you!"

"You misunderstand," Spirit said. "That mark on your face belied the captain's words. Officially he was terminating the alliance, but in reality he was continuing it. *That's* why your father is acting. He knows he must do what the Navy will not do, and that we are backing him in the manner we are able."

Rue nodded, brightening. "Still, my father doesn't have to—"

"Well, it is a question who will be the dominant power in the Belt, once the Navy presence is vacated," Mondy said. "Evidently Straight prefers to assume that mantel himself. It does seem reasonable in the circumstance."

"But he can't take Samoa! Not without her." She gestured to Emerald. "You know she's the reason the Navy has been so successful in the Belt."

"One of the reasons," Mondy agreed. "I could be inclined to give credit also to the accurate intelligence provided by my department, the superior logistical performance of Commander Phist, and the inspiring leadership of Captain Hubris."

"But my father has none of that! He doesn't even have me to command his fleet! He's a gambler, not a warrior!"

"Well, he may have some of it. It seems that the civilian employee Isobel Brinker elected to take employment with Straight, rather than remain as a clerk in the Navy; I gather he offered her command of a cruiser. She happened to have in her possession a dossier I had prepared on the Samoan pirates, including the most recent and accurate intelligence estimates of their strength and dispositions, and a tentative plan of battle worked out by my wife—"

Rue stared at him. "You slimy dog!" she exclaimed admiringly. "You could be hung for that!"

"I really don't know how she got hold of that dossier," Mondy said innocently. "It was securely locked in my file."

"She's a pirate! She knows how to get into a locked file!"

"So it seems. I shall, of course, accept responsibility for the oversight; no doubt I shall receive a stern reprimand ." He shrugged. "But it was a standard Navy security file cabinet, and the material was not relevant to Naval interests following Captain Hubris's deposition, since we have no intention of engaging the Samoans, so I doubt there will be very much of an issue made. In any event, it is useless to bemoan the loss now; the damage is done." Somehow Mondy did not look regretful.

Roulette's brow wrinkled. "How could all this just happen so fast, with no meeting or discussion? How could my father know? *I* didn't tell him! I had no inkling!"

Mondy spread his hands deprecatingly. "A smart commander prepares contingency plans, in case of surprise developments. In the course of exchanging information, in order to ensure proper liaison between our fleets, I may have mentioned something about surprises. Casually, of course; it would not have been my place to make any official statements. But I believe it is generally known that on occasion there are unforeseen consequences for the proper performance of one's job, as was the case with Commander Phist some years back, and Sergeant Smith." His lips quirked wryly.

"You told my father the Navy would bust my husband for doing his job?"

"Naturally not! I merely reminisced about past events. I have had a certain experience with the ways of the Navy.

Your father is an intelligent man, master of the finesse. Possibly he drew a conclusion that should have seemed unwarranted at the time. Certainly I am paranoid about things that no longer exist. I even dream about them."

"I always wonder what Rising Moon saw in you," Rue said. "Why she holds your hand at night. I'm beginning to get a glimmer. You have an obscenely suspicious mind."

Emerald took Mondy's hand. "Isn't it awful!"

"But Commander Phist—he doesn't know? He's not stupid—"

"There is nothing stupid about Old King Cole," I said. "He knows what's going on. He is simply following the letter of the law, as he always has."

"But he could scotch this transfer of ships and personnel and information anytime!" she said.

"He has not been directed to do so. He has been directed to reorganize the Task Force for prompt return to Jupiter, purging it of foreign elements. I'm afraid you have lost Shrapnel, Rue; he'll probably command a ship for your father."

"Shrapnel," she murmured. "I wonder what *his* song was?" Then she reverted to the more vital matter. "But Phist knows what's happening! All he has to do is tell Jupiter—"

"To blow the whistle?" Spirit asked. We all laughed.

"What would he tell them?" I asked after a moment. "About conjectures? Hearsay? Paranoia? Scuttlebutt?" I shook my head. "He would not stoop to that sort of thing. The admirals back home are not interested in sordid pirate gossip."

Rue nodded. "I guess Phist is more man than I figured, too. He's making it all work out right."

"A man can be honest and gentle," Spirit said, "and still be worthwhile. I married him for other reasons, but I would have chosen him for love, had I known."

Rue pondered, considering that. She had been learning a lot about gentle men recently. Then her gaze turned on me. "What will become of you, Hope?"

"I'll be court-martialed," I said. "The responsibility is mine; my officers simply obeyed my orders. They are clean, but there's not much question of my guilt. This has been a remarkably un-Navy campaign."

"But you didn't do it! You're a figurehead!"

"All was done in my name. I take the credit—and the blame. I would not have it otherwise. The record shows that I have indeed pursued my mission beyond my authority and did indeed flee before the enemy for six days—"

"But that was strategic!" she protested. "And you turned around and destroyed them when a conventional approach would have decimated your forces!"

"But it looks like cowardice, and that is bad for the Navy image. Appearance is more important than reality at times. And I have certainly consorted with pirates."

"Such as my father—and me."

"I'm afraid so. So I will be found guilty of at least one count and probably stripped of my commission, or at least be reduced in rank."

"But you've done everything they wanted! You wiped out the pirates of the Belt with few losses, and freed the base—"

"Captain Hubris has done *more* than they wanted," Mondy said. "There's the key."

The key. That reminded me of the one I carried, that QYV still wanted.

"But if they didn't really want the Belt cleaned up, why did they send him?" Roulette was still having trouble with the background.

"They thought he would fail," Mondy explained. "As he would have, had he insisted on planning strategy himself, as most commanders do. Hope has no special talent for that. He is intelligent and motivated, and his men are devoted to him—I'm sure Sergeant Smith has his hands full, now, keeping them in line—but he is no strategist."

"But—"

"But the salient quality he does have does not show well on the standard tests," Mondy continued. "Hope is a born leader, not by rhetoric or force of personality or ruthless application of power, but by his inordinate talent to grasp the true nature of men and thereby to inspire their loyalty.

Thus he lacks the overt abilities of a conqueror but has established those abilities in his staff."

"He hasn't shown much understanding of *me!*"

Emerald laughed. "His talent fails when his emotion gets in the way. I was always able to fool him."

Rue's eyes narrowed, then relaxed. "I told him I hated him—"

"And he believed you," Emerald said, nodding knowingly. It was as if I wasn't there.

"My father had it figured," Rue said. "He had Hope picked out for me from the moment the fleet set out from Jupiter. God, I was angry!"

"Your father sought the best possible match for you," Mondy agreed. "He knew you would submit to no ordinary man either in body or emotion, but Hope has the ability to—"

"To conquer unruly women," Rue concluded, glancing at Emerald. "But I still don't see why Jupiter wanted the mission to fail. First they sent a man they thought couldn't do the job. When he started doing it, they cut off his supplies. When he fled before the enemy, they let him be. But when he turned about and beat the pirates, they deposed him—right before final success. *Why?*"

"They had to act when they did," Mondy said. "The other pirates are expendable, but the Samoans control the drug trade."

"Which is why they must be destroyed," Repro put in. "The drug trade is more insidious and damaging to our society than piracy itself. It does to the society what the drug does to me."

Now Rue focused on Repro. "My father said if he had wanted to destroy the true threat to piracy in the Belt, he'd have sent an assassin after you. But you're the least effective officer in this bunch! You're slowly dying!"

"True," Repro agreed. "I'm only a dreamer."

"Whose dream almost came true," I murmured.

"I still don't get it," Roulette said. "Why does Jupiter want the drug trade to continue?"

"You see, many legitimate elements of the Jupiter society use those illegal drugs," Mondy said. "They can't afford to have their major source of supply cut off. So while public pressure required that the Marianas be punished for stepping on our base, it was never intended that piracy itself—particularly the Samoans—be extirpated from the Belt. Had Hope gone straight to the Marianas and liberated the base, or had he bungled the job, all would have been well. But when he forced their hand by succeeding too well, the powers that be acted."

"Seems to me there are worse pirates in Jupiter than in the Belt," Rue muttered darkly, and I was surprised to see the others nod agreement. "But now my father will do the job, anyway. He has no truck with drugs."

"So it seems," Mondy agreed. "The Jupiter authorities will be furious, but fortunately our fleet will be safely out of it before the final battle occurs. They will not be able to blame us for that."

"They'll try, though!" she said. "They'll crucify Hope!"

Mondy shrugged. "Hope always knew that—as did we all, including Phist. Phist more than any of us! Now it is Hope Hubris's turn, and Phist, ironically, will achieve honor for delivering Hope into their hands."

"And so Hope tried to void our marriage before he got canned."

"He gave you that last chance, knowing you would have been better off with your father, in the Belt, though he knew we still needed you for the alliance."

Rue turned to me. "Hope, I have a gift for you."

Mondy stood up. "We'll be leaving now."

"No!" Rue said sharply. "All of you were witnesses to my rape; you must be witness to this, too."

Mondy sat down again. "None of us liked what we had to do then. We are not of your culture."

"But I am joining yours." Rue took my hands in hers. "For you, Hope. My tears."

I was startled. "Your what? You never cry, Rue—" Actually, I had felt her tears during the wedding rape, but those had been of frustration, not grief or love.

"I never had reason before." Already they were starting, brimming at her beautiful eyes as if the tide had risen in her body, overflowing to her cheeks, and down to her mouth and chin.

"I don't understand," I said, hesitating to take her into my arms; she was not necessarily partial to open gestures of affection. "I haven't really voided our relationship; I'll never do that without your consent."

"You raped me and won my body," she said through her tears. "But you never conquered me. I swore no man would do that. I knew I could take or leave any man, and never love him. But you—"

Now I took her in my arms. "I never required your love, Rue."

"Well, you got it." And she sobbed into my shoulder. "You tamed the shrew, you monster."

Mondy stood again. "Congratulations," he said to us both, and led the way out.

Yes, we made love, and she was able to respond without even token violence. I would never have to hit her again. She had indeed given me a rare gift.

Yet what would I have for her when I was stripped of my rank and perhaps my freedom? She still would be better off returning to the Belt. But she could not—and I knew that if she could, she would not. The loyalty of a pantheress is not easy to obtain—or to end.

We were well on our way back to Jupiter when the final battle was fought. We were able to follow it only approximately, by monitoring erratic news reports from the Belt. I reconstruct here in minutes what we learned piecemeal in the course of many hours. The rest of us had no notion of Emerald's strategy, and she refused to tell; she wanted it to be a surprise. Well, it was certainly an adequate distraction for the occasion.

The fleet of Samoa was ensconced within the shelter of a great, curving, cup-shaped cloud of debris from a defunct comet or fragment of an ancient supernova. They had mined the cloud, using a camouflaged variety of mine that looked exactly like space refuse; it was impossible to tell with the equipment available in the field which chunks of rock were natural and which were mines. Any ship attempting to pass through this region would contact a mine; if the explosion did not hole it, the attention attracted by the detonation would set it up for a shot from the battleship at the fringe of the cloud. A ship inside the cloud would be practically invisible; the dust and debris interfered with radar. But an explosion emitted radiation that penetrated the rocks and was readily detectable from nearby. Thus the cloud was considered impassable, and the ships in the cup were secure from any flank or rear attack.

With that protection, the Samoans needed only to cover the region of space in front of their fleet. It was like the pincushion defense without any planetoid for the pins to anchor to; thus it was more versatile. Since this was the only feasible channel through the Belt leading to their main base, they seemed secure. The Solomons fleet could not occupy the Samoan base without traveling this channel, and the cloud-backed Samoan fleet guarded it. But the Solomons could not afford to ignore the base; Samoa was far from the Solomons' home region, and the moment Straight departed for home, as he had to do before long, the Samoans would come out and take over whatever they wanted. More frustrating to us, they would continue their drug trade, the worst of the pirate activities in the Belt.

Oh, I realize that some people would question that, suggesting that the slave trade was worse. But slavery was limited, with very specialized markets, while drugs penetrated to the heart of the leading governments of the Solar System, corrupting them—as our present situation showed. The power of the drug trade was much greater than showed in the Belt; the Samoans were only the visible projection of it. Only now was I coming to appreciate the sinister magnitude of that business. Even the Jupiter Navy danced to its tune!

So now we watched, hoping Straight could do what we could not. Oh, there would be an outcry in private circles if he managed it, but what could they do? Court-martial him? He was technically a pirate, beyond their jurisdiction. No, they would have to deal with him, his way; a new power was forming in the Belt. Straight would probably obtain the legitimacy he craved. Provided he took out Samoa.

Would Emerald's strategy work without Emerald there to oversee it? A battle was not something one set up and let fall, like a row of dominoes; proper implementation was critical. Could Straight provide the proper tactics? I was not at all easy.

The Solomons fleet came straight down the channel, decelerated, and drifted just beyond combat range. It seemed that Straight was hoping the Samoans would come forward to fight, deserting their cloud-cup rear protection. That, of course, was foolish. The Samoans had an excellent defensive position, their guns covering the full breadth of the channel, and they were surely stocked for a siege. Straight, with his makeshift fleet and skeletal crews, could not wait them out; he had to win quickly, or give it up. He could not even restock at the Jupiter base, for the alliance was off and the commander there was no longer permitted to associate with pirates.

There they waited for a day in seeming indecision. Straight made some feints, but these were unsuccessful. The Samoans, though their fleet was as strong as Straight's, were too canny to budge. They were forcing him to attack their prepared position and suffer ruinous losses, or to retreat and suffer similarly.

Then news of another fleet came. The remnants of the other pirate bands were sending their ships to support the Samoans, and in two days these would come down the channel behind the Solomons' fleet. That was trouble indeed; Straight would have to commence withdrawal immediately if he was to avoid being caught in the middle. Obviously things had started to go wrong the moment Emerald was disassociated from the effort.

Our fleet's night came, and I slept, holding Rue's hand. I still had much joy in her final gift to me—the gift of her tears, her unrestrained emotion—but I feared for her father, and for her if she lost him to battle just when she was losing me to Navy discipline. She had given herself at last to me, but at what cost to herself and her band?

I dreamed, in that special fashion I sometimes do when

under stress. Rue and I were in space, in the Belt—an impossibly crowded section. We were perched on boulders, carrying pugil sticks. All around us were other members of our crew, each person riding a rock and bearing a pugil stick. Sergeant Smith, and Shrapnel, and Juana, and Brinker, and all the other Hispanics and Saxons and just plain, good people. We waved cheerily to each other, but no one deserted his rock.

Then something floated toward us, huge and cylindrical. It was a spaceship—a cruiser! There is no good reason for spaceships to be rounded or cylindrical, apart from the convenience of construction, since there is no atmospheric friction in space, but the Navy somehow never felt free to deviate far from the streamlined form. The cruiser nudged so close to my rock I could touch it, and, indeed, I did touch it, reaching out with the padded end of my pugil stick to shove the huge hull away. Of course, the mass of the cruiser was much greater than mine, even including the rock I perched on and braced against; all I accomplished was to shove my platform away. I retreated from the cruiser, waving my stick, and now I saw that on the hull were hundreds of other people, each with a similar stick, and all of them waved cheerily back at me. We seemed to be having one big, crazy party in space, the rockworms and the hullnuts pushing each other away. Odd game!

But now I was drifting away also from Rue. She stood on her stone, gesturing helplessly, proffering respect and love but unable to reach me or draw me back. I knew, with the certainty that only a dream provides, that neither of us could leave our rocks, lest some horrendous disaster occur. We were bound to go with our pieces of real estate, wherever that might be.

"Rue!" I cried.

"Hope!" she cried back. The vacuum of space was all about us, yet our voices carried.

"I'm worried about you!" I called.

"My garden is waste!" she replied.

"Thank you for your tears!" I cried. But our boulders were rotating, and hers had turned to face her away from me, or maybe mine had spun, and we were lost to each other. And now I cried, inheriting her tears.

I woke, and she woke, and we hugged each other. We were together after all! But still I felt the premonition of the dream, and the chill of outer space seeped through my bones. This lovely girl, not yet out of her teens, would surely be lost to me, and I could do nothing to prevent it.

There was a knock. I recognized the touch of my sister and called her in. "It's happening," she said. "Turn on your vid." But she did it for me, then sat down on the edge of the bunk. There was plenty of room, this being the outsize nuptial bed. Now it reminded me of a space boulder.

A Jupiter-Network news spot was in progress. Of course, reception was poor, this being several light-minutes distant from the source, but we were used to that. ". . . activity behind the Samoan battleship," the announcer was saying.

Emerald arrived. "Hear that, Worry? They did it!"

"Did what?" Rue demanded, not bothering to cover herself.

"Sneaked through that cloud with a cruiser," Emerald explained. "Fired point-blank into the Samoan battleship, taking it out. Now the cruiser commands the field. Those lesser Samoan ships are pointed the wrong way; they're sitting ducks!"

"Through the cloud?" I asked. "Your plan, did it include setting men on space boulders with pugil sticks?"

"Oh, you found out!" she said, annoyed.

"I think I was there," I said.

"Where?" Rue asked.

"You were there, too."

"That's nice. Does this mean my father's all right?"

"He's in control," Emerald assured her. "My plan was to infiltrate the mined cloud by moving very slowly, matching the velocity of its internal currents and posting men on every rock in the path of the ship. It didn't matter whether any given rock was natural or a mine; none were allowed to touch. So the cruiser did what the enemy thought was impossible: It ambushed their battleship from behind."

"God, I'm glad to hear that!" Rue said. "But what will the drug merchandisers do now?"

"First they'll have Hope's head," Spirit said, taking my free hand. "Then they'll set about developing other avenues of supply. But it will be much harder for them to operate now."

Rue pulled me back down with her and enfolded my head in a bosomy embrace. "They can't have his head," she said. "It's mine!"

I liked this new mannerism of hers very well. But I suspected the colder vision of my dreams was closer to reality. Powerful external forces were bearing us apart, and we could not resist them.

Commander Phist brought the fleet safely back to the Jupiter System and duly turned us all over to the military authorities. It was a measure of his integrity that he had never met privately with Spirit since the directive came, though she was his wife and he loved her. In this respect his ordeal was harsher than ours, but it would have been an abuse of his position to socialize with any of those who were under arrest, and this he would not do.

We were separately interned; there was no more camaraderie in captivity. I had a good month in virtual solitary confinement while they prepared their case against me. Here I was denied access to external news, and that was almost as painful as the separation from my staff and friends.

I put that time to use: I commenced writing this narrative of my military career. There is nothing like solitary confinement to sharpen one's appreciation for past experience! I have written this in Spanish, to refresh my skill in my native language and to protect its privacy at least somewhat from my English-speaking jailors. They don't care what I do, but they do peer over my shoulder, as it were.

I fear I have focused too much on personal aspects, neglecting the technical ones, but in this time of isolation and loneliness, it is these personal experiences that assume the greatest meaning. The officers of the prosecution will surely be assembling many volumes of technical data; I cannot do better than they in that respect. But when I write of Juana, Emerald, and Rue, they seem to be with me again, and I can almost believe that I loved them each. Yes, surely I did!

Before I completed my narrative, I was interrupted. Without explanation I was conducted to a mortuary section. For a moment I feared I was to be summarily executed without hearing or trial; but, of course, that is not the way the Navy works.

The reality was almost as bad. I was here for the stark private funeral service for Lieutenant Commander Repro, who had suffered a circulatory failure. Ha! I knew what had killed him: deprivation of the drug to which he was addicted. Naturally they had not provided him with it in prison. Whether there was specific malice in this I cannot be sure, but they must have realized that he, more than any other person, was responsible for the campaign that cut off the major source of supply for most of the illicit drugs, and there were those in the anonymous echelons who were angry and perhaps hurting privately. The fact that Repro had been slowly dying, anyway, did not much alleviate the ugly shock; he had been the guiding genius behind the unit I had formed and commanded. It was his vision, more than my own, that I had implemented. Now Beautiful Dreamer was gone. What was his reward? An anonymous extinction. No mention was made in the spoken service of his addiction, for theoretically no officer of the Jupiter Navy indulged in drugs. At least they had had the grace to see him out with the honor befitting his rank.

Poor Repro! He had wrought so well, from the depths of his own captivity by the drug, and had so effectively struck back at it. He had had the immense courage to dream and to shape reality to that dream, all the while slowly dying. He was truly a great man, doomed to be unrecognized for his most singular accomplishment.

The other officers of my staff were there. I stood beside them for the somber service, glad for their company, sad that this had to be the occasion for it. I knew they shared my emotion, and that they were crying, too.

Afterward, we were permitted a brief grace period of reacquaintance. First to come to me was Captain Phist, at long last promoted for his sterling service to the Navy, who had the privilege of rank, though he seemed almost ashamed of it. Gravely he shook my hand. "Your work will continue, sir," he said. "And his." His eyes flicked toward the coffin. "If we can just preserve the liaison with Straight, on whatever basis . . ."

Yes—here was an important element. Straight now controlled the Belt, and if Phist retained command of the unit, as seemed to be the case, he could preserve what remained of our nucleus unit and hold the loyal lower officers and enlisted men. He was not Hispanic, but they knew him and trusted him, knowing that he had done what he had done because he had had to. But only my marriage to Straight's daughter had secured our uncertain and unwritten treaty of alliance; without that, the cooperation would be lost. I knew, now, that the Navy would never let me resume command, of this unit or anything. The Navy never forgave a transgression of this nature. Only Phist, who had obeyed their directive so perfectly, could retain his power. How could he relate to Straight?

Next came Mondy. "But there is a way," he murmured as if reading my thoughts. "You know they will never let your sister return, any more than you, sir. So Phist loses his wife, too. He loves her, but he is a realist. If Rue is willing . . ."

I understood him. Trust Mondy to see the vital connection!

Roulette came next, her eyes brimming with those tears she reserved for me. "They are making you the scapegoat this time, Hope," she said. "Everyone else gets off, except The Dear, if you—"

"Yes, of course," I agreed gently. "My sister and I are finished in the Navy. But you need not be. Rue, for the sake of the unit and the mission, will you let Old King Cole tend the garden?" Naturally the Navy guards did not grasp the significance of what I was saying; our songs became our code.

She looked startled. *"Him?* After what he—?"

"He obeyed orders," I reminded her. "By so doing, he made it possible to complete our mission, help your father, and preserve the unit. King Cole had loved The Dear, he could love the Ravished. If your father accedes to the connection—"

Her chin lifted. "Yes, of course. Now I understand. I will . . . facilitate the alliance. But I won't cry for Cole."

"Don't expect him to lay waste the garden, either," I said. "He is a gentle man."

She smiled wanly. "I know the type. Don't worry, Hope; you tamed me. I can play the game. I will serve the post."

"Thank you. I believe you will find the game worthwhile, for yourself and your father. You are the only way this alliance can be held. I wish I could have been the one . . ."

Her tears began to spill. Slowly I leaned toward her, and we kissed a chaste kiss. That was all we could get away with here.

Before we separated, she whispered: "Hope, would you—would you—one last time?"

I glanced around. The guards weren't watching us at the moment. I brought my right fist up in a short, concealed uppercut and clipped her on the chin. Somehow she bit her lip in the process, and blood welled out. She backed away, her eyes shining with more than tears.

Emerald came up, blocking the view of the nearest guard who had thought he had seen something. "That was a nice thing you did, Hope," she murmured.

"She won't cry for any other man," I said. "I won't strike any other woman." No one outside this unit would grasp the significance. If I had tamed Rue, she had taught me her way, too.

"Your tactical position is better than you might think, sir," Emerald continued. "The news had been full of the Hero of the Belt, the Hispanic Scourge of Piracy. The Navy has been stalling, waiting to bring you to trial until the notoriety dies down; they don't want to make a martyr of you. But it hasn't died down; you're becoming a cult figure. In fact, there are growing rumblings about their failure to give you a medal and promote you to admiral."

"Admiral!" I stifled a laugh.

"Just don't give in, Hope; you can win the final battle."

I hadn't thought of it as a battle, but perhaps it was. "Thanks, Rising Moon," I said with feeling.

"And I bring a message from Used Maiden," she said. She took my head in both hands, set her mouth against mine, and gave me a kiss that sent me right back to that first session in the Tail. That was from Juana, all right, who was not privileged to attend this officer's funeral. Sweet Juana!

Last came Spirit, who had just completed an impassioned parting with Captain Phist, the severance of their marriage. I held her and she held me, and we did not speak.

As I started back to my cell, an anonymous officer gave me a box. "The Deceased bequeathed this to you," he said curtly.

Back in my cell, I opened the box. It was the structure with the five steel balls. I put my head down and cried.

In due course I resumed my narrative manuscript, feeling somewhat better. Between bouts of writing I knocked the balls about, grateful to Beautiful Dreamer for this remembrance. He had made of his life a better thing than others knew. He had understood force and counterforce.

Perhaps a week later I had a visitor: Reba Ward of QYV. "The forces are finely balanced at the moment, Captain," she said, setting on the table a device I knew was there to guarantee security from electronic surveillance. "A small nudge at the correct nexus can change history. Will you deal now?"

"You!" I exclaimed with angry revelation. "You had me deposed and recalled, just when victory was at hand!"

She shook her head in negation. "A natural suspicion, Hubris, but unfounded. We oppose the drug trade as strongly as you do."

"You tried to addict me!"

"I do not condone my predecessor's acts. The end does not justify the means. Otherwise I would have had your item long ago."

I saw that she was speaking truly. "Kife did not—?"

"We hoped you would succeed. The Navy acceded to our nudge and gave you the command because it thought you would fail. We protected you as long as we could, but in the end your success was too great and we could not act without exposing our interest. But we did do this: We had one of your officers assume the command, instead of the martinet they planned to appoint. That enabled you to do what you did to the Samoans, and to avoid a mutiny by your loyalists."

Still she spoke truth. QYV was on my side now. "Go on."

"We can't restore your command, but we can engineer a compromise. If you will agree to resign from the Navy, with your sister, with no adverse publicity, you will be granted a medal, full Jupiter citizenship, and a perfect military record. You will retire a documented hero."

I did not quite trust this. "And my unit?"

"Captain Phist will retain command. But there will be no more pirate fighting; he will have a mission elsewhere."

I realized that it would indeed be expecting too much to have my unit returned to the Belt. "And the Solomons?"

"They have delegated the chief's daughter, Roulette Phist, to be liaison to Jupiter. The Navy is interested in peace in the Belt. As long as no outbreaks of violence against Jupiter interests occur, the existing order will not be challenged."

It seemed a fair offer. Slowly I reached down to my left shin, where flesh tape bound the key invisibly. As a ranking officer I had never been subjected to a physical shakedown. I separated the key and handed it to her. The terms of this deal had been set before I went to the Belt; now I had to accept them.

Reba smiled as if this were a routine formality. "When you arrive at Jupiter, our representative will provide you with the background on Megan. She is, at this point, exactly what you need."

"Need for what?"

"To become a politician."

"Why would I want to go into politics?"

"That is the only way to pursue your life mission. We want you to succeed."

So it seemed I had gained an ally in QYV. But I had lost my last physical memento of Helse, my love. That cut me deeply. Yet I knew that loss had been replaced by the prospect of finding new love, in the form of the one woman in the Solar System who could replace the old one. My emotions were mixed.

Editorial Epilogue

This manuscript, unlike the prior one, titled *Refugee,* survived complete. Perhaps Hope Hubris intended to write a few more paragraphs, since he never quite caught up to the present tense, but he did not.

As is, of course, well known to history, he did resign from the Navy, together with his sister Spirit, and came to the planet Jupiter as a hero. That is just about the only particular in which the official Navy record of the event coincides with the presentation by this manuscript. Readers are now free to choose which version to credit. Certainly this manuscript helps clarify the passion and determination with which the Tyrant pursued piracy and drug dealing throughout his later career, and the unfailing support he received from the rising echelons of the Jupiter Navy. Probably never in history have these evils been as thoroughly suppressed as during the Tyrancy. But as the following manuscript shows, Hope Hubris had an extraordinary account to settle with these forces.

Note the continuing influence of the Tyrant's sister Spirit. Hope himself was courageous in his dealings with others, whether they were his erring superior officers or fleets of pirates, and he had more personal magnetism than he credits himself with. His men respected him, and his women loved him. But when Spirit was not with him, he had very little initiative; he simply survived, taking things as they came, responding to the passions of the moment. But once he discovered that Spirit was alive, his whole ambition was to recover her. That, rather than any initial interest in ascending the military ladder, was what caused him to cooperate with Commander Repro's grand design. Once Hope had Spirit, who sometimes seems more like a lover than a sister, he pursued other interests, but she was always there to implement them. She was in many respects the true leader of his outfit, having subtle but enormous power. He gives credit freely to the other officers of his staff, and certainly they deserve it, but it is literally true that he could not have run the unit without Spirit. He needed her, in both the business and emotional senses; she was his better half, the competent reality behind his figurehead. The failure of others properly to appreciate this reality turned out to be critical to the Tyrant's career, as will be seen. It was to Spirit's wordless embrace that Hope went last, at the funeral; no words were needed.

Hope Hubris, at the age of thirty, professed to have only two loves: Helse in the past and Megan in the future—but, in fact, he had one: Spirit in the present.

Hopie Megan Hubris, daughter of the Tyrant
January 4, 2671

BIO OF A SPACE TYRANT
Piers Anthony

"Brilliant...a thoroughly original thinker and storyteller with a unique ability to posit really *alien* alien life, humanize it, and make it come out alive on the page." *The Los Angeles Times*

A COLOSSAL NEW FIVE VOLUME SPACE THRILLER—
BIO OF A SPACE TYRANT
The Epic Adventures and Galactic Conquests of Hope Hubris

VOLUME I: REFUGEE   84194-0/$2.95 US /$3.50 Can
Hubris and his family embark upon an ill-fated voyage through space, searching for sanctuary, after pirates blast them from their home on Callisto.

VOLUME II: MERCENARY   87221-8/$2.95 US /$3.50 Can
Hubris joins the Navy of Jupiter and commands a squadron loyal to the death and sworn to war against the pirate warlords of the Jupiter Ecliptic.

VOLUME III: POLITICIAN   89685-0/$2.95 US /$3.50 Can
Fueled by his own fury, Hubris rose to triumph obliterating his enemies and blazing a path of glory across the face of Jupiter. Military legend...people's champion...promising political candidate...he now awoke to find himself the prisoner of a nightmare that knew no past.

Also by Piers Anthony:
The brilliant Cluster Series—
sexy, savage interplanetary adventures.

CLUSTER, CLUSTER I   01755-5/$2.95 US/$3.75 Can
CHAINING THE LADY, CLUSTER II   01779-2/$2.95 US/$3.75 Can
KIRLIAN QUEST, CLUSTER III   01778-4/$2.95 US/$3.75 Can
THOUSANDSTAR, CLUSTER IV   75556-4/$2.95 US/$3.75 Can
VISCOUS CIRCLE, CLUSTER V   79897-2/$2.95 US/$3.75 Can

Fantastic Worlds of Adventure
FROM AVON BOOKS!

The Best Collections of the Best Short
Science Fiction and Fantasy Stories

Silverberg
SCIENCE FICTION HALL OF FAME,
volume I   00795-9/$3.95

Bova
SCIENCE FICTION HALL OF FAME,
volume IIA   00038-5/$3.95

Bova
SCIENCE FICTION HALL OF FAME,
volume IIB   00054-7/$3.95

Clarke & Proctor
SCIENCE FICTION HALL OF FAME,
volume III   79335-0/$4.95

Boyer & Zahorski
FANTASISTS ON FANTASY   86533-x/$3.95

Boyer & Zahorski
THE FANTASTIC IMAGINATION   41533-x/$2.50

Asimov, Greenberg, & Olander
100 GREAT SCIENCE FICTION SHORT   50773-0/$2.95
SHORT STORIES   US/$3.75 Can

Asimov, Carr, & Greenberg
100 GREAT FANTASY   69917-6/$3.50
SHORT SHORT STORIES   US/$4.50 Can

Haldeman
STUDY WAR NO MORE:
A Selection of Alternatives   40519-9/$2.95